A Promise to the Past

A Promise to the Past

A Genealogical Mystery

James G. Brown

Writer's Showcase
presented by *Writer's Digest*
San Jose New York Lincoln Shanghai

A Promise to the Past

Writer's Showcase
presented by *Writer's Digest*
an imprint of iUniverse.com, Inc.

For information address:
iUniverse.com, Inc.
5220 S 16th, Ste. 200
Lincoln, NE 68512
www.iuniverse.com

Credit for Graphic: James G. Brown

ISBN: 0-595-12798-3

Printed in the United States of America

ACKNOWLEDGEMENTS

Cover image of Union soldier courtesy of Library of Congress, Prints & Photograph Division, ship image courtesy of Department of the Navy, Naval Historical Center, other photos from author's collection.

PROLOGUE

West of Cape Horn
November 14, 1784

The ship rolled heavily to larboard, another wave cresting on her starboard quarter. She was laboring under a dark gray overcast sky even though she was carrying only her lower canvas, the southwesterly wind gusting occasionally to thirty-five knots. She surged ahead at nine knots in the gusts and, although they were making a fast passage, Abigail Steele Smith still felt the gnawing fear that she had had since before the historic voyage began. *Eagle of America*, a three masted ship of 220 burthen tons from Portsmouth, New Hampshire had left Boston, Massachusetts in January on what would be the first trading voyage by an American ship to China. The outbound passage had taken 138 days with mostly fair winds and even the rounding of Cape Horn was relatively easy and not the terrible ordeal that had been expected.

The great cabin canted to port as the ship rolled and Abigail looked down at the chart, then up at her husband, Captain Jacob Smith who thoughtfully traced out the previous 24 hours run. He had been just able to take a noon sight through a brief break in the heavy cloud cover and was marking the new position on the chart. After studying the chart for a moment he picked up the dividers to measure off the distance between the two positions.

"Looks close to 180 miles," he said opening the logbook to record the latest position and distance traveled.

"That means we're about 100 miles west of Cape Horn," she replied.

Jacob looked up at her. "That should put us there at about midnight. I'll be glad to have that behind us." They both grabbed for the chart table as the *Eagle* rolled once more, another wave crashing aboard. Recovering his balance, Jacob tapped the glass on the bulkhead; it had dropped again.

"I don't like the looks of this," he said. "I think that we're in for a big blow and it couldn't come at a worse time. We may have to hove to before we get to the Horn."

Abigail glanced down at the chart again and nodded her agreement. "If we do, at least we'll have some sea room. What do you think about taking in more sail now?"

Jacob smiled at her. "Probably a good idea."

She smiled back at him. Secretly she knew that she was as good a seaman as her husband. She suspected that Jacob knew this also but knew he would never speak to it. He understood her and respected her abilities and she loved him desperately because of this.

"I'll go on deck to take in the fores'l and mizzen," Jacob said. "We could probably stand a second reef in the main too. Maybe then the motion will be a little less violent." He bent over to give her an affectionate buss on the mouth. He went out of the small chartroom to the companionway and climbed to the quarterdeck.

Abigail moved to the settee and sat down feeling a sudden chill. She pulled her pea coat tight around her fighting another pang of fear and foreboding. It was odd she thought, she had seen death before but this time the dark aura seemed to be all around her.

She was twenty-nine and had been at sea since the age of twelve when her father, Captain James Steele, had first taken her with him. She accompanied him on most of his voyages and learned the trade from him until, at nineteen, she became a master herself. It was, of course, very rare for a woman to do this and she had to fight constantly for the respect she deserved with a strong-willed passion.

In addition to his more conventional seafaring ventures, Captain James Steele was a smuggler and this occupation allowed him to become very rich. He began smuggling goods from Nova Scotia before the War of Revolution and during the war, managed to keep many of the old contacts alive to help supply the colonists with essentials in their bid to defeat the British. The profits reaped from these efforts helped him to accumulate a sizeable fortune and he used some of this to build a fine house at Rosemary Point, north of Kittery in the District of Maine. The house was located on over two hundred acres near the sea and Abigail, who now owned the property, thought it was the most beautiful place in the world. She thought of her two children who were there now with a nanny; Jacob Jr. who was five and Content, almost two. Normally she would have brought the children with her on the voyage, but the danger involved with this trip and the terrible sense of foreboding she had made her leave them at home.

She looked around the chartroom and smiled to herself. The ship was still a tie to her father and she thought it ironic that the man who was such a good sailor with an innate sense for profit had been killed because of a sudden attack of patriotism. The *Eagle* had been built in Kittery as a privateer. In 1779, just after she had been contracted for and the keel laid, her father felt compelled to join the ill-fated Putnam Expedition to Penobscot Bay. In the ensuing catastrophe he was killed, leaving Abigail as his only surviving child to look after her mother. Her father willed her both the unfinished *Eagle* and the Rosemary Point property.

The *Eagle* was never used as a privateer because her completion was delayed by the time needed to settle James Steele's estate. She fitted out just before Cornwallis' surrender in Virginia but did not go to sea as intended to seek British prizes. But, even though she had not been used as originally intended, she still carried ten 12 pound long guns for defense.

She was a fast ship, recording several profitable and swift trans Atlantic crossings. One of these passages had come right before the Treaty of Paris which formally ended the war and Jacob Smith had insisted on a stop in Plymouth, England to show the new nation's flag. They were one of the first American ships to trade with the former mother country. Abigail had given birth to Content that voyage and she still thought of the trip with a fondness that made her smile.

She returned home to find her mother remarried to a well to do merchant from Boston named William Marston. She was happy for her mother, who she knew, found little to be happy about because of her sour disposition. However, the marriage also brought with it children by her new husband's first marriage. One was a son, Jonathan Marston, who Abigail now found to be a very disagreeable annoyance.

Her thoughts of Jonathan caused the pangs of fear to return and she involuntarily shivered again. She tried to fathom why she had ever allowed him to participate in financing the voyage. Jonathan Marston was a merchant like his father and Abigail asked him, at her mother's prompting, to help finance the voyage. She knew she and Jacob could have done this easily themselves, but in the interest of family harmony, she reluctantly agreed. From the beginning, she always felt that Jonathan was jealous of her wealth and would do anything to get her property, including Rosemary Point. The business association only helped to magnify these feelings and she knew this was one of the reasons why she left the children behind. She had also taken what she thought to be prudent measures to protect her assets if something happened to her on the voyage.

Abigail got up from the settee and went to the bulkhead, tapping the glass as Jacob had done; it had dropped again. She buttoned her jacket, taking a scarf from her pocket and tying it around her head. She left the chartroom and climbed the companionway ladder to the quarterdeck.

The wind velocity had increased and Abigail guessed the gusts were now over forty knots. She glanced forward to see that the crew had taken in the foresail and had just finished reefing the main. The *Eagle* was running under only the reefed main and the smallest jib. Still, she was rolling in the building sea, making a steady eight knots. Abigail looked back at the wheel and was glad to see that the helmsman seemed to be having no difficulty steering the ship. Next to the helmsman Jacob was in deep conversation with Adam Davies, the First Mate. They looked off the starboard quarter at the sea, then at the skies that had darkened even more than when Abigail had gone below an hour before.

She walked toward them, adjusting to the rolling deck, yet another wave hitting the ship sending spray and spume flying through the air. Jacob and the First Mate turned as she approached.

"I think it's getting worse," she stated.

The First Mate nodded in agreement. "Yup."

Jacob said, "I think we're in for a bad time, Abby. We're going to rig life lines and I want to get chains on the lower yards."

Abigail nodded knowing the chains would add a margin of safety to the heavy rope lifts, which supported the huge yardarms on the masts.

She was about to speak when she noticed movement at the companionway and Nathan Malin came on deck. Malin was Jonathan Marston's representative traveling as supercargo to look after Marston's interest in the voyage. Malin was almost comical in appearance. He was of medium height, thin with a narrow face and a rounded nose that was much to big for the face. But, he had cold green eyes and Abigail felt the dread again as she saw he was very pale, the cold eyes wide with fear. He came toward them stumbling as the *Eagle* abruptly came off a wave.

"Are we in danger?" he blurted out.

"We've seen worse than this," Jacob replied.

Abigail and Davies nodded in agreement.

The answer didn't seem to help Malin and the mask of fear remained frozen on his face. He looked out at the white foaming sea pondering the gale around them. "I wonder where the *Empress of China* is?" he said.

Abigail looked at Jacob and said, "We had at least a two week head start on her and we're probably faster, but if she has caught up to us then she will be having the same problems that we have!"

Jacob nodded and agreed. "It really doesn't matter. Anyway, we're headed back to Boston and the *Empress* will go back to New York. We can each claim a record voyage."

Malin gave him a blank look, moving to the weather side of the quarterdeck where he leaned against the bulwark. Jacob shook his head and gave Abigail a wink; he had little use for the man. Malin was nothing more than a toady for Jonathan. He motioned to Davies saying, "Let's go forward and check on the rigging!"

They left, making their way toward the bow, leaving Abigail alone on the quarterdeck with Malin and the helmsman. She thought of the *Empress of China*. The *Eagle* had been in Macao for three weeks when the *Empress* arrived after a voyage from New York. The endeavor was a joint effort of New York and Philadelphia interests. Jacob and Abigail were glad to see them and a friendly visit cemented relationships. As a result of the visit, a wager was made between the vessels on who would have the fastest return passage and who would arrive home first to establish the record of the first voyage to China.

The *Eagle* carried a cargo of mixed merchandise to China and was already loaded with a new cargo of tea and silk that would fetch a rich price in New England upon their return. Because of this, she was able to leave just three days after the *Empress's* arrival. Jacob thought the *Empress* would need at least two weeks to unload, get cargo and provisions before she could follow.

Abigail couldn't quite figure why it bothered her so much, but she thought that Malin had almost expected the *Empress* to be there. It was another reason she now felt even more addled by everything. She tried to calm herself but the pangs would not go away. She walked aft to the stern, gazing out over the transom at the ocean and the violent white wake that the *Eagle* was leaving. She rested her head on her arms thinking of her children. She missed them very much. They would both be so changed when she returned, if she returned. She caught herself, don't think that way you foolish woman. Still, she knew her feelings were very real. Once again she was glad she had taken measures to protect her fortune for her children.

*   *   *

The gale gained strength through the afternoon and was now near hurricane force. Jacob had reduced sail again during the afternoon watch and hove to under only a small jib which was backed. The *Eagle* was riding fitfully, almost head to wind, rolling as the giant seas played with her. Abigail climbed the companionway ladder to the quarterdeck dressed in oilskins. She guessed that the wind was a steady sixty knots with gusts that were much stronger. She bent to steady herself against the wind and the motion of the ship, moving to where her husband stood near the wheel. Dinner had been a hit or miss affair because the galley fires could not be lit, so a glass of port, some ship's biscuit and cheese were all Abigail could eat. She still felt hungry and this gnawing feeling in the pit of her stomach only added to the foreboding with the reality of the storm now justifying all her fears.

She put her hand on Jacob's shoulder and stood on her toes to speak in his ear above the wind's howl, "I don't like this one bit. The roaring forties are as bad as any place on earth!"

He leaned to her, "I never thought I'd see anything as bad as the North Atlantic, but this is worse! Still, we seem to be holding our own. She's a fine ship and we're riding well, considerin'."

"It's a shambles below," Abigail said. "I'm afraid that Mr. Malin is a bit under the weather!"

Jacob laughed, "At least he knows what he's doing now!"

Abigail laughed also and Jacob held her close. "We'll be alright in the end. The *Eagle* will see us through this," he said.

Abigail felt the need to speak. "You know that I've had a bad feeling about this voyage from the beginning, but having you with me has made it bearable. You know how much I love you Jacob." She smiled as she tried to shield her face from the driving spray.

"And I you," he replied. "I'd not have had things any other way. My eight years with you have been the best I could have asked for."

They stood together, balanced as one, the *Eagle* rolling and pitching in the storm.

Adam Davies made his way up the companionway ladder almost falling as the ship took a severe roll to starboard. He went aft to where Abigail and Jacob stood and tapped Jacob on the shoulder.

"We have a problem," he said his voice calm but his eyes were wide. "I've been below to take a look. The cargo has shifted a mite."

Jacob looked at Abigail and then back at Davies. "How bad is it?"

Davies blinked, spray hitting his face. He wiped the salt from his eyes with the back of his hand and answered, "The shift isn't too bad, but that's not the worst of it! We're taking water. As best I can see there is a bad leak around the sternpost. Every time she comes off a wave the stern rides down and water sluices in. I reckon that we have near two feet in the bilges. I put a couple of men to work at the pumps and so far I think we're holdin' our own!"

"I better go below and take a look," Jacob said and tried to smile. "Adam, you stay here with Abby and keep an eye on things. 'Specially the main mast, it's whippin' around a bit!"

Davies nodded in return and Jacob moved across the bucking deck to the companionway ladder. He made his way down two decks to the hold. He saw that there was indeed water in the bilge. He lit the lantern he had picked up and carefully made his way aft to the sternpost. As the *Eagle* rocked each time, the stern came down, shooting a stream of water through a large leak in the planking. Jacob walked carefully to keep his footing and moved as far aft as he could to examine the leak. He saw it was about three feet long and he saw the planking flex as the ship worked in the storm. He held the lantern closer and his blood chilled at what he saw. The space between several of the planks showed signs of chipping as if someone had taken an axe or another tool to purposely knock out the caulking. Even as he watched, the opening moved again, spurting another stream of water that hit him in the face and snuffed out the lantern. In the dark he tried to focus on who could have done such an insane thing. Clearing his head, he felt his way back to the ladder. He climbed back up to the lower deck.

Jacob focused hard to quell the panic that he felt. He knew the leak had to be plugged quickly and he quickly retraced his route up the companionway ladder. He went on deck where he had left Abigail and Adam Davies.

He looked at Davies. "Get Chips," he said referring to John Derry, the ship's carpenter. "Get him below with some men! We stop it now or it will get worse!"

Davies looked at him, nodded and went carefully forward to get John Derry to work on the damage aft.

Jacob put his arm around Abigail. "We're in trouble."

"How bad is it?"

"We're taking on a good amount of water, but perhaps we can control it, I'm not sure. In any event the storm is still building and the ship is having a rough time of it!" He did not lie to her for he knew she had already made her own assessment of the situation.

They both turned to see Nathan Malin come up the ladder, stumble to the deck and fall down. He struggled toward them on his hands and knees. As he came closer they could see that, sick or not, he had been drinking. He pulled himself up clinging to the bulwark next to them and the fear spilled out of him.

"We're going to die, all of us!"

Jacob looked at him with a mixture of hate and revulsion. Abigail felt his fear as if by contagion and her own foreboding took hold once again. She held herself to Jacob.

None of them saw the huge rogue wave that had grown seventy feet high as it had moved three thousand miles unimpeded by land through the lonely roaring forties. Abigail looked forward in the spray and gloom just as it crested high above the bow of the *Eagle*. She tried to cry out but there was no sound to her voice and she pulled Jacob to her with desperation. Jacob turned seeing it also, knowing what would happen. He looked into Abigail's eyes and held her as *Eagle's* bow gallantly tried to rise into the towering solid wall of water.

The wave crashed aboard over the *Eagle's* bow pushing the ship over on her starboard beam. She slew around, the force of the wave pulling the fore mast out of her. As she rolled, the main and mizzen masts followed. The wave was so brutal, so powerful, that the *Eagle* stood no chance of surviving. The leak around the sternpost did not matter in the end.

The ship was broken by the wave and as the masts went by the way, the hatches gave way like boxwood, water cascading below. What the rogue did not finish, several more huge cresting breakers did. Within a minute, the *Eagle of America* foundered and as she died her crew perished with her. Abigail's fears and foreboding came true and what might have been died with her. As a consequence, many lives would be changed for generations to come.

CHAPTER ONE

Spring 1990

Pilgrim Village is located south of Boston near where the Mayflower colonists first settled. It is a faithful recreation of the original settlement during the Pilgrims' early years and the Village uses interpreters to assume the roles of the early Pilgrims. The role-playing is extensive and detailed and the interpreters go about routine daily chores, faithfully recreating the lives of those who were actually there. Visitors may ask the interpreters questions about their community and way of life and the interpreters will answer as though they were in the 1625 time period. It is a very popular, well run living museum that educates by historically correct demonstration. Like any other such organization it takes many people of different skills to make it work successfully. Pilgrim Village has many talented people and, as a multi-million dollar enterprise, it must function as a business to prosper.

David Baker looked out the window from his second floor office in the main museum building and watched the early visitors enter the grounds. He was very much aware of what it took to make Pilgrim Village work because as Development Director he knew the day to day details as well as anyone. He was responsible for a great variety of functions including publicity, fund raising and special projects.

He yawned and leaned back in his chair stretching his arms above his head. It was a bright clear early May morning, a rare spring day given the chilly soggy streak Massachusetts was experiencing. The buds on the trees were beginning to open into leaves as though surprised by the sudden change in the weather.

David stood, still looking out the window toward the water of Plymouth Bay on which the recreated village was located. He liked the view and the contrast of the hutch roofed dwellings of the village with the modern homes that could be seen in a distance to the south at the far edge of the museum property.

He yawned again coming to the same conclusion he had already reached ten times that morning; he didn't feel like working today. He knew he was lazy; it seemed to be his nature and if he could put it off until tomorrow he'd do it. Yet he knew his image was one of a motivated go-getter and he admitted to himself that once properly stimulated, he worked like a dervish. This trait had made his reputation but it was the lazy times, like today, which made him indifferent and sluggish. This happened to him more frequently of late and he wondered again why he felt this way.

He watched the early visitors make their way down the path to explore the 1625 replica dwellings. The crowd was not large for such a nice a day but he rationalized it was early in the season and knew attendance would pick up once the tourist season was in full swing.

His apathetic attitude bothered him because although he had always gone through periods of uninspired activity lately they seemed to be the rule rather than the exception. He'd always been able to find motivation somewhere. Perhaps it was the fact that he was getting older, he thought. But still he couldn't shake the feeling something was missing. Something he needed to do but could not sense an answer.

David was thirty-seven and that fact didn't bother him, but he was conscious that he would be thirty-eight later in the year and wondered if he was facing the beginning of the mid life crisis he had heard so much about. He dismissed the idea. I'm not that crazy, yet, he told himself.

David sat back in his chair putting his hands behind his head raising his feet to the desk. He took stock of his life, a ritual he had done often of late.

He was a native Midwesterner from a town just west of Des Moines, Iowa and was the youngest of three children raised by his mother after his father died tragically in an auto accident when David was seven. Perhaps this fact accounted for his periods of apathy, he reflected. It was probably a good reason for the way he felt as anything else, although his older brother and sister had shown no similar traits.

He managed to be an over achiever in high school, making the honor roll. At six feet two he had the natural ability to be a standout guard on the basketball team that had gone to the state finals his senior year. Losing that game still bothered him. He liked basketball but remembered how the coaches constantly tried to stimulate his desire to play, the intensity of his game often measured by the quality of the "psyche job" delivered by his coach. He still played in an adult league doing it to keep in shape more than for a love of the game. Apathy again he reflected, or something more? A deeper problem?

David shrugged off the thought and turned in the chair to look out the window again before trying to get to work. He could not stop himself from thinking and resumed his train of thought. He had attended Northwestern University where a major in business with a degree in marketing and a minor in economics led to a job as a copy writer for a Chicago advertising agency. His work earned a steady stream of good reviews punctuated by occasional raves when he became particularly creative. David smiled with satisfaction remembering those simpler days.

Behind him the phone rang and he swiveled around from the window to pick up the receiver.

"Dave Baker," he answered.

"It's Jack. Do you have some time to go over the plans for the annual fund?"

"Sure. When?"

"Come on down in twenty minutes or so. I want to finish something first."

"I'll be there," David replied hanging up the phone.

If there was one reason to get motivated he reflected, it was Jack Pierce. Jack was the most enthusiastic person David had ever known. He inspired those around him with infectious excitement generated by his sheer physical presence and animated gift of gab.

David stood once more to stretch, hoping to stimulate his sluggish brain to consciousness. He needed to be on his toes to talk with his boss and friend, Jack Pierce.

His thoughts wandered as he mentally shifted gears. It had been Pierce who had brought him to Pilgrim Village. David's early good reviews in Chicago led to a promotion to account executive. Shortly after, at a client presentation, he met Mary Dunbar; a career oriented merchandise buyer. They fell for each other immediately and David soon found himself married.

David shook his head remembering.

The union produced no children and a divorce two years later when it became apparent Mary Dunbar Baker was more interested in her career than a family. She also found David's outwardly visible success a threat to her own ego and aspirations.

He stopped and imperceptibly shook his head again, the details of his failed marriage vivid in his mind. He felt the doubts once more about his own abilities and motivation. Was he still bothered by the divorce after nearly twelve years? He didn't think so, but the hurt remained nonetheless.

He turned, absently looking out the window again seeing his reflection in the glass. He considered the image. He was still fairly good-looking he reasoned, turning his head to check his profile. Not too bad for thirty-seven, going on thirty-eight he reminded himself.

David had been stoic about the conclusion of his marriage and accepted the inevitability of the divorce. And some good had come from it since the divorce had spurred in him a need for a change of scenery. He used his growing reputation to take a new job as an account executive with Doyle, Nelson and Weed, a Boston advertising firm. Upon arriving in Boston, he immersed himself in work to put the failed marriage behind him. One of his clients was Pilgrim Village and he soon crossed paths with Jack Pierce.

With Pierce's stimulation and a vague personal interest in history he found that the Village fascinated him spurring his own enthusiasm. While the Village was not his largest or most profitable account, it quickly became his favorite. He gladly spent his own time working on advertising and promotional campaigns. When the Development Director left for greener pastures Jack Pierce invited David to dinner. After a second round of drinks he asked David if he'd be interested in the job.

David mulled the offer over for about ten seconds before deciding he wanted to work for Pierce. Besides, he told the Executive Director of Pilgrim Village, he needed a new one-on-one opponent on a regular basis. They sealed the deal over plates of linguini with white clam sauce and a dessert of chocolate cream cheese cake.

That had been four years before, David knew, and the arrangement had been more than satisfying. He loved what he did, so why was he feeling so listless and down?

His eyes focused again on the visitors entering the Village. A particularly attractive woman walked past in a short skirt and David admired a shapely pair of legs that extended below the hemline. He felt a rumbling in his stomach that moved to his groin.

"Maybe that's what bothering me?" he mumbled out loud to himself. His current love interest was Carol Tandy and she had terrific wheels too. That made him smile.

He followed the visiting woman's legs until they disappeared past the entrance gate. David pondered his relationship with Carol. There had been a number of women in his life since the divorce but this latest relationship with Carol seemed to be the most promising. He shook his head. They had lived together for the past year at his house in Duxbury but lately doubts were pressing on his mind. Carol seemed more noncommittal each day and her mood swings were becoming more unpredictable.

Carol was from New York. She worked as a municipal bond broker for Merrill Lynch in Boston and made fairly good money, David thought, but he also knew she complained every day that selling was getting more difficult for her. He suspected this was part of the reason for her mood swings. Could this be the reason he felt as he did?

At thirty-four Carol was three years David's junior but at times she acted as though she were still a child. She pouted when she couldn't have her own way and this trait was particularly apparent when dealing with a personal problem.

David had talked with her many times attempting to help find a solution to a problem; with little success, he rued. Still, he knew he was satisfied with the relationship and he reflected she was certainly a beautiful intelligent woman who was also shapely and well proportioned. In fact, he'd thought a lot about marriage again lately. He grinned at his reflection in the window.

He looked at his watch. He'd daydreamed for almost fifteen minutes and it was time to get his file to go see Jack Pierce in his office down the hall. As he gathered up the manila folder, he thought once more of Carol. Maybe that was it; the reason he felt so out of it. He yawned, stretching again.

David thought about putting his jacket on then dismissed the idea; Pierce was a firm believer in casual dressing. Carrying the files, he went out of his office past his assistant, Jane Flynn, telling her he was going down the hall. Intent on her PC screen she nodded her head without looking up. David walked the length of the building going into Jack Pierce's two-room corner office suite. Pierce's aide, Vickie Collins, waved him on through to the inner office.

David winked at her as he went into the office. Even though she was in her mid-fifties Vickie Collins was very attractive and as usual, she blushed when David did this. "Stop that Dave Baker! You don't need to get on my good side! You're already there!"

"I'm glad to hear that. You're still the best Vickie!" he smiled. It was always good to have the boss's assistant on your side. Never knew when you'd need some help.

John Bradford Brewster Pierce was very tall; six feet five. He had been named after three of his Mayflower ancestors, John Alden, William Bradford and William Brewster and Pierce was already something of a legend at the age of fifty-three. Coming from a very well to do old line Boston family, David knew Pierce worked because he wanted to, not because he had to. He had gone to Yale to get away from the family, and as he put it, "to piss off his father and grandfather who had gone to Harvard". He had majored in history and wrote his senior thesis on the development of the United States into a world power in the late 19th century.

A naturally gifted honor student at Yale, he played basketball with abandon, making the All-Ivy Team his senior year. David had played him one-on-one numerous times and was hard pressed to beat him despite the age difference.

After graduation, Pierce won a Rhodes scholarship where his year in England resulted in some serious hell raising and his first book published at the age of twenty-three. A three year hitch in the Army followed, "to build my character", as he put it. Once discharged, he moved into a teaching position at Yale where he became a very popular assistant professor of American History. During his nine-year tenure, he managed to publish six more books on various subjects, a record many viewed with jealous envy.

It was an astonishing academic achievement David knew, but there was more to the man. Jack Pierce was one of the rare academics who not only had the credentials to write and teach but he was also a most effective business manager and inspiring leader. He became Executive Director of Pilgrim Village at age thirty-five when he tired of academic life.

Eighteen years later he had built the organization into an energetic progressive model of what he thought a museum should be. As a final touch, his ebullient zeal promoting the village spurred those who came in contact with him to extra effort.

David was proud of the fact that they had a great working relationship, but happier that they were close friends. He also knew that in addition to his many accomplishments Pierce maintained a respectable golf handicap and had a consuming passion for genealogical research. As a blue-blooded descendant of no less that seven proven signers of the Mayflower Compact he was very involved The Society of Mayflower Descendants.

Despite his success in life, Jack Pierce let none of his academic, personal or business achievements go to his head. His ego was amply satisfied by his own ardor. He came across as just another person to those who met him. All in all, David reflected, Pierce was a very unique man.

"Baker, how are things today?"

"Pretty good Jack. I haven't heard for sure but I think we may be getting the Phillips Foundation grant to add the new exhibits. Herb Jacobs gave me a call last night and said the board would meet Friday. He didn't come out and say we'd get it but he did tell me he thought we made a terrific presentation. I'm hopeful."

"That's great!" replied Pierce. "You did a good job on that one. It was pretty easy to do the color at the dog and pony show. You produced a well-prepared proposal. I'll keep my fingers crossed. What else?"

"Just some routine stuff. You?"

"I was meeting in Plymouth with the Mayflower folks last night wearing my Village hat. We may try to do some more joint work with them, at least that's what I suggested. Some of them tend to be pretty stuffy and set in their ways but who knows, they might have a divine vision and see the wisdom in my ideas. It might be a way for both our groups to get some more revenue. It's a natural fit, it helps us and helps them. I hope the board goes for it."

He paused to look at David. "Have you done anything about researching your family yet?"

David hesitated. At least once a month Pierce had this conversation with him trying to interest him in tracing his roots and at least once a month David thought hard to find an excuse why he had done nothing about it. It wasn't as if he didn't have some curiosity about where he came from. No, it was just another example of his lethargy. It just didn't motivate him.

"Yeah," he lied, "a little. I talked to my mother. She says my aunt had some information. She's supposed to send it to me. I've been real busy though."

"Well," Pierce lectured, "you really ought to follow through on it. It helps a man to know where he's going when he knows where he's been."

"Yeah, I know," David said feeling he had been scolded.

Pierce smiled at him knowing that David was lying to him. "Now sit down and let's talk about the annual fund. We've got a lot riding on it."

*   *   *

Like many other workers, David's routine was predictable as he arrived at his house in Duxbury about 6:30. He pulled his Honda into the driveway and braked to a stop in front of the garage. Grabbing his jacket from the back seat, he went up the back stairs into the kitchen. He threw the jacket over a chair and went to the refrigerator for a beer.

He popped open the beer and, sipping the can, went through the dining room to the front porch where he took the mail from the mailbox. Returning inside to the living room, he switched on the television, kicked off his tassel loafers, settled into the recliner and began going through the mail. Sorting out the junk mail, he tried to pay attention to the national news on the screen in front of him. He glanced up at the clock comparing the time to his watch. He had some time to wait for Carol, who normally returned around seven after doing battle with her carpool partners on the congested Southeast Expressway and Route 3.

The mail contained nothing of special interest; two bills the only items worth saving. David rose, walked into the hallway placed the bills on the shaker desk and tossed the junk in the wastebasket. Putting the can to his lips he realized it was empty and went to the kitchen for another.

The news was just over when he heard a car pull up out front. A door opened and closed. He twisted and looked out the curtained window to see Carol climbing the stairs to the porch.

He called out to her as she entered. "Hello!"

He heard the screen door slam and knew she was unhappy again. David cringed and waited for Carol's outburst.

"The goddamed business is no fun anymore! I'm sick of trying to peddle goddamned municipal bonds! Even when I get an order it's for bonds I can't find! And on top of everything else, I've got that weasel, Blackman, on my ass to produce! I just can't take it from both sides!"

She broke into tears.

David went to her and held her as she started to cry. She continued to sob on his shoulder for another minute then pulled away, kicked her briefcase and ran up the stairs taking them two at a time. If she held true to form, David thought, she'd be back down in fifteen minutes to say how sorry she was. He thought about another beer but decided against it.

A half-hour later Carol had not reappeared. David finished watching the rerun on television and looked at his watch, tonight something was really wrong. He took a deep breath, stood and went up the stairs turning right into the master bedroom. Carol was on the bed laying on her back staring at the ceiling. She didn't move as he came into the room.

"Want to talk?" he asked.

She shook her head.

"Damn it Carol! You know it doesn't do you any good to do this! Let's talk this out."

She pawed at her eyes wiping away the remaining tears. Clearly there was a lot on her mind. She sat up slowly.

"You're right. Seems like you're always right," she sighed but didn't look at him. "God I feel so lousy Dave, the business is nothing like it used to be! It just feels like everything is closing in on me! I don't have any room anymore!"

She looked at him, softening her tone. "I'm sorry for acting this way Dave, it's not fair to you."

"Hey", David said, as he sat on the edge of the bed, "that's what I'm here for. But Carol, you've got to stop beating yourself up, nothing is worth doing this to yourself all the time!"

The tears started again. "I know," she pouted, "I keep trying to ease up but it's not easy!"

"Would it help if we could get away for a few days?" David asked. "Maybe a change of scenery would be good? We could take a drive, maybe New Hampshire or Maine? Go shack up for a couple of days?" he leered at her.

That small joke broke the ice bringing a slim smile to her face and he hoped the crisis had passed.

"Could we?" she asked, her eyes brightening somewhat. David could see she was still troubled though.

"Sure, I can take a couple of days. We can make it a long weekend. We'll leave on Thursday night or Friday morning and come back on Monday or Tuesday. How does that sound?"

"I'd like to do that," she said, showing signs of returning to normal. "I need to get out of the office for a while, maybe that will do some good."

"Great," David said and put his hand under her chin and leaned to kiss her. As often happened after one of her mood swings, she responded passionately.

"Let's make love," she whispered in his ear smiling.

"Okay," he said. And they did.

*   *   *

David and Carol left Duxbury at mid-morning on Friday and after the usual traffic tie up at the Central Artery in Boston they crossed the Mystic River Bridge onto Route One. David felt no need to hurry and he drove at a leisurely pace up Route One to I-95. He took the exit at Newburyport and drove into town to the waterfront area that was full of shops and restaurants. They walked down the street to a small restaurant and ordered lunch. Carol seemed more at ease and David smiled as the waitress brought the food.

"Well," David asked, chewing a bite of his jumbo cheeseburger, "you feeling a little better?"

He thought she seemed more relaxed but he sensed there was more working at her than just the dissatisfaction with work.

"I'm better," she smiled, holding her hand out to him across the table. It was a tentative reaction on her part, he thought, but she was trying.

"I'm glad," he said taking another bite, "want to browse some of the shops after we finish?"

She nodded and smiled uncertainly. "Yes, I'd like that. Shopping always helps take my mind off of things."

David paused to swallow again, washing the cheeseburger down with a gulp of soda. He hesitated before speaking, afraid to continue his train of thought.

"Is there something else bothering you?" he asked after a moment.

Carol stopped chewing, her eyes not betraying her inner feelings.

"No," she said, an uncertain smile reappearing on her face, "I'm still just down and tired. You can cheer me up though," she added as an afterthought. "Let's go window shopping or something."

He grinned at her. "I think I like "or something"."

They both laughed and David thought, maybe this trip was a good idea after all.

After browsing through some of the shops in the old town section, they headed north on 95 exiting at Portsmouth. David wanted to spend the balance of the day at Strawberry Banke, a collection of old homes and buildings near the river. The area had once been a rough and dirty maritime section of Portsmouth and at one time it included the red light district and attracted sailors and other rougher types. Strawberry Banke had been rehabilitated and restored and was now a working museum similar in intent to Pilgrim Village. David had visited several times, both as a tourist and on business and he knew several people who worked there. He had in fact, done a joint project with the Development Director who was a good friend.

Carol had not been there before though and David took great pleasure in showing her around explaining details about some of the houses. He watched her as she examined one of the flowerbeds just coming to life in the fresh spring weather and marveled at her beauty. She had a classic oval face set off by light brown hair cut medium length. She was about five feet six with a shapely body that, he admitted, was as nice as he'd ever seen. He was staring at her when she looked over to him and smiled when she discovered he was staring at her.

"What are you looking at?'

"You."

"Do you like what you see?" she said coyly.

"What do you think?" he leered.

"Let's go find a place to stay," there was mischief in her voice.

He grinned at her but wondered at this latest change in her disposition. Oh well, why not enjoy this while you can he thought.

"Let's go," he said.

They checked into the Sheraton thirty minutes later and they were soon in each other's arms.

*   *   *

It was sunny and bright Saturday morning and the sky a deep blue indicating that perhaps the streak of wet weather was at least temporarily at an end. David and Carol continued the drive north electing to take scenic Route One rather than the turnpike and crossed the Piscataqua River Bridge into Maine.

"Where do you want to go today?" David asked, taking a turn in the road.

"Believe it or not, I'd actually like to go see the President's house in Kennebunkport," Carol laughed.

"Sure. I'll call ahead and see if we can get in for a tour," David joked. "I just hope there isn't too much traffic."

They drove along, detouring right on Route 103. Neither of them spoke intent on absorbing the scenery. David had his mind on Carol's apparent mood change and wondered if it was only temporary or if there had been a sea change. He was still thinking about this several miles later when he saw a sign along the road. "Hey! I've read about this place!"

He automatically switched the right turn signal on and hit the brakes. He turned right onto a narrow road and stopped the car. To the right was a sign that read: ROSEMARY POINT MUSEUM-1/2 MILE. An arrow pointed ahead.

"What's this?" Carol asked.

"I read about this in one of the publications we get," he explained. "It's an old house that's been maintained as a memorial to the family who owned it. The house is supposed to have been restored and the grounds are still in a natural state with walking trails, if I remember right."

"Do we have to?" He sensed she was distracted.

"Humor me for a few minutes. Call it professional curiosity if you want."

"Okay, but I still want to see Kennebunkport."

David nodded, putting the car in gear. He drove down the winding road finally arriving at the entrance. The sign read: ROSEMARY POINT, HOME OF THE SHERWOOD FAMILY, BUILT 1775.

David pulled into a parking space in the lot at the bottom of a small hill where there were several other cars. He switched off the ignition and they got out of the car.

"Which way?" Carol asked showing a bit more interest now.

David looked around and saw a sign with arrows pointing to "The House" and "The Ocean Walk".

"Let's take a quick look at the house and then walk down to the water."

Carol nodded and started for the house. David followed. They walked through an opening in the thick hedge that fronted the house and made their way up a neat brick path. At the top of the small rise they stopped.

The house was not as big as he expected but it was imposing. It was a classic colonial garrison with massive brick chimneys at both ends. Another sign on the porch informed them the house had been built in 1775. David saw that the front of the house faced southeast. He studied the front deciding the porch that ran the length of the house was not an original part of the building but had probably been added later in the home's life.

Because of the hill, the porch gave a magnificent view of the ocean. A wide ribbon of lawn bordered by gardens surrounded the house. On the side facing the ocean a meadow ran down northeast to the sea where a small sandy beach lay between the rocky coastline. To the south David estimated there were about twenty acres of what appeared to be real natural saltwater marsh. From his experience at the Village he knew that very little of this type of grassland existed anymore. The view was breathtaking and they both stopped, taking in the panorama, enchanted by what they saw.

"Can you imagine having this view every day?" Carol wondered out loud, clearly interested now.

"Yeah, it's something, isn't it? Let's see what it looks like inside," David said turning back toward the front door. He started up the stairs to the porch and stopped when he saw a sign on the door that said; CLOSED FOR PAINTING. WILL REOPEN JUNE 1ST.

"Oh shit!" he said, "the house is closed!" Disappointed, he turned to again look at the view and Carol joined him.

"It's almost perfect, isn't it?" Carol said smiling.

He leaned to kiss her. "They must have been very happy here. Whoever the Sherwoods were."

They stood together, quiet for a moment, taking in the natural beauty of the land.

Finally David said, "Well, come on, let's take the ocean walk. Then we'll head for Kennebunkport."

"Okay. You know, I could be happy in a place like this," she said.

David looked into her eyes and saw a calm that had not been there for a long time. "Yeah, I know what you mean. It's a real gem. I doubt there are any other places quite like this left anywhere along here anymore."

He took her hand and they walked back to the parking lot then took the dirt path down toward the sea. Climbing a short set of stairs, they walked across a boardwalk on pilings that crossed the virgin salt marsh.

On the other side they descended another set of wooden stairs to the small beach. The panorama was beautiful.

They saw another couple who were also holding hands turn to go back to the house. The young couple smiled a greeting at David and Carol as they passed.

It's pretty and peaceful here too, David thought, but after the view from the house it was almost a letdown. He sat on the beach digging his hand in the sand. He played with the fine granules between his fingers. Carol came and sat beside him reaching for his hand.

"I'm glad we stopped," she said. "This is so wonderful. If life could be this serene I think it would be great. It would make everything so easy, nothing to worry about." She sighed and looked away at the water.

"I guess I know what you mean," he offered. "Are you okay?"

Carol didn't answer, apparently deep in thought. Was this another mood swing?

"Yes," she said after a moment, "I'm fine. Just thinking again. I guess that's my problem lately, too much thinking. Want to go?"

"Sure," David said, not really understanding the woman by his side.

He stood up, brushing the sand from his pants. He held out his hand to help her. Their eyes met for a moment. Carol looked away quickly, not able to meet the questions his eyes asked but he could see the earlier calm gone. The same tight-lipped grin appeared on her face but she took his hand rising to her feet.

She squeezed his hand and the smile becoming genuine again.

"Stick with me Dave. I know I've been a little confused lately but things really have me down. Just hang in for awhile, I'll be okay."

"Sure. I think I know how you feel. I'll be here," he said not sure just what she meant.

He sounded reassuring even though he hadn't the faintest clue how she really felt.

"Ready to go?" he asked.

She nodded and they walked back to the parking lot. Sitting in the car, David started the motor but didn't put the car in gear.

"I'd like to come back and see the house sometime," he said.

"Yes," she said, "me too. Let's come back later in the summer. This could be a special place for us," she said with little conviction.

He touched her thigh and smiled then shifted into reverse and backed out of the parking space. Moving the gearshift into first gear he headed out of the lot and they drove on to Kennebunkport.

*　　　　　　*　　　　　　*

The visit to Kennebunkport was interesting if somewhat disappointing. They viewed the Walker's Point house from a distance, limited by barricades and security guards. Television, they decided, provided a better panorama of the property.

Driving north they arrived in Portland late in the afternoon checking in to the Regency Hotel in the Old Port section of town. The hotel building had formerly been an armory for the state militia and this fascinated Carol. After settling in they strolled the Old Port, stopping to look in the many shops.

Hungry, they walked finally to DiMillo's Restaurant on the waterfront. The restaurant attracted their attention because it was located in an old ferryboat snuggled between pilings. Recently built condominiums surrounded the restaurant and a marina full of yachts on adjoining piers to the east and west gave the area a nautical setting. The condos were a token of the real estate boom of the 1980s.

DiMillo's dining room featured a view of the inner harbor and from their window table David and Carol could see the Fore River and Casco Bay to the east. They ordered cocktails and looked over the menu. Neither spoke as the drinks arrived. David stirred his scotch and raised his glass to Carol.

"Us?" he said smiling.

"Sure," she replied, but with that same tentative smile on her face. What was on her mind now?

They both drank. David set his glass down pushing the menu aside.

"I don't need to look at it anymore. I'm having the double lobster!"

"Are you sure?" Carol fussed. "You know how rich food sometimes gets you."

"Yeah, I know, but this is Maine. Got to have a lobster in Maine! I'll be fine," he laughed then said, "you know me too well!"

"Well, don't say I didn't warn you!" Carol clucked at him but smiled.

She stared at him, deep in thought. She was bothered by something again, he guessed. She sipped at her drink.

"Maybe I do know you too well," she said emotion in her voice.

Once more David didn't know what to say. He was unsure what she meant.

She saw the puzzled look on his face. She smiled the genuine smile again.

"Don't worry Dave. I'm not out of it yet. I'll be okay. You know I sometimes I say things without thinking. I don't mean them. You okay?"

"Yeah," he hesitated, "but are we still okay?"

"Sure," she said looking up at him. Her eyes met his but she could not hold his gaze and she looked away out the window.

David still didn't know what to make of this latest emotional swing. He wished he understood what was going on with the woman he loved. Strangely though he thought, while he was very much in love with Carol he felt that same ambivalence he felt earlier in the week. Maybe that's what's missing. Could that be what is bothering me?

Maybe he needed to make a commitment to her, he thought. They'd discussed marriage on a number of occasions in the last year but neither of them ever really seemed serious about it. They were both content to let the arrangement take its course. Neither had been willing to make the first move towards commitment.

Maybe that is what I need to do, David reflected. Could that bring her out of her unhappy state of mind? He'd have to think about that some more but he resolved to do something. Even with his recent lack of motivation he knew he had to do something to help Carol and he reflected, perhaps for himself.

He snapped out of his reverie as the waitress came to take the dinner order. He grinned at Carol and he knew he had to do something, but what to do and how to do it?

*   *   *

They slept late on Sunday. David found Carol was not receptive to his amorous advances complaining of a mild hangover, the result of a late night at several Old Port nightspots. They had a leisurely brunch at the hotel, checked out and spent time exploring downtown Portland. The weather had turned again and the day was cloudy and chilly. At mid afternoon it began to rain and they were caught in the downpour. They ran to the car in the parking garage but were soaking wet.

As they stopped by the car David looked at Carol who was fussing with her hair. He had spent the previous night and much of the morning trying to decide what to do about Carol. The idea of making the final commitment seemed more desirable the more he thought about it. Maybe he needed the commitment as much as he thought she did but he wasn't sure how or when to broach the subject with Carol.

While they had been browsing he had finally made up his mind to say something as soon as the opportunity presented itself. Besides, he thought, he had to end his own uncertainty about Carol. He needed to get back on a productive track again.

"Where to now?" David asked, trying to dry off with his jacket.

Carol finished patting her still damp hair. She looked at her watch.

"It's really too late to keep going north. I'd like to start for home. We have to be home tomorrow anyway."

David nodded.

"Okay. It's been fun. How do you feel?"

"Better Dave. This was a good idea. I'm as relaxed as I've been in a long while. Thank you."

She gave him a peck on the cheek.

It seemed like the right time. Now or never he thought and he bent to kiss her on the lips. She met him half way. They kissed briefly.

"You know I love you," David stated. He'd started, no turning back now.

"Yes, I love you too," she said smiling.

Without fanfare, he spoke impulsively, "Why don't we get married?"

Her eyes went wide and the smile disappeared. As soon as he spoke, he knew it was the wrong thing to say by the look on her face. All the hope and euphoria he felt faded in an instant. There was nothing he could do about it though, the damage was done

Carol let out a deep breath. "Oh Dave, we've talked about that before and you know how I feel. Why bring it up again? Just when things were getting better! You know I'm not interested in marriage! Not now!"

David sensed that all the good the weekend had accomplished was now undone. He tried to explain his feelings, perhaps as much to himself as Carol, perhaps salvage what he could.

"Sorry, I just thought that after the last couple of days you might have reconsidered. I thought it might be what you wanted now. I won't mention it again."

"You're right, you won't!" she said, her face grim now and her jaw tight.

She looked away, staring out the passenger window. David watched her, guessing she had returned to one of her blue funks again. God damn it, he thought, why can't I learn to keep my mouth shut?

"Let's go home, now!" Carol said with the emphasis on the word NOW. "I want to go!"

David could only nod. "Okay."

They drove home in silence, neither speaking and David found he was totally deflated. All his careful deliberation of the past twenty-four hours was obviously wrong and he wasn't sure what to do now. He knew he really didn't understand Carol at all anymore and he'd have to wait to see how she reacted when they arrived home.

The silence in the car was discouraging and this only added to the strained feelings and David's confused state of mind. Depression gradually replaced the euphoria he had felt only hours before.

They arrived in Duxbury a little past seven. As they entered the house the telephone was ringing. Carol answered.

"Hello?"

She listened for a moment.

"It's for you," she said handing David the phone.

David took the receiver. "Hello?"

"Dave? It's Jerry."

His brother, Jerry was calling. While they hadn't stayed in close contact, David admired his older brother immensely and was glad to hear his voice but Jerry sounded frayed and tired.

"Hi Jerry. What's up?"

"Where the hell have you been? I've been trying to call since last night!"

"We've been away for a few days. What's up?" He was worried by the tone of his brother's voice.

"I've got bad news Dave. God I'm sorry Dave, but Mom died yesterday. An aneurysm. She didn't know a thing."

David choked on his words as he rasped, "When do you want me out there?"

"When can you get here?"

"I'll leave tomorrow," David said, suddenly cold. He shivered involuntarily. "I'll call you as soon as I know the details."

They spoke for a moment longer, Jerry giving him the sparse details. David said goodbye and hung up the phone, turned to Carol and began to cry.

CHAPTER TWO

David estimated the plane was somewhere over Ohio as he reached for his second Dewars and water. He was jammed uncomfortably into the coach seat on the United 727 and he tried to reflect on all that had happened in the last twenty-four hours. It was difficult to grasp how his life could be so drastically altered in such a short period of time.

First the disaster with Carol had hurt him and he still didn't understand what was on her mind. Then the call from his brother had devastated him and now, feeling totally drained, he only wanted to drown his sorrows.

The previous night, after the shock of his brother's call had ebbed, he had called Jack Pierce at home to explain the situation. Pierce had been more than understanding and had told David to take all the time he needed to be with his family. David ended the conversation by thanking Pierce and said he would call as soon as he knew what his plans were.

Even Carol had been sympathetic, her mood had changed abruptly and she consoled him as he cried over his brother's news. She offered to accompany him to the funeral but they had talked while he fought to get his emotions under control and David decided there was no need to put her through the emotional stress of the funeral given her present state of mind. He thanked her for her concern. Moreover, she even made an effort to make up for her actions earlier in the day by trying to pull him into bed.

David appreciated her real, but halfhearted effort and preoccupied by his sorrows, he was not surprised to find he wasn't interested. Rebuffed, and perhaps somewhat relieved he suspected, Carol satisfied herself by mothering him.

Once he made the decision to go alone, he called United Airlines to book a flight and found a non-stop from Logan Airport to Des Moines that left in the early afternoon. After making a reservation for the next day, he called his brother to give him the flight information and then packed with Carol's help. She apparently sensed his need to be alone, staying in the bedroom as he returned downstairs. He mixed a drink and watched television until he fell asleep on the couch.

In the morning Carol had called in to take the day off so she could drive him to Logan. The Boston traffic provided only a minimal delay, much to their surprise and they arrived early. They sat silent in the car in front of the terminal building each waiting for the other to say something.

"I'm not sure what to say," Carol offered, breaking the silence.

David shrugged. "I'm not sure either. I'll call when I know my plans."

"Okay. I'm really sorry Dave. It's a lousy thing to have happen."

"Thanks."

He didn't want to add anything more, afraid of saying the wrong thing again. Instead, he only repeated, "I'll call when I know my plans."

Carol leaned toward him and he responded. She gave him a long shallow kiss and he couldn't help measuring her ardor, realizing there was little intensity to her efforts.

"Goodbye Dave. I hope everything's okay."

He watched her face.

"I'll call," he repeated for the third time.

David got out of the car, grabbing his luggage and shutting the door behind him, glanced into the car interior. He thought he saw tears in Carol's eyes and turned away to walk into the terminal. He didn't look back instead walking purposefully to the glass doors in front of him. He sighed, knowing he would have to deal with whatever was left of their relationship when he returned.

Now, as the United 727 cruised at 34,000 feet, he sipped the drink that helped deaden the pain he felt and his thoughts returned to his mother. He couldn't believe she was gone. She had always seemed so young, and yet she was dead at only sixty-seven. He remembered her as a tower of strength for him and his brother and sister as they grew up. Although he hadn't seen her as often as he would have liked, he knew he would miss her very much and, in a way, her death was twice as hard to take because he had been so young when his father died. It was like he'd lost his final link to the past, he thought.

That made him blink as he remembered Jack Pierce's monthly admonition that a man must know his past to know where he was going. Maybe it was his sorrow or the scotch, but he felt a sudden twinge of curiosity about his family background. Perhaps knowing more about that would help fill the void he felt over his mother's passing. He would ask some questions while he was in Iowa. Surely he thought his mother must have kept some family information and his aunt probably knew something. Yes, he thought, he would do that.

He looked out the window, swallowing the last of the drink, his eyes misting again.

*   *   *

The Boeing jet set down on the runway five minutes late and taxied to a gate at the terminal building. David waited in his seat until the crowd thinned, then walked up the aisle out of the airplane and made his way up the boarding ramp into the waiting area where his brother was waving at him to get his attention. David went toward him, put his bag down and stood as his brother gave him a bear hug.

"How you doing Jerry?" David gasped; his breathing briefly interrupted by his brother's enthusiastic hug.

"I'm okay. Boy it's good to see you! Even if it's for such a crummy reason. How are you doing?"

"I think I'm dealing with it, but I feel pretty bad about the whole thing," David said.

"Join the club," Jerry said, picking up the carry on bag. "Come on, let's get your luggage and head for home."

"Sounds good to me."

They both smiled, glad to see each other and started to walk to the baggage area.

"How's Sue taking it?" David asked as they went down the terminal walkway.

"I think she's okay too. It's Aunt Beth who seems the worst. She was really close to Mom. You know Beth helped Mom get through Dad's accident? She's taking it real hard. We'll see her later."

"Sure," David agreed. "When's the service?"

"The memorial service is Wednesday morning. Then we'll have a short graveside service and after that we're having people over to our place. Karen and Sue are planning everything."

"And how is my lovely sister-in-law?" David asked as they both stopped at the baggage carousel.

"Fine, as always," Jerry said. "She's looking forward to seeing you. So are the kids by the way."

David smiled. "I'm looking forward to seeing them. After all this, it's nice to be with family again."

Jerry grinned at him as baggage began rattling down the conveyor to the carousel. "How's Carol?"

David looked away. "She's fine. She didn't come with me because I didn't want her to have to go through all of this. She's having problems at work and she needs a break."

Jerry nodded, seeing the vacant look on his brother's face and wondered what was going on behind his mask of sorrow. David watched for his garment bag, which soon appeared on the carousel. He snatched it and together he and Jerry walked out of the terminal to the car in the parking garage.

      *   *   *

The drive west along the Interstate produced the same nostalgic feelings David usually felt when he visited home. He and Jerry talked idly as they drove along and soon the familiar scenery made David feel at ease. Despite the strain caused by his mother's death, he was comforted by seeing the rolling plains and felt the usual wonder at the difference between the Iowa countryside and the hilly New England landscape he was now accustomed to. As they drove along, they passed new subdivisions on, what he remembered to be, farm land.

The Stillman exit came almost before he expected it and Jerry eased the car onto the off ramp. Immediately, they passed a new shopping mall on the right.

"When did this open?" David asked.

"Last year," Jerry replied slowing the car slightly, "how long's it been since you were here last?"

"I don't know. Four years I guess."

"They started this about two years ago. Went up in a hurry. The old guy who owned the land finally got his price I guess." Jerry pressed the accelerator. "Was that the last time you saw Mom?"

"When?"

"When you were out four years ago."

"No, Jer. She came out to see me last summer remember? I think she had a good time. I had a chance to really show her around."

"And she met Carol?"

"Yeah, couldn't help it," David laughed, "she didn't say anything but I'm not sure how she felt about her sharing the house with me."

"That's how Mom was. She didn't say much about it to us though."

David laughed. "And what did she say? I'm not sure Mom liked her or approved of the fact she was there. She never let on though."

Jerry smiled. "Let's just say she had her own opinion about things!"

"Yeah, but I give her credit. No matter what she felt about Carol, she didn't make any judgements. You know, she always treated us like adults even when we didn't act like it. I'm going to miss her a lot," David sighed.

"Me too. She was a classy lady," Jerry agreed. "One of a kind, no doubt about it."

They lapsed into silence as Jerry came to a stop at a red light. He turned onto Main Street.

David was glad the downtown Stillman hadn't changed much since he'd left after high school. It was all so familiar, almost like a welcome home, but he knew that the new housing developments that had blossomed out from the old town center had increased the population to over twenty-five thousand. It was now a full-fledged bedroom community of the city of Des Moines.

Jerry watched him looking at the older downtown buildings. He read David's thoughts. "Some things just don't change, do they?"

"No, but in a way, I like that," David replied.

"Yeah, it kind of gives you a feeling of substance. You still happy where you are?"

Jerry turned left as they left the downtown area onto Spring Street.

"Yeah Jerry, I am," David said. "Moving was the right thing to do after Mary and it's still the right thing. I'm happy and I've been lucky. I like what I do, I'm having fun and I like the area. I feel like I belong in New England."

Jerry wheeled the car right into the driveway of his bungalow style house braking to a stop by the side door. They left the car, collected David's luggage and went into the kitchen. Inside, David was greeted with a passionate hug and kiss from his sister-in-law, Karen Baker.

"How are you Dave? You look great!"

"I'm doing okay, all things considered. You're still as beautiful as ever! I still think my big brother lucked out getting a girl as good looking as you! Good luck is wasted on the dumb!"

Karen laughed. "It's good to see you Dave. It's been too long!"

David laughed, as did Jerry behind him. David turned to his brother and missed seeing the two Baker children, Tommy and Jerry Jr., come tearing around the corner blindsiding him. He gasped as they both grabbed him at the same time. Tommy was ten and Jerry Jr. thirteen. They had both grown so much since the last time David had seen them.

"How are my pals?" he said, hugging them both.

"Good," they both chorused.

"Uncle Dave? I played basketball on the junior high team. Do you think we could play while you're here?" young Jerry asked.

"I think we could arrange that," David replied. "Are you any good?"

"Well, maybe not so good, yet, but I'm practicing!"

David looked up to see his sister, Sue Hubbard, peek around the corner. She smiled at him. "Hi little Brother."

David went to her and gave her the same greeting he had just received from Karen.

"How are you?"

"I'm doing alright. It's too bad we have to get together because of this, but I'm glad you're here. It's awful good to see you."

"Anybody thirsty?" Jerry interrupted.

"I'll take care of that," Karen offered and went to the kitchen for a pitcher of iced tea while the others settled on seats in the family room. She put the pitcher on a tray along with some glasses and went to join to others who were already deep in conversation.

*　　　　　　*　　　　　　*

The memorial service and the funeral had gone well, David thought, as people gathered at his brother's house for refreshments. The church had been packed, a sign of his mother's reputation in the community and good old Reverend Adams, who showed no signs of slowing down at age seventy-two, gave a moving eulogy. Jerry and Sue had done a terrific job of organizing the service and the flowers from family and friends overwhelmed the altar. The graveside rites were also nicely done and many of the same people at the memorial service had continued on to the cemetery. The day was sunny and warm and this helped make the service memorable. David thought his mother would have been happy with the way it had all been done.

Regrets and sympathy gushed from friends and acquaintances, almost to the point of embarrassment to the family. Nevertheless, it gave David a good feeling to know his mother had been held in such high esteem. He was bewildered by the many people who came up to him to offer condolences at the church, the cemetery and now here, in Jerry's living room.

He was talking with an old high school friend who now ran the local lumberyard.

"I was so sorry to hear Dave. I always liked your mom when we were growing up."

"Thanks," returned David. "We did have a lot of fun when we were kids. You were nice to come."

"I wouldn't have missed this," his friend replied putting his hand on David's arm. "I hope we get the chance to spend sometime together before you go."

David shook his head, smiling. "I'll try."

The afternoon went by rapidly, faces stopping briefly to speak, before moving on. To David, it became a blur but finally the guests were gone, leaving David, Jerry, Sue and their spouses with Aunt Beth in the living room. David moved over to sit next to his mother's younger sister.

"You okay Aunt Beth? I haven't really had time to talk with you yet."

"I'm a lot better than I was the other day. This hit me pretty hard. Jan and I were very close."

"Yes, I know, almost like you were sisters."

She laughed at the small joke.

"You always could make me laugh!" Beth said.

"Well, I'm glad some things don't change," he replied. "Beth, can I ask for your help with something?"

"Sure, if I can."

"Losing Mom started me thinking. It's like I missed something."

"How so?" Beth asked.

He thought for a minute. "Well, I guess it's also that Dad died when I was so young. I never really got to know him. I guess what I'm saying is I'd like to find out more about the family. You know, who Mom's parents were and Dad's. Can you help me?"

Beth smiled, interest brightening her eyes. "I think I can help you some Dave, but I'm not really sure how much I know. I do know that Grandma Mead, your great grandmother was descended from someone on the Mayflower."

"She was?" David asked surprised. "Mom never said anything about it."

Well, she probably didn't know about it. Our mother, your grandmother, had no interest in the whole thing, so she never mentioned it that I know of. I only knew it because I spent time with Grandma Mead when she was sick before she died. She told me once and I think she was even a member of that Mayflower club. But that was a long time ago."

Sue joined them, pulling up a chair.

"What are you two talking about?"

"Family history," David answered, "I guess I'd like to know more. Beth just told me our great grandmother was a Mayflower descendant."

"You mean the Pilgrims? Really? I didn't know that," Sue said and looked at David. "That's interesting, considering where you work!"

They laughed.

"What about the Bakers? Know anything about them?" David asked.

"Well I really don't know much," Beth said. "But there are probably some things at you Mother's house. I think she put some stuff away in boxes after your Dad died. I guess the only thing I do remember about the Bakers is the crazy family tradition that Baker men pass on the rights to the "stolen family treasure", whatever that is. I always got a laugh from that but there might be something to it because it's even mentioned in their wills!"

David and Sue looked at each other, "What!"

"You didn't know that?" Beth asked surprised.

"No," said Sue.

"I sure thought your mom would have said something to you about that," Beth continued. "Your dad included the treasure thing in his will, so it must have been important to him."

She paused to think a moment. "There's probably a copy of his will still in your mother's things."

Sue regarded her aunt. "We've got to start going through the stuff at the house anyway. Maybe we could start tomorrow? Could you come over and help? I'd like to find out more about this myself."

"Sure, I'd be delighted to do that. I'll meet you at the house in the morning."

David sat back on the couch smiling to himself, if this Mayflower business was true it would surely interest Jack Pierce and, he thought, this does kind of peak my own curiosity.

*   *   *

David awoke early the next morning anxious to get over to the old house. He ate breakfast with Jerry before his brother left for work in Des Moines and David told him what he was going to do. Jerry seemed genuinely interested and admitted to having had similar thoughts. Jerry, at age forty-five was the oldest and had known their father the best.

"Did Dad ever mention this 'lost family treasure' to you?"

"No, he never did, but he must have thought it was important enough if he included it in his will. I didn't know about that either, by the way. Mom never said a thing to me."

"You think that's kind of strange?" David asked.

Jerry thought for a moment "No, not really. I guess if what Beth says is true, Mom was like Grandma and she didn't care about this family stuff. So she probably never even thought to say anything. If we'd asked, I'm sure she would have told us." He paused. "You know, maybe the will brought back bad memories for her. That could explain it."

"Yeah, you're right I guess. I know Mom was still felt Dad's death. She told me once she missed him more each day, even thirty years later."

"Yeah, she told me the same thing. You know Dave, I'd like to see the will too. I hope you find it."

"Sue thinks she knows where it is."

"Hey that reminds me," Jerry said. "Joe Delany from church, you remember him?" David nodded.

"He's Mom's lawyer," Jerry continued, "he told me yesterday he's got a copy of Mom's will and said to call him when things calmed down. Might as well get going on that I guess, I'll call him today and see what we have to do to settle the estate."

"Good, let me know if you need anything from me."

Jerry nodded and thought for a minute.

"Jesus Dave, I wonder if there really is a treasure? And what do you think it is?"

"Search me," David replied, "it's probably just an old tale. If the "treasure" existed someone would probably have found it years ago. But if it's true, it might make a good story. I'm curious about that."

"Me too. If you want to work on it I'll help you all I can," Jerry offered.

"I'll try," David said. "Maybe if there is a treasure we can both retire. Huh?"

They both chuckled over the unlikely possibility of undiscovered riches.

*   *   *

Later, after Jerry left for work, David called Carol at her office. He thought she seemed glad to hear from him, asking about the funeral. David briefly gave her the details but again sensed that she was once more preoccupied by something.

He told her he would probably stay a week to help start to settle his mother's affairs. Carol became defensive at this, but he chose to ignore it. He told her he would call her in a few days, saying "I love you" as he said goodbye. This received no response only silence and the click of the phone disconnecting.

Trying to ignore Carol's response, he called Jack Pierce.

"How are things going Dave?" Pierce asked, after they connected.

"Fine, all things considered. It's been tough, but I'm having a good visit with my brother and sister. I'm going over to my mother's house today to start going through things. You know, all the talking you've done over the years may finally be getting results. I'm going to try to look for family records. My Aunt Beth has already given me some interesting stuff and I may have a surprise for you when I get back."

"Hey that's good news," Pierce said. He was glad to hear David in such a good frame of mind. "Remember, I always told you I'd help you, if you want."

"I remember. I think I'm going to take a week or so to help Sue and Jerry get things organize here. That okay?"

"I told you Dave, take all the time you need to get things squared away. Everything is covered here."

"Thanks Jack, you're a good friend."

"Keep in touch. If you need something, call."

"I will. Goodbye."

David hung up the phone, returning to the kitchen where Karen was finishing the breakfast dishes. She looked up from the sink as he came over to her.

"Give me ten minutes and I'll take you over to the house," she said.

"Thanks, but I think I'd like to walk," David said. "It's a nice morning."

"Suit yourself. I'll try to stop by later."

"Okay, see you later," David said, giving her a peck on the cheek.

David walked the six blocks through the old neighborhood, feeling nostalgic and remembering many childhood adventures. For the fist time in three days he was alone with his thoughts. Family and the rush to get everything ready for the memorial service had left him with little time to think. Now, the nostalgic feelings made him focus on his own sorrows over his mother's death. He felt sad but was somewhat relieved the rites were over. With the services over he was left to manage his own grief and he thought he could manage that well enough.

But he knew that the unsettled sensation in his stomach had returned and as he walked, the nostalgia faded and was replaced by the indifference he had felt before. Would his mother's death make that worse now? He hoped not.

At the same time, he had a growing curious fascination about his aunt's sketchy tickler about the "family treasure". Was it real and if so what was it? How had it come into the family? Who was responsible? Did it even exist?

David went over each of these questions rapidly several times and he felt invigorated by his increasing interest in his ancestors. Maybe he shouldn't have scoffed when Jack Pierce delivered his monthly sermon on family history.

He suspected that the "treasure" was only a lure, but he admitted to himself that he now really did want to know more about his predecessors. He knew he could rely on Jack for help.

Thoughts of the Village and home broke his reverie. Carol. He was back to her again and he knew something was really wrong by her reaction to his phone call. Whether it was the same old thing or something new he wasn't sure. He tried to put her out of his mind, returning to the project of the moment.

He wondered what he would find at his mother's house. It was like the beginning of a journey with an unknown destination he decided and he felt elated and suddenly excited about where the journey might take him.

He looked at his watch, noting that it was five past nine as he walked up the steps at his mother's house. He used the key Jerry had given him to let himself in.

"Hello," he called, "anyone home?"

"I'm upstairs," yelled Sue, "be right down."

A moment later she bounded down the stairs giving him a kiss. "I was just getting started in Mom's room but we can go back later after Beth gets here. Let's go into the den now and see what we can dig up. I've been thinking about this Mayflower thing all night!"

"Me too," David said, "but I'm just as curious about the "treasure".

"Yeah me too. Do you think there's anything to it?'

"Probably not," David said. "I said the same thing to Jerry, but I'm going to try and find out. It's funny, 'til Beth mentioned it last night I really didn't care much about family history. Now though, I want to know more, even without the treasure."

"I'm curious too and I'll help you Dave. Come on, let's get to work," she said, leading him from the hallway.

The closet in the den yielded several boxes tied with string marked "photos and scrapbooks". They opened the first box, each taking one of the large books and paged through them.

"This is a photo album," said Sue, "the pictures are of us growing up."

"Yeah, I remember. I'll bet Mom put together at least a dozen of them."

They went through the first box as quickly as they could, making sure they missed nothing. As they finished, they heard the front door open and Beth came in.

"Hi kids," she said, "find anything yet?"

"We just started," replied Sue.

"Yeah, dig in and help," David invited.

The trio began looking through the other boxes and two hours later they had found nothing. The boxes contained photos and clippings from their childhood, but there was nothing related to earlier generations.

They took a break and in the kitchen, sipping coffee Beth made, David spoke. "Well, nothing yet. Where do we go from here?"

"I think we should try Mom's closet next," suggested Sue. "I know she kept some things up there."

"Sounds good," David said. "Beth?"

"I'm no help," she shrugged. "I don't know what's where around here. Let's do what Sue says."

They finished the last of their coffee and went upstairs into Janet Baker's bedroom and found something almost immediately. There was a box in the closet marked 'Mead family'. Their mother, whose maiden name was Janet Mead, had apparently saved the information from her grandmother after all. They opened the box and sat down on the floor to inspect the contents.

David took the first item from the box. It was their mother's birth certificate. Born in 1923, she was the daughter of Robert Mead and Susan Neale.

"I knew that," said Sue. "I remember Grampy. Do you Dave?"

"Sure, he died right after Dad did. I never knew Grammy though."

"Neither did I. She died before I was born."

"She died in 1947," offered Beth. "Jerry would have been only one or two at the time. Neither of you ever knew my mother, your grand-mother. But Sue, you know you're named after her?"

"Yes Aunt Beth, Mom told me. I remember looking at pictures of her wondering what she was like."

Beth smiled at her. "I think you would have liked her. She was a tough bird at times but I know she would have liked you. All of you! Let's keep looking."

"Right," David agreed.

Next they discovered two memorial books for John and Sarah Button Mead.

"There!" exclaimed Beth, "that my Grandma Mead."

They noted the vital information given in the memorial books.

"Keep digging, this is getting interesting!" said an excited Sue.

They went through the rest of the box, the contents of which consisted of old photos and newspaper clippings, including obituaries for John and Sarah Mead.

"My mom must have saved those," Beth explained.

The best, though, was at the bottom of the box in an envelope. It was a membership certificate for the Society of Mayflower Descendants in the name of Sarah Button Mead, dated June 1915. It indicated she was eighth in descent from John Howland and included a national membership number.

"Wow!" exclaimed Sue, "so it is true!"

"I never knew this stuff existed," said Beth. "My mother must have given this to Janet since she was the oldest. This is great, I don't remember her ever mentioning it."

"What do we do about this?" asked Sue.

"I have a friend who can help us, David said. "Jack Pierce is involved with the Society back home. He'll tell me what to do."

"I remember meeting him when we were out to visit you three years ago. He's a nice guy."

David nodded.

"You know, it's lunch time," Beth said, looking at the clock on the table by the bed. "Take this stuff downstairs and come over to my place for some food."

"You're right. I'm hungry," David agreed. "We can come back after lunch."

        *   *   *

They returned to the house early in the afternoon and resumed the search. The closet did not yield any additional information and the attic was next. Sue led the way to discover there wasn't much in the large open space.

"Looks like Mom cleaned house," observed Sue. "I remember this as being almost wall to wall with things."

But they looked around quickly and found a trunk in the corner under the eaves.

"This must be it," David said.

Ducking to avoid the low rafters, he bent to examine the old navy trunk that bore the name, Lt. William Baker.

"That's your dad's trunk from the war," said Beth. "I think Jan stored a lot of his things in here after he died."

David and Sue carried the trunk down to the living room. Sitting on the couch, they opened the lid and peered inside. On the top was a dress blue U. S. Navy uniform with two gold striped on the sleeves.

"That's you Dad's," Beth said, "it may be the uniform he wore when he married your Mom in 1943."

Sue lifted it from the trunk, examined it carefully, and set it aside. There were some other clothes under the uniform and Sue removed then and put them aside. This uncovered a box with a label that was written in Janet Baker's handwriting. The label read: "my husband, William Baker's records".

Sue handed the box to David who opened it. On top was an envelope marked 'Last will and testament of William Baker'. David removed the will. Sue and Beth watched while he read it.

"Well, I'll be damned!" he exclaimed, "here it is. "Listen to this, *'Finally, I leave and bequeath to my sons, Gerald and David, in equal shares, any rights to the stolen family fortune.'* How about that?"

He looked at his sister.

"What about me?" Sue asked, "he didn't mention me!"

"I know, but remember what Beth said. The treasure was left to the Baker men."

"That's right," acknowledged Beth.

"And it was before women's lib Sue," David added with a smile on his face.

Sue laughed despite herself.

"Okay. I don't like being left out though. The will kind of gives me goose bumps. It's like Dad is talking from the grave, sort of. He called it a "fortune" not "treasure". Do you think that means anything? I really wonder what's behind it?"

I don't know," David replied, "it's another wrinkle to contend with. Beth? Any ideas?"

"No, I don't remember much about you dad's family except the "treasure" thing. Remember, your Grandfather Baker died in World War I and your Grandma Baker died right before you were born Dave. I don't think she ever spoke about her family or the Bakers. You know she never remarried and your Dad was an only child."

"Yeah, I knew that," David said. "Dad didn't have a father growing up and I always thought that gave us something in common after he died in the accident."

"I think you are a lot like him in a lot of ways," Beth told him. "He was a good man. So are you Dave."

David smiled at his aunt.

"I think she's right," Sue added. "I mean from what I remember about Daddy, you are like him. He made me laugh too."

She reached for the small pile of yellowed clippings that were next in the box.

"Here's Dad's obituary."

Sue read the aged newsprint.

"It says he was the son of William Senior and Anne Henry Baker." She looked up. "I knew that."

"Your dad was real young when your grandfather was killed. You knew that though, didn't you?" asked Beth.

"Yes," David replied, "he was killed in World War I when Dad was about two I think. Mom always used to tell me how ironic it was that Dad grew up without a father and that I had to do the same thing."

"Maybe that's why you're like him," Sue suggested.

David shrugged, reaching into the box. He continued digging, opening and envelope with "U.S. Army" printed on the upper left-hand corner. The envelope contained a copy of a certificate for the Distinguished Service Cross. It had been awarded, posthumously, to his grandfather for action above and beyond the call of duty at Chateau-Thierry, France, July 1918. He found his eyes were misting. He showed the heavy paper to Sue and Beth.

"Wow!" Sue said, "Mom did say that Grandpa Baker was a hero, but I never saw this. I'd love to know the full story about the medal. It's really too bad no one in the family ever paid any attention to this stuff. I wonder what else there is that nobody bothered to remember?"

David shook his head wondering the same thing and removed the last envelope in the box. It was an obituary for his grandfather. The short two-paragraph item gave notice of the death of William Baker in France and mentioned his wife and parents.

"This says that Grandpa Baker was born in Logansport, Indiana and his parents were Joseph and Martha Williams Baker. Too bad there isn't more information."

"Well, at least you've made some progress," Beth offered, looking at the empty box. "Yes, I'd call that a good start."

"Yeah," Sue agreed, "a start, but that's it. The box is empty and there's nothing more in the trunk either. There's nothing about the "treasure or fortune" or whatever."

David examined the envelope that contained his father's will. At second glance he noticed that there was another, smaller, envelope inside it. He removed the envelope and opened it, finding a note written in his father's hand. He read it.

"Listen to this," he said, "it's a note from Dad dated in 1958. It says that if anything happens to him he wants to be sure his children, and I guess that includes you too Sue, receive the letter his father wrote him from France. I didn't see anything like that did you?"

Sue and Beth both shook their heads no.

"How could he have written to Dad if he was only two?" David wondered.

"I don't know," Sue said, "let's go through things again."

They went back to the attic, tried the basement, again went through the den and their mother's closet. Then they searched the desk, but at days end they could not locate the letter.

Frustrated, David sprawled on the couch in his mother's living room "I wonder if the letter even exists anymore. Maybe Mom threw it out?"

"She would have kept something like that," Sue said. "I don't think she would have thrown that out, at least not on purpose."

"I don't know," David replied. "Beth?"

"I told you, I'm here to help but I can't help with that. I think she would keep something like that though. Where else can we look?"

"We've torn the house apart," Sue pointed out. "I don't think we've missed anything here. Maybe it got lost?"

"Well, I'd like to find it," David said. "It might have some answers about the "treasure.""

Sue looked at the clock on the wall. "Come on Dave. It's time we got back to Jerry's. You coming Beth?"

"No. I think I'll go home and catch up on a few things. I've spent too much time with all of you. You need some time to yourselves."

Sue gave her a kiss. "You're special Aunt Beth. We like having you around."

"Well, I'm going home anyway," Beth said. "See you tomorrow."

David rose from the couch, still disappointed by the missing letter.

"Thanks for your help Beth, it its a good start and you're still my favorite aunt."

"Is that a compliment? If I remember right, I'm your only aunt!"

David laughed; Beth had cheered him a lot. He was now very curious about the "treasure" and wanted to get to the bottom of the mystery more than ever. The desire to know where he had come from was growing within him and his indifference was beginning to give way to a new purpose.

*   *   *

After dinner that night David excused himself and went to the Stillman Library to copy the information from his mother's house. Even though the letter from his grandfather was missing, he knew the information they had found was a good beginning. He admitted to himself though, he didn't know what to do next but his growing curiosity made him wonder just what to do next. When he finished making the copies he went to the front desk and waited while the librarian finished checking out some books for an elderly lady.

She looked over to him as the lady left. "Can I help you?"

"I hope so," David smiled. "I'm not sure what I want though. Could you tell me where books on family history might be?"

"You mean genealogy?"

"Yes I guess so."

"That would be 929.1," she pointed, "go down the aisle to the last row, the shelves on the right."

David nodded as he mentally followed her instructions. "Is there any one book you might recommend to someone who doesn't know anything about the subject?" he asked.

"There are a number of good ones I think. I know we have several on the shelf. Timothy Beard's book is good, *Shaking Your Family Tree* by Ralph Crandall is very good and one of the most popular ones is an old one called *Searching For Your Ancestors* by Gilbert Doane. Just browse and see what interests you."

"Thanks, I will," David said and wandered down the aisle, going into the last row of shelves looking until he located 929.1. There were at least a dozen different titles dealing with genealogy and he paged through several, studying them. He found Crandall's book interesting and Doane's book also caught his eye. He took both volumes to a chair at the end of the aisle.

David sat reading for an hour, engrossed by what he found, until the lights dimmed to announce closing time. He rose to replace the books realizing he wanted to know more and decided to see if he could find copies of them in at the bookstore in the morning.

He returned to Jerry's house and sipped a glass of iced tea while talking with his brother about what he and Sue had found at their mother's house.

"Sounds like you two had a fairly successful day," Jerry said.

"Yeah, I'm pleased. It's a good start I think but I wish we'd found that letter."

"It'll probably turn up somewhere, Jerry said. "We'll keep looking."

"You know Jerry, I hate to admit it, but think I'm hooked on all this."

Jerry laughed. "Better you than me. But you always were the one who just bulled ahead when you found something that interested you and you haven't changed one bit!"

"Yeah, I guess you're right. The old "how do we motivate Dave Baker" thing."

"You said it, I didn't," Jerry laughed.

"I guess it's true though," David shrugged. "It's funny though, with Mom gone I really feel like I do have to get to the bottom of this!"

Jerry smiled at his younger brother. "You mean like little voices?"

David laughed too. "No, just big time curiosity. Besides," he smiled, "we may all get rich!"

Jerry chuckled again. "Well, I'll drink to that. Want something a little stronger than tea for a nightcap?"

"I think I'll pass, but I could use a refill on the tea."

"Sure." Jerry got up to go into the kitchen.

"Jer?" David said.

"Yeah?"

"I'd like to get going on this stuff as soon as I can." He pointed to the copies of the material he'd made earlier in the evening. "I think I'll leave for home earlier than I'd planned, change my reservations to leave on Sunday. I've got a few other things that I need to take care of too. Is that a problem?"

"Shouldn't be," Jerry replied. "I'd like you to stay longer though but Sue and I can take care of things here. Do what you want."

"I think I will then."

David thought about the puzzle facing him, then about Carol. His thoughts were interrupted as Jerry spoke returning with a full glass.

"Incidentally, I did talk with Joe Delany today. He says Mom's will is pretty straightforward. She named me as executor, so I'll have some work to do. The will basically divides everything between the three of us. I'll make sure everything is inventoried and if there's anything you want let me know. I think Mom's estate should be fairly substantial, she invested wisely over the years."

"I'm not surprised," David laughed, "she was a remarkable woman. Let me know if I can do anything."

"You bet I will."

David got up to call the airline. After confirming the flight and the time of arrival, he called Carol to ask her to meet him at Logan. The phone rang eight times before she answered. David thought she sounded tired.

"Hi Hon," he said, "I'm coming home on Sunday afternoon. Can you pick me up?"

"I thought you were staying until at least Wednesday," she mumbled, irritation in her voice.

"I've got some things I want to do before I go back to work."

"I wish you'd stay until Wednesday. I can't pick you up on Sunday. I have plans."

What the hell was this all about David thought "Carol, are you okay?"

"Yes, I'm fine," she snapped, "we need to talk."

God she's in one of her moods! "Okay, we'll talk when I get home. Try to stay cool, everything's going to be fine. Don't worry, I'll get a limo home. No problem, I'll see you then. I love you Carol."

He heard the silence at the other end of the line and then the phone clicked dead.

CHAPTER THREE

It was overcast and cold in Boston with a fine rain in the air making it the kind of late spring day that tried the souls of most New Englanders who hoped to forget winter. The cold dampness pervaded everything and the gloom generated a depression that weighed upon David as he sat in the back of the car that had met him at Logan Airport and wondered what to expect from Carol when he got home.

It could literally be anything he decided. She was becoming more irrational all the time and he conceded that his patience with her was wearing out. He would have to resolve things soon and he knew he couldn't take too much more, he knew this wasn't doing him any good either. While he thought he loved her, her Jekyll and Hyde mood swings had worn him and his patience out and made him doubt his feelings.

He shook his head. At least the rest of his stay in Iowa had been great. He'd had dinner the night before at Sue's house with Jerry's family. David had enjoyed himself kidding and teasing his nieces and nephews. After the events of the last week the familiarity of family life was a comfort and a contrast to his own situation at home.

Most of all though he had enjoyed talking with Sue and Jerry at length. They discussed the family information they'd found at their mother's house and speculated on where it might lead them and what the treasure might have been. David had purchased copies of the genealogy books he had found at the library and despite the fact that he had only scanned them he felt he knew something about the topic.

From her enthusiasm, he was glad that Sue seemed as curious as he was and he thought he could count on her support and help no matter where the quest led him. He felt sure he could count on his brother and aunt to contribute also. Beth, he suspected, had been waiting for this supporting role for a long time and he was glad she could be a source of help. Now he needed to get home and resolve a few other things.

The limo slowed briefly at the Central Artery but the Sunday traffic caused only minimal problems and the car accelerated onto the Southeast Expressway.

David's thoughts returned to his departure that morning. Sue and her family had come to Jerry's house for breakfast. Through the meal they had all laughed a lot and the strain and grief they all felt began to ebb. David had asked Sue to keep looking for the missing letter from their grandfather and she agreed, saying she would be spending a lot of time at the old house going through the rest of Janet Baker's things.

Beth arrived after the early church service and her infectious good humor adding to the upbeat feeling. When the time came to leave, good-byes were exchanged all around. David noticed Sue, Beth and Karen all had tears in their eyes and he found his own eyes misted also. Even though he would see them again he felt as if he was saying good-bye to something important now that his mother was gone.

Jerry drove him to the airport, giving him a bigger than usual hug and had promised to visit when he could. The United flight had been on time; landing at 5:15 and now the morning's warm memories had left David apprehensive. He had not idea of what to expect when he got home. What would he find when he saw Carol?

*   *   *

The limo stopped in front of the house in Duxbury and the driver got out to open the door for David. As David got out, the driver went for the luggage in the trunk. David paid the driver and then stood in the rain watching as the car pulled away. He hesitated at the curb for a moment then walked to the front door which was open.

He entered the house. There were moving boxes on the floor of the living room and next to a large wardrobe box was Carol's luggage. She was sitting on the couch, a glass of wine in front of her. She had been crying and wet tears were still on her face.

"Hello," David said warily.

"Hi," she sniffed.

"What's this?"

She looked at him and the tears started again rolling down her cheeks.

"I'm leaving," she sniffled. "There's no easy way to say it Dave. I'm sorry to do this to you so soon after your mother, but this is something I have to do."

"Why don't we talk about it?" said David, trying to fight the sour taste in his throat, his head spinning.

"We can talk all you want Dave, but it won't do any good now. God knows that you've tried to help me so often but I know what will happen. You'll only postpone what I have to do!"

"I love you," he said, not knowing what else to say.

"You're more serious about this relationship than I am Dave. I think I love you too, but not the same as you if you can understand that. You know sometimes you get so lazy, take things for granted including me. Then you're always eager to help when I get in one of my moods. I just don't think that's what I need. I need something more than this, I just don't know what."

She sobbed out loud twice. "I'm moving back to New York. I quit my job on Friday. I guess I just wasn't cut out for the securities business and I'm going home to straighten myself out."

"You could stay here and do that, you know," David offered. He wanted to take her in his arms, to hold her, make it better. He sensed though that this time there was nothing he could do.

"No Dave, you're part of my problem. You're so goddamned good. You're too understanding, but you have no passion in your life. You're too easy going. You've protected me and tried to help me, but I've got to solve my own problems. Damn it! I'm thirty-three! I've got to grow up and I can't do it here!"

David reflected on this, thinking some of what she said was true. He was easy going. His success had come relatively easy and this had given way to the lack of motivation he had felt recently. Perhaps he had no passion as she said, but he knew that the recent events in his life had somehow changed that. He felt a new challenge stirring within him and he was excited about something other than work for the first time in a long while. But he knew he couldn't explain this to Carol though, she just wouldn't understand that part of him.

"Carol, I want to do what's right for you. I owe you that at least."

"No, I owe you a lot Dave," she said. "We've had something good and you've been supportive and I really think I do love you. That's why I'm so sorry to do this to you!" She broke down again sobbing.

David went into the bathroom, returning with a handful of tissue. He handed the wad to her and she dabbed her face stemming the flow of tears.

Satisfied he'd done something; David went into the kitchen removing a can of beer from the refrigerator. Sipping it, he went back into the living room. Carol had managed to compose herself.

"What now?" David asked, "would a hug help?"

She smiled a faint smile. "Yes, maybe. Once anyway for good luck."

She stood and they embraced for a moment.

"Now," she sniffled, "I rented a U-Haul van. I could use some help loading it. It's in the driveway."

David knew it was over and he realized that he'd known it since the trip to Portland. The pain was bad, but not, he reflected, as bad as it might have been, certainly not as bad as the divorce.

"Sure, I'll help you," he smiled.

He pointed to the glass of wine on the table. "You sure you can drive?"

"I only had one waiting for you. I'll be okay. I should get home in four hours or so. If I have a problem, I'll stop."

Together, they loaded the van in the rain. Finished, David closed the rear door and they stood facing each other in the soaking drizzle. He hurt inside but tried not to show it.

"Kiss?" he questioned.

"Sure."

Their lips met. It was the kind of kiss a sister gives her brother. In the final hour the passion in their relationship had evaporated, David thought.

"Good-bye," she said climbing into the van.

He shut the door. "Good-bye. I really do hope things work out for you Carol."

She tried to smile, then looked down as she started the engine. She glanced up at him one last time, tears beginning once more. Unable to return his stare she backed out of the driveway put the transmission in drive and left.

David watched her go, aware of the same misting in his eyes he'd felt in Iowa that morning. He wiped them as the van disappeared down the street. He turned to go inside.

"Shit," he said aloud.

He remembered the immortal words from one of his friends: "Life sucks and then you die."

He found he could laugh at the thought. Maybe tomorrow would be better.

*   *   *

David awoke late the next morning, bright sunlight shinning through the open window. He blinked to clear his eyes, moving his arm to his side to check the bed. The fact that he was alone did not surprise him as he remembered the events of the previous evening. He sat up, too quickly, suddenly aware of the aching pain in his forehead. He was terribly hung over, the result of the attempt to wash away the hurt of Carol leaving.

He had finished the remains of a bottle of scotch the night before while sitting in front of the television trying not to feel sorry for himself. He had not succeeded he reflected as his stomach protested and a wave of nausea swept over him. His appetite gone, he had barely finished the steak he had taken from the freezer at 10:00 p.m. He had cooked it on the gas grill and had managed to burn the still frozen sirloin badly. At least, he complimented himself, he had remembered to eat.

David sat on the edge of the bed looking at the clock. It was nearly 10:30 and he got up and went into the bathroom, his head throbbing. After relieving himself he studied his face in the mirror and was surprised that he didn't look as bad as he felt.

He opened the medicine cabinet to get a bottle of aspirin and he shook two tablets from the bottle. He swallowed them with a sip of water then replaced the bottle and closed the mirrored cabinet door.

His reflection reappeared in the glass and he took stock of himself. He knew he wasn't handsome, but was satisfied with what he saw. His boyish sandy brown hair gave his angular face a good look, he thought. He was aging well, he decided, even though there were strands of gray hair beginning to appear to mix with the brown.

He contemplated his image. Shit, day one without Carol, Da Dum. He was hurt, but this time he thought he was ready for it. He twisted the handle turning on the water to wash his face. The water made him feel better as he lathered up and shaved, planning the day as he drew the razor across his face.

After dressing, he went downstairs to make coffee. Holding a mug of instant, he went into the living room, picked up the telephone and dialed Jack Pierce who answered on the third ring.

"Jack. It's Dave. I'm back."

"Dave! I didn't expect to hear from you until later in the week."

"I came back early. I've got some things to do and I need your help. You have lunch plans today?"

"No."

"I'll swing by the office and pick you up. I need to talk."

"Okay, see you around twelve-thirty or so?"

"Good. I'll be there." David replaced the receiver and tried to organize his thoughts. What do I do first?

                    *   *   *

They sat down at a table in Godfrey's, a restaurant near the Village where they often ate. David had picked Pierce up at the Village late due to his throbbing head and the conversation in the car was measured, but David suspected Jack knew something was troubling him.

A waiter came to the table with menus. "Can I get you gentlemen anything from the bar?"

David eyed the waiter who smiled politely and almost said no, but Pierce spoke first.

"I'll have a light draft. Baker?"

David shrugged. What the hell, maybe he'd feel better. "Bloody Mary," he responded.

The waiter smiled again and scurried to the bar. After watching the man walk away, Pierce shifted his gaze to David. He broke the ice.

"What's the problem Dave?"

David hesitated. Damn! The man could read his mind.

"Carol left," he said.

Pierce stared at him. "That's pretty shitty Dave. Especially after losing your mother. You okay?"

"Yeah, surprisingly I think I am. I guess I saw it coming. You know Jack, I'm hung over, hurt and feeling pretty lousy but the bottom line is I feel sort of relieved that this has been resolved."

"You mentioned before that she was under a tremendous amount of pressure. Was that the problem?

"Some of it," David hesitated, "but there's more to it. I'm damned if I could figure the woman out."

He paused as the waiter brought their drinks. The man told them he would return for the lunch orders and went to another table. David picked up his glass taking a swallow of the spicy tomato juice blend.

"She was having problems at work Jack. Pressure to produce, but I told you that already. It got to her but it's funny though, I really thought we were okay until a week ago. In the end I guess the problem was me or maybe us. The problems at work were just the last straw. She told me I too easy going, that I took too much for granted.

David paused to sip the drink, then continued.

"She said she needed to get away. I really wonder down deep if she doesn't have a real problem?"

"I repeat," said Pierce, "are you okay?"

David smiled at his boss.

"Yeah Jack, I'm going to be fine. I've just got to accept the fact that I'm oh for eleven or something like that when it comes to women, including my marriage."

"Nonsense," laughed Pierce, "you just haven't met the right girl yet. And when you do, it'll be a knockout. You won't know what hit you!"

"Oh Christ, if I hear that again I'm going to puke. Which I may do anyway, the way I feel!"

Pierce chuckled but David got very serious.

"Jack?"

"Yeah?"

"Am I too easy going?" he asked.

Pierce though it over for a second. "Yeah, sometimes you are. But I've got to say that, as far as I'm concerned, it's an endearing quality in you. You seem to know when to get excited and you know when to work. The important things make you excited and when that happens I usually know I'm on to something. Especially when I've been the one to motivate you!"

David laughed despite the returning headache.

"You've got a good sense of humor Dave. Don't ever change that. You're going to be fine, it'll just take some time."

The waiter returned with a basket of hot rolls and they ordered lunch.

Buttering a pumpernickel hard roll, Pierce spoke. "Tell me about the visit home. Everything okay there?"

"Yeah. I've resolved that part of things better than what happened with Carol. I had a great visit and I've got a new project to work on. I need your help."

"You know I'll do anything I can. What are you up to?"

"Well," David smiled, "I think I've been bitten by your damned genealogy bug!"

A surprised Jack Pierce looked at him. "No kidding, you mean all my years of subtle brainwashing have finally produced some results?"

"Remember I told you on the phone I was going to look for family records?"

"Sure, I remember," Pierce said.

"Well, I think that I can join the Mayflower Society."

Pierce blinked in surprise. "You're kidding! Fill me in!"

They stopped for a moment as the waiter set plates in front of them. While they ate, David related the whole story. How he had found his great-grandmother's Mayflower connection, the Baker family information, the curious reference to the stolen family "treasure" and the missing letter from his grandfather. He told Pierce that his brother and sister were anxious to help and he wanted to get to work as soon as he could to see what he could find.

"Where do I start?"

"That's quite a story," Pierce said between bites. "But actually you've made a good start. Let's take the Mayflower relationship first. Do you have a copy of your great grandmother's membership certificate?"

"Yes."

"Let me have it. I'll get a copy of her application from the Society. It'll cost you thirty-five or forty bucks but the application should give you her lineage. You'll have to add the information for your grandparents and parents and you'll have to document everything though, even you great grandmother's data. The information in a lot of the old applications from the early days of the Society can be suspect. I'll look it over for you though to see if it needs work. Once I see where you stand we'll get a preliminary application for you. I'll be your sponsor and we'll go from there."

"Thanks," replied David.

"Now, this Baker business. The treasure story is very interesting! You say the rights to it have been passed to you?"

"I guess so. My brother and I anyway."

"No other relatives?"

"None that I know of. My father was an only child. So was my grandfather, I think. If there are any other Bakers I don't know about them."

Pierce thought a second.

"There could easily be others Dave. You don't know how far back this thing goes. Maybe someone already found the treasure, whatever it is or was."

"Yeah, I thought of that but if that had happened though, would my grandfather or father have bothered to mention it? Even if someone's found it I'd like to know what it was. I'm curious about it and besides, I really want to know more about the Baker family now."

Pierce watched him as he spoke.

"You really have caught it haven't you? You know, I haven't seen you so excited in a long time. You're really getting into this, aren't you?"

David grinned. "Yeah, I am."

"Well, just so you know, it can be a lot of tedious work. A long and difficult task and you're going to have problems because Baker is a very common name. Don't expect to be as lucky as you've been with your mother's side of the family! Now, tell me your grandfather was born when and where?"

"1892 in Logansport, Indiana," David replied.

"And you know his father's name?"

"Yes."

"I suggest that you start with the 1900 Census for whatever county he was from in Indiana. If you can find you great grandfather, the information will give you the state where he was born and where his father was born. That will get you started. Also try the 1880 Census to see if he's listed there."

"Why not the 1890 Census?"

"Not much of it left. Almost all the records were burned in a fire. So you have to work around the void."

"That's right," remembered David, "I read that in Doane's book. Where do I go to start?"

"You've read Doane's book?"

"Half way through."

"Good beginning book. It was the first one I read as a kid. You could probably rent the census microfilm through inter-library loan at the Duxbury Library, but if you're going to get serious about this you really should join the New England Historic Genealogical Society in Boston. They're on Newbury Street in town and they have most of the census records on microfilm. They have a whole lot more and I'd suggest you become a member to save you money because they charge non-members each time they use the library."

"I'll do that," said David. "Jack, I'd like to take the rest of the week off if that's okay with you?"

"Dave, as far as I'm concerned, you're still on bereavement leave. I'll see you at work next Monday. Call me tomorrow, I may be able to expedite getting your great grandmother's papers. In the meantime, I'm ready to help you all I can. I wish you luck and I'm absolutely fascinated by this idea of a stolen family "treasure". Just remember there are probably other lines of descent from whoever had the treasure and if it existed it's likely someone has already solved your mystery and claimed the "treasure", or whatever. It may be a wild goose chase, but I know how you feel, I'd like to know the details too."

"Thanks, Jack. I want to find answers if I can." He looked at Pierce. "And thanks for being a friend, I needed to talk."

"You're a good guy Dave. I'm glad to do it and if you run out of things to do give me a call and I'll kick your ass in a game of one on one!"

David laughed. "Anytime, old man!"

They paid the tab and left the restaurant. David thanked Pierce again as he dropped him off at the Village and although his head was still fuzzy, he felt a hell of a lot better.

Satisfied with the start he'd made David Baker drove home making plans to begin his research.

*   *   *

David reviewed what he knew one more time the next morning as he drove into Braintree to catch the Red Line. He had spent the previous afternoon organizing the Baker information. As the genealogy books suggested he made a pedigree chart for his father. This family tree graphically showed the father and mother of each of his parents through the preceding generations. The Baker chart was only partially filled since David had only information going back two generations from his father.

He arrived at the "T" station in Braintree and after finding a place to park in the packed lot, he boarded the train, taking it into the city. He transferred to the Green Line at Park Street and rode to Arlington where he got off. He walked over to Newbury Street and went west to the turn of the century six-story brick building that housed the New England Historic Genealogical Society.

He entered the building and stopped at the front desk where a young woman greeted him.

"I'd like to use the library," David explained. "And I'd also like to become a member."

The young woman smiled. "Sure, that's easy. Here, full this out. Annual dues are fifty dollars for a regular membership. Ever been here before?"

"No," replied David, as he filled out the membership form. "I could use some help finding things."

"Sure, library is on the sixth floor," she pointed to the elevator. "Ask one of the librarians for specific help. There's an awful lot here."

David finished the form and wrote a check for the membership dues.

"Thanks," said the young woman, taking the form and the check from David. "Welcome to the New England Historic Genealogical Society. We're glad to have you as a member and good luck in your research!" She handed David a brochure and a copied guide to the library.

David nodded. "Thanks," and put the material in his briefcase. "Thanks for the help."

David went up to the sixth floor library. Taking a quick glance around the reading room he took in the high ceiling, the old aged paneling and the massive worktables with nameplates memorializing the names of donors. He went to the librarian's desk and asked to use the microfilm for the 1900 Census of Cass County, Indiana which was where Logansport was located. The librarian directed him to the fifth floor stacks where giant gray metal cabinets held the various rolls of microfilm. Here another librarian helped David find the microfilm he wanted and demonstrated how to load and use the microfilm reader. After supervising him for a moment, she left leaving David in front of the machine.

He called up the beginning of the census record, which he noted was sort of like a giant ledger book. The entries were written in a scrawling script that was hard to read on some pages and unclear because of the microfilm on others. He slowly scrolled through the film until he came to Logansport and scanned the information more carefully reading the names as he went down each page. As he went down the pages he realized that he was looking at history. This was the way things had been ninety years before.

Thirty minutes later, near the end of the listings for the town, he found what he was looking for. On the page in a neatly penned script was the census taker's record of the family of his great grandfather. David carefully copied the data into the notebook he had brought with him.

Joseph Baker	Head of Family	White	Male	Nov. 1860	Age 39
	Born Ohio	Father born NY		Mother born NY	
Martha Baker	Wife	White	Female	July 1861	Age 38
	Born Indiana	Father born NY		Mother born Penn.	
Mary Baker	Daughter	White	Female	May 1887	Age 13
	Born Indiana	Father born Ohio		Mother born Indiana	
Susan Baker	Daughter	White	Female	Jan. 1890	Age 10
	Born Indiana	Father born Ohio		Mother born Indiana	
William Baker	Son	White	Male	May 1892	Age 8
	Born Indiana	Father born Ohio		Mother born Indiana	
Martha Baker	Daughter	White	Female	Aug. 1895	Age 4
	Born Indiana	Father born Ohio		Mother born Indiana	

David read and reread the record of his ancestors and felt as if he was glimpsing the past. Funny how that felt. He finished copying the information, noting that Joseph Baker's father had been born in New York. This surprised him, but the information was important as he reasoned that Joseph's father, whoever he was, had left New York for Ohio before Joseph was born in 1860 and that was a good clue.

He rewound the microfilm and went back to the storage cabinets to locate the 1880 census for Cass County. He hoped to find the same family in the same place and returning to the reader, he loaded the new roll of film into the machine. He advanced the film to Logansport and again scanned the old records. It took him almost the same amount of time but he found what he was looking for, this time the record of his great-great grandfather.

Charles Baker	Head of Family	White	Male	Age 46	Born 1834
	Born New	York Father born		NY Mother born NY	
Jane Baker	Wife	White	Female	Age 44	Born 1836
	Born New York	Father born NY		Mother born NY	
Joseph Baker	Son	White	Male	Age 20	Born 1860
	Born Ohio	Father born NY		Mother born NY	
Abigail Baker	Daughter	White	Female	Age 18	Born 1862
	Born Indiana	Father born NY		Mother born NY	
John Baker	Son	White	Male	Age 14	Born 1866
	Born Indiana	Father born NY		Mother born NY	
April Baker	Daughter	White	Female	Age 10	Born 1870
	Born Indiana	Father born NY		Mother born NY	
Betsey Baker	Daughter	White	Female	Age 6	Born 1873
	Born Indiana	Father born NY		Mother born NY	

David was excited by this discovery. He had found the next generation and now had the name of his great-great grandfather. In addition, he had discovered that the family had moved from Ohio to Indiana some time between 1860 and 1862 because of the birthplaces of the first two children. What had made them move? He wasn't sure what to do next.

He went back to the microfilm cabinets and found the 1870 census for Cass County. He viewed this film and easily found the family again in Logansport. The information was the same as in 1880 but everyone was ten years younger and the younger children had not been born as of the 1870 census date.

David took a break for lunch at a nearby deli and returned to the library. He spent an hour getting to know the layout of the library and the location of the vast amount of material available. The NEHGS library really was a tremendous resource, he thought. There was information from all over the country and even from some foreign countries.

Later in the afternoon David searched the genealogy catalog file looking up the name Baker and found about twenty titles on file. He recorded the information in the notebook he'd started and spent the balance of the afternoon going over the material in each book. He was unable to find his great grandfather or great-great grandfather in any of the published genealogies. He made notes to use as a reference in the future if he discovered new information because Pierce had told him he might be eventually be able connect his line of descent into one of the published lines.

Late in the afternoon he left, retracing his route to Braintree, excited about the progress he had made.

*   *   *

David arrive home about 5:30 and he quickly checked his mail. Finding nothing of interest, he went to the telephone in the kitchen. He knew Jack Pierce would still be at work so he picked up the receiver and tapped out Pierce's direct number.

"Jack Pierce."

"Hi. It's Dave. I had some good luck today. I found my great-great grandfather in the census records!"

"Hey, that's great! I did okay too. I've got a copy of your great grandmother's lineage record from her Mayflower application. It's pretty straightforward. The whole family was from Connecticut so you should be able to document it all with a trip to the Connecticut State Library in Hartford. The Barbour Collection has vital records from most of the towns and that should provide you with most of what you need. If you can find the documentation, you can tie you great grandmother to John Howland. It should only take you a day."

David absorbed what Pierce told him.

"Stop by in the morning," Pierce continued, "and I'll give you a copy of the lineage papers and directions to the library."

"Okay, I think I'll stop in early and then head for Hartford. You sure I can do it in a day?"

"Yeah, Dave, even you can do it in a day. It probably shouldn't take more than a couple of hours."

"Okay. By the way Jack, there were other children. My grandfather wasn't an only child."

"Oh?" Pierce questioned.

"Yeah. According to the census, he had at least three sisters. He was the only boy though."

"That's interesting."

"I guess that's why my mother thought he was an only child. I wonder what happened to his sisters? Any way I can find out where those relatives might be? Maybe someone else is interested in this too?"

"Could be. There are a few ways to track down other lines. First I'd try to find an obituary for your grandfather."

"I found one in Iowa. It mentioned that he died in France. It also gave me the names of his parents though."

"It didn't mention the sisters as survivors?"

"Not that I remember. I can have my sister check it again though."

"Actually, that's not unusual. Early obituaries often didn't mention anyone other than wife, children or parents. I'm not surprised. Do you have an obituary for you great grandfather?"

"No. Do you think there is one?"

"Could be. Do you know when he died?"

"No."

"Well, see if you can find out. Then you might be able to find his obituary. That might mention where the his daughters, your grandfather's sisters were."

"Good idea. Anything else?"

"Yeah, but one thing at a time. You're going to Connecticut first. Start with that."

"Yeah, okay. I'll call my sister later to see if she can help. I'll see you tomorrow. Thanks."

"Early?" Pierce asked.

"Yeah, early," David said.

"I'll be here Dave. See you."

David chuckled, returning the phone to the cradle.

*   *   *

The Connecticut State Library is located in a large stately marble building across the street from the State Capitol and, in addition to the library the building houses the Connecticut State Supreme Court. David took in the local scenery as he started up the stone steps that led to the entrance. It was late morning, but the sun was already beating down and he thought it would be a very hot humid day.

The directions Jack Pierce had given him earlier had been easy to follow and he knew the Genealogy and Local History section of the library was in the basement on the eastern side of the building.

He entered the building and turned left to go down the marble steps into the library. Entering the large reading room, he set his briefcase on a table and looked around. He was unsure where to start and went to a man with thinning hair who sat at the librarian's desk.

"Hi. I need some help," David said.

"Sure, what do you need?"

"I want to use the Barbour Collection to verify some records. Could you show me where to find it?"

"Sure come this way," the librarian said and rose from the desk. He led David to a hall corridor that was lined with shelves and catalog card files.

"This is the Barbour Collection," he explained, pointing to the bound volumes on several shelves. "Church records are here also and to the right is a catalog of census records. Have you used a catalog file before?"

"Yes."

"Good. If you need anything else, let me know."

"Thanks. I will," replied David.

Stopping only for a sandwich in the library cafeteria, David rapidly went through the vital records for Ashford, Colchester, New London and Waterbury Connecticut. He found what he needed with relative ease and spent almost ten dollars at the Xerox machine making copies of the documentation.

As he finished with the copier he glanced at the clock and found it was only 2:00. There was time left to see what else he could find.

The card catalog listed a large amount of Baker material including most of the same genealogies he'd looked at in Boston the day before. Disappointed at this dead end he spent an hour browsing through the many volumes lining the walls.

As he read part of an early history of Connecticut, he found that his new interest in genealogy had given him a new perspective on history. The fact that some of his ancestors had been alive and had participated in the events of the times made it seem all so real to him. David became so engrossed in reading that the time went by rapidly and the announcement that the library was closing took him by surprise.

He packed up his things and left the library satisfied that he had what he needed for the Mayflower Society. Now he looked forward to joining and he would give Jerry and Sue the information so they could join the Iowa chapter if they wanted to. He felt a sense of accomplishment and knew he had done a lot in a short period of time.

David left Hartford just at rush hour and as he sat in the car crawling along in rush hour traffic, it occurred to him that he hadn't thought of Carol for most of the day. Genealogy was apparently a good release for him. Therapy for the broken hearted, that's what it was. Shit he thought, it was time to go back to work.

*   *   *

David Baker indulged in his favorite method of time killing by looking out his office window. He had been back at work for nearly two weeks now and May had turned into June. It was June, but the weather had turned cloudy and chilly once again. However, the weather did not scare the visitors away he thought. There were six different tour groups scheduled for the Village today, including a Japanese group of over two hundred people.

He smiled to himself glad to be back at work. Upon his return he had pushed himself to tackle several different projects at once. Hard work he found, was the best cure for the pain he suffered. He was sure he was getting over Carol but his mother's death would take longer. But he was confident he would deal with that too.

Jerry and Sue were a big help in this respect. David had talked with them frequently over the previous three weeks and they had helped each other work through the void left by their mother's death. Jerry and Sue were beginning to inventory their mother's estate and Sue had called on several occasions to tell him of a new treasure that had been discovered at the house. Each tale of a childhood memento brought with it a pang of sorrow, but by confronting his feelings David found he could deal with his mother's death. He suspected he would never get over the loss, but each passing day made it seem less painful.

He had spent most of the day working on the budget for a new television advertising campaign scheduled to run in the West Coast market. The ads would extol the virtues of New England, encouraging Westerners to return to their East Coast roots.

The telephone rang and David picked up the receiver. "Dave Baker," he answered.

"Dave? It's Sue."

"Hey, how are you?"

"I'm great!" Sue sounded excited. "I've got terrific news!"

"What's up?" he asked.

"I feel really stupid," she said. "I don't know why I didn't think of it before. God Dave, it should have been the first place to look!"

"What are you talking about?" David asked.

"The letter!" Sue bubbled, "I found the letter. Or rather Jerry and I found the letter. We finally went to the bank to clean out Mom's safety deposit box. Geez, I should have thought of that when you were here. I'm so stupid but anyway the letter was there!"

"Hey, that's great news!"

"I found something else too," Sue said.

"What?"

"With the letter is the detailed citation for the medal Grandpa Baker won. God Dave, this is some story!"

"Wow!" he said.

"David?"

"Yes?"

"The whole thing is kind of eerie. It's kind of like you're there watching it all happen. I think our grandfather was quite a man, even if we never knew him. I'll FedEx a copy of the letter to you but I'd like to read it to you. Do you have time now?"

"Sure," David said and sat back, put his feet on his desk and listened as Sue read to him.

CHAPTER FOUR

July 24, 1918
La Ferte-sous-Jouarre, France

First Lieutenant William Baker, U.S. Army, late of the Iowa National Guard, put his pen down and tried to ignore the distant rumble of artillery. He yawned then stretched and rose from the campstool he had been sitting on and went to the window of the partially demolished stone farmhouse. The muted thunder of the distant guns faded and he took stock of his immediate surroundings. He was standing in a small farmhouse to the west of Chateau-Thierry where his unit, the 168th Infantry, was bivouacked.

He was the Assistant Company Commander of D Company and 2nd Platoon Leader. The 168th Infantry was a part of the 42nd Division, nicknamed the Rainbow Division because it was made up of National Guard units from twenty-seven states and the District of Columbia. The division, composed of ready state units, had been among the first troops called up and organized into division strength after war was declared in 1917.

The troops had moved into the reserve area during mid afternoon on the 24th and now the soldiers were waiting for the evening meal to be delivered from the regimental kitchens. Baker again sat on the campstool and picked up the letter he had just finished and read it one more time.

My Dear Son:

I am writing this letter to you with the hope that you will never read it. However, I am mindful of the risks of war and fate, so I want to take this opportunity to tell you some things you should know.

Although you are only two years old now, you will be a man someday and while I hope to be able to tell you in person, there are some family traditions that, by a promise to my Father, I am bound to tell you.

My father was Joseph Baker and he was born in Ravenna, Ohio in 1860. He moved to Logansport, Indiana at the beginning of the Civil War and his father, my grandfather, Charles Baker, served in the Union Army during the war. My grandfather died when I was very young so I don't remember much about him, but I think he was born in Ohio also. My father died in Stillman, Iowa in 1906 during the measles epidemic that year.

On Father's deathbed, he related a family tale of the stolen family treasure that had been taken through treachery and deceit. He didn't know when or where this happened, but his father told him that it was back east somewhere. My father also told me it was a family tradition for Baker men to bequeath the rights to this treasure to their sons. By doing this, Baker men are always to remember the treacherous deed and pass the rights forever to each succeeding generation. As my father spoke to me I promised him I would pass this information on to my children.

I do this for you now as my only child and I might add that I have questioned the legend of the family treasure, thinking that something so important should have been a better known tale. My father did mention something about a cousin who had pursued the treasure but he became tired and mumbled this part so that I could not understand his meaning. I wish I had for he lapsed into a coma and died the next morning without being able to tell me more.

Whether this tale is true or not, it has been important enough that our ancestors have passed this tradition down to each subsequent generation. I feel I have now honored my commitment and I fervently hope that I will be able to tell you this in person. If not, your mother has instructions to give you this letter when you reach the age of twenty-one. I love you very much and know you will be the kind of man of whom I would be very proud.

> *With Much Love, Fondly,*
> *Your Father*

1st Lieutenant William B. Baker

Satisfied that he had fulfilled the promise to his father but with an uneasy sadness, William Baker folded the letter, inserted it into the already addressed envelope and sealed it. The mail orderly would be by later. He stretched his arms one more time wondering what the morning would bring.

*   *   *

The 42nd Division moved into the line on July 25th, relieving the 26th Division. The Americans were counterattacking the Germans in the Chateau-Thierry salient that had resulted from the German attacks in March and June. The German onslaught, planned to produce a quick victory before massive numbers of American troops arrived to sway the balance of power, had been a near thing. Exhausted French and British soldiers, reinforced by a few newly arrived Americans, managed to stop the thrust near the Marne in an action reminiscent of early battles of 1914. Now, the Allied Armies were attacking to regain the lost ground taking the battle to the Germans and the Americans were making their presence felt.

The Allied offensive had begun on July 18th with the 26th Division as a spearhead unit acting as a pivot near Soissons. The American soldiers were proving to be good troops, earning the grudging respect from the battle hardened French Poilus they fought beside.

The 42nd and the 168th had first seen action in March at Badonviller; Baker remembered and had been in action many times since. A hardened veteran now, Baker knew the fear and apprehension were still the same no matter how many times you went through the shattering experience.

Now, in the early morning of July 26th, he reflected on the task ahead of them. They would attack the German lines shortly and the men of the 168th were to take the ground in the center of the area assigned to the division. The Hawkeyes were anxious for the assault to begin, confident and proud of their competence, but were anxious to get it over with and be one more step closer to home.

Baker laughed to himself and shook his head thinking of the remark made by his Platoon Sergeant, John Woodward. Woodward, a small thin man with a narrow face like a ferret, was from Cedar Rapids, but his outlandish outward appearance in no way diminished his abilities; he was a tenacious fighter. He was a very proud man and had remarked that no matter what the Iowans did, the men of the 165th Infantry, formerly the 69th New York Irishers, seemed to get all the publicity from the newspapers. Baker shook his head. There should be plenty of attention to go around after today, he thought.

It was getting lighter in the east. Baker looked at his watch. It was 4:40 a.m.

Any time now.

In the distance, behind him, the dull booming began and across a wide front the batteries of artillery started the barrage that would precede the attack. The freight train thunder announced the presence of the first shells, which crashed into the German positions. Soon the German trenches were covered with smoke and bright flame as the artillery observers adjusted fire and walked the barrage back and forth along the enemy positions.

The barrage would be a short one, Baker knew. It was designed to do maximum damage to support the attack without allowing the German artillery a chance to respond with an effective counter barrage on the advancing troops. In front if him he watched the men of the 2nd

Battalion, who would be the first wave of the attack. They were fidgeting, nervous and tense, anticipating the end of the barrage.

All at once the firing and echoing explosions stopped. Silence covered the field then the company commanders of the 2nd Battalion were on their feet now, whistles blowing, yelling "Attack, Attack!"

The Hawkeye soldiers, bayonets fixed, obeyed the order climbing out of the friendly trenches. They walked at first, but responding to the whistles, the excitement and their own adrenaline soon broke into a run. Yelling wildly, they crossed the No Mans Land. Mortar rounds landed on the German trenches to assist their advance. Men dropped here and there at random hit by weak rifle and machine gun fire suppressed by the effective opening barrage but the Americans were soon in the first line of German defenses.

Baker watched the action from his observation post, glad to see there was little apparent opposition from the enemy. He put his field glasses to his eyes scanning the German position through the murky smoke. He saw the first wave make headway through the Germans, bayonets flashing occasionally in the early morning light.

His stomach tensed and he was aware of his own fear. He expected it now knowing he would never get used to it. Still it gnawed at him.

Captain Walter Heinz, the company commander, yelled, "Fix bayonets!"

Around him the men in his platoon complied, metal scraping on metal as the long knives locked onto rifle barrels. Baker looked again and saw the attacking Americans move up out of the first line of trenches and run toward the main German line of defense. A green flare rose above the enemy position. This signaled the successful completion of the first part of the attack. It was also the signal for the second wave to move up in support.

"Hawkeyes, let's go!" Heinz ordered.

Baker was up and moving, pistol in hand. He put the whistle in his mouth and blew. The shrill noise pierced his ears.

"Second Platoon! Move out!"

In a staggered line abreast, they went forward at a trot. Behind them, several explosions announced the arrival of the German counter fire. Baker was glad it was late. They rapidly crossed the field into the first German trenches. Dead and wounded soldiers, German and American, lay everywhere.

The carnage confirmed it had been a fierce violent struggle. Baker would never get used to it he thought. He concentrated on his front and D Company continued forward following the first wave. They moved quickly two hundred yards to the second line of German trenches that had also been taken now by the leading attackers. As they came up, the men of the 2nd Battalion were sorting prisoners, dressing wounds and resting from the ordeal.

Heinz came over the Baker, almost out of breath.

"We'll jump off in three minutes," he puffed. "It's our turn now. Remember Will, the objective is the last line of defenses in those woods!"

Baker nodded as Heinz pointed to the sparse forest that lay in front of them.

"From the briefing, it should be about another two hundred yards! Stay close to my right flank!" he smiled. "Good luck Will, this will be hot work, make no mistake about it!"

"Good luck to you Tom. We'll do our best!"

"I know you will," Heinz said and the two officers shook hands. Then Heinz ran off to the left.

Baker called Woodward to him, outlining the plan of attack. The wiry Iowan nodded.

"We'll get it done, Sir!" he replied.

Next to them trench mortars began popping, a small attempt to help support the advance to the next objective.

Heinz was on his feet now, blowing his whistle.

"Let's go! Attack! Attack! Attack!"

Along the line, the men of the 1st Battalion rose to their feet and they advanced as a mass toward the woods at a fast walk, the excitement building. Overhead, mortar rounds flew, crashing into the trees in front of them shattering what was left of the forest. Deadly splinters sprayed down on the German defenders inflicting casualties.

Company D was running now, wet with sweat and already exhausted but the call of battle made them ignore this. They plunged over downed trees and a line of barbed wire. Through the air, they could feel the passing of bullets. The Germans were firing at them. Several men dropped, hit by fire, screams unheard.

The woods opened and Baker could see the German breast works. To his left he could make out the rest of the company running slightly behind. A figure came from the flank tugging at his sleeve. He recognized the concerned face of PFC Sajeski from the first platoon.

Baker stopped to listen.

"Sarg'nt Jackson sent me! Cap'n Heinz's dead!" the young soldier yelled panting, sweat pouring down his face. "Caught one in the chest. You're in command!"

He took a deep breath adding a hesitant, "Sir!"

Baker nodded, the implications of the message not yet registering. Not thinking he reacted automatically. "Get back to your platoon. Tell Jackson to keep pushing forward. I'll be over as soon as I can!"

The messenger bent to catch his breath then stared at Baker with a forlorn look of hope on his face.

"Everything okay Sajeski?" Baker asked trying to sound confident although he wasn't sure what he would do next.

"Yessir, I'm okay. Just need to catch my breath. I'll tell the Sarge to keep going. Yessir!"

The young soldier crouched and ran back toward the left flank.

Baker paused for a second to get his bearings.

I'm in command, he thought. How in hell did I let that happen? He looked to his right where his platoon was still advancing slowly. He knew what he had to do and ran to Woodward.

"Heinz's down! I'm in command and you're in charge here! I'm going to the left flank to finish the attack. Keep the platoon moving forward!"

"I'll keep 'em movin'!" Woodward said eyes wide.

Baker hurried to the left where the rest of the company was attacking. The Hawkeye doughboys were at the breast works. Machine guns and rifle fire echoed throughout the woods. Men fell everywhere. The Americans were over the breast works now, the fighting hand to hand. The Germans were tenacious, but could not stop the crazed Americans.

Gasping for breath, heart pounding, Baker leaped over the breast works, Colt Automatic ready. He shot a German who lunged wildly to bayonet him and saw the man collapse like a puppet with severed strings clutching his neck which spurted red. The Iowa men madly continued on chasing the retreating Germans. Realizing his men were in danger of going too far, Baker blew his whistle to stop the insane dash. He had to bring the troops back to consolidate the hard fought ground they had just gained.

Slowly the American soldiers returned and as the weary soldiers sat to rest, Baker organized the company along the old German position ready to repel the counter attack that he knew was certain to follow.

The battalion commander, Major Francis Ivery, ran to him.

"Where's Heinz?" Ivery demanded, coughing as a whiff of gas caught him.

"Dead," Baker said simply.

Ivery faced the Lieutenant, shaking his head, accepting the fact that the man he had come to find was dead.

"They'll come soon," he said, his voice even. "Be ready. Have you positioned your men?"

Baker responded. "Yes, the machine guns just came up. We'll be settled in a minute!"

"Okay Baker, hold your ground!" Ivery ordered. He touched his hand to his forehead and trotted off to the right to seek out C Company.

Baker surveyed his position and saw the men had settled in behind the breast works and found good cover. The company machine guns were setting up on the flanks to provide cross fire when the attack came and judging by the number of men in line, Baker estimated they had suffered ten percent casualties in the attack. As bad as that was, it was less than expected.

Baker's head rose to watch as German mortar rounds began to land on the American position and he quickly ducked to avoid flying shrapnel. The attack would come any minute now. Firing began on his right. A Browning Automatic Rifle chattered briefly behind him then abruptly stopped and Baker looked to see the Germans come down the gentle slope attacking his flank. But the massed fire of the Iowa soldiers stopped the Germans in their tracks; many gray green clad soldiers falling before the American line.

Baker focused back to his front. They would come at him now he thought, the flank attack just a diversion. Why do I know that he thought as a mortar round exploded near him throwing more shrapnel. He felt the hot sting as he was hit in the left forearm. Looking down, he hoped it was superficial.

In front of him he saw the Germans appear over the rise coming straight toward him. They began to charge through the woods at the Hawkeyes but on the flanks the machine guns opened fire, cutting into the Germans.

I think we can beat this off, Baker thought.

The German attack had been badly timed with the diversion. The Americans on the right added their firepower to rake the Germans.

The attacking wave hesitated, then broke. Men turned running in retreat past dead and wounded comrades and did not stop to help.

The counterattack blunted, whistles blew. Baker was on his feet again yelling.

"Counterattack! Counterattack!"

The men of D Company moved quickly over the breast works, running forward. Again Baker was in the lead with a group of ten or twelve men. They were exhausted, but were spurred on by the narcotic effect of pumping adrenaline and the excitement of battle. Others followed. The attack was general; the men wild with the desire to come to grips with the enemy.

The Germans continued in retreat, running to whatever safety they could find pursued by the crazed Americans.

Coming to the edge of the woods, Baker and the men near him stopped as they attracted clattering fire from a hidden Spandau machine gun. Baker dove to the ground as bullets buzzed around him and three of his men were hit by the fire. The rest of the soldiers fell, hugging the ground.

"Where is he?" Baker yelled to no one in particular.

A grimy soldier next to him peered out from under his helmet and looked at him. "I think he's in the field by the edge of the forest! I think I saw flashes!"

More men came up behind him and flopped on the ground breathing hard.

"Okay," Baker said looking around, "let's flank the position! First squad, second squad!"

He pointed to the squad leaders making a motion to move to the right and left. The men acknowledged the command and spread out crouching low into two groups to attack.

In position, they waited for the signal. Baker raised his arm and as he brought it down the Americans rose to attack. Running bent over, bullets flying around him, he almost to made it to the machine gun nest. Then another gun to the right opened up on them. Eight Hawkeyes fell tumbling backward and the others were pinned down by the machine gun fire. Baker saw this.

Lying on his belly Baker rolled over as Woodward came over to him.

"Give me some cover," he said, "I'm going to try and see if they're still alive! Get another bunch ready to try and flank the bastards!"

Baker crawled forward on his belly, hugging the ground Spandau bullets whined overhead but he ignored them. Slowly creeping forward, he reached the first man who was still alive and groaning. Carefully, Baker began to drag the unconscious soldier back to the American position. As he neared the line of men, willing hands pulled the man to safety.

"I'm going back for the next one. Are you ready yet?" Baker asked Woodward.

Woodward shook his head. "Give me another minute, the boys are a mite winded."

Baker nodded and crawled forward again. He went back three times retrieving three more wounded Iowa soldiers. Returning with the last man, he called Woodward to him.

"I think there's one more that's still breathing. I'm going back again," he panted. "You ready now?"

"Any time you say Sir!" Woodward tried to smile.

"Okay," Baker said touching Woodward's arm. "As I go out this time send your two teams to attack both nests at the same time. I think I can draw their attention!"

"You sure you want to do that Lieutenant? Seems like you've done enough already!"

"Don't argue with me," Baker said. "Now get going!"

Major Ivery came crawling forward.

"What's the holdup? What's going on?"

Baker looked at the man, couldn't he see what was going on?

"Ran into a couple of machine guns but we're about to storm their positions! I'm going after the last of my wounded as they do."

The battalion commander nodded. "Okay."

Baker crawled off again and Woodward, who had stayed when the battalion commander arrived, spoke.

"It's the fifth time he's gone after one of the boys Major. He's pushing his luck!" He paused for a moment and looked Ivery in the eye. "Seems like the kind of thing a man should get recognized for!"

"I think you're right Sergeant," Ivery said watching as Baker crept forward.

Touching his hand to his forehead, Woodward nodded and went off to lead the attack on the machine gun nests.

Baker moved slowly to the remaining wounded man. He moved carefully because he was starting to draw sniper fire and several bullets whined and slapped into the ground around him. He reached the wounded man who had taken a round in the chest and was wheezing badly. Baker began to drag him to safety aware of the added noise and gunfire as Woodward launched his assault on the German guns. Pulling the wounded man he made his way back to the American line.

The attack was successful. With the pop of grenades and a final crack of gunfire, Woodward's men overran the machine guns. As they mopped up, Baker reached the safety of the American position. The attack behind him was ending. He handed the wounded man to several Hawkeye soldiers who reached for him.

Baker pulled himself up into a sitting position, strain and fatigue on his wet face. Ivery was there.

"That was neat work Baker! I'm going to put you in for a medal for that!"

Exhausted, Baker could only gasp and shake his head, "It wasn't much."

The Americans began to march the few prisoners to the rear. Relieved the close quarters fighting was over and realizing they had survived the vicious fight, the men did not notice a lone German rifleman who drew a bead on the American officers sitting across the field.

Carefully he squeezed off a round and as he fired, the sound alerted the Americans. Too late they saw the rifleman. Aiming from the hip, three Hawkeyes open fire and the German died instantly from wounds in the chest not knowing what he had done.

Major Ivery had been the target, but the bullet found Lieutenant William Baker in the temple and killed him instantly.

From the ground where he had dived as the shot rang out, Ivery pulled himself erect and saw Lieutenant Baker, lifeless eyes open, lying in his own blood. He shook his head in sorrow.

"A very brave man," he said to no one in particular, "this is such a waste!"

He vowed to put the brave young man in for a posthumous Distinguished Service Cross. It was the least he could do.

CHAPTER FIVE

David put the phone back in the cradle feeling that he had seen a glimpse of the past, at least it felt that way to him. His grandfather's letter had been written just two days before he died in action and the full length citation for the medal he received told the story of a man who died trying to save others. Reading the citation Sue had said was almost an eerie feeling and it was also very special to them both.

David had talked with Sue at length after she finished reading the letter and the citation. She was very emotional about the content of the documents and he suspected that she was near tears. He told her he felt the same way. It was funny, he thought, the impact of the death of their Grandfather was still having an effect on the family seventy-two years later. He told Sue that he would call her soon and thanked her for the important discovery he said good-bye.

David leaned back in his chair, taking stock of the information the letter gave him. He now knew that his great grandfather, Joseph Baker had been born in Ravenna, Ohio. One fact did not ring true though he thought, although his grandfather's letter said that he thought Charles Baker was born in Ohio, David knew, from the census records that he had, in fact, been born in New York. However David still didn't know where though but the most interesting new information was the fact that Charles Baker had been in the Union Army during the Civil War. David thought that this might be an important clue. Finally and most tantalizing was the part that told him the family fortune had been lost somewhere in the east.

David wasn't sure what to do next but he thought that he should check the 1860 census for Ravenna, Ohio. There might be something there to help him and the Union Army connection should provide a lead, he thought since he had read that old Civil War records existed. David picked up the phone, tapping out Pierce's extension. Vickie Collins answered.

"Vickie, it's Dave. Is he busy?"

"No, not really, I'll put him on."

"No," David said, "I'll come down. Okay?"

"Sure, I'll tell him you're coming."

A moment later David walked into Pierce's outer office and nodded at Pierce's door.

"Go right in," Vicki told him.

David knocked at the door, heard Pierce's voice and entered the office.

"Dave! What can I do for you?"

"A little help, if you will. I'm still a little shook."

"About what?" Pierce asked, not sure he should be concerned.

"You remember the missing letter from my grandfather?"

"Sure."

"Well, I just got off the phone with my Sister. She found the letter in Mom's safety deposit box. She just read it to me."

"What was in it?" Pierce asked relaxing.

"It turned out to be a letter he wrote just two days before he died. It had some information about my great grandfather and great great grandfather and then he mentioned the family fortune again. God I've got to get to the bottom of this! Also, it turns out that my great great grandfather was in the Union Army in the Civil War."

"More progress," commented Pierce.

"Yeah, but more questions too. I've still got to find out where in New York my great great grandfather was born. Would his Civil War records show that?"

"They might," said Pierce. "There could be muster records with that information. Also, his pension application might give you that information, if he filed one. When did he die?"

"1896."

"The Pension Act went into effect in 1890, so there's a good chance he probably filed. There could be a widow's application if his wife outlived him," Pierce explained.

"What do I need to do?" David asked.

"You can write the National Archives for the information, but that takes anywhere from two to three months now. You'd better use a professional researcher. I have a good friend, Rose McKenzie, who does research work there. I'll give you her phone number. Give her a call and tell her what you know. She can take it from there. She'll charge you an hourly fee but it's worth it," Pierce said.

As David watched Pierce pulled a small card file from his desk and He looked up the number, writing it down on a slip of paper for David.

"Thanks," David said.

"You doing any real work?" Pierce asked only half joking.

"A little here and there," replied David, "I'll let you know how I make out. Thanks Jack."

"Okay Dave, let me know how you make out."

David walked out the door. "See you later Vickie", he told Pierce's assistant and she smiled back at him.

David walked back to his office and sat at his desk. He took the telephone number from his pocket and picked up the telephone tapping out the number in Georgetown.

A telephone answering machine announced that no one was home but Ms. McKenzie would get back to you, if you left a message. David gave both his work and home phone numbers and he went back to work.

*   *   *

David was just thinking of leaving for home when the telephone rang and he picked it up on the second ring.

"Dave Baker."

"Mr. Baker, this is Rose McKenzie returning your call."

"Yes, Ms. McKenzie. My associate, Jack Pierce, suggested that I call you."

"You know him?"

"I work for him. He's a friend."

"In that case, my name's Rose," she laughed. "How can I help you?"

"I need some research done at the National Archives. Jack thought you might be able to help me?"

"I'd be delighted. I usually charge fifteen dollars an hour, but since you know Jack it'll be twenty," she laughed again.

David laughed too. He thought he liked this woman.

"Seriously," she said, "I usually work with a hundred dollar advance. If I don't spend that much time I'll refund the balance. Is that agreeable with you?"

"The check is in the mail as soon as you give me the address."

"That's fine. Now what do you need to find?"

"I want to know what Civil War records are available for my great great grandfather."

"Tell me what you know?"

"His name was Charles Baker. Most likely, he was living in Logansport, Indiana when he joined up. He died in 1896. From the census records, he was born about 1834 in New York. I don't know where and I'm afraid that's all I know."

"That should be enough," she said slowly obviously jotting down the information he had given her. "Today's Monday. I should be going to the Archives on Wednesday or Thursday. I'll let you know if I find anything."

"That's great."

"Say hello to Jack for me. He's a special guy."

David agreed. Rose McKenzie gave David her address and they exchanged good-byes. David hung up the phone feeling just a bit excited. What would Rose McKenzie find, if anything? He gathered up his things and headed for his car in the parking lot.

*　　　　*　　　　*

Two days later David drove for the basket past a sweating Jack Pierce who fouled him trying to stop him from scoring but David made the lay-up anyway. They were playing in a schoolyard in Duxbury near David's house. Since David had returned from Iowa, Jack Pierce insisted on a game of one on one at least one night a week. He wanted to be sure that David was handling the double shock of his Mother's death and the break up with Carol.

"God damn it Jack! You fouled me!"

"I've got to find some way to make up the fifteen years I've got on you!"

"Yeah, but don't cripple me in the process! That makes it twenty-four to nineteen. Your ball."

Pierce took the ball, dribbling it twice, then moved to his right. He faked left then pulled up, lofting a jump shot from twenty-five feet. The ball swished through the hoop. Nothing but net.

"Twenty-four twenty, shithead," he smiled.

David retrieved the ball from the fence where it rolled to a stop. He slowly dribbled back to the head of the key.

"It's getting to be Miller time, Mr. Pierce!"

"Put up, or shut up!"

David put the ball in motion, moving to his left. Pierce went to block him but, sensing the movement, David spun, dribbling through his legs and drove for the basket. Pierce could not change his direction. David drove for the basket, making the lay-up.

"How's that old man?" he laughed.

"Good game, Mr. Baker. Want another?" Pierce said panting but smiling.

"Gee, I'd like to, but, I'm thirsty."

"Your place or mine?" Pierce asked.

"Mine's closer," said David.

They both picked up towels wiping away the sweat from their faces and walked to Pierce's car, bantering as they went. They got in, driving to David's home two blocks away.

David removed two beers from the refrigerator and gave one to Pierce as he went into the bathroom. While he was there, Pierce took a moment to reflect that David was all right. He had adjusted to the grief of his Mother's death and to the disappointment of Carol's departure. Pierce was also pleased with David's interest in genealogy and he knew only too well how the bug could grab a person.

David returned and they went into the living room where David took the recliner and Pierce collapsed on the couch.

"Good game," said David. "You satisfied yet that I'm okay?"

"What do you mean?" Pierce said defensively.

"In case you don't know it, you've been trying to be a father to me for the last several weeks. You may be a genius, but you're a shitty actor!"

Pierce laughed, "It's that obvious?"

"Yeah, but I appreciate it."

"I'm concerned. So is Jenny," Pierce said alluding to his wife Jennifer.

"And I'll be okay," David said. "I think I'm taking Friday off to go to the library again."

"What are you working on?" Pierce asked, finishing his beer.

"The Baker's still," David said as he got up to get a copy of the letter Sue had sent by Federal Express. He handed it to Pierce and went to the kitchen coming back with fresh beers for them both.

"I want to read the 1860 census for Portage County, Ohio. That's where Ravenna is."

Pierce finished reading the letter.

"You know," he said, "you told me about this, but reading it though, I can almost feel the goose bumps too! This is a hell of a story. Still no clue as to what the fortune was or where it was taken?"

"No, not a hint," David said.

"While you're at the library, you might check to see if they have microfilm of the probate records. You know when your great great grandfather died from the letter?"

"Yeah I do, that's a good idea."

"If the library has the probate records you can try the index to see if you can find his will. It might help."

"Okay, I'll try that," said David sipping from the can.

"How about a pizza?" Pierce suggested.

"Don't you have to get home to Jenny?"

"Nah, she gave me the night off. She's worried about you too," he repeated as he went to the telephone. "Pepperoni, Sausage and Bacon?"

"And onion," David added going into the kitchen for refills.

*   *   *

The visit to the New England Historic Genealogical Society had not been entirely successful David thought. He had consulted the Accelerated Indexing System Census Index for the 1860 census and after an hour working with the microfilm for Portage County, Ohio David found his great great grandfather. He recorded the information in his notebook.

Charles Baker	26	married	Farmer	born New York
Jane Baker	24	married	wife	born New York
Joseph Baker	1	mo	son	born Ohio

This did suggest that his great grandfather had probably been born in May since the date of the census was June. However, it didn't tell him anything else that he didn't know but it did confirm that his great great grandfather was living in Ravenna, Ohio though. Still David could not help wondering where in New York he had come from.

Next David tried for probate records from Cass County, Indiana where Logansport was located. He found the records on microfilm but upon viewing them discovered no index existed but there was a note on the film saying that some original records had burned in a fire in 1898. Seeing this, David gave up and spent the rest of the afternoon working on several lines on his Mother's side. He found some helpful information and again he was impressed with the vast amount of information available in the library.

He left early and driving home from the "T" station in Braintree, his mind wandered. Rose McKenzie hadn't called him yet and he wondered when he would hear from her. Had she found anything?

He turned on the radio and several minutes later heard the weather forecast for the next day. The forecast for the Boston area called for a beautiful sunny day for the first day of summer and David thought that really called for him to do something special.

David tried to think of something appropriate but instead a summer memory of Carol came to him. He frowned, he hadn't thought of her all day, he realized. Things were getting better but the prospect for a beautiful summer day made him remember the trip to Maine the previous month. He thought of the Rosemary Point house and despite the association with Carol he realized that he wanted to go back. Not to relive a memory of their visit, but because he wanted to do it, to see the house again. And why not? He could leave in the morning and with luck he could make it in less than two hours even with the expected traffic jam downtown. The prospect of seeing the magnificent house and grounds again filled him with a sense of anticipation.

*   *   *

The day turned out to be a New England gem. There was not a cloud in the sky and the dark blue summer sky stood out against the horizon. The predicted high temperature would be in the low eighties with low humidity and the conditions filled David with elation as he drove north along Interstate 95.

Once more he exited at Portsmouth onto Route One and glanced at his watch. It was 11:15 and he wondered if he should stop to eat or go to the house first? Reasoning that he wasn't that hungry, he decided to visit the house first.

He drove through Kittery to where the sign pointed to Rosemary Point and turned right onto the road, driving the half-mile of curving dirt to the parking lot. There were more cars in the lot than there had been in May and he thought that was probably a sign of the tourist invasion, he thought.

David got out of his car and looked toward the path to the board-walk. He thought of Carol for a moment and the memory hurt him briefly but then it passed. He would go down to the marsh later he decided.

David took the path up the rise toward the house that seemed even prettier than it had been in May. The grass was greener, the flower beds in full bloom and there were other people exploring the grounds. He walked the lawns stopping at the edge of the flowerbed to look out at the sea. It was beautiful, the water glimmering in the sun as the water rippled in the gentle breeze. He turned and looked back at the house. In May he had thought it imposing, but smaller than expected. Now, however, it was truly a dominating presence. What a place it was.

He walked slowly up to the front porch taking in each detail of the house. The six over nine windows were most impressive as was the full-length porch and massive front door. The porch was probably a later addition, he remembered.

David walked up the stairs to the open doorway and as he entered, it was like walking into another time period. The exterior of the house was faithfully restored to the 1790 era and the interior was the same, a moment frozen in time.

An older woman with a nametag identifying her as Norma Lord was sitting at a simple rectangular table to the right of the doorway.

"Welcome," she said smiling.

"Hi, I'd like to look around," David said.

"Sure, admission is five dollars."

David paid her. In return, she handed him a brochure.

"This will give you the details on the house. I'm sorry but I'm the only one in the house today but if you have questions I'll do my best to help you."

David nodded. "My name is Dave Baker. I work at Pilgrim Village. Tell me about this place it's really something!"

"Oh, I've been there," Norma Lord said. "Pilgrim Village is truly a wonderful place. You folks do a great job! We can't touch it for size and historical significance, but this house is very special!"

"Do you work here?"

"Yes, I'm a volunteer actually. The Rosemary Point Society has about six hundred members and a lot of us are active doing one thing or another."

"The society owns the property?" David asked.

"Oh no, it belongs to the Sherwood family. They've owned it for almost two hundred years. They lease it to the Society for a dollar a year. Up until about twenty-five years ago they paid for all the upkeep but now they can't afford it anymore or they don't care, we really don't know. The current family members don't seem to have the interest in the past that previous generations did. The society does fundraising to help maintain the house and grounds. Would you like to join?"

"How much are the dues?"

"Thirty dollars for individuals. That plus admissions helps us defray expenses."

"Sure, I'll join," said David, feeling a sudden need to do this. "Let me have an application. I'll send you a check when I get home."

"Great," replied Mrs. Lord and handed David a blank application.

David folded it putting it in his pocket. "Thanks, I'll take a take a look around now."

"I must stay here," Mrs. Lord said, "but the brochure will help guide you through the house."

David nodded and went to the right into the front sitting room. It was large with a stone fireplace on the East Side of the house that was the natural focal point of the room. The room was furnished with nineteenth century furniture. He read the brochure finding that the room represented the 1840 time period and the furniture was Oriental. David walked to the front windows looking out at the magnificent view of the ocean. And again marveled at the natural beauty of the setting.

There was a door to the pantry that connected to the kitchen on the rear wall of the room. David poked his head in to look and decided to visit the kitchen last.

He went back into the entry hall past Mrs. Lord and nodded a greeting to a man and woman who were leaving the house. David went into the Library and noted the same terrific view out these windows. The room was lined with bookshelves and momentos and the brochure described the furnishings as being from the Civil War period. David told himself that he would be sure to tell Jack Pierce about this place thinking he would really enjoy it.

David went through the open double doors to the dining room where a large mahogany table dominated the room that was decorated and furnished in the Victorian era. He thought it was nicely done.

David retraced his steps to the entry hall and went up the stairs to the second floor. There were six bedrooms on the floor; all were done in different motifs that spanned the years. It was very impressive. There were also two baths that had been created from what had apparently been a seventh bedroom. The brochure noted that this conversion was done in the 1890's. There was a stairwell at the rear of the house that led up to the loft and down the back way to the kitchen.

David climbed the stairs to the loft. There were two finished rooms, one on either side of a hallway that led to a large loft storage area. There were two dormers on the front of the house and David looked out one of the windows. The view, which from the first floor was magnificent, was even more powerful here because of the elevation. David could see the lawns, flowerbeds and the boardwalk over the salt marsh where a number of visitors were enjoying the view. The setting was extraordinary he thought. Probably nothing like it anywhere along the coast.

He reluctantly left the panorama from the window and went back down the stairs to the second floor. David paused for a moment and then continued on down the back way into the kitchen. As he entered what had been the winter kitchen, he noticed a woman in period costume sweeping the floor. She turned to him when he stepped off the last stair.

"Hello," she smiled.

"Well hi," replied David. She was very pretty, David noted. Then thought, no she's beautiful. She was probably in her late twenties and her piercing deep blue eyes were perfectly oval. They accented her long brown hair and her high cheekbones and smooth skin gave her an almost regal look. David felt his heart pump faster. "Who are you?" he asked.

"I live here," the woman answered.

"What year is it?" David asked as he realized the woman was an interpreter/guide, like those they had at Pilgrim Village.

"Why it's 1800," she smiled at him, her eyes dancing brightly. "Are you a visitor to the house?"

"Why yes I am. I sure would like to know more about the house. Tell me about it."

"Well Sir," she said, "it was built in 1776 by Captain James Steele. He was a very successful sea captain and made a great fortune but alas he was killed during the Penobscot expedition in 1779."

David glanced at the brochure.

"He was also a smuggler, wasn't he?"

"Yes," the woman continued in character, "but he smuggled contraband goods before the fight for independence and then during the war he was able to beat the British blockade to bring in supplies that the colonists badly needed. His daughter, Abigail, often sailed with him. In fact, she owned this house at one time, before she died."

"What happened to her?" David asked mesmerized by the woman's manner. He wanted to get to know her better.

"Ah," she smiled, "Abigail never returned from a voyage to China in 1784. The ship was presumed lost at sea."

"So the Sherwoods's then bought the property? Is that right?" David asked glancing at his brochure.

The woman lowered her eyes then raised her head, staring at David. She looked him in the eye, the dark blue orbs burning.

"No!" she said angrily. "Another took it first! And now it would seem they want to sell most of it!" The woman appeared to break out of character then regained her composure.

"What do you mean?" asked David amazed by the woman's theatrical talent.

"I can say no more, I have said enough on that subject," the woman said mysteriously. "But you may ask me something else about the house or the grounds."

"You seem very knowledgeable," David smiled but wondered at this angry momentary break in character. "You're very good by the way and if I may say so you're very beautiful. Tell me about the kitchen?"

The woman smiled coyly, her face reddening slightly.

"This was the winter kitchen," she explained, "in the summer most of the cooking was done in a shelter out back but that no longer exists. The baking and cooking was done in the fireplace on the east side of the house." She pointed to where the huge fireplace was located on the outside wall.

"Is that a bake oven?" David asked.

"Yes, the iron enclosure to the left of the hearth is where the baking was done and it worked very well indeed."

David watched her as she talked. She was beautiful, he decided and he thought that she was the first woman he had been attracted to since Carol. It was nice to know that the feelings were still there but, none the less, he felt there was something vaguely familiar about her. He couldn't quite put his finger on what made him feel that way but he had a strange feeling in the pit of his stomach. He must have grimaced because she asked.

"Are you all right Sir?"

Yes," David said relaxing, "I'm just fine. You've been very nice."

She looked at him as if also trying to remember a previous meeting and then she spoke. "I hope you will come again Sir. I sense you are a good person and would hope to see you again."

"Well, I'm going to join the Society so you just might see me again."

"I'm glad", she said, "I would like to see you again."

David smiled was she flirting with him? He wasn't sure but it made him feel good and he nodded goodbye to her and went through the pantry into the siting room. He thought of the woman's remark about the Sherwood's wanting to sell the property. What was that all about? He went back to the entry hall where Mrs. Lord was still seated behind the table.

"Well," she said, "what do you think of the place?"

"It's terrific! I'll be sure to send in my application as soon as I get home. Thanks!"

"We were glad to have you and also glad to have you as a new member. You keep up the good work at Pilgrim Village and I'll look you up the next time I'm down."

"Please do that," David responded.

"You come and see us again," Norma Lord said.

"I will," David said and started for the door, then stopped and turned. "By the way, I want to compliment you on your guide. She's great. Very knowledgeable and helpful and good entertainment! She really added to my visit. Thanks!"

He waved and went out the door, going down the stairs.

Mrs. Lord looked after him with a puzzled look on her face. What did Mr. Baker mean, she wondered? She looked around her. She got up and looked into the sitting room. Then she went quickly up the front stairs checking each of the bedrooms. She returned to the first floor and made a fast tour of the rest of the rooms. As she walked slowly back to the table in the entry hall she shook her head just what was going on for just as she thought, she was alone in the house.

CHAPTER SIX

January 21, 1865 Near Savannah, Georgia

The 74th Indiana Volunteer Infantry was on the march north. They had crossed the Savannah River the day before, leaving the vanquished city of Savannah that General William T. Sherman had taken as a Christmas present to President Abraham Lincoln. Sherman had spared the city from the torch and now the 74th Indiana was marching toward the Carolinas with the rest of Sherman's Army. The 74th Indiana had participated in the campaign to take Atlanta, the fighting against General Hood after the city fell and then Sherman's march to the sea. The Regiment was experienced, battle-hardened and proud.

They were proud, but hardly parade ground presentable. In fact, they were a rag-tag bunch after several months in the field because the army was marching light and living off the land. They had left the supply trains behind and, as a result, the last two months had taken a toll on their appearance. Most of the Indiana soldiers were dressed in a mixture of government issued uniforms and foraged civilian clothing

At least he had boots that were still good, thought Corporal Charles Baker.

"Hey Sarge!" he yelled to Sergeant Thomas Welsh, "how soon before we rest? I'm some tired!"

Others in the ranks echoed his thoughts and the big burly Sergeant turned to look at the men. He did not break step, walking backwards.

"We'll stop when we're told, an' not before. Why, I thought you heroes could march forever!" He smiled at his own joke showing gaps where several of his teeth were missing.

"Only when we have to Sarge!" someone yelled, "and I don't want to!"

Laughter broke out in the ranks and Welsh smiled. As he turned to face forward again. His men were a cocky bunch now because they were winning and they knew it.

It was late in the afternoon when the column stopped and the men scattered off the road into the fields and woods next to the road where they sprawled on the ground. Most of the men were sipping from canteens or nibbling from rations that came from their haversacks. Small fires were started and coffeepots came out to boil the ever-present army coffee. As badly clothed as they were the soldiers found food plentiful along their path. What they could not eat or take with them, they destroyed and most of the rag tagged soldiers thought it was great fun.

Baker observed Sergeant Welsh talking to Captain Kimball, the company commander. When they finished, Welsh walked over to him.

"Baker, I've got a job for you."

"Hell Sarge, why me? I do all your damn errands for you!"

"Ah, that's because I trust you laddie. You can be counted on to do the right thing. Besides," the big man smiled, "I like you."

"Thanks for that singular honor Sarge," Baker said grimacing.

Welsh grinned because he really did like the lanky corporal. Baker was one of the few soldiers who had a decent education and he was also a natural leader. He could have been an officer Welsh thought but he knew Baker had resisted any promotion past corporal. Welsh knew that Baker didn't want to leave the men he had joined with, although there weren't too many left after over two years of hard campaigning. Welsh got to the point.

"I want you to take a squad of men on a foraging party to the west of the here. Cavalry told the Captain that there's a farm about a mile to the west and he wants whatever food you can find. Simple job Baker, out and back."

"Why can't the Cavalry do it?" Baker complained.

"None around right now," Welsh explained. "They're mostly at the front of the column screenin' us or scoutin' on the flanks. Pick your men and get movin'!"

"Yes Sarge!" And Baker turned to the group of men near him.

"I need a dozen volunteers. Who wants to go for a walk?"

None of the veteran soldiers responded.

"Well now," he said with a growing smile, "if you don't volunteer I figure I'll have to volunteer you."

He looked at his best friend, Walter Hanson. Hanson smiled a laconic smile, shook his head and slowly stood, picking up his rifle and haversack.

"Might as well get some exercise," he said.

Several others got up and joined Baker and soon he counted fourteen, all veterans. He thought the two extra men would come in handy if they found a supply of food. Baker glanced at Welsh who nodded.

"Okay let's go find some food. At least if we find anything we'll have a chance to fill our bellies before the rest of these bastards eat!" Baker laughed.

He moved the soldiers into the woods to the west of the road and the veteran Indiana soldiers automatically spread out in a skirmish line. The soldiers advanced cautiously through the sparse winter vegetation, in no particular hurry to locate the farm.

Baker was alert, aware of the danger of Rebel outriders who shadowed the Army's flanks. While these units were not large enough to pose any real threat to the Army, the danger to small groups like his foraging party was real.

They came to the edge of the woods and found a cleared field in front of them. There was a farmhouse, barn, chicken coop and smokehouse on the other side of the field. The line of men halted at Baker's hand signal and he motioned for the men to come to him.

"I'll take five men in to check the farm," he said across the field. "Hanson, you're in charge of the rest. Find some cover. I want you hidden so's you can us supporting fire if something happens. Understand?"

"Yep, Charlie, we'll cover you."

Baker nodded and pointed to five of the men saying, "Come with me."

Baker spread his men out in a loose skirmish line and took up position on the left flank. He motioned for them to move forward and they started across the field, wary of any movement near the farm. The day was cool and cloudy, none the less and sweat flowed freely from nervous tension.

The thin line neared the farm and Baker looked carefully for any sign of danger but did not see anything amiss. He halted the line at the edge of the field motioning the soldiers to remain where they were. He continued on past the stock pen slowly walking to the farmhouse. He cautiously looked for cover as he moved to the porch at the front of the house. He went to the door that was slightly ajar and, using his rifle butt, he pushed it open.

Baker entered the house and discovered whoever had lived there was gone. The house was empty. He quickly went through the small rooms finding no food. He went back to the front door out onto the porch and pointed at two of the soldiers motioning them to the barn. As they went to search it he pointed at two others, then at the smokehouse. They nodded in acknowledgement and went off to investigate and Baker joined the remaining man, Private Joe McCarthy.

"Come with me Joe and we'll see if there are any chickens left!"

McCarthy nodded. "Hope so, I could use me a drumstick Charlie!"

Baker smiled at this and the two men went to the ramshackle chicken coop. They looked inside and finding it also was empty, Baker and McCarthy went back to the stock pen. They were joined by the other soldiers from the barn and smokehouse.

"Nothing in the barn," one of them reported.

"We found some hams in the smokehouse," said another.

Baker looked at him. "How many?"

"Maybe a half dozen or so Charlie. Won't need no help, I think we can carry them ourselves."

"Good. Go get them and I'll tell Hanson to stay where he is."

As he said this, he was aware of a disturbance in the wood to the west of the farm. He heard the sound of a galloping horse and the Indiana soldiers looked in surprise. A group of motley brown clad riders emerged from the woods. Confederate irregulars! One of the Baker's men raised his rifle and fired.

Several of the Rebels returned fire with pistols as they came charging toward the Yankees. Baker felt a sting as one of the bullets grazed him in the right calf. He fell to avoid another volley but to his right Joe McCarthy fell clutching his chest, mortally wounded.

The Southerners were all around them now and the Indiana men had no choice but to surrender, throwing down their rifles and raising their hands.

From the woods on the other side of the field Hanson's group loosed a well-aimed volley at the horsemen and several of the Confederates dropped from their saddles. Fifteen or twenty of the riders kicked their mounts and went chasing off across the field toward the source of the rifle fire. Baker rose to his feet and watched. Half way across the field another volley banged out, felling four more of the Rebels. The Indiana soldiers were good, Baker noted with some pride. The riders slowed to a stop not wanting to face another volley from the troops in the woods and they turned, retreating to the farm.

Several of the Rebels dismounted and roughly searched the captured Yankees. One turned over McCarthy's body, which now lay in a spreading pool of blood.

"This one's a goner Cap'n," said the Rebel.

Another went to Baker and looked at his leg.

"He's only grazed," he said taking Baker's haversack. Opening it, he let out a laugh. "Hey, lookee here, damned if he ain't got a good sackfull! Even coffee and sugar! Don't seem fair. Hey Cap'n, we caught 'em looting right? Can we shoot 'em?"

The man apparently in charge didn't reply as the riders rode up and dismounted. One of them looked up to the tall rider who seemed to be in charge. "Cap'n Johnson, whoever they were they got away. Too many of 'em for us!"

One of the Indiana soldiers spat. "You dumb cracker. There was only ten of them!"

The Rebel soldier walked over to him and looked the Hoosier in the eye.

"You callin' me yellow you Yankee son of a bitch?"

The Indiana man said nothing, spitting onto the ground and the Rebel hit him in the belly, doubling him over.

"That's enough!" yelled the Rebel Captain, "we'll take them with the others. It's Andersonville for them. I don't think they'll look forward to that!"

Charles Baker felt those words in the pit of his stomach and a cold fear went through his body. As the Rebels laughed at them Charles Baker did not want to think about what lay ahead.

*   *   *

The Union prisoners were being herded west along a road that Baker guessed was about ten miles from where they had been captured. The last twenty-four hours had been the worst of Charles Baker's life and he was growing more apprehensive at the thought of imprisonment in Andersonville for he had no illusions about his chances of surviving what he knew to be a Rebel created hell hole. The combination of overcrowding, disease, unsanitary conditions, no shelter and little food meant a significant chance of death to every Union soldiers who was sent there.

Fighting off the depression he felt, Baker looked around him. There were about fifty Union soldiers from various regiments in the group. Most had been captured while foraging and they were guarded by about thirty mounted Confederate irregulars. The Yankees had been given no food and there had been only one stop at a small stream to fill canteens.

Most of all, Baker thought, the prospect of dying in Andersonville meant that he would fail to pass on the family tradition to his young son. He had not left a record of the stolen family fortune before he left to join the regiment. He once mentioned the tradition to his wife, but knew that he could not depend on her to pass it on. He reflected that he really knew few details of the whole thing, but still had promised to pass the tradition on. If he died in Andersonville the tradition would also die with him.

He glanced at the man to his right noted they were about the same height. The other man had dark brown hair and was of slender build like Baker and he was dressed in the same type of rag tag uniform that Baker wore, signifying a soldier who had been in the field a long time. The other soldier looked at Baker.

"I'm John Bedford," the man offered.

"Charles Baker," he replied.

"I'm from Michigan. 1st Artillery. Got caught two days ago. Pretty dumb luck. How 'bout you?"

"74th Indiana. Got captured yesterday. Bad luck too!"

"Farmer?" asked Bedford.

"Yep. You too?"

"Yeah, near Calhoun Michigan. Been there all my life. My Dad settled there in '34. Good place to be from. Sure wish I was there now!"

"Yup," Baker agreed. "I'd like to be home too. I'm from Logansport, Indiana."

"Lived there long?" Bedford asked.

"Been there a while. Moved from Ohio but I was born in Delaware County in York state."

Bedford nodded and the two soldiers continued to talk quietly as the prisoners trudged down the road. Later the Confederates allowed them to take a rest break and the Union soldiers dropped to the ground tired and dirty.

"How's the wound?" Bedford asked looking at Baker's leg.

"It's all right. Really only a scratch," replied Baker, tugging at the kerchief he had wrapped around the wound. "I cleaned it up some when we stopped for water before. It hurts some, but I can walk on it easy."

A soldier Baker did not recognize slid over to where he and Bedford sat.

"You two brothers?" the soldier asked.

Baker and Bedford exchanged glances and they laughed.

"No, why?" asked Bedford.

"I've been watching you that's all," the stranger said. "All day, you both look alike."

Baker eyed Bedford more closely and Bedford did the same. There was a strong resemblance he thought.

"No," said Baker thinking. "We're not brothers, but maybe we're cousins."

Bedford laughed at that.

"Sorry to bother you," the stranger said and turned to go.

"No bother," Bedford offered, "join us."

"I'm Tom Wilton, 40th Illinois," the other man held out his hand.

The three sat talking, trying to assess their chances of surviving what lay ahead of them and the possibility of making an escape.

"Sure could use a bottle of whiskey," mused Wilton. "I'd share it if I had one."

"Thanks," said Bedford. Baker didn't reply, hesitant to admit that he did not drink.

"I wonder if we could escape?" Wilton said, again looking around as if to judge the chances to run.

"I been thinkin' about that too," Bedford said. "Don't think so though, too many Rebs. I'd sure be willing to give it a try though if we had half a chance, but I'd also like to stay alive!"

"You know," Baker reflected sadly, "I'm sure put out by this. Damn, I won't be able to do something I promised my father now."

"How's that?" asked Wilton.

Baker related the tradition of the Baker men and the legend of the stolen family fortune. When he finished, he looked at Bedford and saw the man from Michigan had a peculiar look on his face.

"Strange," Bedford said slowly. "My family had the same tradition. Only difference is it's the stolen family land. Must be a coincidence!"

"Maybe we are cousins," laughed Baker. "Where were your people from?"

"Originally from Massachusetts, I think. How about you?"

"New York, but before that I don't know," replied Baker. "I guess anything is possible though."

"Well cousin," Bedford laughed shrugging his shoulders, "we'll stick together anyway and take care of each other." He held out his hand to Baker who took it in a firm grasp and smiled.

"Reckon I'll stick with you two. If that's right with you?" asked Wilton as he watched the two men.

"Sure," they both agreed.

The Confederates soon rousted up the captured Union soldiers and put them back on the road. Bayonets prodded them and they marched on, not knowing where they were or how far they had to go.

Baker walked along next to Bedford and they continued their conversation as they walked. The more he talked to the man, the more he realized how much he liked him and he hoped they would stay friends, if they survived.

The ragged column walked up to road to a slight rise that led to a wooded ridge. Baker looked at the line of trees, squinting into the late afternoon winter sunlight and thought he saw a brief reflection in the trees on the ridge. He focused on the spot where the reflection appeared and saw it again. There was something or someone on the ridge and he moved closer to Bedford, touching him lightly.

"John, I think I saw something on the ridge up ahead. I don't know what it is, but I reckon we should have our wits about us!"

"What do you think it is?" asked the man from Michigan.

"I don't know and I don't want to guess." Baker whispered the same warning to Wilton at his left.

They walked on, wary of what was waiting on the ridge.

All at once a bugle blared and from the woods a mass of blue clad cavalry came charging down the slope yelling and waving their sabers that flashed in the low afternoon light.

The Confederates were surprised and they did not know what to do. In a panic, they started to run and the Yankee cavalry followed in hot pursuit. Pistols cracked and bullets flew after the running Rebels.

Several of the Southerners tried to stand their ground, drawing pistols in defiance but their return fire made no difference as the Union formation drew nearer. Several of the Southerners were hit and fell from their horses.

At the first sound of shooting most of the captured Union soldiers dove for the ground and were hugging the dirt to avoid the gunfire. Baker and Bedford tried to follow the action, as they lay on their bellies elated and excited by the arrival of the Union Cavalry.

In front of them one of the Rebel horses fell dead, the rider still in the saddle and they saw it was the Rebel Captain. Before he knew what he was doing, Baker was on his feet and he ran toward the motionless animal with all his frustration and anger of the last day focused on the downed rider. He rushed the Rebel officer, who was getting to his feet. The Southerner saw him coming and drew his pistol. Baker was quick, jarring the weapon from the Rebel's hand. He threw his body into the man pushing him down and in the process got the wind knocked out of him. He lay stunned on the ground trying to catch his breath. The Rebel

Captain drew his saber and moved toward him. Charles Baker could do nothing to protect himself and still gasping for breath he watched the Southern officer come towards him knowing there was nothing he could do. There was nothing for him to do except die. He felt hot and his eyes would not focus.

Unexpectedly, the Rebel officer stopped, his head jerking down, then up and Baker was aware of a snapping sound, followed by wood splintering. The Rebel officer gave a low moan collapsing on the ground his head askant, his neck broken. In his place stood John Bedford, a carbine with a splintered stock in his hand. Baker realized that Bedford had taken the carbine from the saddle holster on the Rebel's saddle and knew that the Michigan man's actions had saved his life.

Bedford dropped to the ground next to Baker, exhausted and put his arm on Baker's back as his friend began to breath again. Around them the Union Cavalry rode in pursuit of the remaining Rebel irregulars and a group of blue clad soldiers stopped to tend to the former Yankee prisoners. Bedford sat up to look at their saviors.

"Hey!" he exclaimed, "they're Illini!" He recognized the troopers of the 15th Illinois Cavalry, who had rescued them.

"From now on, I will revere the men from our sister state to the west!" Baker panted.

Bedford laughed and Wilton came up behind them

The rest of the Illinois troopers were returning now the chase after the fleeing riders successful. They were herding most of the Rebels with them and the commanding officer of the three troops of blue cavalrymen led the formation. He reined in his horse as he approached the rescued soldiers and dismounted in front of them.

"I'm Major Thomas, 15th Illinois," he announced. "I'm sure glad we found you!"

"Lucky you happened along!" one of the former prisoners said smiling now with the realization they had been saved.

"No luck to it," the Union Major explained. "We were sent out on a foraging mission early this morning. We had a report from some Indiana men that prisoners had been taken near here and we were ordered to look for you. We were successful, it seems!"

An Illinois sergeant gave Bedford a flask and the Michigan man removed the stopper, taking a long drink. He passed it to Baker who hesitated, but he took the flask after a brief second. He held it up to Bedford.

"You saved my life John and I think I'll save that broken rifle stock from the carbine to remind me how close I came to dying today!"

John Bedford grinned at Baker and slapped him on the shoulder. Charles Baker took a drink from the flask and almost choked as the unfamiliar liquid burned his throat. He fought the urge to cough successfully and felt the warmth flow into his empty stomach. His eyes teared and Bedford looked at him laughing. But Charles Baker did not mind it was the taste of life.

CHAPTER SEVEN

David finished reading the last of the documents Rose McKenzie sent him by Express Mail and shook his head. He had returned home to find the packet in the mailbox. The Civil War documents contained muster and pay records, which told the basics of Charles Baker's service. There were his pension records also, including Charles Baker's original pension application filed in 1890. The application was accompanied by several affidavits attesting to his service and David noted that Walter Hanson of Logansport, Indiana, Thomas Wilton of Champaign, Illinois and John Bedford of Calhoun, Michigan had submitted affidavits. These three had all been with Charles when the Confederates captured him in 1865. David shook his head again as he thought that the whole thing read like a novel.

Finally, there was a widow's pension application filed by Charles Baker's widow, Jane Baker, in 1897. With it was an affidavit from a William Peck who stated that he had witnessed the wedding of Charles Baker and Jane Peck on June 24th, 1858 in Farmington, Ohio. From this David now had gained Jane's maiden name and he thought that William Peck would prove to be Jane's brother. According to the pension records, Jane Baker had died in 1902 in Logansport and David made a mental note to write for a death record for her. He also thought he might find an obituary that would give him some information.

All in all, the Civil War documents contained a wealth of information but the most important data was the information in Charles Baker's pension application that he was born in Delaware County, New York. That was the real breakthrough and now David had a place of birth for his great-great grandfather. He thought that the next thing to do was to check the 1850 census for Delaware County to see if he could find Charles Baker. He would have been sixteen in 1850 and most likely would be listed living with his father. If David could find this, it would give him another generation.

Also since he now had Jane Baker's maiden name, David wanted to see if there was a Peck Genealogy which might give him information on that line. He thought about this and decided to call Sue to ask her to get a copy of their great grandfather's will from the Stillman Probate Court. Finally, as a long shot, David also decided to write to the County Clerk of Cass County, Indiana on the off chance that Charles Baker's will had survived the Logansport courthouse fire, which he had noted at the library the day before.

David decided to take Wednesday off and put in another day at the library. He got up, putting the Civil War records on the desk and went to the telephone to call Sue. It was his turn to relate an exciting story.

*   *   *

Following his usual route, David arrived at the library early and went directly to the newly published index to the 1850 census for Delaware County, New York. He recorded all the Bakers listed and taking this information he found the microfilm and settled down in front of the microfilm reader. One hour later he was terribly disappointed because he could not locate a sixteen year old Charles Baker anywhere in the county. David was very frustrated and unsure what to do next.

Returning the microfilm to the storage cabinet, David decided to try another tack and see if he could find some information on the Peck family. Perhaps that might give him a clue. He looked through the card catalog and discovered several Peck Genealogies. He searched out the books in the stacks and sat down at a table to study them.

He felt his disappointment turn to joy when the second volume gave him the information he wanted. He found Jane Peck, daughter of Jonathan and Martha Gaines Peck listed. She had been born in 1835 in Sullivan County, New York but the most important information was the notation that she had married Charles Baker on June 24th, 1858 in Farmington, Ohio. This information agreed with the data in the Civil War records but the Peck genealogy did not include a record of the family of Charles Baker. Nevertheless David was able to get the Peck line all the way back to William Peck, the immigrant who lived in New Haven and Stamford, Connecticut and he felt very satisfied.

David copied the information from the book on the copying machine. While he copied the pages, he wondered what he should do next about the Baker line. Jack Pierce's warning about the difficulty of tracing a common name like Baker seemed prophetic now but as he finished copying the last page, his course of action was clear in his mind. He would find each Baker in the 1830 and 1840 census' for Delaware County, New York to see who could have been Charles Baker's Father and by process of elimination see where that led him. Of course that assumed Charles Baker's father had been in Sullivan County in 1830 and 1840.

Using the new indexes, David recorded the Baker heads of households for both the 1830 and 1840 periods. Then, viewing the microfilm records, he then looked up each one of the male Bakers listed. The 1830 and 1840 census records listed only the head of household by name and the rest of the occupants were broken down by sex and age groups only. David finished this time consuming job just as the library was closing.

He would organize his findings when he got home, he thought and a quick glance at his notes told him there were twenty-six Bakers listed in the 1830 census and thirty-one in the 1840 census. Several in the 1840 census had sons in the 5 to 10 year age group and he reasoned these were good candidates for the father of Charles Baker.

Satisfied that he had accomplished something, David put his notebook and papers in his briefcase and headed for home.

*　　　　*　　　　*

The next morning David looked up to see Jack Pierce enter his office. "Hi Jack," he smiled pushing back his chair. "What can I do for you?"

"Just paying a house call," Pierce explained, "how's the research going?"

David updated Pierce on the work he had done the previous day.

"Still making progress, that's good," Pierce said.

"Yeah, but you were sure right about the Bakers though. It's taking forever!" David lamented.

"I know, but there is really no other way to do it right," Pierce agreed. "In the end you'll be glad you took the time. Besides it's the only way to figure out what the family fortune is."

"Yeah I know and that's still working at me. I think I told you that my great great grandfather was born in Delaware County, New York? Well, I checked the 1850 census but couldn't find him. I know that his father could have moved anywhere during the sixteen years since he was born, but I don't have a clue where to look. Got any ideas?"

Pierce thought for a moment. "Did you tell me you found a marriage record for your great-great grandfather?"

"Yeah," David said, "in the pension records and also in the Peck Genealogy."

"Where were they married?"

"Farmington, Ohio."

"Is that in the same county as Ravenna? You know, where you found him listed in the 1860 census?"

"Shit, I don't know," David said and got up going to his file cabinet. He picked up the road atlas that lay on top and opened the atlas to the index. Finding what he wanted he turned the page to Ohio.

"No, different county," he said studying the map of Ohio. "Farmington is in Trumbull County, right next to Portage County where Ravenna is."

"Well," Pierce suggested, "it's probably a longshot, but, try the 1850 census there. You might find something."

"Good idea. I'll get back to the library on Saturday and I'll check."

"You're spending a lot of time there. Becoming a real regular," Pierce laughed.

"Yeah," smiled David, "you know how this hooks you."

"Only too well Dave," Pierce returned the smile. "Listen Dave, I've got a proposition for you. I've been asked to speak to the Portsmouth, New Hampshire Chamber of Commerce on Saturday, July 20th. They're having a fundraising dinner and they want me to talk about the Pilgrims and how they helped settle the Portsmouth area. I guess it starts about 5:00 followed by dinner and I'd like you to come with me to help organize and answer questions."

"Sure, be glad to," David said looking at his calendar, "I sure as hell don't have anything else to do these days. I might even get you over to see the Rosemary Point house I told you about."

"If we have time," Pierce said, "I'd like to go see that but anyway put the Portsmouth date on your calendar."

"Okay. Incidentally, Jack, the gate yesterday was over a two thousand people. That's one of the best days we've had."

"Yes, I know. You'll probably tell me it's all because of your marketing genius."

"It is."

"I'll see you tonight," Pierce laughed again, "and we'll see how your marketing genius holds up on the basketball court!"

✳   ✳   ✳

The following Saturday night David sat in his recliner sipping a beer feeling very proud of himself as he reviewed the information he had discovered that day. He was happy and elated because the information gave him more answers to some of his questions.

Pierce's suggestion to look at the 1850 census records for Trumbull County, Ohio had been a good one and David had found what he was looking for:

James Baker	Head	Male	Age 47	Born New York
Deborah Baker	Wife	Female	Age 46	Born New York
James Baker	Son	Male	Age 20	Born New York
Content Baker	Dau	Female	Age 18	Born New York
Charles Baker	Son	Male	Age 16	Born New York
Abigail Baker	Dau	Female	Age 13	Born Ohio
John Baker	Son	Male	Age 11	Born Ohio

This information solved the mystery of why he had not been able to find the family in the 1850 census for Delaware County. The place of birth for the last three children indicated that the family moved from New York to Ohio sometime between 1834 and 1837. This was good to know, but most important though, was the name of Charles Baker's father. David looked at the record again and the name on the paper, James Baker. He was back another generation. It seemed that James Baker had been born in New York also so David thought that the next step would be to try and identify who James Baker's father had been. That might be difficult David thought but he didn't want to worry about it now. He felt just felt too good.

He picked up the manila envelope and removed the contents. Upon arriving home he had found this bonus. Sue had located their great grandfather's will and a copy of this document was waiting for him in the mail. He looked at it and felt that another piece of the puzzle was now in place. The will was very straight forward leaving shares of Joseph Baker's estate to his wife and children. There was also the reference to the stolen family fortune, but no details. While David knew that it gave no real new information he was glad to have the will anyway.

He sat back, satisfied with the warm glow he felt inside.

              *   *   *

The next three weeks passed quickly for David Baker. He was very busy with work as Pilgrim Village experienced the height of the tourist season and as much as he wanted to, he could not get away to do more work at the library. Even his Saturdays were occupied dealing with problems that turned up at the office.

When he returned on Friday night, David checked the mail and found a manila envelope from the Cass County, Indiana County Clerk's Office. Opening the envelope, he was very surprised to find a copy of a will.

Sitting down, David read the cover letter that explained that in response to his letter, the Clerk's office had located a copy of Charles Baker's will. Although there had been a fire in 1898 that destroyed some of the probate records, most of the record books were saved. David smiled at this and noted that there was a twelve-dollar service fee for the copy of the will.

He unfolded the photocopy of the will not knowing quite what to expect and scanned the page quickly, then returned to the top to read the document more carefully. This will was also straightforward like the others he had seen and he found the familiar reference to the stolen family fortune. But he stopped when he read the next paragraph and whistled out loud.

"*I give and bequeath to my cousin, John Bedford, of Calhoun, Michigan the broken rifle stock which he used to save my life. I also leave him the sum of twenty-five dollars cash money to help him research the full story behind the stolen family fortune in Massachusetts.*"

David read the paragraph a third time and then went to the desk to get Charles Baker's Civil War records. He found the affidavit he wanted and saw that was signed by John Bedford. It had to be the same person he thought. Were they really cousins? They must have been for Charles Baker to include him in his will. But David wondered just how they were related and why was Bedford interested in the stolen family fortune? I have no clue, David admitted to himself thinking it was supposed to be Baker men who were interested in the fortune. The whole mystery had now deepened and he could only wonder where the trail would lead him now.

David reflected on how the family moved west from New York to Ohio to Indiana and later to Iowa. It was almost like reading a history book about the westward expansion of the country he thought. The family information made it seem very real, even personal as he relived it through his ancestors. David went to the phone thinking, I've just got to call Sue.

*   *   *

The following day was the Chamber of Commerce dinner in Portsmouth and as he drove up with Jack and Jennifer Pierce David related the newest twist in the Baker saga.

"What do you think?" he asked.

"Wow," Pierce replied, "I've got to think about this for a while."

Jennifer Pierce, who was in the back seat asked, "This was your great great grandfather's will?"

"Yeah," David replied.

"So this John Bedford and your great great grandfather had to have had a common ancestor if they really were cousins. But what about the broken rifle stock?" Jennifer asked.

"As near as I can figure," David said, "Bedford broke the stock on some one or something to save Charles Baker's life. I know they were captured by the Confederates near the end of the war and then rescued shortly after. My great great grandfather was wounded and he claimed a disability from it in his pension application."

"Bedford was from Michigan and your Charles Baker was from Indiana, right?" Pierce asked.

"Yes."

"Then the relationship could have been in New York or some place else earlier than that. You can try finding information on Bedford, just like you've done on the Baker Family."

"I'll try to do that when I get the time."

Pierce nodded and they soon pulled off the Interstate and drove into Portsmouth.

*   *   *

The Chamber of Commerce fundraiser occupied the large function room at the Sheraton. The turnout was good David observed, perhaps about two hundred people attending. The program began at 5:00 with Jack Pierce as the featured speaker. David listened while Jack spoke of the Pilgrims and their coastal trading efforts. Jack Pierce was a relaxed and easygoing lecturer who usually entertained an audience with a combination of wit and expertise. Pierce used many anecdotes that drew laughs and was careful to keep the talk short, the real secret to keeping an audience attentive. He even managed to get in a few plugs for Pilgrim Village and finishing the talk, he introduced his wife and David explaining that Jennifer had given him instructions to be brief. David, he said, was here to answer questions.

There were a few perfunctory questions that David easily fielded and then the President of the Chamber closed the meeting and the crowd broke for the two bars that were set up at opposite ends of the room.

A man and a woman made a beeline for David.

"Mr. Baker, I'm Tom Atwood and this is my wife Lucy."

"Glad to meet you," David said smiling.

"We'd like to give you a few suggestions for Pilgrim Village," Atwood said. "We're members of the Mayflower Society and there are some things we'd like to see you do."

"What are your thoughts?" David asked. Well meaning folks did this all the time he thought and resigned himself to listening as politely as he could.

It was fifteen minutes before David could pry himself away from the Atwoods. They wanted to build memorials to all the signers of the Mayflower Compact at the Village and David listened patiently, finally agreeing to look into it. To himself, he doubted that he would find any support for the idea, but he would at least broach the subject at the next staff meeting.

Thirsty, he went to one of the bars, where the lines had thinned and ordered a scotch and water. Taking a sip, David looked around to room for Pierce to congratulate him on a good talk. He saw him in a corner surrounded by a group of admirers so he walked into the crowd to mingle. David chatted idly with the President of the Chamber of Commerce who thanked him for coming and he nodded a goodbye and started to move on when from behind he heard Jennifer Pierce.

"Dave, wait!"

David spun around and looked into the greenest eyes he had ever seen. He glanced right to Jennifer Pierce then back to the green eyes in front of him. The hair was blond but he decided that it was not her natural color and the girl, no woman, was very attractive. She was tall, about five feet eight, he guessed and a rumble in his stomach told him he was attracted.

"Dave, this is Abby Palmer," Jennifer said, a puckish grin on her face. "I thought you two should meet."

Abby Palmer looked at him, a smile forming on her face. "Hi Dave, everything check out okay?" she said apparently amused by David's stare. David blushed.

"Sorry, I was just looking," he mumbled trying to regain his dignity. "But I do like what I see."

Abby Palmer laughed and he decided he liked the natural ease she radiated. *God she looks so familiar. I feel like I've seen her somewhere before.*

"Abby works in real estate, Dave," Jennifer explained. "I just met her. She's also involved with Strawberry Banke as a volunteer so I told her you had done some work with them."

"That's true," David agreed trying to decide what it was about Abby he liked the best.

"And you're Development Director at Pilgrim Village?" Abby asked.

"Yes, I'm afraid that includes doing a lot of different things though."

He examined her more closely as they talked. He thought she was about thirty and he could see she had a pleasant shape and was nicely proportioned. He could see there was no ring on her left hand but he couldn't see her legs.

"I've got to go rescue Jack," Jennifer Pierce said and excused herself leaving Abby and David alone.

"Are you staying for dinner?" Abby asked.

"Yeah," replied David finishing his drink. He pointed at the bar. "Want another?"

"Sure, I'll come with you," she said and they walked over to the bar.

"Tell me about yourself," she suggested.

David ordered refills

"Not that much to tell."

"Oh there must be something you can tell me!" the green eyes beckoned him.

He was definitely interested and he handed her the glass. They moved to the side of the room and found two empty chairs along to the wall.

"Well," David said warming to the woman, "I'm from Iowa and I went to Northwestern, marketing and economics. I've been in Boston now for about eleven years, at the Village for five. I'm divorced, no children. I guess that covers the basics." He sipped at his drink. "How about you?"

The smile flashed again. "I grew up in Portsmouth," Abby Palmer said. "I live in town and I work for Crown and King, they're real estate developers. We do work in New Hampshire and southern Maine. I went to the University of New Hampshire and got a degree is in history, so of course I went into real estate!"

They both laughed and David knew that he liked her. He found himself hoping she felt the same.

She got serious. "Can I ask you how old you are? Or is that a no-no?"

"Sure, I'm thirty-seven," David said, "that's no secret."

"I'm thirty-three," she replied, "just wanted to get the rest of the basics on the table." Her green eyes flashed moist and inviting in the bright lights of the function room. They both fell silent.

"Hey you two, it's dinner time!" called Jennifer breaking the silence. Jack Pierce was with her.

"Honey this is Abby Palmer," Jennifer said introducing her husband.

"Nice to meet you. Will you join us?" Pierce asked Abby.

"Sure I'd love to," she smiled and flashed the sparkling eyes again.

They went into the dinning room at a table where places had been reserved for Jack, Jennifer and David. The Chamber President graciously gave up his place for Abby and the Pierces, David and Abby introduced themselves to the others at the table.

One couple was Herb and Kathy Dials. David already knew them because Herb was the Development Director for Strawberry Banke. Abby of course knew him too and the other couple at the table, Bill and Grace Johnson. Grace Johnson was a Trustee of the Portsmouth Historical Society.

While they ate the shrimp cocktail to start the meal, they made small talk, comparing jobs and experiences. As he ate, David could not keep his eyes away from the woman on his right and across from him, Pierce noticed this. He nudged his wife with his elbow and they exchanged amused smiles trying hard to keep from laughing at David's obvious interest in the woman. Abby listened to Grace Johnson talk about a recent problem that her daughter had and glanced toward David to find him staring at her. She blushed and bent down to finish her shrimp. She knew she was attracted to this man. He was easy to talk to and fun to be with and it had been a very long time since she found someone who made her so comfortable. It was somewhat apparent that he was of the same mind. She laughed to herself but I'm not getting my hopes up, I've been burned too many times.

The main course was prime rib and as they finished, David asked Herb Dials how things were going at Strawberry Banke.

"Good, Dave, we're having a good summer so far. But, I'm kind of unhappy with you. I understand you visited us last May but you didn't stop in!"

"Sorry Herb, but I was a tourist. How'd you know I was there?"

"My secretary recognized you and she told me about it later. Next time make sure you say hello."

"Sure, I just stopped in for an hour or so. I was on a weekend trip and stopped here then went on to Kennebunkport and Portland. We also stopped at a place called Rosemary Point. What a marvelous place!"

"Yeah, I've been there too. It's great," agreed Dials.

Abby looked at David. "I do volunteer work there," she said. "I'm a member and most of us pitch in one way or another, but most of all I just like to walk the grounds, it kind of relaxes me."

David focused on the woman. "Yeah, I'm a member too. I joined after I saw the house last month. I just kind of thought the place felt like home."

"For me it is," Abby said, "I've got Sherwood blood in me. An ancestor way back."

"Dave's doing his family history," Pierce interjected.

Abby looked at Jack Pierce then back at David. "That's interesting, my grandmother has done that for our family. She is really something. She's ninety-one, still sharp as a tack and knows everything about the family. How far back have you been able to go Dave?"

"On my mother's side I've got several lines back to the immigrant, including John Howland from the Mayflower."

"Then we're cousins!" Grace Johnson interrupted, "I'm descended from John Howland too."

"See," said Pierce, "how insidious this all is!"

They laughed and David returned to Abby.

"I've been able to trace the Bakers back to New York in the early 1800's but haven't been able to get back from there yet."

Jennifer Pierce spoke up, "Abby, Dave's got this terrific mystery about a stolen family fortune. Each Baker male passes on the rights to the fortune to the next generation. Even if there is no truth behind it, it's a wonderful story!"

"Tell me about it Dave," Abby asked.

"Sure," he said responding to her interest.

David told her what he knew about the legend. He briefly talked about each generation trying to give her the story without boring her to death.

"That's some story," she said, "would you give me more details later?"

"Sure, if you really want to." She nodded.

Dessert came and they finished eating, settling for coffee to end the meal. The President of the Chamber spoke to close the evening, thanking the people for attending. He thanked Jack Pierce for participating and a round of applause followed. Then the dinner broke up and the crowd thinned out.

Jack Pierce looked at his watch. "It's only 9:30. Anyone want a nightcap? We don't have to leave for a while."

"You're not staying over?" Abby asked sounding disappointed.

"No," Jennifer Pierce said, "we're going back tonight."

"Then I'm having a nightcap!" Abby declared, rising from the table. She took David by the hand and walked out.

The Dials and Johnsons declined the invitation and said goodnight. The Pierces along with David and Abby walked into the hotel lounge and found a table. A waitress appeared and they ordered aperitifs.

"This was fun," Jennifer said, "I really had a good time."

"Me too," agreed Abby.

"Well, I certainly had a good time showing off," Pierce said, "any time I get to ham it up it's fine with me!"

They laughed at Jack Pierce's easy manner and the waitress returned placing glasses in front of them. Pierce paid her and lifted his glass. "A toast, I think. To good times," he said looking at David and Abby, "and to good friends."

They raised glasses and echoed Pierce's sentiments. "To friends".

"I suppose Abby is short for Abigail?" David asked the green-eyed woman as he put his glass down.

"Yes," she said.

"I think it's a beautiful name."

"I used to hate it when I was a kid," Abby said. "Other kids used to tease me about it. I like it now though."

"You know," David responded, "there's a very interesting lady connected with Rosemary Point whose name is also Abigail."

"I know," she said," Abigail Steele Smith. I think she must have been a remarkable woman."

"Tell me about her," asked Jennifer Pierce.

Abby told her the story, as she knew it. "My grandmother knows a lot about her," she said as she finished. "She's been involved with Rosemary Point for a long time."

"I'd like to come back and see it," Jack Pierce mused, "from what Dave has told me it must be a terrific place."

"It really is beautiful," Abby agreed. "I know you'd like it."

They finished their drinks.

"We should hit the road," Pierce said looking at his watch.

They got up from their seats and when the women went to the ladies room Pierce looked at David. "She's something!" he said.

"Who?" David asked absently.

"Abby Palmer you dope! Jesus, you've only been making moony eyes at her all evening you know."

"Oh," David said reddening, "she is nice."

The women returned and David excused himself, taking Abby aside.

"I'd like to see you again?" he said it was both a question and a statement.

"Yes, I think I'd like that," she smiled, "here's my phone number," and she handed him a slip of paper. She rose on her toes and impulsively gave him a light kiss on the lips. My God what came over me? This man will think I'm a flake! "I would like to see you again." She blushed.

David nodded a smile and said, "me too." Then he took her hand while they walked to the parking lot. He let her lead him to her car and waited while she unlocked the car door. He held it open for her and she paused before getting in. David kissed her, returning the kiss she had given him earlier. She smiled.

"I'll call," he said.

"You'd better," she replied.

She got in, started the engine and drove off. David walked back to where Jack and Jennifer were waiting by their car.

A few minutes later as Pierce eased the car up the on ramp onto the Interstate, Jennifer turned to David in the back seat.

"I'm a terrific matchmaker," she laughed, "in case you don't know it, Dave, that woman has fallen for you like the proverbial ton of bricks!"

"Jennifer, you truly have a way with words!" David smiled. "I think she's nice, but we'll just have to see if this leads anywhere."

But, deep inside he knew he had fallen for her also.

CHAPTER EIGHT

David Baker could not get the woman out of his mind and spent most of the following day thinking of her. She was attractive and there was something about her that attracted him. Something that made him want to know her better. So David called Abigail Palmer that evening.

"What took you so long?" she joked.

"I thought I'd play coy," he laughed, a bit self-consciously. Why do I feel so drawn to her?

"What did you do today?"

"Exciting day," David said. "Read the paper, cleaned the house and did some laundry. I even tried to watch the Sox for a bit. How about you?"

"About the same David. My life isn't too exciting these days," she said. "I did go over to have lunch with my parents. My mother says she wants to meet you."

"Aren't we rushing this?" David asked.

Oh God Abby thought I've gone too far. "No, she's interested in Pilgrim Village, not you!"

"Oh," David said deflated, he really did want to see Abby. "How about meeting for dinner some time this week?"

"I'd love to."

"You want to come down here or me go up there?"

"Why don't we meet in the middle someplace," Abby suggested. "Neutral territory?"

"Where?"

"Well, we could always go to the Hilltop on Route One," she joked.

"Too many people," David replied, "I demand a quiet romantic setting. I need to have the right atmosphere."

"Then where?" Abby asked.

"There's a place in Peabody called La Maison just off of Route One. It's easy to get to, you go on Route 114 and it's on a side street. Northern Italian cooking. It's quiet, just the place to sit and talk. I'll give you directions. That okay with you?"

"That would be nice. When?" Abby asked. I really do want to see him.

"What's good for you?"

"Wednesday okay?"

"Sure, fine with me. What time should I meet you?" David asked.

"What's okay for you?" she said.

"Give me some time to get through traffic," David said thinking. "Say 7:00. I'll make the reservations."

"Great!" God I do want to see him. Please don't let this guy be another turkey. It feels so right so far but please don't let me rush this.

"I'll see you then," he said.

"Dave?" Abby asked.

"Yeah."

"I'm really looking forward to this." Oh shit, that sounded lame.

He paused, "Me too. I'll see you Wednesday."

David found he was almost counting the minutes and was glad when Wednesday finally came. He left work early and worked his way north through the downtown traffic. He surprised himself and made good time arriving five minutes early. He entered the restaurant and was surprised to see Abby sitting at the bar. She saw him come in and started to laugh. He went over to her and smiled a greeting.

"Hi."

"I wish I wasn't so obvious," she said, "I gave myself extra time so I could get lost and still be here on time. I always seem to get lost wherever I go, except tonight that is. I got here a half hour ago!"

David laughed and she responded with a grin. He was glad and watched the tension in her face fade away. He saw that she was dressed in a white lace blouse and tan linen skirt. Her hair was pulled back in a ponytail making her look young and vibrant. David guessed she was very comfortable with herself and would look good in just about anything. He thought that quite a contrast to Carol, who worried forever about the way she looked.

"You look terrific," he said.

"Thanks, you're not too bad yourself," she replied, giving him the once over. He saw her do this and she laughed. "I can do that too you know!"

"What are you drinking?" he asked.

"Tonic water, I've got to watch myself."

"Let me go check if we can get our table early," David said and left her at the bar. David returned in a moment.

"Come on they're ready for us."

She slipped down from the barstool. She was wearing low-heeled shoes and the added height brought her up a bit so that David could look directly into her eyes.

"You have the most incredible eyes," he said. "Do you know that?"

"Why thank you Sir. Those are the result of great genes!"

The Maitre de showed them to the table and they ordered drinks. Abby scanned the restaurant. "This is a nice place. Good choice."

"I've eaten here several times before. If you like veal it's one of the specialties of the house."

The waiter served their drinks and David raised his glass. "To dinner with a beautiful woman."

She smiled at him, "I'll drink to that, thank you. You say the nicest things!"

They both sipped at their glasses, their eyes not moving from each other.

Finally she spoke. "How long has it been since the divorce?"

"Eleven years," he said.

"So it's been that long. I don't want to pry Dave. Do you mind talking about it?"

"No, I don't mind Abby. She wanted a career and I wanted kids. I was reasonably successful in the ad business; she had a difficult time with that. No, she resented it and I guess the end was predictable. How about you?" he asked, "you never married?"

Abby looked down at the table. I guess I deserved that she thought, I started this conversation. "No," she said, "I never found the right man. I've had chances. Some wonderful relationships, but they always seemed to be star-crossed for one reason or another. I guess sometimes I'm too demanding, hoping to find the perfect man."

"Are you?" David asked.

"Am I what?"

"Too demanding?" he said trying to read her eyes.

She paused for a moment, not really thinking for she knew the answer only too well. "Probably," she admitted, "I used to get my expectations up every time I met someone new. I got hurt a lot."

"That's too bad," David said and smiled, "you're very honest. A lady as nice as you shouldn't be hurt."

"We'd better check out the menu," she suggested changing the subject. They studied the menu in silence.

"Anyone in your life now Dave?" Abby said finally.

"No not now. I was living with someone but we broke up two months ago."

"Painful?" she looked concerned.

"Isn't it always that way? I think I've accepted it. I just seem to have a lousy record when it comes to relationships!"

"The right girl just hasn't come along for you yet," she replied, then regretted saying it.

"Damn! You sound like Jack Pierce. He tells me that all the time. Did he coach you?"

"No," she laughed again, "I like them. They're very nice."

"Yeah, he's a good friend and Jennifer is the best. How about you? Are you seeing anyone special?"

"No Dave. I took the pledge not to fall in love again a year and a half ago. I've dated some but nothing steady."

"I'd think a woman as beautiful as you would have her pick of men?" he said meaning it.

She laughed, "No, beauty can be a handicap. Besides, I'm very demanding, remember?"

David laughed and thought that the evening was going well. He was aware of the feeling that had been growing in the pit of his stomach; it was a longing to be with this lovely woman. That feeling was at once soothing to his damaged psyche and a disquieting ache.

The waiter came to the table and they ordered dinner, including a bottle of wine.

"Tell me about your family?" Abby asked.

David told her of his brother and sister. He told her about the accidental death of his father and his mother's death in May.

"I'm so sorry Dave," Abby said. "It must have been difficult for you, I wish I had been there to help."

David stared at her and knew she meant it. She blushed.

"I know I would have found that to be a big help," he said and smiled at her.

The waiter brought the food and they continued talking while they ate.

"Tell me about your family," David asked between mouthfuls.

"Well, my mom and dad are still alive. He's a retired marine engineer, used to work at the Portsmouth Naval Shipyard. I have a brother, Tom, who's forty-one. He's married and lives in New York. My sister, Charity, is thirty-eight. She's married and lives in Maine. I'm the youngest."

"So we're both the babies of the family?"

"I guess so," she said.

They finished dinner and sat sipping the last of the bottle of wine and she watched him closely. David Baker certainly wasn't movie star material, she decided, but he looked good enough. His sandy hair and blue eyes gave him a boyish look and she had the impression of a rascal just waiting to pull a practical joke. She suddenly realized that what she was experiencing were the beginnings of genuine feelings for him. He made her feel so good, so at ease, but God don't let me go too fast. I don't want to screw this up.

"A penny for your thoughts?" David said looking into the green eyes.

"A penny doesn't buy much any more," she replied playfully.

"Okay, I'll take inflation into account. A dime for your thoughts."

"I was just thinking," she said, "that I almost didn't go to the fundraiser the other night. Life's funny, isn't it?"

"Yeah, you're right. Just think Abby, you would have missed this terrific free dinner!" They both laughed.

"Yes, and the chance to dine with a nice guy." She said trying not to sound anxious.

"Watch out, you'll turn my head and I'm very susceptible to flattery by beautiful women. Soon I'll be putty in your hands!"

"I think I'd like that," she said and David just smiled at her.

They finished the wine and ordered coffee with the dessert. As they finished, Abby spoke.

"This was really nice Dave, I had a wonderful time."

"Me too," he said mesmerized by the woman across the table. "I feel like I've known you for years. You're great to talk to."

The eyes twinkled. "I feel the same way. I'd like to do this again."

"Count on it," David said grinning.

The waiter came with the check and David paid the bill. They left the restaurant and he walked her to her car. The night was warm and muggy and it felt as if rain was in the air. A large sodium light illuminated the parking lot and they stopped by her car. David took her in his arms and gave her a slow careful kiss. She responded by moving her body close to his for just a moment and then they parted.

"When can we get together again?" David asked, aware of the way Abby smelled. He thought it the scent of roses.

Abby caught her breath. "Soon."

"Would you like to come down for the weekend?" David offered. "You know, come visit me?"

"Let's not go too fast," she said wary of rushing things.

"No strings," David explained, "I could show you around the Village and Plymouth. We'll take it by the book Abby, slow and easy."

She thought for a minute and decided she wanted to be with him, but at the same time she was afraid of getting in too deep, too fast.

"What do you say?" he asked hopefully and leaned to kiss her again.

Another tender inviting kiss touched her lips and she trembled slightly in his arms. He let her go and looked deep into her green eyes that gave off a blue reflection in the sodium light. He saw her eyes were moist.

"Okay," she sighed, "but promise me that we'll go slow."

"You have my word as a gentleman," he assured her, "and as a former Boy Scout."

She laughed and gave him a peck on the cheek then got into her car. She rolled down the window.

"I really did have a great time with you tonight Dave."

"Me too," David said. "I'll call you tomorrow with directions to the house. See you Friday night, I'm looking forward to it."

"I'll see you then," she winked at him and drove off. She watched him standing in the parking lot in the rear view mirror as she pulled away. He waved after her and she could not stop looking at him. She turned onto Route 114 and focused on the road aware of her thoughts and feelings.

She knew that she was falling in love with David Baker and could only pray, please don't let me screw this one up.

$$*\qquad\qquad*\qquad\qquad*$$

Abigail Palmer arrived at the house in Duxbury late Friday evening. The traffic on the Southeast Expressway had been bumper to bumper for most of the drive and the normal rush hour crush of cars was almost doubled by vacationers headed for Cape Cod. It was almost 8:00 when she finally pulled into David's driveway.

David had anxiously awaited her arrival and spent a good two hours worrying about her. He was glad to see her and went out of the house to greet her. She was dressed in a blouse and green shorts and as she got out of the car he finally got a good look at her legs. He was not disappointed. They met with a brief kiss.

"I was getting worried about you," he said.

"The traffic was really bad," she said. "God I hate it! How do you deal with it?"

"I don't," David reminded her, "I work ten minutes south of here. Boy you look terrific!"

"Thank you," she said reddening slightly. "This is a nice house."

"Yeah it's comfortable. I've been here five years. I bought it when I went to work at the Village. You have any luggage?"

"In the back," she motioned to the trunk of the car.

David retrieved the overnight bag and took her into the house through the back door. He had managed to clean things up the night before and was satisfied that the place at least looked presentable. He put down the bag on the kitchen floor.

"I'll take it up to the guest room later."

"Guest room?" she asked.

"Sure, I told you everything by the book. You set the pace Abby. Go slow, that's my motto!"

"Like a Boy Scout?" she asked. "God David, you're too good to be true!"

"Just wait until later after I've plied you with liquor. Then see what you say!"

She laughed again. "Where's the bathroom?"

David pointed to the room off the kitchen.

As she went, he asked, "Can I get you something to drink?"

"Sure, a glass of wine would be fine. White if you have it?"

"Blush okay?" he asked.

"Sure that's fine."

David poured a glass of wine for each of them and waited for her to come back. He handed her a glass of blush wine when she returned.

"We're doing steaks on the grill, if that's okay with you?"

"Sure," she said smiling.

"Let's go into the living room for a bit. You must just want to kick back and relax after the drive."

"Fine."

They sat in his living room and Abby curled up on the couch tucking her legs under her. They talked quietly and laughed frequently again finding they enjoyed each other's company. They were both at ease and found it easy to open up to each other.

Later, in the kitchen, Abby helped David make a salad and he put a roll of garlic bread in the oven. Then he went out to the grill to start the steaks.

They ate by candlelight in the dinning room with the flames flickering in the breeze that blew through the open windows. They talked of childhood memories and experiences and David was surprised to discover that Abby had been a terrible tomboy as a young girl. She was surprised to learn that he hadn't dated a girl until his senior year in high school.

They shared these secret memories willingly with each other. They were getting used to each other now, two friends who found they could talk about anything.

Abby helped him with the dishes, drying as he washed and it seemed perfectly normal that they should do this together.

It was past midnight when David led her up the stairs to the guestroom.

"You're in here," he said, "sleep as long as you like tomorrow. I'll take you to the Village later to show you around."

She looked around the room and then at him.

"This is nice. You really are being a Boy Scout, aren't you?" she smiled.

"Just playing it by the book Abby, as requested. Bath's down the hall, so I'll see you in the morning." He gave her a long soft goodnight kiss and she nodded absently, as if trying to decide what to do.

"I'll see you tomorrow," he said and that made up her mind.

He left the room, closing the door behind him. Walking to the master bedroom he wished he could go back in and do what he really wanted to do. He was in love with Abigail Palmer and that was almost too much to hope for.

*   *   *

David awoke at 8:30 the next morning to the smell of coffee coming from downstairs. He shaved and dressed quickly and went down the stairs.

He found Abby in the kitchen reading the *Boston Globe*. She wore no makeup but still she was beautiful he thought. She smiled as he entered the room.

"Good morning," he said.

"I didn't start breakfast yet," she said, "I didn't know if you eat in the morning or not?"

"I usually don't," he said, "I never seem to have time, but God Abby, you're very domestic. I am impressed!"

She laughed. "Actually, I'm pretty good in the kitchen."

David poured a cup of coffee and sat next to her.

"And you're beautiful," he said, "even without makeup." And he kissed her lightly on the lips.

"Why Sir, you overwhelm me!" she mimicked with a southern drawl.

"When you're ready, I'll take you over to the Village. Then we can visit Plymouth. Have you been there?"

"Once when I was a kid but I don't remember much about it."

"We'll have dinner later at a place I know on the water. The view's great and the seafood is very good." He paused, "I'm awful glad you came to visit. I like having you around."

"And I like your company, Mr. Baker. Let me go put on my face and we'll go sightseeing."

An hour later David took Abby through the second floor offices above the museum. They passed Pierce's office suite and saw the door was open and the lights were on. David stopped and went into the inner office. Jack Pierce was at his desk and he looked up from his work at David and Abby.

"Hey you two! How's everything going?"

"Great," replied Abby, "it's very nice to see you again."

"The pleasure is mine," Pierce said, "that I assure you. You two want to join Jennifer and I for lunch?"

David and Abby looked at each other. He shrugged and she nodded.

"Sure," replied David. "Godfrey's?"

"Yeah, meet us back here at 12:30."

Agreeing to meet later, David took Abby back downstairs to the display museum. He walked her through the exhibits, stopping occasionally to show her something. As a former history major, she was very interested and knowledgeable and asked good questions.

They went out of the museum building to the recreated village. The attendant nodded a greeting to David and gave them visitor passes. He also gave Abby an approving smile and they went down the dirt path past wooden homes, some which were little more than shacks, with thatched straw roofs. Abby marveled at the sight.

"It seems so real!" she said.

"That's the general idea."

They stopped to talk with one of the interpreters. David knew him as Joe Perry, from Sharon. Today, in character, he was Miles White, a 1623 immigrant to Plymouth Colony from Bristol, England. With a marvelous accent, he explained why he had come to the colony. Then another visitor asked him what breed the pigs he was tending were.

"Why Sir," he replied in a rich accent, "they are but swine!"

David turned to the tourist. "There were no breeds 370 years ago," he explained.

"Oh," muttered the tourist absently.

David and Abby spent two hours exploring the Village and Abby found she enjoyed the visit.

"This place is so neat!" she bubbled. "It must be a real kick to be part of it."

"It really is," agreed David. "Most of the time anyway."

They met Jack and Jennifer Pierce at the museum building and then drove to Godfrey's for lunch.

They ate and picked up their conversation from the previous Saturday as if they had never stopped. David observed that Jennifer was taking Abby under her wing. She was the consummate matchmaker he chuckled to himself.

After finishing the meal the Pierce's dropped David and Abby at the Village, bidding them goodbye. As they drove away, Abby told him, "I really like them Dave. Jennifer is so friendly that I feel I've known her for years."

"She likes you too," David said. "I think you bring out her motherly instincts. Let's go visit Plymouth."

They traveled the short distance back to the town on the bay and parked on a side street. They walked down to the water, stopping first at the famous rock.

"It really isn't very big, is it?" Abby observed.

"No, but it did use to be bigger," David explained. "A large piece cracked off years ago and in the 1800's people were even allowed to take chips away as souvenirs."

"You're kidding!"

"No, it's true," David said and Abby shook her head.

They walked along the waterfront toward the replica of the Mayflower. They held hands and once again passed tourists, hardly noticing them. David looked at her and she smiled flashing the eyes. Christ, he thought, she makes me feel like I'm eighteen years old again.

They took the tour of the *Mayflower II*, marveling that 102 people, plus the crew could have made it across the Atlantic in such a small vessel. Finishing the tour, they walked north past several restaurants towards the Sheraton Inn.

"The town has a slight honky-tonk atmosphere to it, doesn't it?" Abby asked.

"Yes, I guess so, like a lot of other tourist meccas. But, there is a lot of history here to offset the outward appearance. You just have to be aware of it."

"That's very profound, Professor." She reached up to kiss him on the cheek and he just smiled at her mesmerized by her face. They continued on to a small shopping mall and spent some time browsing through the stores. Finally they strolled back to the car.

*   *   *

Later they ate dinner at a restaurant at the south end of town overlooking the water.

"This is beautiful," Abby said. "Thank you for a wonderful day Dave. I really enjoyed myself and I'm so glad I came."

"I'm glad too," he said. "You know, I've lived here for five years, but I'd never taken a tour of the *Mayflower*. And now that I've joined the Mayflower Society, it gives me a sense of what the people on the ship did. Over half of them died the first winter, did you know that?"

"I probably read that somewhere in U.S. History 101," she said, "but I don't remember that. Makes you appreciate the risks they took and the sacrifices they made for what they believed in. I'm glad you took me."

She looked at him, eyes expectant and felt the need to tell him how she felt about him, but she decided not to press the issue. Not too fast, she warned herself one more time.

They ate, talking quietly and David once again noted Abby's intellect. She could discuss any subject with depth and perspective and that only made her all the more attractive to him.

This could not have happened so quickly, he thought. But it had and it seemed too good to be true. He could only hope the bubble would not burst.

They returned home later and Abby kicked off her shoes. David went to the kitchen for after dinner drinks. She was sitting on the couch when he came back into the living room and he handed her a glass. He held his up.

"To us," he said simply.

"Yeah, I'll drink to that," she said and they clinked glasses. They sat together on the couch talking and finally Abby said, "You know what would be a perfect way to end the evening?"

"I can think of several things!" David laughed.

She returned his laugh with a leering grin, "I suppose you could. I'd like to dance."

"Ah, that was not one of the things I was thinking of," David mugged. "But I think I have some old Lettermen albums around here somewhere."

"You mean David Letterman has recorded dance music?"

He burst into laughter.

"Come on Abby! You're not that young. The Lettermen, they were big in the 60's. Lovey dovey slow songs. Good to dance to. Jesus, I got my first kiss at a dance in Junior High while they played a Lettermen song."

"Another interesting puberty story," she exclaimed, "you're telling me all your secrets. Dave you better watch out, I might steal your heart!"

He held her, suddenly serious. "You may have done that already Abby, but I'll take my chances."

She broke loose and went to the stereo where she turned the radio on and switched to the FM band. She played with the tuner and finally found some slow music that suited her purposes. She went back to David who had turned the lights down.

"Now, dance with me!" she ordered.

They danced slowly in the darkness and he was aware of her perfume and the smell of her hair. She felt his strong embrace as he held her and when the music stopped they kissed softly.

"Still going slow?" he asked, willing to be patient for this beautiful green-eyed woman.

"Yes," she said, putting her head on his shoulder.

Another tune began and they danced slowly.

"This has been a perfect day Dave," Abby murmured. "You're a very special guy. Thank you."

"I feel the same."

They danced slowly through several more tunes, saying nothing, holding each other close.

"I think it's getting late," she said finally. "I'm going to bed. Thank you again, especially for being so understanding."

He nodded and saw in the dim light that she had tears in her eyes.

"Are you okay?"

"Yes, I'm just very happy Dave. This is all too good to be true. I'll see you in the morning. Good night," she said wanting him but not trusting herself.

She gave him a kiss, turned and went up the stairs. David watched her go, his heart aching and went into the kitchen where he poured a glass of water. He sat in the darkened living room and tried to read his own thoughts. He knew he was in love with her, that was as plain as day. But he didn't want to ruin this beginning by rushing things. He would wait. He knew he had to wait because it was obvious to him that Abby was holding back due to the ache of previous hurts. But Abby was a woman worth waiting for and he understood. He'd gladly wait.

David left his empty glass and climbed the stairs, going down the hall past the closed door to the guestroom. He resisted an urge to go to her.

He went into the bathroom where he washed and brushed his teeth and he turned off the light as he went into the master bedroom. He was about to turn on the lights to see when he became aware of the smell of perfume.

"Don't turn them on," her voice was nervous and perhaps uncertain.

"Abby?"

"Yes." Quiet now the voice low.

His eyes adjusted to the darkness and a dim shaft of light coming in through the window from the street light outside helped him to see her. She wore a long nightgown and her hair was brushed down falling on her shoulders. In the pale light she seemed unreal, like an aura in a dream.

"I wanted to be with you," she said simply.

"What about going slow?" he asked as his heart beat faster.

"To hell with that!" she laughed surer of what she was doing now. "I want to be with you and I need you. I love you Dave."

"I love you too, Abby," he said and felt his body shiver at his own words. It felt so right. "You're the most wonderful woman I've ever met Abby and I want you so much."

He went to her and carefully embraced her kissing her tenderly. He tried to be gentle and caressed her face with the back of his hand.

David asked, "Are you sure about this? I'm patient. You're worth waiting for Abby. It can wait until you're sure."

"No, I made up my mind," she said, "I need you Dave and I need this. So much has been missing from my life and now I meet you and you fill the void for me. You're quite different from any other man I've met. If we need to put things in perspective, we can talk tomorrow. Tonight, I want to be with you. Now, shut up and kiss me!"

He kissed her again and she responded to his slow passion in kind by moving her body hard against him. Neither of them was a first time lover and they both took their time savoring each other, exploring trying to explain the reason for the attraction each of them felt. David let her go for a moment.

"You're beautiful you know, quite beautiful. You're giving me a special gift."

"Do you always get this corny?" she laughed.

"Yeah, I'm a Boy Scout, remember?"

He reached for her, dropping the straps of the nightgown down around her arms and he slipped the lacy garment down her body letting it drop to the floor. She stepped out of it and stood in front of him.

David gave her an appraising look. Her body was every bit as beautiful as she was. If he had any doubts they were gone now.

"Wow! You're terrific!"

"Shut up and kiss me!" she said, and he embraced her, his hands caressing and touching her body. She giggled as he nibbled gently on her neck and he continued to kiss her.

She started to undo his shirt and ran her hands up his chest. She reached down and undid his pants. He pulled away.

"Fair is fair," she said. "I get to do that too!"

"Boy, women are getting tougher every day."

"Shut up and take your clothes off," she giggled.

David helped her to undress him and they stood together naked. They embraced and David tenderly held her chin, giving her another slow searching kiss. He moved his hands down her front touching her lightly with his fingertips until he reached her waist. She pulled back abruptly.

"I take it back, you're no Boy Scout!" she said.

"But, I am prepared, aren't I?"

Laughing, they fell onto the bed, giving each other the intimacy they both so desperately wanted.

CHAPTER NINE

May 14, 1835 Buffalo, New York

Buffalo, New York was the western terminal for the Erie Canal. Since the canal opened in 1825 it had been the primary route taken by those from the east who were migrating to new lands in the west. Buffalo had experienced phenomenal growth because of this traffic and had developed into a busy port city. Along with the growth and the money it attracted, it also became a very rough town with a pervasive criminal element that was all too real.

James Baker knew this and was aware of the dangers that might threaten him. He reflected on the events of the past three weeks and the preceding nine months. His mother had died the previous fall and she had died young of a broken heart. The doctor has said consumption, but he knew that it was really a broken heart that had killed her. With her death, he no longer felt that he must remain at home in Walton, Delaware County, New York since he knew his father, James Baker Senior, could get along well enough living with his older sister. He also knew that he had to respond to the urge he felt to move on to the western lands. After several years of deliberation he had finally made the decision to move his family to Michigan and satisfy the destiny that drew him. His cousin from Massachusetts, who he had never met, had settled there the previous year and had written letters extolling the virtues of the land.

James Baker felt the urge to move but still the decision had been a hard one. Even harder since his mother had told him on her deathbed of the mysterious family fortune that had been taken from her years before. She had been near death when she made him promise to someday reclaim the fortune but had not given him any real details. His father had told him some more of the details and had extracted a promise to pass this request on to future generations.

He felt drawn to this promise but the attraction of the rich and fertile lands to the west beckoned him. The decision to move and join the ever-increasing number of people moving west had the full support of his wife of eight years, Deborah. They said their good byes the last week in April and traveled down out of the Catskills, by road, north to Utica. There they purchased passage west on a canal boat. The trip on the Erie Canal took nine days, the journey governed by the speed at which the mules, struggling on the towpath, could pull the boat.

James Baker, Deborah and the three children; James age five, Content age three and Charles age one had arrived in Buffalo at mid day. The first order of business was to book passage on a lake steamer to Detroit, where the final leg of the journey would begin. Baker made several inquiries about safe vessels and secured space for his family on the side-wheel steamer *Michigan* that would depart at noon the next day.

He checked several large trunks with the freight agent and, family in tow, he now searched for accommodations for the night. He led them down a street near the waterfront, lugging their remaining belongings in a smaller trunk and several canvas bags. They came to a boarding house in a building that looked fairly respectable and advertised clean rooms for rent.

"What do you think?" James Baker asked his wife.

"It seems nice from the outside. We need to find a room James, it's getting late."

"Yes I know. I'll go and see if they have room."

He went up the three front stairs and entered the wooden building going into a room with a low ceiling. It was plain but neat and a woman sat on a stool behind a tall desk and she smiled at Baker showing gaps where her top front teeth had once been.

"Hello, Gent, lookin' for a room for the night?"

"Yes, do you have a room with three beds for my wife and children?"

"Why sure, Mister. Fix you right up. Nice room on the back of the house. Three beds even a window. Dollar a night. You want it?"

"That's a lot," he said.

"This is a nice house, Gent. Take a look around and find a better place!"

Baker thought this was true and knew it was only for one night. "Guess so," he said and paid her from the small purse he kept on a rope around his neck.

"Want some help with your things?" the woman ginned a toothless smile. "My boys can help you upstairs."

Baker thought her just a little too friendly and was suspicious of her intent. "No, we can manage, thank you," he said.

Disappointed, the woman gave him the key to the room. "Number nine. Upstairs, to the rear of the house on the left."

Baker nodded and went out to Deborah. "We're set, I'll take our things up to the room. You bring the children."

James Baker carried their belongings into the house and climbed the stairs to the second floor while Deborah followed with the children. He put the key into the lock but before he could turn it, the door opened by itself. He saw the lock was useless and he went into the room. Deborah led the children in and Baker put their belongings on the floor then went back down to the front desk and confronted the woman.

"The lock's broken," he said as indignantly as possible.

"It is? Why, I'll send one of the boys up to fix it."

Baker nodded saying, "Please do that."

He returned to the room where Deborah was waiting for him.

"This room's a mess!" she said stating the obvious. "It's filthy!"

"It's not nice," he agreed, "but it's only for one night Deb. We can stand it."

She gave him a look and went to work to settle the family in for the night. The window proved to be small, only a foot square and through it, the setting sun threw an orange light. There was a noise at the door and James Baker opened it to see a pale man with a terrible pockmarked complexion standing in the doorway. The candle in his hand made him look even more sinister.

"Ma says your lock is broken, Mister."

"Yes."

"I'll look at her," he offered.

He held the candle in front of him and while he did this, he looked around the room, trying to size up what the visitors might have that was worth taking. He pretended to look at the lock.

"Sorry Mister, it's broken. Can't fix her tonight but don't worry though, you're safe here, I'll see to that."

"I'm sure we'll be fine," Baker said as confidently as he could. "Thank you for your concern."

"Don't think nothin' of it," the man said. "I'll be checkin' on you durin' the night. Sleep well." And he left them going back down the darkened hall.

Baker closed the door and Deborah came to him. "We should leave," she said firmly.

"I think it's too late," he replied.

"James, we've almost six-hundred dollars in coin and silver in my basket, plus your purse. You know he'll be back later to take it from us!"

"We'll deal with it, somehow Deb," he said but was clearly worried. "Let's get some food into the children and get them to bed. I need to think."

They gave the children some bread and cheese from one of the baskets and a flask of water provided drink to wash the food down.

Finished, the tired children lay on the bed in the corner of the room and quickly fell asleep.

James and Deborah nibbled at some of the same food in the dim light of the candle they had lit but did not have much of an appetite. Worry showed on both their faces and James Baker went to one of the boxes and removed a long fillet knife. He tested the blade with his thumb and satisfied with the edge on the blade, he went back to where Deborah sat on the rough bench. He put the knife down beside her.

Next he went to one of the beds and lifted the straw filled mattress. He took one of the supporting slats from the frame and hefted it. The slat wasn't much, but would get the attention of anyone who got in the way of it.

"We'll get by," he tried to smile. "I'll stay up to watch the door Deb. You try to get some rest."

"Yes, James," she said kissing him softly, "call if you need some help."

"I will," he said trying to sound more confident than he felt.

Deborah Baker lay down on the other bed and tried to relax but the tension in her would not allow her to do so.

James Baker sat on the bench by the door and waited in the dark, tense and alone with his thoughts. An hour later the floorboards outside the room creaked and instantly alerted, Baker was wide-awake. It was dark, the candle long since extinguished and he heard, rather than saw, the door latch move.

"Who's there?" he demanded.

There was no answer.

"Who's there?" he repeated.

Still no answer but behind him he heard Deborah stir.

"James, here are the pistols! They're both loaded!" she spoke as loudly as she could hoping her lie would confuse whoever was at the door.

James Baker looked at his wife in the darkness and smiled. He could always count on Deborah Wolcott Baker to do the unexpected.

"Thank you my dear!" he said in a voice that he hoped sounded defiant. "Whoever is on the other side of the door, I have two pistols cocked and aimed at the door! Now, who's there?"

The only response was more creaking sounds from the floorboards and heavy footsteps going back down the hall.

"That was quick thinking, Deb!" Baker said. "They're gone but I think they'll be back."

"We can bluff them," she said quietly, "but I really wish we did have a brace of pistols." James Baker nodded and settled back down to wait.

Baker thought it was about 1:00 in the morning when he again heard footsteps in the hall followed by scratching at the door. He waited for a moment and now there was just enough moonlight to see the door move slightly. A hand and forearm appeared. Holding the bed slat as a club he struck at the arm with all his might. The blow struck home and a man swore loudly.

"Here are the pistols dear!" Deborah said loudly behind him.

Outside they heard the footsteps go back down the hall, once more in retreat. One of the children whimpered from the bed and Deborah went to comfort the child.

It was almost dawn when the strangers tried again to enter the room. Baker had dozed off for the last hour but the first light of a cloudy morning and his farmer's morning alarm woke him.

He heard the creaking and shuffling in the hallway. Angry now, he called, "I have two pistols leveled at the door. Go away you bastards!"

Once more the door latch moved and a hand appearing as the door opened slightly. This time Baker slashed angrily with the knife. He knew he had struck the man because a scream came from the other side of the door.

"God damn, I've been cut! Oh God, help me!"

Another voice whispered urgently and Baker heard two sets of footsteps scurry down the hall, one man moaning.

"Let's get packed and out of here!" Deborah pleaded.

They hurriedly repacked the few things they had removed the night before. The children, now wide awake because of the commotion begged for something to eat but Deborah quieted them, promising food after they left. Baker, sticking the bloody knife in his belt, gathered their bags together.

Cautiously, he opened the door and saw the hallway was empty. He carefully made his way to the stairs, then beckoned to Deborah. She followed, carrying the two youngest children while young James walked beside her holding her skirt.

As Baker crept down the creaking stairs he noticed drops of blood on several of the risers. Finally at the bottom, he warily looked around the corner to the front desk. Strangely, no one was there but a trail of blood went from the stairs to the door that led to the rear of the house. Deborah came down behind him and he put his finger to his lips to warn her.

He made for the door and carefully opened it, alert for any footsteps behind him. Quickly Deborah was out the door with the children and Baker followed shutting the door quietly behind him.

James and Deborah hurried down the street relieved to have made good their escape from the evil boarding house. They did not mind the wind and rain that began to fall on them.

"Are you hurt?" Deborah asked.

"No, I'm just fine. You?"

"I'm well James but we must find some shelter quickly and food for the children."

"Yes," he agreed, "as soon as we can. You were a tower of strength Deb. I will never doubt your bravery or judgement as long as I live!"

*　　　　　*　　　　　*

The sidewheel steamer *Michigan* ploughed into another wave and seemed to stop abruptly, shudder and then start on again. The shallow depth of Lake Erie made for short steep waves that came close together. They were not at all like ocean swells that rolled under a ship so the *Michigan* pounded into each wave with a crash, making little headway.

Michigan was rolling from side to side as she hobby-horsed in the storm that blew from the northwest. Making conditions worse was the fact that the ship had two steam engines, each one driving a paddle-wheel. This created great noise and vibration each time the ship rolled and one of the great paddlewheels would come out of the water, free-wheeling pushing only the air. The combination of all these unpleasant sensations caused a great deal of discomfort to the passengers and crew.

James Baker experienced the same discomfort, ruing the fact that he had opted for the cheapest steerage accommodations for his family. Everyone on the lower deck was seasick from the violent motion. Children cried and women shrieked each time the steamer ploughed straight on into a wall of water. Baker was no exception and he had been violently ill several times. The slop buckets provided as precaution against this possibility had long since overflowed so the stench and mess below was unbelievable. He watched his wife, who was also sick, try to comfort the children and saw she was not having an easy time.

He swore to himself and retched again. The motion on the cabin deck would have been just as bad but at least the ventilation would have been better. The putrid smell on the lower deck was more than a match for the undersized ventilating funnels that brought a small amount of air, and a considerable amount of water, into the berthing space.

Baker was ashamed of the fact that he was sick. Particularly because he remembered his mother saying that there had been sailors in her family.

The steerage space was crammed with over two hundred souls, most of whom were settlers on their way to Michigan. He hoped that the Captain and the crew knew their business because all their lives depended on their skills.

Baker thought back to the events of the previous night and morning. After escaping the boarding house he and Deborah had found their way to a simple but clean eating place several blocks away. Wet and cold they dried the children as best they could and ate. They warmed themselves at a fire in a grate at the end of the room and James and Deborah worried that the children would catch pneumonia. They had lingered in the eating place and had a second pot of tea to warm up; passing time until the ship sailed at noon.

Finally they donned their rain gear, which had gone unused earlier and they left the eating place and walked to the waterfront careful to see they were not being followed. The rain was intermittent, the wind increasing in force.

Arriving at the pier where the *Michigan* waited, they found shelter in a terminal building that the steamship company provided for those awaiting passage. The schedule called for the *Michigan* to make the trip from Buffalo to Detroit in forty hours and the ship was scheduled to arrive early in the morning of the second day.

They boarded the ship late in the morning and settled into settees and rudimentary bunks in the crowded steerage hold. James Baker took young James on deck to watch the departure and, as the *Michigan* was warped from the pier, he noticed two men run along the dock looking at the ship. One of them had his right hand bandaged and the other was the man with the bad complexion.

Baker moved back with his son so that he could watch without being seen. The two men were looking for someone and they were excited, gesturing toward the ship. Finally as the ship drifted away from the dock they walked back down the pier.

Baker was sure these were the two who had tried to rob him last night. They were undoubtedly interested in revenge for the wound he had inflicted on the one with the bandage. He was glad to be leaving the tough port town.

That had all taken place twelve hours before and now, just past midnight, Baker sensed that the ship was in trouble. Water sloshed in the bilge under the floorboards beneath where he sat. Even though he was no sailor he knew there were signs of trouble all about him.

Two crewmen came down to steerage, a look of fear on their faces. One of them had a lantern and they went forward to a manhole hatch. They opened the hatch and the one with the lantern got down on his hands and knees to lower the lantern into the bilge. After examining the bilge for a moment he stood and Baker overheard the man tell his companion, "More than two feet, we'd better tell the Cap'n."

"Christ, we'll do 'fer her yet!" the other man muttered louder than he intended. The two crewmen hurried off up the ladder to the main deck.

James Baker slid over on the settee to where Deborah sat stroking the head of young Charles who lay on the narrow bunk. He was too young to know but the other children were clearly frightened.

"We're in trouble," he whispered to her.

"Yes, I thought as much," she said.

"I just heard two crewmen say the ship is taking water," he continued. "How bad is it?"

"I have no idea, but they went to tell the Captain. I wish there was something I could do!" He grabbed for her and held her arm.

"The Lord will see us through," Deborah responded. "Make no mistake about it, I've been praying."

"I hope you're right," Baker said, "but I'm not sure."

"One thing, James," Deborah vowed, "If I ever get on dry land again, I am never leaving. I promise you I mean that!" and she retched once more in the overflowing slop bucket.

James Baker almost laughed despite the way he felt. "I understand how you feel Deb. Stay here and I'll go and see if I can find out what's going on."

Baker could stand it no longer, he had to find out what was going on and he went to the ladder that led to the main deck. Bracing against the motion of the ship he climbed the ladder and came out of the shelter that protected the companionway. In the dim light of the ship's night-lights he saw the spray and rain flying through the air.

Seeing that no one was about he looked aft past the paddlewheel boxes towards the stern of the steamer. There was a dim glow that he took at first to be from the ship's night-lights. But as he watched, a flicker of flame shot out from the side of the cabin trunk.

Oh God! The ship was on fire!

Baker watched for a moment, fascinated and transfixed, unsure what to do. The flame flickered again. Water crashed down the deck as the ship hit another wave and water rushed between his legs. He went to the ladder that led to the pilothouse and climbing quickly, he went into the small rounded house where the ship was steered. Bursting in, he saw a man at the wheel and another peering out the window. A third man stood at the chart table that was attached to the aft side of the pilot-house. He decided the man at the chart table was the Captain.

"There's a fire!" he warned.

The Captain, an older man with a white beard, looked at him, eyes wide at the sound of Baker's words.

"Where?"

"Back by the cabin on the main deck," Baker panted.

"Come show me!" and the Captain pulled him out the door rushing down to the main deck.

Another wave of water washed down the deck as Baker pointed toward the stern. Flames shot out of the passageway.

"There!" he yelled and pointed.

"That's near the boiler uptakes!" the Captain yelled above the storm. "You Sir, stay here while I get some help! You've done well, I'll need your help!"

He went off and Baker held onto a handrail on the cabin trunk as the ship bucked into another wave. The out of water paddlewheel sent vibrations throughout the whole vessel as if she was shaking herself to death.

The Captain returned with a half dozen hands and he pointed at Baker. "Come with me!" he ordered.

They went aft to where the flame had appeared. There was a pump attached to the deck with a fire hose connected to it. Two men took the hose and others began to work the pump. Baker watched as one of the men with the hose opened the door to the passageway near the flame. As he did, a blast of flame shot out and the man backed off, letting the blast subside. The two horsemen pointed the pulsing hose toward the flame and entered the passageway followed by the Captain who supervised.

One of the men on the pump tugged at Baker's arm. "Spell me!"

James Baker traded places with the man and began pumping up and down drawing water for the hose. His arms tired quickly and he was weak from being sick. Nevertheless, he continued with a will and felt the bile rise in his throat but he ignored it.

Behind him, the fire fighting crewmen were making progress against the fire. One of the hose handlers came coughing from the passageway and another man replaced him.

How much time passed Baker did not know. He kept working the pump and ignored his leaden arms. Finally, he knew he could not go on and looked at a man near him. The look on his face was enough and the other man took his place at the pump. Baker dropped to the deck exhausted and too tired to notice the water that washed over him every time the ship hit a wave.

Other crewmen now appeared to help in the battle against the fire and slowly, they contained the blaze. Fresh men entered the passageway to help the two with the hose and others beat at the flame with canvas covers. Little by little the fire died.

James Baker lay with other exhausted and spent men on the sodden deck oblivious to the storm and waves crashing around him. He was much too tired to be sick, although he felt the urge to do just that and he tried to nod as the Captain came to him.

"Thank you," the Captain said. "That was a very near thing. We were lucky you found the fire when you did!"

Baker shook his head and the Captain spoke to one of the crew. "We're in a bad way!" he said. "We'll hove to for the rest of the night. At first light we'll run for safety at Cleveland!"

The fire fighting party broke up and the tired crewman returned to their regular duties. The Captain faced Baker once more.

"Thank you again," the Captain smiled. "If there is anything we can do for you please let me know."

Baker felt drained by his efforts but struggled to his feet. "I'd like to get my family away from the mess in steerage, Sir. Is there any place else we could go?"

"That's the least I can do," the Captain replied, "I'll get one of the crew to help you. You can use my cabin until we put into Cleveland."

Baker nodded in thanks and followed the Captain forward, ducking as another wave broke over the bow of the ship. The Captain motioned to a crewman and pointed to Baker.

"Help this man bring his family to my cabin."

The crewman shook his head in agreement and trailed Baker down the ladder to steerage. Baker was sure that the sight that greeted him was a scene straight from hell. The steerage hold was even worse than before with a thick pall of smoke hanging in the air. Smoke from the fire must have been sucked into the compartment through the ventilation funnels. He went to his wife and children who were coughing.

"Where have you been?" demanded Deborah. "Are you all right? What happened? Are we on fire?"

"I'm all right," he assured her. "There was a fire, but it's out now and I helped put it out. How are you?"

"I'll live," she said relieved to see her husband alive. "The children are very sick James!"

"I can see that. Come with me Deb, we're going to the Captain's cabin."

She looked surprised but saw he meant what he said. They gathered their belongings and with the crewman's help went to the Captain's cabin on the upper deck. While it was still rough, with the ship hove too into the wind, the motion was easier and the vibrations less noticeable. The children rested easier as James and Deborah fretted through the rest of the night.

Dawn found the ship deeper in the water but the storm had abated during the night. The Captain turned the vessel south at first light and ran for the safety that lay in the harbor at Cleveland.

Pumps clanged constantly in an effort to keep up with the water the ship had taken aboard. The crew was making progress because the ship was running with a quartering sea now with only an occasional wave breaking aboard.

Baker was awake, feeling tired and very dirty from the night's hard work. He noticed the change in the ship's motion and saw Deborah and the children sleeping in the Captain's bunk. He did not disturb them and went to the porthole to look out at the water. The sky was still gray and the rain was still coming down but the wind velocity seemed to have dropped. He took this as a good omen and went through the door, careful not to wake his family. Climbing to the pilothouse he entered the steering space.

As he entered, the Captain turned to him. "Good morning Sir. Thank you again for your efforts last night."

"Happy I could help," Baker said. "How are we doing now?"

"We're keeping ahead of the water," the Captain explained. "With luck we can make Cleveland in a few hours to make repairs."

The Captain proved correct in his estimate and the *Michigan* entered the harbor at Cleveland just after noon, docking at a pier on the Cuyahoga River. The crew, with the help of local ship fitters, immediately went to work repairing the damage from the storm and the fire.

The passengers, who were grateful to be alive, staggered ashore to rest and recuperate.

Baker took his family to the warehouse building that the steamship company made available to the passengers. The children were showing signs of bouncing back from the rough trip, their young constitutions remarkably robust. Deborah was tired and still sick though and Baker worried about her knowing that the trip had been particularly taxing on her.

"Is there anything I can do to help you?" he asked her.

"No, James, I'll be fine. I just need some time to rest, I'm very tired."

"We'll have at least a day to do that. One of the crew told me that we can't possibly leave until tomorrow at the earliest."

Deborah Wolcott Baker crossed her arms on her chest and stamped her foot. "James! I will not get back on board this, or any other ship! And I will not travel one step further! The Lord has spared us for a reason and has brought us here. I will go no further James and we are staying here!"

James Baker knew that she meant every word of what she said and, in fact, he could not blame her. When Deborah Wolcott Baker made up her mind there was nothing he could do except agree with her. They would not be settling in Michigan he thought and knew Ohio would be their new home.

CHAPTER TEN

David paged through the index to the History of Delaware County, New York and found several references to James Baker. He turned the pages of the book to the first reference and could not believe his good luck. In a chapter that told of the westward migration of former County residents, there was a letter dated in 1836 from a James Baker in Farmington, Ohio to his father, James Baker Sr. The letter related the story of the move west that the younger James and family made the previous year. They had started out for Michigan but had ended up in Ohio. The book noted that this letter had survived because it had been donated to the local historical society by a grandson in the late 1870's and had been reproduced in the book.

David looked at this in disbelief and knew that with this one lucky find he had found the next generation. The story of the trip taken by the younger James Baker was truly amazing and he went to the copier to make a copy. He knew he was finding more than he ever expected to find and had discovered that his ancestors had truly been made of strong material.

Back at the table he found the next page with a reference to James Baker. This section was devoted space to early settlers in the County and there was a notation that James Baker Sr. and his wife had come from Massachusetts and had settled in the Walton area about 1800. James Baker was a farmer and a millwright and the book mentioned that his wife had died in 1834 and James in 1845. Also mentioned were five children, including as son James who had gone to Ohio. This was another important find and David copied the material realizing just how lucky he had been and how useful the new data would be.

The family was from Massachusetts, he thought that was very interesting. Somehow he never felt that the trail he was following, would take him there. But that was the lure of genealogy; you never knew where you would end up.

He looked at his watch. He still had time to do some more work before he headed north to Portsmouth to visit Abby. He smiled at that, just the thought of her made him feel happy.

David decided to see what he could find on John Bedford as Jack Pierce had suggested. He located the microfilm for the 1850 Census for Calhoun County, Michigan. He checked the printed index and noted two Bedfords listed in the town of Calhoun. He scrolled to the first listed page but this did not contain the family he sought. Moving to the next listing, he found what he wanted:

Nathan Bedford	Head	Male	Age 46	Born Mass.
Abigail Bedford	Wife	Female	Age 45	Born Mass.
Jacob Bedford	Son	Male	Age 20	Born Mass.
Susan Bedford	Dau	Female	Age 17	Born Mass.
John Bedford	Son	Male	Age 14	Born Mich.
William Bedford	Son	Male	Age 12	Born Mich.
Elizabeth Bedford	Dau	Female	Age 10	Born Mich.
James Bedford	Son	Male	Age 8	Born Mich.

The census information gave him the basics of the Bedford family. John Bedford's father was Nathan Bedford from somewhere in Massachusetts and the coincidence that both the items he found led to Massachusetts did give him some evidence that the Bakers and the Bedfords might be related. He decided he would do more work on the Bedfords later.

He looked at his watch and noted it was nearly twelve noon. It was time to go visit Abby so he put his papers in his briefcase and left the library.

*   *   *

The Saturday traffic wasn't too bad, David reflected as he crossed the Mystic River Bridge onto Route One. He wanted to see Abby again and he was impatient to get to Portsmouth.

The last three weeks since her visit to Duxbury had been the best time of his life. They had made a joint decision to not rush the obvious and move in together right away. He understood that she did not want to leave her job yet and they both knew that they each needed time for the relationship to grow naturally. They had seen each other on the intervening weekends and had met for dinner once each week. Their nightly phone calls made him worry about his phone bill but he didn't really mind, he was in love. He smiled to himself as he thought how he wanted to spend every minute he could with her.

The drive north took an hour and he pulled up to a parking spot in front of her apartment west of Portsmouth. She must have been watching for him because she came out the door to greet him. They met on the walk and David gave her a long ardent kiss.

"How are you Abby?" he asked as he let her go.

"I'm wonderful, now that you're here. I missed you."

Then he kissed her again and told her, "I love you, you know that?"

"Of course. And I love you. Now how are you?"

"Good and I had a productive morning at the library. I got back another generation in the Baker family."

"Hey that's great Dave. Let's go inside and you can tell me about it."

Holding hands they walked inside her apartment. David had been there twice before and he liked the way she decorated the small one bedroom unit. It was clearly a woman's apartment, but the colors and style set it off in a way that would satisfy anyone.

"Have you eaten?" she asked.

"No, I wanted to get here as fast as I could."

"I'll make you a sandwich then," she smiled. "Ham and cheese okay?"

"Sure, just fine. You have a beer?"

"Yes, I'll be right back."

She returned in five minutes with sandwiches and beers for both of them. David took a hungry bite of the sandwich and washed it down with a sip of beer.

"Tell me what you found this morning?" she asked.

Between bites he told her of the information in the Delaware County History.

"Wow! That's a really neat find Dave. The trail leads back to Massachusetts, huh?"

"Yeah, it's funny, I never would have guessed that," he said. "It is truly amazing how the family went west. From Massachusetts to New York to Ohio then on to Indiana and Iowa. The Bakers seem to have been really mobile!"

"Well, look at you. You went the other direction in less time!" she joked.

"Yeah, I guess you're right but it really is an interesting story."

"I'm glad you did move east," she smiled and the eyes twinkled. "Otherwise, I never would have had a chance to meet you."

She sat down next to him.

"What are we doing today?" David asked.

"I thought we could go for a walk in town this afternoon, if that's okay?"

"Sure."

"Then tonight Mom and Dad have invited us over. They want to meet the man who has swept me off my feet. Is that okay too?"

"Yes," David smiled, "I'd like to meet the people who had such a lovely daughter."

She leaned over and kissed him. "You know what I like best about you?"

"My superior intellect or my good looks?"

"No," she laughed. "You always seem to know the right thing to say to me. I love you for that Dave."

"Are you sure you really want to go for a walk?" he asked. "We could stay here and mess around."

"Oh David, we can't do that all the time! God you have a one tracked mind!"

"Oh why the hell not?" Then he grinned at her. "Okay, let me make a pit stop and I'm ready for a walking tour. I'd much rather mess around though!"

She laughed as she watched him go to the bathroom thinking he was a terrific guy.

*   *   *

David and Abby arrived at the Palmer house in Newington at 6:15 and a slim woman in her sixties greeted them. She was an older version of Abby. David immediately decided and knew where Abby had received her terrific looks.

"Hi Mom," she said, "this is Dave Baker."

"I'm very glad to meet you Dave. I've heard so much about you for the last month, I feel like I know you already."

"I'm glad to meet you too, Mrs. Palmer," David said a bit self-consciously. "I can see where Abby gets her good looks."

"He's good at flattery," she said to her daughter, "I like him already!" Then she looked back at David, "Please call me Jan."

"Fine with me," David said.

A man with gray hair in his late sixties came up behind Jan Palmer and Abby gave her father a kiss.

"Dad, this is Dave Baker. Dave, this is my dad, Bob Palmer."

"Glad to meet you Sir," David said.

"Likewise and you can drop the Sir. Name's Bob. Come on out to the back porch. Like something to drink?"

"Are you having something?"

"Already have a bourbon and water. What would you like?"

"Scotch would be fine."

They settled into comfortable chairs on the screened in porch. It was typical late August weather and the evening was warm and humid. They talked and David found himself answering questions about his job and background. While he talked and watched their reactions, he decided that he liked Abby's parents.

"We're doing chicken on the grill," Bob Palmer said, "would you like to help me Dave?"

"Sure, I'd be glad to."

They went to the kitchen to get the chicken for the grill and Abby's eyes followed David as he left. Her mother noticed this and laughed. "I like him," Jan Palmer told her daughter. "It's about time you found someone that's as nice as you are."

"Thanks, Mom. I really like him. I've never met anyone like him before."

Jan Palmer just smiled at her daughter's obvious happiness.

"Is Grandma coming over?" Abby asked.

"She should be here any minute. Dad offered to pick her up but she still insists on driving herself. She just won't admit she's getting old."

They both laughed. Jan Palmer's Mother was the source of many family tales and jokes. At the age of ninety-one she acted thirty years younger and though she was the target of the good-natured jokes, she was still the source of a great deal of family pride.

"I'm glad she's coming," Abby said. "I want Dave to meet her. Maybe she'll tell us some of her famous stories."

"You know it won't take much to get her going Abby."

The doorbell rang and Abby went to the front door to greet her grandmother, Susan Taylor.

"Grandma! How are you?" she said to the woman with short gray hair. Susan Taylor still stood tall, as tall as she could at five feet two. She was thin and wiry and did not look her age.

"Just fine Dear. Is this new young man of yours here?"

"Yes, I want you to meet him."

Susan Taylor greeted her daughter asking, "How about a glass of wine Jan?"

Jan Palmer laughed and went to get her Mother a drink while Abby led her grandmother out to the patio where the men were cooking on the grill.

"Grandma," she said proudly, "this is Dave Baker. Dave, this is my grandmother."

The older woman gave David a friendly grin. "Very nice to meet you young man. I seem to have heard a lot about you."

"It's nice to meet you too," David said looking down at her.

Jan Palmer appeared with a glass of wine and then went back into the kitchen to finish preparing the rest of the dinner. While the chicken cooked, David chatted with Abby and her grandmother.

They ate in the dinning room of the tastefully furnished house. David was enjoying himself and as he finished the meal he sat back in his seat.

"That was delicious. Thank you for a fine meal."

"Sure you wouldn't like anything more?" Jan Palmer offered.

"I couldn't eat another thing. Thank you."

"You'd better," laughed Abby, "Mom's got a blueberry pie for dessert that you have to try."

"I'll make the effort," David said. How could he refuse?

"Grandma, Dave's working on his family history," Abby said. "I told him that you did ours. I've never seen all the stuff you did. Could I see it sometime?"

"Yes Abby. Anytime you want to copy it I'll loan it to you. I did it years ago with my mother."

"Thanks Grandma, I'd like to do that. You know, Dave has got this strange family tradition," Abby related. "All the Baker men pass on the rights to the 'stolen family fortune' down to each generation. He's trying to find out what that is."

"What did you say?" Susan Taylor asked.

"I said he was trying to find out what the family fortune was," Abby said as saw her grandmother pale slightly.

"Are you all right Mom?" Jan Palmer asked.

"Yes, I'm fine. It's just that my mother told me the same story about the Bedford family," the older woman said.

"Bedfords?" questioned David.

"Yes," Susan Taylor continued, "my mother was a Bedford. All the Bedford males did the same thing, only it was the 'stolen family land'. She never knew what it was either, although she told me though that one of her uncles did a lot of work on the mystery."

David felt the hairs on his neck stand up and his heart quickened. "Where were they from?" he asked.

"My mother was born right here in Portsmouth," Susan Taylor said looking a David with a new interest. "Her father was born in Michigan though and returned back here in the 1860's, before she was born. It's very interesting, my mother's Grandmother Bedford was from Salem Massachusetts and she always said the she was related to the family that owned Rosemary Point."

"Is that where the relationship to the Sherwoods comes in?"

"No, that's another line," Susan Taylor said. "This one goes back to the original owners."

"What!" Abby exclaimed, "you mean the Smith family?"

"Yes, my mother's grandmother was Abigail Smith, she married Nathan Bedford. She was the daughter of Jacob Smith whose family owned the land at Rosemary Point in the beginning."

"Does that mean that I'm related to Abigail Steele Smith?" asked Abby.

"Sure does," her Grandmother replied.

"How come you never told me this before?" Abby said.

"I guess I never thought to. All my material was always available and you never asked. I didn't think you were interested, most young folks aren't you know. But I guess as you get older, you tend to want to know more about where you came from."

David had a very strange feeling as he sat listening to this conversation. Susan Taylor's story was just too much of a coincidence. It just couldn't be the same family. Could it?

"You know," David said, "you won't believe this, but when I was at the library this morning, I looked up the family of a Nathan Bedford of Calhoun, Michigan. I was trying to get answers to some questions I had about the relationship between his son, John Bedford, and my great great grandfather."

"What?" asked Grandma Taylor.

"That's right, I'd forgotten that puzzle," Abby said getting excited now as she recalled David's earlier story. "Tell them about it Dave."

David told them what he knew from the Civil War records and the will that Charles Baker had left. He finished with what he had discovered at the library that morning and when he finished the table was silent. Bob Palmer spoke first.

"That is one incredible story Dave. Jesus, what a coincidence!"

"It really is," Abby agreed. "From what you found today there seems to be a connection in Massachusetts. It must be the same family, don't you think?"

"It is," Susan Taylor spoke shaking her head in amazement. "Remember the uncle that my mother talked about?"

"Yes," said Abby.

"It was John Bedford."

"Absolutely amazing!" muttered David. "Mrs. Taylor could I borrow your information and copy it?"

"I'd be delighted to share it with you. She looked at David and Abby. "You two could be cousins a few times removed. Maybe now you're kissin' cousins?" she laughed.

David looked at Abby seeing her face color slightly at her grandmother's comment and they both burst into laughter.

*   *   *

David and Abby had talked long into the night discussing the bombshell that Susan Taylor had passed on to them. They both agreed that the neatest thing was that Abby was clearly descended from Abigail Steele Smith and that filled her with pride. They were not quite sure what they should do next, but before going to bed they decided to visit Rosemary Point the next day. The implications of the new information were not clear and he would have to talk things over with Jack Pierce to understand where it might lead. Finally, he and Abby had fallen into exhausted sleep in each other's arms.

They awoke the next morning and made love spontaneously, giggling and laughing and then joked about their incestuous relationship. They ate breakfast and left Abby's apartment at ten-thirty, knowing that the house at Rosemary Point would not open until twelve on a Sunday, but they both felt the need to walk the grounds. Abby said that it was as if the place was hers now and she wanted to get to know each square foot of the property.

They drove down the dirt road to the parking lot and parked the car. The day was overcast and they were early so there were few cars in the lot and there were only a few tourists with whom to share the grounds. They walked down to the boardwalk and past the salt marsh. It was low tide and the smell of the wet lands was in the air. They looked up at the rise that ran uphill to the house.

"I think the view from the house in better," David said.

"I've always thought so too," Abby agreed, "but this is pretty nice too."

"No, it's not. Especially with you here." He kissed her.

"God you can't get enough, can you?" she giggled.

"There's no one around!" he protested.

They laughed and held hands tightly.

"Come on," he said, "let's go back to the house."

They walked back along the boardwalk to the parking lot and went right up the path to the house. They walked the grounds from end to end enjoying the natural beauty of the land.

"Whoever acquired this knew what they were doing. It's the most beautiful place I've ever seen," David stated.

"That would have been James Steele," Abby said, "he bought the property in 1774. I've seen the deed and the house was built two years later."

"It must have been something, even then. Now though, it's just short of marvelous. I don't think you could replicate this now considering the environmental laws and all that. And I'm glad that you know you're a part of this place, it somehow seems important," David said.

"It does," she smiled and squeezed his hand. "I've always liked being here and now I know that maybe it's because I have a tie to both the Sherwoods and the Steeles. In a way I kind of feel responsible for the place. You know what I mean?"

David nodded and they sat on the edge of the grass overlooking the sea. It was a calm quiet setting and they lay on the grass for an hour talking.

David looked at his watch and saw that it was past twelve, the time had passed quickly.

"The house should be open now, let's go look around," he said.

"I'll show you a few of my favorite things in the house," Abby said rising.

They walked into the house and David noticed a different woman was at the desk in the entryway.

"Hi Jane!" Abby said greeting the woman.

"Hello, Abby, how are you?"

This woman was in her early twenties, tall and very thin. She had a friendly, cute face and a volunteer nametag labeled Jane Webster.

"Jane, this is my friend Dave Baker," Abby said. "Dave, Jane Webster. She's a volunteer."

"Hello," the woman said greeting David and giving him the once over.

"Nice to meet you," David smiled.

"Dave's a member too Jane. We'll just look around for a while, if that's okay?"

"Sure suit yourself."

David walked off to the library and Jane pulled Abby aside whispering, "is this something serious?"

Abby laughed, "God I hope so, he's a pretty neat guy."

"Well, it agrees with you Abby, you look great!" Abby smiled and went to catch up with David in the library.

"Here," she said, going to one of the bookshelves, "this china plate came from the Orient. One of the Sherwoods shipped a consignment sometime back in the early 1800's. They made a lot of money from it."

David nodded and he followed her into the dining room.

"See the silver tea service?" Abby asked pointing to the silver on the sideboard, "that was a gift from President John Quincy Adams to the family in 1826."

"No kidding? The Sherwoods must have been pretty well connected then?" David asked.

"From what I have seen, yes. But, they seemed to lose their power just before the Civil War. I'm not sure why, but it's almost like they ran out of money and influence at the same time."

"That's interesting, I wonder what happened?" David mused.

They walked into the kitchen and looked at the period cooking utensils that decorated the room. As they were examining the hearth the back door opened and the interpreter/guide David had seen in June entered.

"Hello," she smiled.

"Hi," responded David, "remember me? I was here couple of months ago. You made my visit a great experience."

"Oh yes, I remember you. You were the one who was so nice and polite. And who is this you have with you today?"

"I'm Abby Palmer," Abby said. "I've been here before. I'm a member of the Society."

"You have a kind face too," the woman said studying Abby. "Both of you will be able to help me."

"Help you do what?" David asked, a puzzled look on his face. What was this all about?

"A great injustice was done here years ago," the woman said. "And another is about to be done."

"What do you mean?" Abby asked suddenly alert to this woman and the way she spoke.

"This property was stolen from its rightful owners by ancestors of the family that now owns it. There are plans afoot to sell the property to another. Many houses will be built here and it will be an even greater injustice to lose the heritage of this land."

David looked at the woman, then at Abby and wondered just what all this was about.

"Do you mean that the property was taken from the Steele and Smith family years ago?" Abby asked, feeling drawn to the woman.

"Yes that is what I relate."

"Who did this?" asked Abby.

"I am bound not to say, so you must find the answer yourself. In fact, I cannot tell you because I do not know. I know only that it was taken by another."

David was puzzled and confused by the woman's words. "Abby is descended from the Smiths and Steeles," David said hoping that might loosen the woman's tongue.

The woman looked at Abby and considered this new information. Then she smiled at her.

"Yes Abby Palmer, I should have known, I should have felt the presence. You have her qualities I think."

"Who?" asked Abby trying to understand what the woman was saying.

"Why Abigail Steele Smith," she replied.

Abby blinked, "How do you know?"

"Ah," she smiled, "I have spent a great deal of time with her."

"What do you mean?" David said wondering if this woman was a mental case.

"Oh, I've studied her for years," the woman explained, amused at the reaction her words were causing. "I know all about her."

"Well, you're very good, you know," David said relaxing.

"Why thank you," and her eyes twinkled.

"Can you tell us more about what is happening to the property?" Abby asked.

"I'm afraid I do not know the details, but the property is to be sold to a man who will build many houses on the grounds. The land will be ruined! Please, you must help me stop it from happening!"

"Who is doing this?" David asked glancing at Abby who was as puzzled as he was about this strange unexpected conversation.

"I believe it to be a member of today's Sherwood family who controls the rights to the land. I do not know his name so you must find out who it is!"

"Why do you need our help?" asked Abby. "Can't you find out for yourself?"

"No," the woman said sadly, "I cannot. So I must ask you to help me." She focused on Abby. "You, as a descendant of the Steele family must do it to help right the great wrong that took place here."

David and Abby looked at each other and a chill went up her spine. She shook it off, but David saw her pale and he grabbed her hand holding it tight.

"Are you okay?" he asked.

"Yes, I'll be fine, I just felt faint for a moment."

"Yes you will be all right," the interpreter said. "I know in my soul that you both are the right people to help me. I think you care about Rosemary Point and you will not disappoint me. You know you owe something to what is past and you will do the right thing."

She smiled and nodded goodbye and then went out the back door toward the garden.

Abby and David stood holding hands for several minutes, not knowing what to say. They both knew that something strange had just happened, but just what they didn't know.

Partly dazed by the experience they walked through the pantry into the sitting room and said goodbye to Jane Webster. They went back to the parking lot and stopped by the car, leaning against the hood.

"Do you feel as strange as I do?" asked Abby.

"Yes," replied David, "that was very confusing. Do all your interpreters go that far in pursuing their roles?"

Abby blinked. "It was as if I had lost control of my body Dave. I felt a force or something overcome me for just a moment. It was so strong and yet I think I wanted to feel it more."

"I saw you," David said, "I saw something on your face. But," he hesitated, "I think I felt it too Abby."

Abby shook her head. "You know Dave, I didn't even think about it, but as far as I know the Society doesn't employ any interpreters."

"No? Then who was the woman?"

"I have no idea," Abby said realizing what she had just implied. "Let's see if we can find her out back."

They walked up the path going to the rear of the house where the vegetable garden was green and abundant. They searched the garden area looking for the woman who had been in the kitchen and they went to the back door and peered in to see if she had returned to the kitchen. The room was empty and the woman was no where to be found.

"How about that?" David said.

"I just don't know," Abby shook her head and they slowly walked back to the car bewildered by what they felt happening to them.

*   *   *

As they drove back to Abby's apartment they tried to figure out just who the woman could have been and what had motivated her to tell them what she suspected. They could think of neither motive nor explanation for her actions. Abby made lunch and as they ate, they reviewed everything that had happened to them.

"Any way you can check and see if there is any truth to the possible sale of Rosemary Point?" David asked.

"Sure, I can do some checking I guess. I can use my contacts at work to do that and if something's in the wind, I should be able to find out about it."

David took a bite of his sandwich and asked the question once again. "Who do you think the woman was?"

"I just don't know Dave," Abby said chewing. "We've gone over this again and again so many times I've lost count. I don't have a clue. Maybe she's a member of the Society who likes play-acting. She seemed so real though didn't she? It gave me chills and I felt something happen to me."

"I know, I felt the same thing. There's one other thing you can do if you like."

"Sure. What?"

"After what your grandmother said yesterday, could you go to Salem this week and see if Jacob Smith left a will? If he did, I've got a hunch there may be some clue in it."

"You really think so?"

"Who knows," David shrugged, "it might."

"Sure, I'll go tomorrow. Dave?" she asked.

"Yes?"

"I felt something earlier when we were talking to the woman. It's like she chose us to help her. Like it's important some way. Did you feel that?"

He paused for a second. "Yes, I did. I felt it too and with all the coincidences that have popped up I think this is something I have to do."

"We have to do," she corrected him.

He smiled at her, "Yes, we have to do."

He pulled her toward him and she smiled kissing him.

"Abby, I know we agreed to go slow but I've never felt so close to anyone before. I guess this isn't the most romantic moment, but I want to marry you. We don't have to do anything about it now, but I'd like us to be together forever. I feel that strongly. I love you that much."

She grinned and held him close.

"Dave, you're not the first one to ask me that, but this is the first time I accept. I love you Dave Baker and we can set a date any time you like."

Embracing each other they rolled on the couch.

*   *   *

Late the next afternoon in his office, David picked up the ringing telephone.

"Hi Dave, it's Abby."

"Hi how are you?"

"Fine. Are you sitting down?"

"Sure," he laughed, "why? Where are you?"

"I'm in Salem. I just had to call you right away!"

"What's up?" he felt a shiver travel up his back.

"Dave, this gets weirder and weirder all the time. You and I really are cousins!"

"What!"

"It's true. I found a will for Jacob Smith. He died in 1840 and apparently he was pretty well to do since he left a large estate."

"What's this about us being cousins?" David asked almost afraid of the answer.

"I'm getting to that. But in the will Jacob Smith mentions his children, including Abigail Bedford of Calhoun, Michigan. That's my ancestor, my great great grandfather I think. But, there's a reference to the family of his sister Content, who married James Baker. That's your family, isn't it?"

David was stunned and sat speechless for a moment. "Oh my God!"

"Dave, are you there? Are you okay?"

"Sorry", he mumbled. "Shit Abby, I wasn't ready for this. Do you mean that Content Smith married James Baker?"

"That's exactly what I mean. We should can check it out further, but it appears that Content moved west somewhere and disappeared. Her brother says in the will that he *'hopes her children will get what they are entitled to if she is ever located, although there is nothing I can do now to right the great wrong done to her.'*"

"No shit?"

"I've made a copy so you can read it. Dave?" she asked.

"Yes?" he said quietly, a dozen different thoughts racing through his mind.

"Do you think the stolen family fortune in the Baker family could have been Rosemary Point?"

"Shit, I don't know Abby. My great great grandfather thought that the fortune was in Massachusetts. I suppose it could be possible though."

"Oh my God Dave!" Abby exclaimed, "I just remembered something. Maine was a part of Massachusetts, until 1820, when it became a state. Dave, it could be Rosemary Point! Couldn't it?"

The chill ran up his spine again as the reality of what was happening overwhelmed him.

"Sure Abby, it's certainly possible, especially if someone left before Maine became a state. It's easy to see that things could have become confused when the tale was passed on down to each generation."

"Dave? Like I said yesterday, it's kind of like we've been chosen to solve this mystery. This is almost scary you know and it really does involve both of us."

"Yeah, I know. Nice going Abby, you did good work. Shit I need to think on this. I'll call you tonight. I love you."

"I love you too. This makes me feel even closer to you now, if that's possible. And," she said, "the answer is still yes."

He smiled at that and hung up the phone thinking that there was much to be done.

CHAPTER ELEVEN

July 23, 1800 Kittery, District of Maine

Content Smith despaired for herself and the new life that was growing inside her belly. She was pregnant and she was broken hearted, but that was not the worst of it. Her legal guardian had used her condition as an excuse to disinherit her and now she would get none of the estate to which she was entitled. The loss of the money her father and mother had meant for her didn't hurt as much as losing the house at Rosemary Point. The wonderful house and the land meant so much to her because it was a tie to her parents. She loved the place more than she thought her mother had loved it.

She also knew she loved James Baker, the young farmer and millwright from Newburyport, Massachusetts. He had already asked her to marry him and the fact that they had made love and she was now growing with child did not alter that.

The fault was hers, for she had made a mistake in trusting her guardian even the least bit. He had given her just enough leeway to hang herself she reflected and she should have seen that possibility sooner. Her guardian had encouraged the relationship with Baker and even as he did, she knew now, he must have kept a close watch on her. No matter what she did though, eventually he would have found some reason; some excuse to disinherit her and claim the fortune her parents had left her and her brother Jacob.

The thought of Jacob brought with it another feeling of revulsion and disgust. The guardian had bought Jacob's cooperation and loyalty cheaply. That was plainly obvious to her now. Jacob had become of legal age in April and he knew full well that their guardian wanted the fortune and property that was theirs. Through the years the guardian had always courted Jacob, enticed him with praise and presents while at the same time he sparred with Content who rebelled against him at every turn. He attempted to pit the two siblings against each other. In the end, she thought, he had been successful.

Jacob had settled for two thousand dollars, which seemed a goodly sum, but hardly a fraction of what he should have been entitled to. Content despised him for his weakness. But despite her scorn she realized she still loved him as her brother.

It was at times like this that she wished her mother and father were still alive. Growing up without them had been difficult for her and the absence of her mother's love had left her vulnerable and with an inclination to fight whenever provoked. She needed someone to talk to, to help her, but there was no one since her mother was gone. Content cried herself to sleep many nights wishing her mother could be with her.

She could not remember her mother or father at all and that bothered her, leaving only an empty feeling inside her. So she had grown up sad, longing to feel that someone needed her. She yearned for a love that she had always wanted.

Now, she had nothing in the world. Fate and her own rebelliousness had caused her to lose everything.

Everything, she thought, except James Baker. The lanky tall good-looking man from Newburyport had come into her life almost a year ago. He had come to Rosemary Point to build a gristmill and Content took to him immediately. They became fast friends, even though he was five years her senior.

With her guardian's encouragement the romance had bloomed and culminated in an act of love three months before. Content remembered how on a warm April night they made first time love in the loft in the barn. It ended an evening in which James Baker had asked her to marry him and she had accepted. She had found the love she so desperately sought.

Now, sitting at the Kittery home of her friend, Amy Warring, she pondered what to do next. She could not go home again, her guardian had made that abundantly clear and her final defiant fight only sealed her fate. She had damned the man and told him he would be cursed with bad luck and that no good would ever come to him or his children.

As she thought of what awaited her, the anger built inside her and she was filled with a terrible resolve that she would find a way for her unborn children to someday claim what was rightfully hers. Somehow, someday she would find a way to make that happen. Now she needed to get to James Baker and let him know what had happened. That was the most important thing but some day she would extract her final revenge. She was sure of that no matter how long it took.

*   *   *

Accompanied by Amy Warring she traveled from Kittery in a wagon driven by Amy's brother Tad. They arrived at James Baker's small farm in Newburyport shortly after noon. There were tears in Content's eyes as she kissed her friend goodbye and promised to write when she could. Amy and Tad left and Content sat down to wait for James Baker to return to the farm west of town. She settled in on the steps of the small farmhouse.

It was late in the afternoon before she saw the broad shouldered man come down the road riding his bay gelding. He was very surprised to see her.

"What are you doing here?" he asked dismounting.

She burst into tears. "I've been thrown out James! I've been disinherited!"

"What?"

"I'm pregnant James! Oh God, I think I'm three months along."

"Me?" he asked.

"Who else?" Her eyes flashed at him.

"I'm sorry," he said recognizing the hurt in her eyes. "Of course I love you Content and we'll marry as soon as we can. What else happened?"

She sobbed and told him the rest of the story. He took her in his arms and held her tight.

"The man's a bastard! I'm sorry I ever went to work for him. But," he smiled, "I'm not sorry I met you though!"

"What shall we do James?" she asked with tears rolling down her cheeks.

"Don't worry, we'll get by well enough. I've some money saved and I've been thinking of moving west anyway. They say New York offers good land. I think we can try that. Besides, my neighbor Jonas Clark has asked several times to buy this property. We can be off quickly if we want!"

"It means leaving everything!" she sniffed.

"What's left for you now? Do you really want to stay here?"

She shook her head. "No, you're right. The only thing left for me is Jacob but he's made his dirty deal. Still James, he is my only blood relative and I must see him before we go."

"As you wish," James Baker said. "First we must marry. You can stay with me, I'm taking care of you now. Tomorrow we'll go find Mr. Welton, the Justice of the Peace and he'll marry us. Come inside with me so we can make plans."

He kissed her. "I do love you Content. God, I do wish you had not been hurt so but this will all work out in the end, you'll see."

*   *   *

The weeks that followed were busy ones. James and Content were married immediately in Newburyport and James agreed to sell his farm to his neighbor and felt the agreed price more than fair. He gave Content money to buy clothing to add to the meager belongings she had taken with her from Rosemary Point.

He knew that she was heartbroken about leaving the land and house she loved so, but at the same time he was determined to give her the best he could; the kind of life she deserved.

Mentally, James Baker went over what still needed to be done. Their possessions were reduced to what would fit in the wagon they would use to travel to New York. Whatever else they needed could be purchased with the cash hidden in the bottom of the chest his father had given him.

One of the last things to do was to say goodbye to his parents, Francis and Elizabeth Baker. It would be difficult, but his father would understand the need to go west, James knew he felt the same desire for elbow room. The elder Baker was a dreamer and saw a great future for the new nation. He also understood that the future lay in the west.

James Baker reflected that this vision of what might be had cost his father his arm. He had been among the first militia, the Minutemen, to arrive in Boston after the British marched in April 1775 to confiscate arms in Lexington and Concord. Two months later he had been on Breeds Hill, in what became known as the Battle of Bunker Hill. He had received a wound in the left arm that resulted in it being amputated. Yes, James Baker reflected, it would be difficult to say goodbye to such a man but he would understand.

The last thing they would do was stop in Salem so Content could say goodbye to her brother. James Baker did not like Jacob. Compared to Content, who was a spirited fighter when it came to standing up for her beliefs, Jacob was weak and indecisive. James Baker could not help but wonder how things would have turned out if their parents had survived.

He looked up as Content entered the house and he smiled at his wife. She was pretty, he thought and her pregnancy only added to her beauty.

She was tall and slim and he had been told that Content much resembled her mother.

"James, I have finished packing the wagon. We can leave any time."

He looked around the now empty house. "I've just been thinking of what still needs to be done. There isn't much more. We'll sign the agreement on the farm tomorrow and we must visit my parents. Then we will stop so you can see Jacob and then we are free. Are you all right?"

"Yes, James, I'm fine," she smiled. "I'll be glad to leave," she looked at him. "I love you."

He went to her and took her in his arms. "I love you too and I wish I could make up for all the hurt you've been caused."

"I know that James. You give me joy by just being my husband, you should know that."

"Come on," he said, "we'll give the trap one last spin before Clark gets it. We'll go to say goodbye to my parents, the ride should do us good."

"Yes. I'd like that. Let me wash up and we can go."

He watched her go to the wash basin in the kitchen feeling proud of this special woman. He thought she must have inherited the best from her mother and even if she lost the family fortune, they would make life work. Together they would be successful. He knew it.

*   *   *

The wagon, pulled by two draft horses, clattered along the brick street in Salem. On the driver's bench sat James and Content Baker. Two days before they had said their good-byes to his parents. It had been an emotional time for them because his parents knew this was most likely the last time they would see him. In the end though, Francis Baker had given his son his blessing with tears in his eyes. That was life, the Revolutionary War veteran had explained.

The farm changed hands with the proceeds from the sale increasing the cash hidden in the bottom of the wooden chest. Now they were on the way west to New York; Delaware County in the Catskill Mountains. They would take the road west to Albany but before doing this they would visit Jacob Smith so Content could say goodbye.

James Baker knew she had mixed emotions about this but she kept her thoughts about her brother to herself. He wasn't sure what would happen so he prepared to be ready for any eventuality.

Since receiving his settlement in April, Jacob Smith had invested in a printing business in Salem. He was not yet married and lived in a room on the second floor above the print shop. James Baker reined the horses to a stop and pulled at the hand brake.

The late afternoon sun was hot and bright in their eyes. He wiped his brow and looked at his wife.

"You sure you want to do this alone?"

"Yes James, it's something I must do."

"Wouldn't it help if I was there?"

"James, we've discussed this before, I can do it myself."

"Suit yourself," he shrugged, "call out if you need help."

She smiled, grasping his arm. "Thank you James. I'll always need you, but I can do this."

She kissed him.

Baker got down and helped her from the wagon seat. She brushed his face with her hand and went into the print shop. A man sitting at a tall work desk looked up as she entered.

"Help you Mam'?" he asked.

"Yes, I'd like to see Jacob Smith."

"Not here right now."

"Where is he?" she asked just a bit perturbed by his absence.

"Out," the man replied with a smug grin on his face.

"Out where?" she demanded.

The man regarded her closely. "Who're you?"

"I am his sister! Now, where is he?"

"Reckon you'll find him at the saloon down the street. Usually find him there this time of day but he should be back anytime though."

"Thank you, I'll go and find him. I don't have all day!"

She turned to go out the door and almost collided with her brother. He looked at her in surprise.

"Content!"

"Yes Jacob, it's me. I've come to say goodbye to you."

"What?" She could see his eyes were glazed. He had been drinking.

"I said, I've come to say goodbye to you. I'm leaving with my husband, we're moving west to New York."

"Husband? West? What are you talking about?" Jacob was befuddled.

"You know well enough. Our guardian has thrown me out Jacob. I've been disinherited and I can never go back to our house thanks to that bastard!"

"Don't talk about him that way," Jacob tried to scold her.

"Don't you side with him Jacob. He's stolen from you too!"

"That's not true Content," Jacob whined in protest. "He says that he's had business losses on our account and needs to borrow our funds to offset them."

"You actually believe that?" she laughed. "Then you are a bigger fool than I thought!"

"Yes, why not?"

"Because the man is a meanhearted bastard and a liar! Mother and Father would never have appointed him to look out for us. That alone proves he's a crook and a cheat!"

"But the Court did appoint him to look out for us. I've seen the papers."

"So have I, but that just shows how clever he is Jacob. He used the Court to get what he wanted and now I have nothing but my pride and you have even less!"

"That's not fair! I'm in business now and I will succeed with his help, he's promised."

"Those promises will prove to be empty Jacob. Mark my words!"

"Why did he disinherit you?" Jacob asked this but knew the answer.

She proudly patted her stomach. "I'm going to have a child. That was his reason, but if it hadn't been that, he would have found another excuse. I'm married now and we're going to New York."

"But Content, you could go back. If you apologize he'll take you back."

"I'll not beg for what's rightfully mine!" her anger flashed. "No, Jacob, you lay down with the Devil but I'll have no part of it. I'd rather die!"

Jacob sadly regarded his sister. "I'll probably never see you again Content. After all, we are brother and sister. We're the last of the Smiths."

"No Jacob, you're the last of the Smiths. I'm a Baker now and you'd better think about yourself, because from where I sit, you're a poor excuse for a man!"

"How can you say that?" He looked at her eyes then looked away unable to face her, shamed by the truth she spoke.

"Look at what you've done!" she scolded. "You didn't even fight for what was yours. You gave in to a dishonest crook and now you're apparently half drunk all the time!"

She looked around to see the man at the desk laugh and she yelled at him. "Get out! This is none of your business!"

The man smirked but seeing the look on Content's face he scurried to the back room. Content turned back to Jacob who seemed to be cowering in front of her, a beaten man.

"My God Jacob, you must pull yourself together! You've got to go on. You must stand up for what you know is right!"

"I can't," Jacob said with tears forming in his eyes. "You've always been the strong one, Content. I just don't know how to do it."

"Then you better learn!" she spat.

She watched him stare at the floor. He could not face her.

"Jacob, you must promise me one thing. You must pass on this story to your children, if you ever have children. They must not forget the great wrong that has been done. Will you promise me this one thing?"

Jacob looked up, facing her. "Yes Content, that I will promise you. It's the least that I can do for you."

"Thank you Jacob. You had better watch out for the bastard. I fear he is not done with you yet."

"Content, he has been good to me," Jacob protested.

"But look at what he did to me! You are only fooling yourself!"

There was nothing more that Jacob could say knowing he was beaten. His sister always seemed to win.

"When are you going?" he asked quietly.

"We're on our way now. You were the last thing I needed to do before I go."

"So," he tried to smile, "you have married Baker, the millwright?"

"Yes Jacob, he will be the father of our child."

"Content, I know it's been very difficult for you without a mother or father. You've gotten stronger because of it, but I've only become weaker. You always stood up for me even though I'm older and I'll always thank you for that. I do love you and wish you all the luck in the world. You deserve to have a happy life. Lord knows the first eighteen years haven't been good to you."

She let him embraced her and he hugged her with a will. There were tears in his eyes.

"Come," she said taking him by the hand, "walk me to the wagon."

"Won't you stay the night at least?" he pleaded.

"No, Jacob, we've a long journey ahead of us. The sooner we start the faster we'll get to where we are going."

They went out the door to where James Baker stood by the wagon. He saw the tears in Jacob Smith's eyes and sensed what had passed between brother and sister. "Hello Jacob," he said.

"Hello James, it's good to see you."

Baker nodded but remained silent.

"James, Jacob has wished us luck on our journey."

"That's nice, thank you Jacob."

"Won't you at least spend the night?" repeated Jacob.

James looked at Content who shook her head.

"Thank you for your kind offer but we must start," Baker said.

He shook hands with Jacob and Content went to her Brother giving him a final hug and kiss.

"Goodbye Jacob. I hope life is good for you but heed my warning about the cheating crooked bastard!"

"He's not a bad man," Jacob insisted.

"Jacob, you will never learn," Content said realizing the futility of her words. "The man is a thief. He's stolen our property and our fortune! I do not intend to forget it!"

Jacob looked at her knowing she was leaving forever and he would likely never see her again. She hugged him one last time.

Content climbed to the wagon bench with help from James. He shook hands again with Jacob and stepped up to the seat next to his wife.

He released the brake shaking the reins and the horses started to pull the wagon away. Content waved goodbye to her brother knowing she was saying goodbye forever. There were tears of sorrow in her eyes as she looked away and she felt the hurt and resentment for what had come between them.

But Content Baker knew she would never forget and she swore to herself. That bastard, their guardian, dishonest crooked Jonathan Marston. Someway, someday, she vowed to see him in hell.

She put her hand on James Baker's arm and he looked down at her, smiling and proud.

"You're something!" he said to her. "We've got quite a trip ahead of us."

"And a whole life," she reminded him.

CHAPTER TWELVE

Driving home from work, David tried to go over everything that had happened one more time. The events of the last two days were almost unbelievable and he laughed to himself, thinking that Abby had called it mystical. Maybe in a way it was, but in reality, the mathematical chances of the two of them having a common ancestor seven generations back were not that long. A coincidence, a matter of chance, but not at all important.

He felt very proud of his descent from the woman from Rosemary Point and then he remembered that he was also descended from her father, Captain James Steele who died in the Revolutionary War. He had information about him in the brochure from Rosemary Point and he thought he would have to do some research work on James Steele the next time he went to the library.

David knew that James Baker, who had married Content Smith was from Massachusetts but he needed to find out what town he had lived in. He wasn't sure how to find this information. Maybe he was back far enough to find him in one of the Baker genealogies again and he thought he should try to get to the library soon.

David also thought it was important to find out more about Abigail Steele Smith and her husband, Captain Jacob Smith. Somewhere there had to be some clue that would shed some light on the mystery of Rosemary Point.

His thoughts returned to the woman who had spoken to them at the house. Who was she and what was happening to the property? Or was it all some silly made-up story from some disturbed woman? Abby would check on that and she would also see who actually owned Rosemary Point. Maybe she could trace the ownership of the property back to see if that information would yield any clues to the mystery.

He turned the car into his driveway and pulled to a stop by the back door. He got out of the car, walked up the steps and unlocked the back door. He entered the kitchen and grabbed a beer from the refrigerator.

David turned on the television and was on his way to check the mailbox when the phone rang. He answered it.

"Hello."

"Hi, it's me," Abby said.

"You again? I just hung up on you two hours ago!"

"I know, it's your magnetic attraction Dave. I had to call though, I miss you."

"Me too."

"Actually, I called to tell you that I just sent you a copy of Jacob Smith's will plus copies of all the information my grandmother had. I forgot to tell you when I talked to you earlier. I was kind of shaken."

"Thanks, Abby. I'll look forward to getting the material. I've been thinking, how about a change of plans? Instead of you coming down this weekend I want to come up to see you. I want to take a couple of days off to do some library work and then shoot up to see you. That sound okay?"

"Sure, doesn't matter to me as long as I can get my hands on you!"

"No need to worry about that!" David laughed. "I'll come up on Friday night after I get done at the library."

"Good. I'm going to the Court House in Alfred, Maine tomorrow to check the land records. I'll call to let you know if I find anything."

"That's great! Thanks for your help, I love you."

"Hey, this is a partnership," she said. "We're going to get to the bottom of this. I love you too. Talk to you tomorrow. Bye!"

David returned the telephone to the cradle smiling at the thought of Abby. He got the mail and quickly looked through it, then sat down in front of the TV to watch the national news. Sipping his beer, it occurred to him that he should tell Sue about what had happened.

He reached for the phone and tapped out Sue's number. She answered on the fourth ring.

"Hello?"

"Sue, it's Dave."

"Hey, how are you?"

"Great, but deep in the middle of a real mystery."

"What's happened?"

David told her about the events of the last two days.

"Boy, that sure is interesting!" Sue said. "And how is Miss Palmer? You haven't even mentioned her yet. That is very much out of character for you these days!"

David laughed. "Well, I do have a little piece of news. I've asked her to marry me and she said yes."

"No kidding? Oh Dave that's so wonderful! I've just got to meet this lady. She sounds like she's what you've needed all along."

"Yeah, she is."

"Set a date yet?"

"No Sue, I just asked her and we've agreed not to rush things. I'll let you all know when we do."

"Can I tell Jerry and Beth?"

"Sure. I should probably call Jerry though."

"I'll leave it to you then. But do it soon."

"I'll call them later."

"You'd better. Boy, I wish I could visit you."

"Geez, Sue, I'd love to have you visit. Could you get away?"

"I wish I could, but the kids are going back to school. As much as I'd like too I don't think I can take time but I'd like to see you and meet this woman who has swept you off you feet!"

"Maybe we can come visit at Thanksgiving, or Christmas," David suggested. "I'd like you all to meet Abby. You'll like her".

"Well it'll have to wait. The kids go back to school the day after Labor Day so I guess me coming out there is wishful thinking."

"Okay, I'll let you know later what things look like for the holidays."

"Well, it would be nice," Sue said. I still want to meet this woman. In the meantime, keep me up on what you find."

"Yeah, I will and I'll make copies and send some of the new stuff tomorrow. Call me if you have any questions or bright ideas."

"Good. I'll look forward to getting the new material. Goodbye Dave."

"Talk to you soon, Sue."

He hung up the telephone and went to the kitchen to fix dinner. He really would like to see his sister and the prospect of a trip over the holidays sounded like a good idea.

*   *   *

Abigail Palmer drove north on the Maine Turnpike focusing on the road as she thought about the job ahead of her. The immediate problem was researching the land records pertaining to Rosemary Point but she also needed to check out the possible sale of the property. She thought her boss, Dan King, should be able to help her with that.

She knew that there were other things she needed to do because her role in the Baker family mystery was expanding. She and David shared the belief that meeting each other, falling in love and discovering a common ancestor was more than just a coincidence. Her intuition told her that fate had conspired to put them together at this time and place to right a two hundred year old injustice.

Just what this was though, she didn't know but she hoped that what she was doing today would provide some help in learning just what the mystery was.

She turned off the Turnpike at Exit Four, paid the toll and headed west on Route 111. Twenty minutes later she parked in the municipal parking lot by the York County Court House.

She went inside to the Register of Deeds where she started with the deed index. She turned the pages to the "S" section, looking for Sherwoods. There were many entries and because of this she decided to start with the name Steele instead. Using the same index, she looked up the name, Steele and saw the index contained only two references to James Steele. The first was dated April 1774 and the second dated June 1780. She wrote down the Deed Book and page numbers.

Abby went to the record books on the shelves and located the two volumes she wanted. She opened the first volume and found the page listed in the index. The deed record was the original land purchase record for James Steele. The Deed, dated April 24, 1774, recorded the transfer of two hundred twenty four acres of land, property known as Rosemary Point in the County of Yorkshire, District of Maine to James Steele for the sum of 520 Pounds Sterling. Abby smiled at the record. This was the beginning of the saga, she thought, where would it end?

The later Deed recorded the transfer of title to the land to Abigail Steele Smith. As directed by the Court of Probate, County of Yorkshire, District of Maine, the deed dated June 6, 1780, transferred the title of Rosemary Point from the Estate of James Steele, deceased, to Abigail Steele Smith. The reference to her ancestor made her smile with a familiar fondness. I wish I could have known her, she thought.

She marked the Deeds in both books with slips of paper so she could copy them later and went back to the index. She looked under the name of Smith and found a mention of the Estates of Jacob and Abigail Smith. There was also a separate reference to a transaction involving the Estate of Jacob Smith and Abby recorded the information.

Repeating the process, she went back to the Deed Books and she found the transfers of title. The first record recorded the transfer of Rosemary Point from the Estate of Abigail Smith to a Joseph Sherwood and his wife Tabitha. This Deed was dated October 23, 1800 and the executor of Abigail's estate was someone named Jonathan Marston. The transaction mentioned that the property was conveyed "for love" and this puzzled her. She didn't know what the term "for love" meant and wondered why the delay in settling Abigail's estate since she knew that Abigail and Jacob Smith had been lost at sea in 1784. Why had so much time passed before the property had been transferred? She didn't know and rereading the Deed, she found no clue to help her.

The other record was dated July 12, 1786 and it recorded the transfer of land in Kittery owned by the Estate of Captain Jacob Smith. The executor of his estate was also the same Jonathan Marston. She wondered who he was and she marked the place to have copies made later.

Abby returned to the index again and located the reference to Joseph and Tabitha Sherwood. The Deed Book produced the next transfer of title that was dated May 14, 1835 from Joseph Sherwood to his son Samuel. Abby again marked the page.

Using the index, she followed the trail forward to the last recorded transfer of title. Surprisingly, the last transfer had taken place only two years before and the Deed record listed the transfer of the Rosemary Point property but contained a covenant that the land and buildings were leased to the Rosemary Point Society. This was dated September 14, 1988 and it told her that Thomas Sherwood of New Rochelle, New York had sold the property to the Springbrook Partnership of Kittery, Maine.

Abby paused, puzzled by this because she did not recognize the name of Thomas Sherwood. She had been active in the Rosemary Point Society for almost sixteen years going back as far as her senior year in high school. She knew many of the Sherwoods, both locally and others who had come back to visit but she had never heard of a Thomas Sherwood from New Rochelle, New York.

Also she wondered just what was the Springbrook Partnership and who were the partners? She knew enough about real estate transactions to know that a partnership was a convenient way to hide the true ownership of property to protect owners who did not wish to have their names made public. This might give some support to the assertion by the woman at Rosemary Point that the property was for sale.

Abby closed the Deed Book and looked at the stack of books she had marked and set aside. This was going to cost her a few bucks, she thought and she went to the clerk who was in charge of the records.

"I need to have certified copies of a number of deeds made," she said.

"Sure," the clerk replied. "It's fifty cents a page. How many do you have?"

"Over there," Abby said pointing to the stack of books on the table, "probably ten different records. Maybe eighteen or twenty pages."

"I'll get them done for you," the woman said. "This is some project, what are you doing, writing a book?"

"Yes," smiled Abby, "something like that."

While the woman made certified copies for her, Abby tried to put the information she had just found in perspective. She thought that something was happening at Rosemary Point. She felt it but didn't know why she felt that way. She focused on the property transfers that had taken place one hundred ninety years before and thought it somewhat unusual. How this fit into the mystery, she didn't know.

The clerk came back with the copies. "That's fourteen fifty worth of copies," she said and Abby paid her.

"Thanks," Abby said and looked at her watch and was surprised to see that it was nearly 2:00. She had worked straight through lunch without realizing it. She laughed to herself. This was getting interesting and she needed to tell Dave what she had found.

*   *   *

David walked into Jack Pierce's office and Pierce looked up from the work on his desk.

"And what can I do for you?"

"Got a minute?"

"Sure."

"I want to bring you up to date on what's going on. It looks like I may be involved in something more than family history. I guess I'm trying to solve a real mystery now."

"What's been happening?" Pierce asked.

"You remember the stolen family fortune?"

"Yes."

"Well, here goes," David said and he told Jack Pierce of each event that had taken place in the last few days. When he finished Jack Pierce looked at him with a funny look on his face.

"Jesus Dave, I don't know what to say. Who the hell do you think the woman is?"

"I don't know Jack. Abby thinks she may be a member of the Rosemary Point Society who likes play-acting but she could be anybody. Might even be some kind of a nut case."

"You think your stolen Baker family fortune is Rosemary Point?" Pierce asked.

"Sure, it's possible but we don't know yet. It's really kind of funny though that Abby and I are related. Even if it is a pretty distant relationship."

"That's not that unusual you know. Jennifer and I have three common ancestors eight or nine generations back. Odds aren't so long if you think about it. What have you found out about the Steeles and Smiths?"

"Right now, not much," David said shrugging. "Except what I've read from the Rosemary Point information brochure."

"You need some answers to what happened back in 1784 or so. I suggest you start to work with some primary sources to see what you can come up with. You're dealing with more that family history now and you need to make sure that you have some accurate information to work with."

"Okay, Jack, where do I go to do this?"

"Well, there are literally dozens of good sources. I guess I'd start with some of the marine museums and libraries. I'm no marine historian, but you can start at the Peabody Museum in Salem and they can tell you where to go from there. You might find the Marine Museum in Mystic useful and maybe the Maine Maritime Museum up in Bath. The Maine Historical Society might have some documents on the Smiths so I'd check there too."

David was jotting down notes as Pierce spoke. "That gives me a lot to start with."

"I'll help you if I can," Pierce said. "I'd like to see you find the answers to this puzzle. You sure as hell have my attention on this!"

"Thanks, Jack. I'll let you know when I need help," David said. "I think I'll take some vacation days over the next couple of weeks."

"That sounds like a plan. Are we still on for tomorrow night?"

David looked at him confused. Then it dawned on him. "Oh yeah, basketball night in Duxbury. You're on."

He left Jack Pierce's office planning his next move. A trip to Salem was clearly in order as soon as he could do it. First though, he wanted to see if there was a will for Jacob and Abigail Smith.

Back in his office he tapped out Abby's work phone number.

"Hi, it's me," he said after she answered.

"I was about to call you," she said. "I got the land records this morning."

"Anything interesting?"

"Yes, two things. The land was transferred two years ago from a Thomas Sherwood to a partnership in Kittery, Maine.

"No kidding," David said, "does that suggest anything out of the ordinary?"

"No, not that I can see."

"Any conclusions then?"

"Nothing except the partnership hides who actually owns the property. We've used that tactic before when we wanted to keep a low profile on a project. I'll send you copies of the deeds."

"Okay. Find anything else?"

"Yeah, the other thing is that it was sixteen years after the Smiths disappeared before the property was transferred to a Sherwood and it was transferred "for love". I'm not sure what that means."

"It usually means that it was given to a family member for a token sum or for nothing. It can mean from parent to child for example."

"Oh," Abby said.

"The property never went to either Jacob or Content Smith?" David asked.

"Not that I could see. You know, I didn't think about that, but it is strange. You would have thought one of the Smith children would have received the property from the estate, wouldn't you?"

"Yes, you'd think so. Have you had a chance to check on whether Rosemary Point is for sale?"

"No, Dan King is out of town," Abby said. "I want to start by asking him. He'll be in on Thursday so I'll ask him then."

"Abby, can you go back to Alfred again and see if there is a will or probate record for either Jacob and Abigail Smith?"

"Oh shit Dave, I should have thought about that this morning. I did see a transfer the mentioned the estate and I should have checked that. I'll go back tomorrow."

"Good. The records may not be there since Maine was part of Massachusetts in 1784. If they're not recorded there I'll try and find them here someplace. Sure you don't mind?"

"Not at all. This is my mystery too."

"Thanks," he said.

"I'll call you tomorrow if I find anything. I love you."

"Me too," he said. "Talk to you tomorrow."

*   *   *

Abigail Palmer retraced her journey to the Court House in Alfred the next morning. She entered the building and went to the Clerk of Court's Office. A woman watched her enter and asked, "Can I help?"

"Yes, I'd like to see the index to the probate records."

"Sure, through that door," she said pointing to the right. "Indexes are on the table and the record books are on the shelves."

"Thank you."

Abby went into the record room and sat at the table in the center of the room. She pulled the index book for 1774-86 towards her and opened the book flipping the pages to the name Smith.

She found a listing for both Abigail Smith and Jacob Smith. The two listings were dated October 1785 and Abby jotted down the information. The she went looking for the matching record book on the shelves. She found the volume she wanted and took it back to her seat.

The first probate record was a copy of the last will and testament of Captain Jacob Smith. The will was dated November 12, 1783 and left his entire estate to his wife Abigail. In the event she did not survive him, the estate was to go, in equal parts, to his children, Jacob and Content, when they reached legal age. According to the will he appointed Jonathan Marston, of Boston, as the executor of his estate and as guardian of the two children.

Abby found the information interesting since the children did not get the property and she wondered why. She turned the page and examined the will of Abigail Steele Smith. Her will was dated the same day and was essentially identical to Jacob's will although she did make a specific bequest of jewelry to her daughter Content.

The probate court record that accompanied the wills stated that Jonathan Marston, Executor and his attorney, James Weaver, entered the wills into the public record. It stated that, while there was no official record of death, Jacob and Abigail were overdue on a voyage and presumed lost at sea.

Abby found this interesting in that it corroborated the information she knew from the Rosemary Point Society. She took the books to have copies of the wills made.

Returning to the worktable she checked the index for the 1787-1799 period. There were three more references to the estates of Jacob and Abigail Smith and she had these copied also. On a hunch, she went back to the index and checked under the name Steele. Here she found a reference to the estate of Captain James Steele. She recorded the record book number and page and retrieved the volume from the shelf.

This information included the will of Captain James Steele. The will, probated in 1780, left the Rosemary Point property, eight thousand Pounds sterling and the privateer, *Eagle of America* to his daughter, Abigail Smith, wife of Jacob Smith. The balance of the estate went to his wife, Rebecca.

There was nothing out of the ordinary here either, Abby thought. She had a copy of the will made to have if she and David needed it.

As she packed up her things, Abby tried to think there was anything else she should look for because she didn't want to have to come back again unless she had to. She couldn't think of anything else. Somehow though, she thought she was forgetting something.

*   *   *

Abby called David at home later in the evening and told him what she had found.

"Doesn't sound like anything earth shattering, except for the children not getting the property. But, we already knew that," he said.

"No," Abby agreed.

"Who do you think this fellow Marston was?"

"I don't know," Abby said, "I've never heard him mentioned before. Maybe he was related somehow. I can check with my grandmother and see if she knows anything about it. She's also got a friend who knows a lot about Rosemary Point. Maybe I can check with her too."

"Good idea. I'm taking Thursday and Friday off," David said. "I'm going to do Baker work at the library on Thursday and then I'm going up to the Peabody Museum in Salem on Friday to see if they have anything on the Smiths. I should be at your place before dinner."

"And I'll be glad to see you. I've missed you, you know?" she pouted.

He laughed. "Me too. I'll see you then. Bye Abby, I love you."

She said the same thing to him and put the phone back on the hook.

*   *   *

David Baker could not believe the lucky streak he was having since discovering the Baker data in the Delaware County History the week before. The Baker research was flying by and today had been no exception.

He had spent most of the day back in the New England Historic Genealogical Society Library. He was looking at several of the Baker genealogies that he had examined two months before. Now he paged through the indexes in each book methodically checking each reference to a James Baker.

In a book that covered the descendants of Thomas Baker, from Lincolnshire, England, he unexpectedly found the end of the Baker trail. There was a reference to James Baker, born in 1777, son of Francis and Elizabeth Browne Baker of Newburyport, Massachusetts. He looked at the information in the book and he felt it was sort of like the end of a voyage. He had discovered his Baker roots and this made David feel happy and sad at the same time. Happy that he had discovered the past but sad that the Baker quest seemed finished. However there was much more to do.

Although the line of descent down from James Baker was not continued in the genealogy, the marriage to Content Smith was recorded. The information in the book gave David the Baker line back to the immigrant, Thomas Baker, who had come to the Massachusetts Bay Colony in 1633 and had settled in Cambridge. The book mentioned that Francis Baker, James' father had been at the Battle of Bunker Hill.

Marveling at this discovery and excited by the reality of his ancestor's service, David made a mental note to call Rose McKenzie to see if there were Revolutionary War records for Francis Baker. While he now had names to fill in on the pedigree chart he had started, he knew the Baker line wasn't totally complete because he was still missing some dates. David thought he would double check the information in the book with the vital statistics from the various towns mentioned but he was satisfied that his Baker journey was almost complete.

He went to copy the information and wondered if he could find a copy of the Baker Genealogy to add to his own library. He would have to call Sue and let her know what he had found and he would also call Abby to share this news with her.

He sat back for a moment looking at the ceiling and realized that he hadn't done anything today on the Steele family. They were a part of him too and he needed to do some work on that line.

David went to the cardfile to see if there was a Steele genealogy and discovered that there were two listed. He retrieved both volumes from the stacks.

He looked first at the larger of the two books and in the index he found that a number of Abigails were listed. Methodically he looked each one up in the text. The fifth one proved to be Abigail Steele, daughter of Captain James and Rebecca Parke Steele of Portsmouth, New Hampshire. The book gave the information that she was born August 10, 1755 in Portsmouth and was "missing at sea" in 1784. She had married Jacob Smith in 1776, bearing two children; Jacob born in 1779 and Content born in 1782. The book continued with a record of Jacob Smith who married Cynthia Adams in 1801, but did not contain any information on Content Smith. Jacob Smith's line was continued and

David noted that Abigail Smith, daughter of Jacob Smith had married Nathan Bedford. This bore out the census information he had found and the data that Abby's grandmother had related. He made copies of all the information he found.

He was pleased with his efforts and knew how lucky he had been discovering this information. He was on a roll and he hoped it would continue. Tomorrow he would visit the Peabody Museum to see what he could find there. He would also see Abby and that was the best thing.

*   *   *

Abby Palmer was about ready to leave work. In her role as a project manager, she had spent the day working on a proposal to present to some private investors in Boston. The recent weakness in the real estate market made the banks reluctant to make loan commitments and Crown and King had turned to other sources to finance development projects. This ability was one of the specialties that set the firm apart from other development companies. While many competitors suffered from the weak real estate market and had even experienced bankruptcy, Crown and King still had viable projects in the works.

Abby thought that this performance was a result of the conservative business practices of Dan King and his partner, Ron Crown. They played things close to the vest, never gambling too much on one project and always left a margin of safety. The company had an image of conservative stability in an environment of great upheaval and uncertainty.

Abby knew she was lucky to be working for a strong company in a job she really enjoyed. Although she had studied to be a history teacher she found the real estate business to be both exciting and challenging and to her way of thinking, the current economic downturn only added another problem to be addressed and solved.

Lately though, the family history project that David was working on and the mystery of Rosemary Point had revived her childhood passion for history. She hoped that she could find the time to devote to this while staying current at work.

She waited until the end of the day to talk to Dan King. He had been very busy after returning from a golfing trip to Vermont. Abby wanted to let him get caught up with work before talking to him about Rosemary point. Just before she left for home she went to his office and found the door was open. She saw he was reading some documents and she knocked at the doorframe. Dan King looked up. "Abby!"

"Hi Dan, do you have a few moments? I'd like to talk to you about something?"

"Sure," Dan King said, "come on in and sit down. What can I help you with?"

"I need some information."

"Sure, what's up?"

"I've heard that Rosemary Point may be up for sale. Have you heard anything about that?" she asked.

"Who told you that?" he said measuring his words. But Abby saw the brief look of alarm in his eyes.

"I heard it at the Society," Abby said somewhat defensively.

Dan King paused to let himself calm down. Damn, the woman had caught him off guard. He had been taken by surprise by the question and he had not been ready for anything like what she had asked.

"No, I haven't heard anything about it," he said. "Did you hear any details? I mean were any names mentioned?"

She looked at King, puzzled by that question.

"No, no names were mentioned," she hesitated wondering at his reaction. "I was told the property would be developed for home sites, that's all."

"That's interesting," King said, "but I haven't heard anything like that," he repeated himself.

"Well," she said, "if you haven't heard anything then I guess there's probably nothing to it."

"Probably just a silly story," he agreed. "Some people always seem to start these things. But let me know if you hear anything else."

"I will," she said, just a little uncomfortable now. "You let me know if you hear of anything too. I guess the information I got was wrong. Anyway thanks for the help Dan."

King changed the subject. "Abby, how's the Blackman project going? Ready for the presentation next week?"

"Yeah, it's almost finished. I'll be ready." She got up to leave. "Thanks again Dan."

"Any time," he called to her as she walked out of his office.

King got up from his chair going and went to the door to his office. He watched Abby Palmer walk down the hall to her own office. She walked back out a moment later and went out the front door. King walked down the hallway, making sure there was no one left in the office. When he returned to his office he closed the door.

He took a small notebook from his desk drawer and he opened it to a page near the back, finding the phone number he wanted. He tapped out the number in New York. The telephone rang a dozen times before a voice answered.

"Hello?"

"Tom?"

"Yes?"

"It's Dan King."

"I told you not to use this number unless there was an emergency." The man was angry.

"I know," King said, "but we've got a problem."

"What's that?" the voice demanded.

"Someone, someway has found out about the Rosemary Point plans!"

"What!"

"I don't know how or where, but one of my people just asked me if I knew about it."

"And what did you say?"

"I told her that I didn't know anything. She seemed to accept it."

"Who is she?" the man asked.

"Abigail Palmer," King explained. "She's one of our project managers."

"Watch her! She could be dangerous to us!"

"Yes, I'll do that."

"How in hell could she have found out anything about this?"

"I have no idea."

"Well, you'd better find out and if there is a leak, it better get plugged. And King?"

"Yes?"

"I don't want anything to queer this deal. It's worth too much to both of us!"

"I know, I know," Dan King said. "Don't worry, I'll stay on top of it."

"If there's a problem we'll use as much force as we need to. You understand that?"

"Yes," King replied. Shit, he hadn't bargained for this.

Dan King hung up the telephone shaken by the tone of voice the other man had used. He had never much liked the man but now he was suddenly afraid of him.

Chapter Thirteen

The Peabody Museum in Salem, Massachusetts traces its roots back to the East India Marine Society that was founded in 1799. The building that houses the museum was built in 1824 and is one of the oldest marine museums in the world. The museum was named in 1867 for George Peabody, an early benefactor, and today houses one of the largest maritime archives anywhere in the country.

Armed with this information from the *Guide to New England Historical Societies and Museums*, David Baker drove east on Route 114 toward Salem. The day was hot and humid, the end of August approaching and David smiled to himself as he passed La Maison, the restaurant at which he first had dinner with Abby. He could not help but think how much the green-eyed woman had changed his life.

She had called the night before to tell him that she could find no evidence to suggest that Rosemary Point was for sale. She had spoken to her boss, Dan King and he told her that he knew nothing about it. David wasn't totally satisfied with this information, but he didn't know why he felt that way. A hunch maybe?

He knew he was looking forward to seeing Abby later. He missed her very much and thought that maybe their agreement to delay the wedding hadn't been such a good idea.

He drove into Salem, found a parking spot in a municipal lot and walked the two blocks to the old museum building. He entered the building and asked a receptionist to speak with the archivist.

At Jack Pierce's suggestion he had phoned the museum the day before to introduce himself and explain what he wanted. The receptionist pointed him toward the archivist's office.

David knocked at the door. He heard a voice call to him and he entered the office.

"Are you Sherry Kaminsky?" he asked a middle-aged woman with short brown hair and glasses who sat behind a desk in the cluttered office.

The woman nodded and rose to greet him.

"I'm Dave Baker," he explained. "I spoke with you yesterday?"

"Oh yes, you're the man from Pilgrim Village," the woman said extending her hand. "You folks do a great job! It's nice to meet you."

"Same here," replied David. The woman was of medium height and plump but was not unattractive.

"You mentioned you were researching the Smith family from Kittery, Maine I believe? How can I help you?"

"Actually, I'm more interested in anything you may have on the voyages of Captain James Steele, of Portsmouth, and his daughter, Abigail, who married Jacob Smith."

"Ah, yes," she said thoughtfully, "the Smiths. Quite a nautical couple. They almost made history you know. Actually, they did make history, but never got credit for it."

"What do you mean?" David asked.

"Well, they disappeared at sea in 1784 after attempting the first trading voyage to China. Something happened to them on the return journey and the ship disappeared, lost with all hands. The fame and the credit for the first voyage to China went to a ship from New York, the *Empress of China*. The records say that Jacob and Abigail Smith got to

China first though, three weeks before the *Empress*. They left ahead of the other ship and, by all rights, should have arrived home first."

"What happened?" David asked.

"Like I said, lost at sea somewhere. We'll never know, but the fact is though, Jacob and Abigail did make history. Their vessel was one of the first ships to show the American flag after the Revolution. They were a very daring, intrepid couple. Perhaps the epitome of what this country has come to represent. What's your interest?"

"They were my ancestors," David explained with pride. "I'm working on finding out all I can about them."

Sherry Kaminsky grinned at him.

"I guess I can understand the attraction. I'll be happy to give you all the help I can. We do have some Smith material that you'll be interested in. I think there are a couple of logbooks from the Smiths, plus we've got at least one logbook from Abigail Smith's father, James Steele."

"Wow! I'd like to see them," David said.

"I can arrange that. Come on with me. I think you will be interested, Mr. Baker."

"The name's Dave."

"Okay then, I'm Sherry," she said to him.

The woman led him to a room lined with fireproof metal storage cabinets. Sherry Kaminsky consulted a loose-leaf notebook index, running her finger down several pages. Then finding what she wanted, she went to one of the cabinets and pulled one of the drawers out towards her. She looked through the material and removed a folder. She put this on the table in the middle of the room.

"This is the log from one of James Steele's voyages."

She went to another cabinet removed a large manila envelope that she put down beside the logbook.

"This one contains two logs from voyages of the *Eagle of America*. That was the name of the Smith's ship. I think they're mostly about voyages to Europe in 1782-83, but you can check for yourself. There should also be some household papers from the Smith family I think and there may be some information for you in them. Our catalog doesn't detail what's there but go to it. This stuff is old so I ask that you don't copy any of it on the copier. If you need to have copies made, I can get photos made for you. I'm going back to my office. Call me if you need anything and good luck, I know what you're going through. I've done my family tree also." She handed David a pair of white cotton gloves. "Please use these to handle the old documents."

"Thanks," David said taking the gloves, "if I can ever return the favor, let me know."

Sherry smiled, "Glad to help. Good luck, I hope you find what you're looking for."

She left David alone in the archives room.

David put on the gloves and removed the James Steele logbook from the folder. The fact that he was looking at a manuscript over two hundred years old that in all likelihood had been written by one of his ancestors gave him a strange feeling. His hands trembled as he began to read.

The logbook covered the time period from June 1774 to October 1775 and recorded the events on the brig, *Alice*. The major event was a voyage to France during 1774. The vessel had departed Portsmouth in June and had returned in October. There were many references to Abigail Steele, the First Mate. In fact, David discovered, there were numerous entries obviously in her hand and this filled him with pride as he read them.

David shook his head as he read the entries and thought she must have been quite a woman. After this voyage there were brief entries about several trips to Nova Scotia but with few details recorded. It was clear to David that these voyages were smuggling expeditions and Abigail made many of the entries here also. David felt very proud to be descended from this remarkable woman and he would to tell Abby about this later. She would understand and share his feelings. While the logbook was interesting and informative, it did not give him any help in solving the current problem at Rosemary Point.

He returned the logbook to the folder and opened the manila envelope containing two logbooks and a packet of papers tied together by a faded red ribbon. There was an accompanying note to these papers that William Read, Esq., attorney at law, of Boston had donated some of the documents on July 6, 1831. David recorded this information in his notebook.

He read the first logbook that covered the period from November 1781 to July 1782. The logbook was from the ship, *Eagle of America*. As David read through the material the history it told jumped out at him and filled him full of pride and wonder. Jacob Smith noted at one point that he intentionally made a port of call in Plymouth, England to show the new American flag.

This had taken some guts, David thought, because although the British had surrendered at Yorktown in 1781, there was not yet a peace treaty and Jacob risked internment by doing so. But he had been allowed to leave unharmed. Reading on, he noted Captain Jacob Smith's entry, recording the birth of his daughter, Content. David felt a tug inside as he read this and the logbook took on a personal meaning for him.

The second logbook covered the period from August 1782 to November 1783. There were two voyages to Europe and one to the Caribbean. The entries were interesting but did not give any pertinent information to help him.

David looked at his watch and was surprised to see that it was almost noon. He removed the archive gloves and leaving the material on the table, walked down to Sherry Kaminsky's office where he knocked at the door.

"Hi," she said looking up, "how are you making out?"

"Good," he said, "you have lunch plans?"

"Why no."

"How about I buy you lunch then?" he offered.

"Sure, I'd like that. Give me a minute and I'll be right with you."

David waited while she got her purse and they walked out of the museum.

"I'd like to pick your brain for a bit," David said.

"Sure," Sherry Kaminsky said, "happy to help however I can." And David began to explain the mystery he was attempting to solve.

*   *   *

David returned from lunch and went to work reviewing the packet of loose papers that were mostly a mixed lot of documents. There were a number of letters to Jacob Smith from cargo agents and merchants inquiring about cargo space on the *Eagle*. Most interesting of these were two letters consigning cargo for the final fatal voyage to China.

David read these with interest and made a mental note to have photocopies made. These documents did not provide any direct information, but were interesting from a personal point of view.

As he looked through the sheaf of papers he discovered a copy of the builders contract for the construction of the *Eagle of America*. This was a good discovery because both James Steele and his daughter both had signed it. Because of this, David assumed that apparently Abigail had invested her own funds in the venture. This made him smile and added another insight to the remarkable woman.

There were other documents including baptismal certificates for both Jacob and Content Smith from the Episcopal Church in Kittery.

Finally, at the bottom of the pile was a receipt for services from a John Read, Esq., Attorney of Boston dated January 10, 1784. The receipt, which was addressed to Abigail Smith, itemized services provided by the lawyer. This included the preparation of wills for both Jacob and Abigail Smith and "estate work". David noted this with interest because it was obvious that Jacob and Abigail had put their affairs in order before leaving on the voyage to China. This moved David deeply because he knew what had happened to them. The finality of their death at sea all the more real because of what he had just read. He would get a copy of this document too.

Glancing at the clock on the wall, he saw it was nearly 3:30. He had been so interested in the material that time had flown by. He went down the hall to Sherry Kaminsky's office.

"Hi. There's a lot of material that I need to have copied. How do I do that?"

"Easy, Dave. You tell me what you want and I take care of it for you. We charge two dollars per page to do photo work. Just show me what you want copied."

She got and walked back to the archives room with him. David showed her the documents that he wanted copied. She noted the details on an order form and when he finished, she tallied the total.

"Wow!" she laughed, "seventy-eight dollars, that may be a record!"

"Yeah, well, it's worth it," he said. "Do I pay you now?"

"It's up to you. We can bill you if you want or pay now. Either way it will take a week to have the work done."

"I'll pay you now," David said, taking out his checkbook. He wrote out a check and handed it to the woman. "That should make us even."

"Thanks Dave," she said. "I'll try and get the work done as soon as possible. Did you find anything that helped?"

"Yes, some interesting stuff. Nothing that helps the immediate problem though."

"You mean about Rosemary Point?" He had given her the details over lunch.

"Yeah. A lot of interesting stuff but nothing that helps. You have any other suggestions?"

"Well, there may be some more Smith material around. I don't think it's all been cataloged yet but if I get the chance, I'll check storage to see if I can find anything more for you. If I do, I'll get in touch with you. That okay?"

"Sure thanks Sherry, that's awfully nice of you."

"That's okay, I know how much this means to you. Besides, you bought lunch. I'll call if I find anything."

David thanked her again and she left the archive room to return to her office. David gathered up his notes and left waving goodbye to the good-natured woman.

A half-hour later he was on Interstate 95 headed north. While he hadn't found anything important, what he did find was good background material. He would share it with Abby later.

*   *   *

Abby and David sat on the couch in the living room of her apartment exchanging insults about their culinary abilities. They had just finished a dinner they had cooked together and were now relaxing with the last of the wine and some tender banter.

Finally Abby had crossed her arms and said, "I am pretty good in the kitchen Dave, and I've told you before, I don't appreciate having my chops busted!" She bent over trying to keep from laughing.

David laughed with her enjoying her good-natured reaction to his kidding. In reality he knew they made a good team in the kitchen, or anywhere else. Abby sat back up with a grin on her face and they looked into each other's eyes. Just by doing that they exchanged feelings.

"Where do we stand?" asked Abby draining her glass.

"Well, let's go over what we've found in the last week. First, the rumor about the sale of Rosemary Point seems not to be true, at least according to your Mr. King."

"Yes, I guess so, but, there's something that bothers me Dave. I can't put my finger on it yet though. Call it intuition but I just can't help feel that he was dodging the question. You know, like he had something to hide. I just can't explain it." .

"Okay," David said considering her judgement. "Then we'll say that's still possible, but, unlikely until we know more."

"Okay, that's fair."

"Then we have the wills. Both Jacob's and Abigail's were probated in 1785 which seems to be a reasonable time frame. Agreed?"

"Yes, I think that's fair too."

"Okay," David said, "next, we have the land records, which provoke the big question."

"Yeah," she said, "why the big delay in transferring the land and why didn't Jacob or Content get Rosemary Point? It just doesn't figure."

"Maybe it could be that this Marston fellow, as the executor couldn't transfer the property until Jacob and Content were of legal age?" David suggested.

"But if that's so," Abby argued, "then why didn't one of them get the property?"

David thought for a moment. "Damned if I know and that's the real mystery. What else did you find?"

"The property was transferred to Joseph Sherwood and his wife, Tabitha in October 1800."

"Do we know where Jacob and Content were then?" asked David.

"Wait a minute," Abby said. "Didn't you find Jacob Smith listed in the Steele Genealogy?"

"Yes I did." David went to get his briefcase. He sorted through the papers and found the pages he had copied from the Steele Genealogy.

"It says that Jacob married in Salem in 1801 but there's no reference to Content. But," he remembered, "I did find her in the Baker Genealogy."

He searched the sheaf of papers for the copies he wanted. "Here," he said, "here's the Baker information. It does say that Content married James Baker in July 1800 in Newburyport. That's odd, when did the land transfer?"

Abby looked at the deeds on the table in front of her. "October 1800."

"So Content was probably gone on her way to New York and Jacob was in Salem. Right?"

"That's right. I wonder what happened?" She paused, thinking. "God Dave, do you think that this was when the fortune was stolen?"

"I don't know," David said considering the idea. "Obviously something happened and it sounds like this guy Jonathan Marston was involved. I think we should try to find out more about him."

"Yeah, that's a good idea, we need to know more about him." She paused for a moment. "Hey, want to go out to the house tomorrow?" Abby suggested, "she may be there."

"You mean our phantom woman? Sure, let's give it a try. Maybe that nutcase can give us another clue as to what's going on," David laughed. "I shouldn't say that. She was nice, but I do really wonder who she is?"

"Me too," Abby said and edged closer to him on the couch. She kissed him full on the mouth and David responded eagerly. Together they rolled on the couch, kissing and touching with a will.

"I like this!" he said.

"What's not to like?" she laughed.

*   *   *

They drove to Rosemary Point at noon the next day and went directly to the house. A volunteer who Abby did not know was on duty at the desk in the entryway.

"Hello," the volunteer said, "welcome to Rosemary Point. First time visitors?"

"No, we're repeat customers," Abby told her.

"Members?" asked the woman.

"Yes," David said and he gave the woman the membership card from his wallet.

She examined it. "My name is Helen Worth," and she extended her hand to both of them. "Always nice to meet other members."

David and Abby introduced themselves.

"Oh, I've heard your name," she said looking at Abby, "I'm kind of new but I've only heard good things about you. You're related to the Sherwood family, aren't you?"

"A long time ago," Abby nodded. "The Smith's are also ancestors as it turns out."

"Is that right? That's nice."

Abby held David's hand. "He is too, as it turns out."

Helen Worth nodded.

"Is the lady guide here today?" David asked, wanting very much to talk with her again.

Helen Worth looked at him with a questioning expression on her face. "What woman?"

"The one who did the role-playing," David said. "You know, period dress and all that?"

"Gee, there's no one here but me. I just started as a volunteer though, so I could be wrong but nobody mentioned anything about that," Helen Worth said.

"Well, we've talked with her," David explained, "she's dressed in period costume and is playing the role of one of the Sherwoods I guess."

"Like I said, there's no one here. Today anyway." Helen Worth looked skeptical.

Abby took hold of David's hand and nodded toward the library. "Come on, let's go look at the house. Thank you for your help," she said, glancing at Helen Worth. "We'll just look around and see you later."

"Nice to meet you," the woman said a little confused by David's words.

Abby led David into the library. "Dave, let's take a quick look around the house to see if she's here. Then, we need to talk."

"Okay, but we did see a woman the last time we were here, didn't we?" he asked now unsure of what he had seen.

"Yes we did, now let's just check out the house."

They went through each room in the house searching for the woman but they could not find her anywhere.

David and Abby went out the front door waving to Helen Worth, who repeated, "It was nice to meet you both. I hope to see you again."

Abby led David by the hand down the lawn toward the sea. She stopped by the edge of the garden.

Abby sat on the grass and David joined her.

"What's up?" he asked. "Are you okay?"

Abby pulled her legs up, resting her chin on her knees, deep in thought.

"Are you okay?" he repeated.

"Yes, I'm just thinking." She was very serious now. "Dave, do you believe in spirits?"

"You mean like ghosts?" he asked.

"Yes."

"Well, I've never really thought about. I guess I wouldn't deny the possibility. Why?"

"I've got a feeling Dave and I can't shake it. It was something I felt when we saw the woman last time. What if the woman you saw in June and we saw last week is a spirit?"

"Are you crazy?"

"No, damn it, I'm not! I'm serious. We've got to consider this!"

"You are serious, aren't you?" he said. "But why a spirit or a ghost? Why can't it just be some nut?"

"Yes it could be but think about this logically. When you saw her the first time you were here alone and you said you were attracted to her didn't you?"

"Yes, I guess so," David admitted.

"Okay. Then when we saw her last week I felt something. Also, I told you the Society didn't have interpreters and Helen Worth just confirmed that. So if there are no Society related people doing this, the woman has to be someone else."

"But a ghost?"

"No, a spirit. Was the woman we saw here last week the same woman you saw in June?"

"Yes, I'm sure of it."

"How would you describe her?"

"You saw her. Rather tall, very blue eyes, I remember that from June. Long brown hair and very beautiful. As a matter of fact she looked a little like you, in a way," he said and smiled. "Except the different colored eyes."

"That's the way I saw her too."

"Okay then, if it is a "spirit", and you're going to have to convince me of that, who could it be?"

"Well, it would probably have to be someone who lived here. I don't know much about the supernatural, but it could also be someone who left something unfinished."

"You know now that you mention it, both times I saw her she mentioned an injustice. Do you remember that?"

"That's right," Abby said. "She did say that and she asked for our help too. I felt a tie to her somehow."

"Yes, I did too. What about the probate and land records you got the other day. Content and Jacob didn't get the land. Could the woman be Content Smith Baker?"

"I don't know," Abby said thinking, "where did Content die?"

"In New York, it was in the *History of Delaware County.*"

"Okay, so she's probably buried there and she has a final resting place?"

"I guess we can assume that."

"Then I think we can eliminate her," Abby continued. "She has a final resting place. She may never have gotten her inheritance, but at least she's at peace."

"All right, that makes sense," David said. "You know Abby, you sound like you know something about this."

"I've read some stuff," she admitted and smiled at David.

"Well, if it isn't Content, then who is it?" David asked.

She shivered as she looked into David's eyes and a tear ran down her cheek. "I think it's Abigail," she said quietly.

"What!"

"I think it's Abigail Steele Smith!" she repeated a little more audibly.

"Jesus, you think we've talked to our own great whatever grandmother?"

"Yes, think about it," Abby said warming to the subject now. "Something happened here over two hundred years ago and now she can't rest until the wrong is undone. She was lost at sea and has no resting place so she has to do this! Now she's found us, or we found her and she recognized you first and then me, seven generations later. She knew us Dave and asked us to help her!"

"Shit Abby, that's pretty far fetched," David argued. "I still think it could just be some nut." She poked him with her elbow.

"Sure it could but think about it. What were the odds of you and I finding each other? I already told you I almost didn't go the fundraiser and if I hadn't, I never would have met you. Dave, some things are meant to happen and even if I'm way off on this, we've got to get to the bottom of the mystery. We've got to find out what happened two hundred years ago and we've got to protect this property now! We can't let something else happen to it again, now we owe it to her! Even if it is a nut case who is playing a role."

Abby was speaking with hot emotion and more tears were streaming down her cheeks. David reached for her and pulled her to her feet. He embraced the woman who was now the most important thing in the world to him.

"We'll do it," he said. "You're right, it is important. It's like we have to keep a promise to the past for her."

Abby wiped the tears from her eyes and kissed David on the lips. "I'm sorry to be so teary Dave."

"No, it's okay Abby. We'll get to the bottom of this, I promise you that. And I guess I promise her, whoever she is."

Abby smiled at him and nodded. Behind them, by the lilac bushes in the side garden, a dim figure watched them. She had chosen well, she thought.

CHAPTER FOURTEEN

August 23, 1799 Rosemary Point, District of Maine

Tabitha Marston was angry and full of spite this sultry evening. She was supposed to be the center of attention at the gala party given to honor her engagement to Joseph Sherwood but this had not been the case. She was filled with hatred and not a little envy because Content Smith had become the center of attention of most of the men and a good many of the women at the affair. Content's beauty, natural good humor and feisty spirit drew admirers of both sexes to her and Tabitha hated her for it. Especially tonight.

Joseph Sherwood was the eldest son of a well to do Portsmouth family and was a good match for Tabitha Marston. This engagement to Joseph Sherwood came late in life for Tabitha who was twenty-seven, which was rather old to marry for the first time and she knew it. She had an acerbic disposition and little patience for others. She knew that she was very plain looking and this only added to the frustration she felt as she watched Content dominate her evening. As Content smiled and laughed at some joke, Tabitah reflected that she never received an even chance with her father controlling every aspect of her life.

The engagement to Joseph Sherwood had been the result of her father's efforts. She had resigned herself to life as a spinster and this really didn't bother her since the prospect of child bearing terrified her. However, her father could not stand the idea of an unmarried daughter and she knew this had driven him to reach an accommodation with the Sherwood family to get Joseph to marry her. How much of her father's substantial assets were involved she didn't know.

She reviewed the recent series of events again and knew that Joseph Sherwood was no bargain. He was not very good looking, had a poor complexion, was overweight with a tendency to eat and drink too much and the prospects of life with him weren't much better than her prospects alone. She didn't particularly like the thought of marrying Joseph Sherwood, let alone giving him the chance to make love to her. But she was resigned to the reality that her father controlled her life and there was little she could do about it.

The contrast between herself and Content Smith grated at her constantly. Even though she was an orphan, Content had a natural vitality and optimism that gave her a radiant confident look and Tabitha could not compete with that.

Now Tabitha Marston watched the girl who was ten years her junior as she cocked her head back laughing at another joke one of the men near her had made. The light and easy manner she generated only added to the hate and jealousy that Tabitha felt.

She turned to her fiancé, Joseph Sherwood. "Take me inside please."

"Yes my dear," the heavyset oafish man obeyed.

They went into the house that her father now used as a summer residence. While the Marston family was in residence only during the summer, Content and Jacob lived here the year around. But how long her father would let that go on, she didn't know. She greeted several guests and went into the library where her father was entertaining. Impatiently, she stood next to him and he finally glanced at her.

"Yes Tabitha?" he gave his daughter a patronizing look. "Having a good time, my dear?"

"No Father! I must talk with you!"

"Later, my dear," Marston said impatiently.

"I need to talk to you now!" the spoiled woman demanded.

Marston joked to his guests. "It seems there is no stopping my daughter. Please excuse me."

He walked with Tabitha into the dinning room and Joseph trailed them like a large dog.

Out of the way, Marston faced his daughter, angry by her rude behavior.

"What is it dear that cannot wait? You act ill-mannered!"

"She is being rude Father, she has ruined my party!"

"Who?" asked Marston knowing the answer but wanting to hear it from his daughter. He enjoyed seeing her discomfort.

"Content, that's who. She spites me by entertaining the men Father! She has taken away the meaning of the evening and has embarrassed me. This was to be my special party! I am the guest of honor and she has insulted me!"

"Ah, so that is it," Marston said. "Well, what am I to do about it?"

"You must do something, find some way to punish her! She must be punished for her behavior!"

"Aren't you being unreasonable?" Marston told her, wondering just how he had let his daughter become such a willy-nilly whiner.

"No Father, I have been humiliated at my own party! If you truly love me, you will do something to prove it!"

"All right, Tabitha. I will speak with her," he said annoyed now by Tabitha's petulant behavior.

"Thank you Father. Joseph and I will appreciate you efforts."

Taking Joseph Sherwood, who had remained silent through the exchange with her father, by the hand, Tabitha Marston left the room and went back to the party.

Marston curbed his temper. He knew that his daughter was terribly spoiled and blamed his wife for this. He knew Tabitha was being unreasonable and only wished to spite the younger woman. However, he also knew that he must do something to placate Tabitha and at the same time he knew it would probably precipitate another confrontation with

Content Smith. He usually won these confrontations, but the Smith girl had a fighting streak in her that was hard to combat. Soon he realized he would have to do something to deal with her once and for all.

He had been able to control his other ward, Jacob Smith, simply by manipulating him. In fact, the Smith boy thought well of him and Marston had been ceaseless in playing the brother and sister off each other. Yes Jacob Smith had been easy to control.

Content, on the other hand, fought him at every turn, parrying his attempts to get the rest of the Smith estate that had not been taken before. He had waited fifteen years for the Smith children to reach legal age and now the final asset remaining was the Rosemary Point property itself. Jacob would be twenty-one the next year and Marston planned to buy him off. Marston would make it convincing and Jacob would not be a problem, but Content would be trouble. He knew he would have to figure out a way to remove her as a threat.

In the meantime, he needed to do something to placate his daughter and he went back to the party.

*   *   *

The next morning, shortly after breakfast, Jonathan Marston called Content Smith into the library. He sat at the desk and she stood before him. He looked at her and saw that she was very much the spitting image of her mother. This bothered him for even though Abigail was long dead, the resemblance unnerved him and Content had most of her mother's qualities. He shook off the momentary dread that image gave him.

"Young lady, what you did last night was unforgivable."

"What do you mean?" she asked warily.

"You upstaged Tabitha at her own engagement party. That's what!"

"I did nothing of the kind!" she retorted folding her arms in defiance and standing tall as she adopted a fighting stance.

Marston boiled, she was doing it to him again.

"You did young lady! I saw you flirting with the young men! You did that on purpose to spite Tabitha!"

"I did nothing of the kind. She's accused me because she is jealous of me! Just as you were jealous of my mother!"

The attack struck home and this made Marston tremble with anger.

"I see nothing of the kind! For as long as I can remember you have tried to spite my daughter and me! Content, I'll not put up with it any longer!"

Content Smith gave her guardian a cold calculating stare.

"Just as long as I will remember what you have stolen from my brother and I?"

Marston raged. "How dare you speak to me this way!"

"How dare you do what you have done to me!" she spat back. "You are a crook Sir!"

"You can prove nothing," he returned, but felt her words strike home.

"Yes, that is true," she said fire in her eyes. "You have covered yourself with the law, but none the less, you are a thief!"

Her blue eyes burned with emotion. She was primed to fight.

Marston recognized her mood and knew she had her heels dug in now. He could never defeat her in this state so he shifted tactics.

"Content, how can you say those things?" he said soothingly. "You're like a daughter to me. All I ask is that you give my family some respect."

She stared at him, eyes wild and defiant, wary but saying nothing.

"Just give Tabitha some understanding. She's waited a long time to get married. This should be a special time for her."

Content remained silent and Marston regarded her once more.

"We'll forget this conversation," he said trying to placate her. "It didn't happen, but please try to give Tabitha some consideration."

"I'll not forget this conversation," Content declared. "You may think you can say such things then retract them, but I know what the truth is and I'll not forget!"

"You may leave!" he said dismissing her. He knew the girl had defeated him. Marston watched her go out of the room with her head held high.

Content Smith was dangerous and he must find a way to deal with her and end this constant battle. She must have a weak spot, something he could exploit. He was patient and he would wait until some solution to the problem of Content Smith presented itself. In the meantime, there was something he could do to hurt her and he smiled, thinking just how much what he had in mind would devastate her.

*   *   *

Later Jonathan Marston found his daughter in the summer kitchen behind the house.

"You asked me to do something to show you how much I care about you?" he said.

"Yes, Father?" Tabitha questioned a look of expectation in her eyes.

"How would you and Joseph like to have Rosemary Point as a wedding present? Would that show you how much I care?"

"Oh Father, what a wonderful present! It will also show Content Smith that she is not the princess she thinks she is!"

"Well my dear, I can't give you the property for a while. I must work out some details first so you must say nothing to Content about this. But as soon as I have made arrangements you and Joseph shall have the property."

Tabitha reached to kiss her father. "Oh thank you! This is a wonderful gift Father, it does prove how much you care for me! Joseph and his family will be so impressed!"

She kissed her father again. "Thank you."

Marston was happy that he had pacified his daughter and, at the same time given Content Smith a slap on the face. The transaction would probably have to take place next year, after Content had turned eighteen. He would discuss the matter with his attorney, James Weaver. But the prospect of taking the last of the Smith assets gave him a great deal of satisfaction. Yes, it had all come about and all he needed was a little patience to finish the job.

*   *   *

Content Smith came to him one evening three weeks later as Marston was about to return to his home in Boston. She confronted him in the sitting room on the east side of the house. She was clearly agitated.

"I have heard that you intend to give this house to Tabitha!"

"Where did you hear that?" he said surprised by her boldness.

"Tabitha told me. She taunted me with it! Is it true?" her eyes flared.

Marston paused, wishing that his daughter had kept her mouth shut. This now presented a problem since he could not yet take the property. He had to mollify Content, somehow.

"There is no truth to what she says Content," Marston explained. "I fear Tabitha is merely trying to get back at you," he lied.

"No," Content stated, "I know what you intend! Do not lie to me Mr. Marston!"

"Content, I speak the truth. Rosemary Point is yours, so do not doubt me."

She eyed him angrily and did not trust him in any way. She would not give up.

"I do doubt you Sir! I have no reason to trust you. You've stolen our fortune and now you will take our land, my house! I will not let you do this. Why my mother and father appointed you as guardian, I will never know. You have never done right by Jacob and I and I have no reason to believe you now!"

"But Content, I assure you that I have no intent to do anything to harm you. I have only acted in your best interests. Tabitha spoke in haste. There is no truth to what she says."

Content Smith looked Jonathan Marston in the eye. His words said one thing but his eyes said another.

"You bastard!" she said, "you'll never convince me that anything you say is true! Be damned with you Sir and may you rot in hell! This house will do your family no good and you will be cursed because of it!"

Marston resisted the urge to hit her. She was on target with her accusations but he calmed himself.

"And I'll not forget that you said that Content. You're agitated and you don't know what you're saying. I'll ignore your threats!"

"You may ignore me Sir, but I cannot ignore your deeds! I will never forget and may your family be cursed forever!"

Content turned and stormed from the room, going out the door into the yard. Tears were in her eyes. Why had her parents left this terrible man to be responsible for her? There had to be some way for her to keep what was rightfully hers.

She was so frustrated and did not know what she could do. For all her feisty spirit, Content did not know how to fight this horrible man, Jonathan Marston.

Marston watched her leave the room and knew she now represented a real direct threat. He had miscalculated how much she knew and understood and how destructive she could be. She was very smart, even more like her mother than he had thought and he would find some way to deal with her. Just as he had dealt with Abigail Steele Smith.

In the meantime, he would talk with his daughter and reprimand her for telling Content of his promise to give her Rosemary Point. She had let her spiteful anger control her tongue and that could only lead to trouble.

But again, Marston felt threatened by the young woman. Jonathan Marston didn't like threats and would deal with Content so there would be no doubt about who was in control. He would triumph in the end because Jonathan Marston usually got what he wanted.

CHAPTER FIFTEEN

David's mind wandered again on his way to work and he couldn't help but think that some very strange things were happening to him. On the one hand he was in love with the most exciting woman he had ever met and, all the better, she felt the same way about him. That was good. On the other hand his research into the family history had led to a ghost or at least it looked that way and he could not put that into perspective. David didn't think he believed in ghosts or spirits or whatever you wanted to call them, but he was also sure that this woman was real enough. And, as he told Abby, he couldn't deny the possibility that spirits as she called them, existed.

Still Abby seemed sure of the existence of this spirit and in fact, she had almost convinced him it was true. Could the woman at Rosemary Point really be Abigail Steele Smith, his own fifth great grandmother? If she was it was, then it was a truly unique situation. After all, what are you supposed to say to your ancestor who died over two hundred years ago? David wasn't sure how to deal with that prospect.

His mind wandered again. What was the Springbrook Partnership and what was its purpose? That seemed to be the next order of business. The fact that the ownership of Rosemary Point had recently passed from the Sherwood family to what was apparently a business entity gave some credence to the possible development of the property and David wondered who was involved?

He pulled into the parking lot at the Village trying to decide what to do next. He went to his office and consulted his address book. He found the number he wanted and sat in his chair, then picked up the phone, tapping the numbers. A woman answered, "Phillips, Walker."

"Jim Phillips please?"

"May I say who's calling?"

"Yes, Dave Baker, from Pilgrim Village."

"Yes, of course, Mr. Baker," she said.

David waited while the call was transferred. Jim Walker was a Boston attorney who did most of the legal work for Pilgrim Village.

"Jim Walker?" the voice answered.

"Jim, it's Dave Baker. How are you?"

"Hey Dave, I'm just fine. What can I do for you?"

"Jim, I need a little advice."

"Sure Dave, always. How can I help?"

"I need to check out who's involved in a partnership, a real estate partnership I guess. Where do I go to do that?"

"Is this partnership organized in the Commonwealth of Massachusetts?"

"No, State of Maine," David replied.

Walker paused for a moment. "Dave, I'm not a member of the Maine Bar so I don't know if Maine statute is the same as Massachusetts. I can't really answer that without knowing Maine law."

"What can I do then?"

"Well, you can give me the details. I've got a good friend in Portland who owes me a few favors. I'll give him a call."

"You sure it's no trouble?"

"Shit no Dave, glad to help."

David gave him the sparse information on the Springbrook Partnership.

"Okay good," Walker said, "I'll call you back when I have something."

"Thanks for the help Jim, I'll look forward to hearing from you."

David replaced the telephone and hoped Jim Walker might actually find something.

*　　　　*　　　　*

Later that afternoon David was intently working on a project when he was startled by the ringing telephone.

"Dave Baker," he answered.

"Dave? It's Jim Walker."

"Yeah Jim?" David said hopefully.

"I just got a call from my friend in Portland. I have some answers for you and some bad news, I guess."

"What do you mean?" David asked.

"Well, under Maine Statute a limited partnership must file with the State but a general partnership doesn't."

"Okay," David asked, "so what are we talking about?"

"The law firm that my buddy works for has an office up in the state capitol, Augusta. They have searchers and paralegals over at the State offices all the time. He called one of his people and asked him to check to see if there was anything on this Springbrook Partnership."

"And?" David asked, hoping for an answer.

"Sorry Dave, they couldn't find anything, so apparently Springbrook is a general partnership."

"Shit! No records then?"

"Yeah, that's right. No names, not even an address I'm afraid."

"Shit," David repeated, "any way to get the names?"

"Well my buddy told me that some local municipalities have laws requiring disclosure but apparently Kittery isn't one of them."

"Damn, any other way to do it?"

Walker paused again thinking. "I guess the only way to get the names of the partners would be by deposition, through discovery, in a lawsuit."

That thought interested David. "Hey Jim, what could set off a lawsuit? I mean, what kind of a case would you need?"

"Geez, I don't know. Let's see, breach of contract, breach of good faith, a question of title, something like that. Again, I don't know Maine statute Dave, so it's hard to say. Might be some quirk in the law that might be used I guess."

David stopped to think. "Then there's nothing else to do?"

"No, I guess not. I'm sorry I couldn't help you more."

"You tried Jim. Thanks, send me a bill for this."

"Oh hell Dave, I didn't do much, call this a favor, I was glad to help. Let me know if I can do anything else."

"I will, thanks again, Jim."

David hung up the phone, knowing he was no closer to the truth.

*   *   *

Abby came to visit him for the long Labor Day weekend and sitting in the living room, they talked over the facts one more time. David told Abby about his check on the Springbrook Partnership.

"That's it then?" she said. "It's a dead end?"

"Yeah, looks that way."

"Maybe we could find a reason to file a lawsuit," Abby said hopefully.

"I doubt it," David replied, "we don't have a real reason to. Anything we did would be thrown out in a minute."

She deliberated, looking at him. "I suppose you're right."

"In this case, I think I am. Unfortunately," he said.

They cooked supper in the kitchen and talked about what had gone on during the week at work. They again ate by candlelight in the dinning room smiling and laughing and the magic between them seemed to grow each time they were together.

Doing the dishes, the talk turned back to the problem at Rosemary Point.

"You know," Abby said, "we've got to be forgetting something. There just has to be some way to make some progress. What could it be?"

"Try taking each fact we've found and let's see what it tells us."

"Okay, the first property transfer was in 1774, right?" Abby began.

"Right. Is there anything important there?"

"No, I don't think so."

"Okay, then what happened next?"

"The property went to Abigail in 1780, after her father died. I don't think that means anything either."

"I agree, next?" David said, drying the last plate.

"That would be the transfer in 1800," Abby said.

"That's the strange one, right?" David asked. "The one to the Sherwoods. The land never went to Jacob or Content?"

"That's right."

"Well, could that be significant?" David asked leading Abby into the living room, wine glass in hand. They sat on the couch.

"But Dave, we've talked about that already. I think it's important, but I don't think it has anything to do with Springbrook though."

"Okay, we can come back to that, what's next?"

Abby went through the rest of the property transfers and David asked questions about each of them. When they finished, they sat thinking. Finally, David spoke.

"When was the covenant to the deed attached? I mean, did you see that?"

"No," she said, "I didn't notice that. I can go and check next week. You think it might mean something?"

"Maybe, we won't know until we see it though."

"I guess it's something, at least."

"I love you," he said kissing her and changing the subject. They necked on the couch for several minutes then all at once Abby pushed him away and shouted, "wait!"

"What is it? Did I hurt you?"

"No. God Dave, I know what we've missed!"

"What?" he said, seeing her very excited.

"Dave, who pays the taxes on the property?"

"Oh hell, I don't know! God, I hadn't thought about that. Maybe the Society pays them as part of the covenant?"

"That's a possibility," Abby said calming down. "I'll go to the Town Office and if there's a tax record there has to be an address! Right?"

"Yeah," said David excited now.

"And, if there's an address, we can see who lives there. Right?"

"Yeah. Now I know why I like you," David said, "you're a very smart woman!"

"Why thank you Sir. Now have your way with me so I can show you my other side!"

"I think I'd like that," David said and they giggled like children as they embraced and began to explore each other once again.

*   *   *

Abby had returned home on Labor Day evening aglow in the aftermath of her weekend with David. It had been wonderful, as usual, she reflected and perhaps it was time to set a marriage date as David had been gently suggesting. She smiled to herself and knew he was pushing her to take the step and deep down she knew she didn't mind.

The following morning she was in the office early to clear her desk so she could spend some time at the Kittery Town Office and then back to the courthouse, in Alfred.

Going out at 9:00, she passed Dan King who was going in. She stopped when he spoke to her.

"Morning Abby."

"Hi Dan, how are you?"

"Fine. How was your weekend with your fellow?"

"Just great thanks."

"You on your way out?"

"Yes, I've got to run some errands."

"Hey? You ever hear anything more about that rumor you told me about?"

"You mean Rosemary Point?" she said, wary at King's question.

"Yes."

"No, nothing more about it," she said, "but I'm checking on something else."

"Oh, what's that?" King asked.

"Just checking on some of the history of the place," Abby said just wanting to leave.

"Oh, well see you later," King said and smiled.

Abby went to her car in the parking lot mulling over King's words. She didn't like the prying questions that Dan King had asked and she remembered David's warning. She would have to be careful what she said to the man.

King watched her get into her car and drive off. He felt that Abby wasn't telling him the truth and that her careful answers indicated there was more she hadn't said. He would question her about it later he decided. He had promised his partner that he would stay on top of what she was doing and he meant to keep his promise.

Abby drove through Portsmouth and crossed the bridge into Kittery. She drove to the Town Hall and went into the office of the Tax Assessor. The woman behind the counter watched her enter.

"Can I help?"

"I hope so," Abby said. "I need some tax information on some property?"

"Sure, that should be easy. What piece of property?"

"Rosemary Point."

"Oh?" the woman looked at Abby with a slightly surprised expression. "That just changed hands a few years ago. Not sure who the owner of record is, but we'll get the information for you."

The woman went to a computer terminal and tapped out several commands to the system and information flashed on the screen.

"What specifically do you need to know?"

"Are the taxes up to date?" Abby asked.

The woman consulted the screen. "Yes, they are."

"Does the Rosemary Point Society pay the taxes?"

The woman looked again. "No, the owner of the property is listed here as the Springbrook Partnership. They apparently pay the taxes."

"Is there an address?" Abby asked excited.

"Yes," the woman replied, "a post office box in Kittery."

Abby clucked her tongue against her cheek. "Rats," she said to herself.

"Want a copy of this?" the woman asked.

"Can I?"

"Sure, public record. Let me run a copy of the information."

She typed another command into the terminal and a printer on the other side of the room clattered. The woman went to it as the noise stopped and pulled off the copy then came back to the counter. "Here," she said.

"Thanks," Abby replied, "how much do I owe you?"

"Nothing, that's not official," the woman explained.

"Thanks again," Abby called over her shoulder as she went out the door.

As she walked to her car Abby examined the information. The taxes were current through the tax year and the property description identified the property boundaries. But most disappointing was the address for the Springbrook Partnership which was a post office box in Kittery.

Acting on a hunch, Abby got in her car and drove to the Post Office. She went into the building to the mailbox area and found box number 4701. She looked through the little window and saw there was indeed something in the box. Maybe she could wait and see who would pick it up but dismissed this thought immediately. She knew she could not loiter all day or longer waiting to see who would arrive with the key. God, it might take days so she went to the front desk. She was surprised there was no line and a man in his early thirties waited on her.

"What do you need?" he asked.

"Can I find out who owns a mail box?"

The mail clerk shook his head. "Nope, can't do that. Against the law."

"Oh."

Abby looked at the man more closely. She knew him from somewhere.

"Hey, aren't you Tommy Couture? You went to Portsmouth High?" she asked.

He looked at her carefully. "Oh hi, you're Abby Palmer! Geez, I didn't recognize you. Wow, you look great! Sorry."

"It's okay Tommy. It's been fifteen years. How have you been?"

"Good, I was in the Air Force for ten years. Got a disability and moved back here and I guess I'm still working for the government. Married, two kids. You?"

"Working girl Tommy. I live in Portsmouth. No kids," she smiled.

"Not married?" he asked hopefully.

"Not yet, but probably soon I think."

"Lucky man," laughed Tommy. "I wish I could help you Abby, but, it's illegal."

"Sure, just a longshot. Good to see you Tommy. Hope I see you around."

Abby went to leave, then stopped. "Hey Tommy, is it illegal for you to watch to see if someone picks up the mail from the box?"

Tommy Couture thought for a moment. "No, I don't think so."

"And if you happened to see the license number of the car this person used and you told me about it would that break any law?"

"No, I don't think so."

"Will you do it?" Abby asked trying give him the sweetest smile she could.

"Sure, but don't tell anybody. I'll find out for you if I can but it may take a while though."

"I understand Tommy, I don't know a thing. Here's my number," Abby said handing Tommy her card. "Thanks again for the help and I'll see you around!"

Abby arrived at the York County Court House in Alfred forty-five minutes later and she went once again to the Registrar of Deeds Office. She quickly found the "S" section to the deed index and rapidly turned the pages to the name Sherwood and ran her finger down the page.

She consulted her notebook for the notes from her previous visit and checked the book against the information she had copied before. She found the latest transfer of land that had taken place two years before. Then she found the record book, feeling stupid for not looking the record up before on the copy of the deed she had at home. She was getting too preoccupied with the mystery to think right, she reflected.

She opened the record and found the page she wanted. The deed record briefly described the bare details of the covenant. It also referenced another deed record book where the actual covenant had been recorded at an earlier date. Writing down the information she replaced the book on the metal shelf and located the older volume.

She sat down at the worktable and opened the book. Glancing at the note she turned to the page she wanted.

The covenant was dated October 14, 1945 and the owner of the property at the time was a Roger Sherwood. It was his desire to lease to the Rosemary Point Society the property described as Rosemary Point for the sum of one dollar a year. The covenant stated that he did this to "*encourage the use of the property for the public good and enjoyment*". Sherwood wished "*the property to be maintained by the Society so that the house and grounds would be a park where people may enjoy the benefits of the beautiful natural setting*".

Furthermore, it was his intent that he, or any future owner, would be responsible for any real estate taxes. It was also his intent to contribute a sum of money annually to help offset the costs of maintaining the house. He also expected that the Society would make an effort to raise money to help in this endeavor. He realized that due to lack of funds, he *"could not guarantee that future owners would do this, but, they must agree to keep the taxes current."*

Finally, he gave his reason for doing this. *"I put this covenant in place in memory to my son, William, who died at Iwo Jima."*

Abby looked up, suddenly sad. Once more, it seemed, death had touched Rosemary Point. It was a normal event in life, but somehow, any death at Rosemary Point was magnified by something that had occurred there in the past.

Abby reread the covenant and there seemed to be nothing she had missed. But maybe some of the information would be of use later.

She went to the clerk to have a certified copy made. She paid the woman and left the office, going to her car. Driving away she thought about what she should do next. She decided she needed to know more about the recent history of Rosemary Point and she thought it was time to call her grandmother and her friend. She arrived back at her office before lunchtime.

*　　　　　*　　　　　*

Abby worked late that evening to tie up some loose ends on a project. She didn't mind staying late because her work schedule was flexible enough to give her the ability to take time when she wanted to so she could do things like her research trip that morning. Finishing up, she thought back to the early afternoon and her telephone conversation with her grandmother.

"Hi Grandma, it's Abby."

"Hi Hon, how are you?"

"Good, are you going to be home tonight? I could use some help."

"The Lord willing," her grandmother said, "I'll be here. What do you need Hon?"

"I've got some questions about Rosemary Point," Abby explained.

"I'm not the expert, you know," Grandma Taylor said.

"Yes, I know. Do you suppose you could you see if Betsey could come too?"

"Sure, you come on over after supper. In the meantime I'll give Betsey Watrous a call and see if she can drop by. I don't think that's a problem, she'll usually do anything for a glass of wine!"

Abby laughed. "Okay, I'll see you about 6:30 then." She hung up the telephone.

Abby left the office a little after six and drove west toward her grandmother's house. As she arrived, she saw another car in the driveway ahead of her and knew that Betsey Watrous had accepted the invitation. If she knew the two old ladies as well as she thought she did, they were probably already on their second glass of wine.

She smiled thinking that Betsey Watrous was really Miss Rosemary Point. She was in her eighties and was slightly younger than her grandmother. Betsey had never married and for years she devoted herself to preserving and promoting Rosemary Point and the Rosemary Point Society. In the fifties and the sixties she had served consecutive terms as the President of the Society and she still remained active. If anyone knew the history of Rosemary Point, it was Betsey Watrous.

Abby climbed the front stairs and saw the door was open.

"Grandma, it's Abby!" she called into the house.

"We're on the back porch dear. Get yourself a glass, if you want, and come out and join us. There's a bottle on the table."

Abby stopped at the kitchen table, poured a glass of wine and went out to the back porch. The evening was still warm with a cool breeze blowing through the screened porch.

Abby bent to kiss her grandmother. "How are you Grandma?" she asked.

Grandma Taylor returned the kiss. "Fine dear, and how is that young man of yours?"

"He's good," Abby said, turning to the other woman. "Hello Betsey, it's very nice to see you again."

Betsey Watrous smiled and winked at Abby. "You know, you were always one of my favorites, Abby. Lord but you look radiant! Your young man must agree with you and it's about time. You deserve the best!"

"Thanks Betsey," Abby said feeling her face flush. "I need some help from both of you."

"Sure, how can we help?" Betsey Watrous asked.

Abby went over the story of her interest in Rosemary Point, only omitting the meeting with the woman at the house not knowing if the women would understand that part of the mystery. When she finished, she watched as both the older women carefully looked at each other. Finally, her grandmother nodded to Betsey Watrous, who began talking.

"Well Abby, I've been involved with Rosemary Point for over sixty years. I was a charter member of the Society in 1934 you know. I think I can give you some help but you've asked a lot of questions and maybe have created a few new ones!"

"I have?" questioned Abby.

"You sure have, well, here goes," Betsey said. "I'll try to give you some answers first. Okay, let's talk about the covenant that you located but I guess I should start by telling you that Roger Sherwood asked me to marry him."

Abby nodded. "Oh?"

"Yes he did. He asked me when he returned from the Great War, that was World War I. He loved me I think, but I was only seventeen and he was twenty-two. I was just too young and besides, as it turned out his father had chosen a bride for him while he was in France. I didn't stand a chance Abby, because he didn't try to pursue me and he married the other woman. Then he had the two boys. Billy was born in 1920 and Tommy was born in 1924. I remember them well, they were both full of mischief but Billy was the nicer of the two though and he cared about

Rosemary Point. He joined the Marines soon after Pearl Harbor. I think
he was at Tarawa, Saipan and then Iwo Jima."

"Yes, he was killed there, wasn't he?" Abby asked remembering the
words in the covenant.

"Yes, and the loss devastated Roger. He grieved a long time Abby and
he vowed to do something as a memorial to his son. He talked it over
with me and we hit upon the idea of leasing the property to the Society.
It seemed a good idea, a remembrance that would stay alive."

"Why didn't Roger Sherwood endow the Society with enough funds
to take care of the place?" Abby asked.

"He didn't have the money to do that," Betsey said, "he was almost
broke."

"Why? I thought the Sherwoods were rich," Abby said.

"Heavens no, they lost most of their fortune in the Panic."

"You mean the Depression?" Abby asked.

"No," laughed Betsey Watrous and Susan Taylor joined her. "Long
before that. The family lost everything during the Panic of 1857. They
had invested in railroads and speculated in land out west. They really
weren't too smart I guess and it cost them dearly. They lost almost
everything, except the land they owned around here that was free and
clear."

"So there were no means to support the property then?"

"That's right Dear. The Sherwoods gradually sold off the rest of their
holdings to live on and by the 1930s they were left with only Rosemary
Point."

"But they never sold that," Susan Taylor said, "they always kept the
place."

"Yes," Betsey Watrous agreed. "It meant something to them, it was
the family home, roots if you will. That's why Roger did what he did
back in '45. It was the final gesture to how he felt about Billy. It was
important to him."

"What about the other son, Tommy?" Abby wondered.

"Yes, Tommy," Betsey said glancing aside at Susan Taylor. "Tommy was nice as a child, but then something happened to him. He never cared about the house at all and he never seemed to be bothered by his brother's death either. Some say he just got mean and he moved away. I think he lives in New York somewhere."

"New Rochelle?" asked Abby.

"Yes, I think so," said Betsey Watrous. "It's hard for me to remember some of this but I think I heard he did well in business over the years. Real estate, I think."

Abby blinked at that. "Did you know he sold the property two years ago?"

"Why yes," answered her grandmother, "you mentioned that."

"Frankly, that surprised me," Betsey said, "I thought he still owned it and that bothers me because it could point to the development of the property. Tell me again, where did you hear that?"

"From someone at the house," Abby said.

"There could be some truth to it," agreed Grandma Taylor.

"Do you know anything about this Springbrook Partnership?" asked Betsey.

"No, nothing more than a post office box. But, there's one more thing I need to ask. In studying the deeds going back to Abigail Steele Smith's time there's a puzzle. After she was lost at sea the land passed to the Sherwood family and neither of Abigail's children got the land. Do either of you have any reason why?"

"No," replied Betsey, "I've always wondered about that too. Some have said, over the years, that Jonathan Marston, who was the executor to the estate, had something to do with that. He was a well to do Boston merchant you know, who became very rich. His daughter, Tabitha Marston, married Joseph Sherwood and they owned the property. Maybe they bought it, that may explain it."

"You're descended from them, Abby, on your father's side. That's your Sherwood connection," Susan Taylor explained.

Abby looked surprised. "So that's how I connect with the Sherwoods?"

"Yes, one of Joseph's daughters."

"If you could find out something more," Betsey offered, "I'd be happy to do whatever I can to help you."

"You've been a big help already Betsey. More than you know."

"Well, I ought to be able to do something!" Betsey Watrous replied and she looked at Grandma Taylor. Then they both laughed.

Abby didn't know what to make of this; a shared joke? "What do you two know?"

Again, the older women laughed. "I guess it doesn't hurt to tell you," Betsey Watrous said, "the reason I've been involved in Rosemary Point for all these years."

"Yes?" asked Abby.

"It was my excuse to see Roger Sherwood. You see for over twenty-five years we were lovers Abby, some things are meant to be. He found out he didn't love his wife and came back to me. You're very lucky my dear, to have your young man. So don't let anything get in the way of the two of you. Life is too short!"

Abby blinked in surprise. "Why, I had no idea!"

"That was just a bit before your time Abby. It was a badly kept secret I'm afraid. We tried, but this is a small town really, so it was common knowledge I'm afraid," Betsey Watrous laughed. "You would have been very young when Roger died in 1962."

Abby digested this surprising information but she had one more question and was unsure how to ask it.

"You've told me a lot," she started, "but I need to ask one more thing."

"Yes?" her grandmother replied.

"Have there ever been any traditions or reports of ghosts or anything like that at Rosemary Point?"

The older women glanced at each other once more sharing a knowing look but reluctant to react to the question.

"Why do you ask?" Betsey Watrous questioned.

Abby hesitated but saw the look in the eyes of the older women. There was something to it! But she did not want to tell what she knew fearing that what she had seen was not real.

"I only asked because some old houses seem to come with traditions like that," she shrugged.

"Then the answer is no, nothing like that," Betsey Watrous said carefully measuring her words.

"Well, I just thought I'd ask," Abby explained, "thanks for your help. You're great, both of you, but I may be back for more later if that's okay? I appreciate the help, thank you."

"Not at all," Betsey Watrous replied, "we're glad to help. You know, I really do love the place and it sounds like you do too."

Abby nodded and went to each of the women, bending to kiss them. She sensed a new bond to her grandmother and to Betsey Watrous, who had shared her greatest secret with her. Why had she done that?

"Bye," Abby said getting up to leave. "I'll call you Grandma."

"It was nice to see you Dear. Please let me know if you need any more help."

"I will." Abby went from the porch through the house and out the front door.

The two older women watched her go and they sat in silence for a moment, each of them sharing the same feeling.

"Do you think Abby's seen her?" Betsey Watrous asked finally.

"I don't know, hard to say, but why else would she ask the question? I think she might have. After all Abby's got Smith blood and sometimes I think she could be Abigail Steele Smith herself."

"Of course you're right, I'd forgotten she's descended from Abigail. She is a very special young lady and this young man of hers must be okay too."

"Yes," Susan Taylor agreed.

"Do you think they've been chosen?" Betsey Watrous asked quietly.

Susan Taylor smiled and nodded. "I think so. She had to have seen something, I think I felt that. Did you see how she acted?"

"You know Susan," Betsey said, "no one has ever seen her and yet so many have said they felt her presence there."

"Yes, I know. We've talked about this so many times before and we've always said it would happen some day. Someday when the right person came along."

"Well, if Abby has seen her, then she is someone special," Betsey said. "Of course we'll need to give Abby and her young man all the help we can!"

"But of course we will," smiled Susan Taylor. "We made the promise to each other a long time ago!"

"And to her, I think," Betsey Watrous said. And like two conspirators, the two old women laughed together.

*   *   *

Abby arrived home even more puzzled by the information she had found in the covenant to the deed. In addition, the revelations about the Sherwood family and the other details Betsey Watrous had given her were also fascinating, but Abby wasn't sure where it all fit in.

She needed to talk with David, but first she needed some dinner. It was nearly 9:00 and she rifled through her refrigerator, looking for something that interested her. She settled for a frozen dinner from the freezer and put it in the microwave.

While she waited for the entree to warm, she reread the covenant one more time. Finishing it, she went to the folder where she kept the land and probate records she had found in Alfred. As she began to page through the land records one more time the bell rang, signaling that her dinner was ready. She took the meal from the microwave and placed it on a mat on the table. She poured herself a glass of iced tea and sat. While she let her dinner cool she continued reading the information in the folder.

She began to eat and shifted her attention to the probate records. Between bites she focused on the wills and estates of Jacob and Abigail Smith. Rereading them she noted again that the wills were dated November 12, 1783.

In the back of her mind an alarm bell went off and she sat upright, dropping her fork. Where were the copies of the last notes that David had given her?

She got up and went into the living room where she rummaged through the pile of envelopes on the desk. She found the copies of the notes David had brought the week before and quickly went through the material. The notes from his visit to the Peabody Museum mentioned a receipt from a James Read Esq. for wills and estate work dated January 10, 1784.

This, she realized, was almost two months after the date on the wills filed with the Probate Court in Alfred. Her heart beat faster as she thought about what this might mean. She needed to talk to David.

She went to the couch, picked up the telephone and tapped David's number. David Baker answered on the third ring.

"Dave, it's Abby," she greeted him when he picked up.

"Hi, how are you?"

"I've come across something!"

"What? Did you find anything out about the covenant?"

"Yes I did, but that's not it. Dave, I think there were two wills!"

"Two wills? What do you mean?"

"I think there were two wills Dave!"

"Tell me what you mean Abby? What have you found?"

"I should have seen it before Dave, there's a discrepancy in the dates!"

"What dates?"

"The wills that were probated for Jacob and Abigail Smith in Yorkshire Probate Court were dated November 12, 1783."

"So?"

"You found a receipt at the Peabody Museum that shows the wills were probably drawn some time early in January, 1784 because the receipt for the legal work was dated January 10, 1784!"

"It does? Couldn't that just be a late payment for the work done in November?" David argued.

"Yes, I suppose it could, but remember someone like Abigail Smith probably paid in cash. Also, the lawyer probably would want to wait to get paid, since Abigail was going away. So, the receipt is probably current."

David thought for a moment trying to find a fault with her logic. He had to admit that she made sense.

"So," he asked, "if it's true what does it mean?"

"It means that may be how the fortune was stolen, with altered or phony wills. But who could have done it?" she wondered.

"That guy Marston!" David exclaimed. "I'll bet he probably did it!"

"Could be," said Abby.

"But, if the probated wills were superceded by later ones, what happened to them and do they still exist somewhere?"

"That's not likely two hundred years later," Abby said.

"Yeah I guess you're right. Shit, there's no way to tell, is there? As a matter of fact there's no way to tell if, in fact, there were new wills done after the ones done in November."

Abby thought for a moment, a smile gradually forming on her face and a shiver running down her back.

"Yes there is," she said quietly, "we can go ask her."

"Ask who?" David said.

"Her! Our friend at Rosemary Point!"

"Oh shit, come on Abby! You can't be serious!"

"Yes I am. I'm going out there tomorrow and ask her what happened before she left for China!"

"Well," David said, "spirit or no spirit, you're not going to do this alone. I'm coming too. I'll be up first thing in the morning."

"Can you come tonight?" Abby asked, "I'd like to be with you!"

"Gee, Abby, it's almost 10:00!"

"I know, but I'd still like you to be with me tonight."

"Okay, let me throw some things together and with luck, I can be there by midnight. I'll call the office tomorrow and tell them I won't be in. See you in a bit."

"I can't wait!" with rising excitement in her voice.

Abby replaced the telephone glad the David was on his way. He was right, this was something they should do together and tomorrow would be very interesting she thought. She just hoped the woman would be there.

CHAPTER SIXTEEN

September 27, 1790 Boston, Massachusetts

Rebecca Parke Steele Marston suspected that she was losing her mind. She was nearly sixty, but age was not the cause of her mental decline. No, it was guilt, remorse, sorrow and drink that were taking their toll on her. Adding to her woes were the physical and mental state of her second husband, William Marston who was ten years her senior. He was rapidly approaching complete senility and would only comply with the wishes of his son, Jonathan.

The thought of Jonathan brought with it another wave of remorse and she went to the dressing closet and reached again for her decanter of sherry. Although it was only eleven in the morning she poured a measure of liquid into a small crystal goblet and swallowed the dose in one gulp. This was the fourth glass she had consumed since rising.

She damned herself for her behavior, but she still sought to deaden her pain for she believed she was at least partly guilty of killing her own daughter. She believed she was guilty by marriage. Because by marrying William Marston she had brought Abigail and her family into contact with Jonathan Marston who, she now suspected, had conspired to have Abigail and her husband killed. The sorrow and guilt would not leave her, so she used the bottle to help her deal with the emptiness that gnawed at her.

The root of her problem was the fact that she had only been able to bear one child and she felt terribly inadequate because of this. In her heart she knew that the stress and damage done to her by Abigail's delivery had almost killed her. She was close to death by the time Abigail had been born, so after talking with the midwife, her husband James Steele, had realized another birth would be fatal and he agreed that they would not try again. The resulting sexless life together was not entirely unsatisfying, but still James Steele had remained true to her.

Or at least Rebecca thought that to be true. She could never be sure of James Steele's amorous inclinations; for after all, he was a sailor and had ample opportunity to be with women in many distant ports of call. She rationalized that this was a way for him to satisfy his physical needs and leave her alone, but in the end she also remained very much unsatisfied.

Compounding her feelings of remorse were the pangs of guilt she felt for the jealously she experienced over the relationship that had developed between father and daughter. Deprived of a chance of having a son, James Steele had raised Abigail like the son he would never have.

During her early years, he would tutor her on the rudiments of seamanship and navigation while home between voyages. Then James Steele took Abigail to sea for the first time in 1767, when she was twelve. She proved to be a willing pupil and a natural seaman and her father was very proud of her.

Rebecca, on the other hand, found this relationship not of her liking. Because Abigail spent so much time with her father, there was never time for a normal mother-daughter bond to grow and Abigail developed a definitely non-feminine point of view. Rebecca's relationship with Abigail became worse as Abigail began to spend more time away at sea than at home. James Steele noticed none of this resentment, proud only of his daughter's accomplishments.

Now, Rebecca thought, things had gone from bad to worse. By marrying William Marston she had expected to find stability in her life because he represented all that she felt she needed. Respectability, wealth, social standing all came with William Marston.

Rebecca married him without consulting her daughter, who was away on a voyage that produced her granddaughter, Content. The fact that she did not consult her was a product of all the years apart and Rebecca's need to have a man in her life. But in the end, the marriage had only led them all to Jonathan Marston.

The final blow was the fact that Jonathan Marston now dominated her life. She could not even visit her grandchildren without his permission and his control over the family grew each day as William Marston fell further into complete senility.

All the frustration, guilt and sorrow rose in her at once and she knew she must do something. Some act of defiance for what her life had become and she must confront Jonathan Marston. Her daughter would have done it and she must do it now. She needed to do something if only to restore her own self respect. Yes, she would do something

She went to the dressing closet and again reached for the sherry decanter. Drinking another glass she thought about what she could do.

*   *   *

Jonathan Marston felt very smug indeed and gazed out over the Boston waterfront from the window of his second floor office on Commercial Street. His office had a fine view of several wharves where sailing vessels of all sizes were berthed and he found great satisfaction in the location, for it was another symbol of his own influence.

He focused on the ship, *Columbia*, which was in the final stages of fitting out and provisioning for a new voyage. Marston congratulated himself on his business judgement. Three years before he had been invited to participate in financing a trading venture by the ship, Columbia and the sloop, *Washington*, but had elected not to participate, deeming the venture too risky.

The pioneering voyage by the two vessels had taken them around Cape Horn to the Northwest coast of America. There they traded with the native Indians, exchanging trinkets for furs. Then *Columbia* had traveled on to Canton, China with a stop along the way in Hawaii. In China, the furs were exchanged for tea and the ship returned to Boston via the Cape of Good Hope.

Columbia had returned home the previous month to artillery salutes and a giant celebration to mark the successful completion of the voyage. Yes, Marston thought, the voyage had been successful, but he knew it had not been profitable. He was glad he had not bought a participation in the venture. Now, *Columbia* was to depart on the flood tomorrow to repeat the trip and Marston did not expect this voyage to be any more profitable than the first.

Again, he congratulated himself and he glanced to the left of the *Columbia* to the black hulled three master with the bright green whale stripe; his ship, the *Herald of Boston*. She too had just returned from a voyage to the Orient but unlike *Columbia*, her voyage had been simple, out and back using the same strategy that the Smiths proposed six years before. This venture would not be fancy but would be immensely successful, Marston reflected and the profits should run into the thousands. This fact gave him a great swell of satisfaction because his judgement was better than most of his peers in the business of trade.

He knew that this feeling of satisfaction was enhanced by the knowledge that he had used the assets from the Smith's estates to build the *Herald* and finance the voyage. The anticipated profits would add to the assets he had taken from Jacob and Abigail Smith and he intended to build this into a great fortune in time.

Jonathan Marston thought his plan had been brilliant. Substituting the wills, which had been copied by the scribe from Charlestown had worked like a charm and the Probate Court had accepted the forged documents without question. It had almost been easy he smiled. The lawyer, Read, had proved to be a problem, but a large sum of money had finally bought his cooperation in destroying the real documents. Now Marston knew he must build on this successful beginning and there was no reason he could not parlay the assets he possessed into the largest fortune in Boston. Yes, that would be his goal.

Already Marston had been able to show the city and his peers the tangible results of his success. The most visible example of his affluence was the magnificent house nearing completion on Beacon Hill. Designed by Charles Bullfinch, the talented and socially fashionable young architect, the finished house would be another symbol of Marston's social position. The very fact that he was able to employ Bullfinch, who was just beginning to make his reputation as an architect and whose buildings would be the measure of others for years to come, was in itself a statement of Marston's rising importance.

Behind him there was a knock at the door. "Come," he said.

The door opened and two men entered. One was James Weaver, Marston's attorney and now his business partner. The other was Captain Thomas Foote, the master of the *Herald of Boston*. Marston motioned for them to sit in chairs by the window and he joined them.

"How is the unloading going?" he asked Foote.

"On schedule, Sir. We've cleared most of it already."

"Good," replied Marston, "when can you be ready to sail again?"

"We came through the voyage with little damage, Sir. We can probably turn around in less than a month. I'd say we could leave near the end of next month and that is good timing since it will be the end of hurricane season."

"That is good indeed!" agreed Marston and he looked at Weaver. "Any estimate on the net of the voyage yet?"

"Estimate, yes," Weaver smiled. "We should clear close to twenty thousand I think and that's a very handsome return Jonathan. We've a lot to be thankful for!"

"Yes, of course you're right," Marston said. "The venture was well planned, if I do say so myself, but we must look for other ventures that promise the same return!"

"I agree," replied Weaver.

Marston turned to Foote. "You have done well Captain Foote and you can be sure you will get a bonus on top of your participation for a job well done. You may go Sir, and I thank you," Marston said dismissing the man.

"Thank you Mr. Marston. You are a fair man."

Foote nodded to Weaver and rose to leave. He walked to the door and the other two men waited until he was gone.

"A good man," said Weaver, "he knows his job."

"Yes, that he does," agreed Marston, "he gets the most out of the ship and the crew."

Weaver hesitated for a moment then spoke. "Jonathan, there is something I must bring to your attention."

"What is it?"

"I'm afraid that your father has reached the point where he is no longer competent. As your attorney I must advise you on this."

"I know," Marston said, "but I can control him."

"I know that, but you must think about the legalities of this."

"What do you mean?" Marston asked sharply.

"You must get him to sign a power of attorney so you can legally act for him."

"All right," Marston said, "I think he will do that if I ask him."

"Then do so. I will draw up the papers."

Marston nodded but saw that Weaver had more. "There is one more thing, your stepmother."

"And what about her?" Marston said angrily. His father was one thing, but his stepmother was another.

"She too is at the edge Jonathan. I think she is going insane and it is obvious that she drinks more each day."

"Yes, I have noticed," Marston said.

"Then you must do something. Could you get a power from her also?"

Marston thought. "I don't think so. She suspects me and does not trust me. I do not think she would do that willingly."

"Then we must find another way to deal with her Jonathan. I think she can be dangerous to you!"

"What do you suggest?"

"Well, I'm not sure yet. I have a few ideas, but I need to think about it. In the meantime, watch her Jonathan! She may give you an excuse to deal with her if you are careful."

"I will do that," Marston said.

Weaver got up to leave. "I'll speak with you later Jonathan. On the whole, our venture is coming along quite nicely."

Marston nodded concurrence. "Yes, we have made a good start. Take care James."

Weaver bid him good-bye and left the office.

*   *   *

The following morning found Jonathan Marston in his dressing chamber changing out of his Chinese silk dressing gown preparing to dress for work. Breakfast with his family had been a quiet affair this morning, with his wife and children preoccupied with a social they would attend later in the day. Marston's father ate with a blank stare on his face, neither seeing nor reacting to the people around him. Rebecca Marston sat next to him playing with her food and staring in silence, but with a dull glistening in her rheumy eyes that told Marston she had already started sipping from her decanter.

Marston's body servant, Santos; a fair skinned Jamaican, moved from behind to remove the silk robe. Earlier the man had shaved him and now had finished brushing his hair, tying the long strands into a queue.

Next he helped Marston don a white embroidered shirt which buttoned and tied in the back. Then Marston put on linen drawers and pulled on silk stockings that were tucked into the drawers and held in place by garters. Black nankeen breeches came next over the drawers and were fastened with a gold buckle. Finally a waistcoat and brown broadcloth coat finished the ensemble.

Fully dressed, Marston examined himself in the mirror and smiled at what he saw. He decided he looked every inch the proper, prosperous Bostonian merchant. He knew the image reflected the truth.

"You look's fine Mista' Marston," Santos said.

"Thank you Santos. You know you make me look that way."

"Why thank you Sir," the Jamaican said, clearly proud of the compliment he had received.

Marston left his dressing chamber and went down the steps to the living area of the row house. As he neared the bottom of the stairs, he became aware of a figure standing in the shadows of the hallway that led to the kitchen. He recognized the face of his stepmother.

"Hello Rebecca. Do you need something?" he said puzzled by her appearance here. Usually by now she was ensconced in her room with her bottle.

The woman stayed silent and Marston could sense that she was drunk. Through the glaze in her eyes, he detected a smoldering fire. She clearly had something on her mind.

"Hello Rebecca," he repeated, "can I do something for you?"

"You killed her!" the woman blurted out. "Damn you, you killed her!"

"Who? What are you talking about?" Marston said surprised at this outburst.

"You know well enough!" Rebecca Marston screamed. "You were always jealous of her. So you killed her and stole her property!"

"What ever do you mean?" Marston asked, alarmed by the vehemence in the woman's voice. The hate and anger spilled out of her.

"You killed my daughter. I don't know how you did it, but I do know you did it Jonathan!"

"I did nothing of the kind Rebecca, don't be silly now," Marston said measuring the woman. "Come and lie down. You're sick, you must rest."

"No! You must tell me the truth. Damn you, must admit to what you have done!"

"But I have done nothing," he soothed.

"You lie!" the woman screamed.

Again, the venom the woman spewed stunned Marston.

"Rebecca, I assure you I have done nothing. You are being silly, now come and rest. You're agitated and you are sick."

"Yes, I'm sick!" Rebecca screamed, "sick of seeing you go scott free after what you've done to my family! Damn you Sir, you shall pay for your actions!"

"Come, Rebecca, you must rest," he reasoned.

Marston moved toward the ranting woman intending to steer her back to her room. But he had taken only two careful steps when the woman took her right hand from behind her back revealing a small pistol, which she pointed it at him.

Marston stopped, looking into the short barrel and at the woman's shaking hand.

"You will pay Jonathan, you must pay! As God is my witness you will pay!"

"Come Rebecca," Marston said thinking fast. "Put that away, it will solve nothing. I'm afraid you are very sick. You must let me help you."

The woman blinked, trying to clear her head, to get control of herself.

Marston took time to consider his next step, knowing he had to distract her so he could disarm her. He looked over her right shoulder toward the kitchen.

"Hello Daisy," he feigned speaking to the cook who wasn't there. "Will you please help me with Madam?"

Falling for the ruse, Rebecca glanced over her shoulder for just an instant. As she did Marston darted towards her grabbing her right arm, pushing it up.

Seeing Marston move Rebecca jerked her hand back towards him. When he grabbed her arm she squeezed the trigger on the pistol in a futile attempt to salvage some degree of punishment for the man.

The pistol went off in Marston's left ear and the explosion momentarily stunned him. The ball had missed him, he was sure as he wrestled the pistol from the woman's grip and pushed her roughly to the floor.

Rebecca was sobbing now, blubbering drunkenly and Marston stood erect, looking around. Above him in the wall in the front hall he saw the hole where the ball from the pistol had lodged. It had been a near thing after all. She had almost been successful in shooting him.

Rebecca Marston sobbed because her pathetic attempt to gain some retribution for her family had failed miserably. Even in her drunken mental state, she now had no illusions about what would happen to her. She would be tried for attempted murder and she would go to prison. She no longer cared what happened to her for she was a totally defeated woman.

Jonathan Marston watched the woman and turned as Santos came running down the stairs with Daisy, the cook coming from the kitchen. Marston looked at them and put up his hand to keep them from grabbing the sobbing woman.

"Mrs. Marston is sick," he said oozing compassion. "Please take her to her room."

The two servants complied and helped the slumped woman up the stairs to her room.

Marston smiled to himself because Rebecca's actions now gave him all the reason he needed to deal with her. He would not press charges against the woman because the resulting notoriety would do the family no good. Instead he would see Weaver later in the morning and with

any luck he would have his stepmother declared incompetent and com-
mitted to the asylum for the insane.

By doing this, he could also get his hands on whatever assets Rebecca
Marston controlled. So, all in all, he thought, this had ended better that
he could have wished. His stepmother would be out of the way and his
fortune increased. In addition, he had now ruined one more of the
Smith family and that gave him the most satisfaction of all.

CHAPTER SEVENTEEN

David and Abby tried to sleep late the following morning but the excitement and anticipation they felt would not allow it. David had made a fast trip the night before and had arrived slightly after midnight. Abby had waited for him and they stayed up until almost three talking over a glass of wine, both wondering what they would find in the morning. They were unsure and apprehensive about what to expect, but had finally gone to bed where they fell asleep in each other's arms.

Now, as they finished a very late breakfast, they looked at each other, the enormity of what they were going to do both exciting and frightening. David drained his cup of coffee.

"What time does the house open after Labor Day?" he asked.

"You've only asked me that six times in the last hour!" Abby laughed. "It's still 12:00 until the end of October."

David examined his watch; it was 11:30. "Want to get going then? This is going to be an interesting morning."

"Yes, let me make go to the bathroom and then we can go."

David waited for Abby to return and then, holding hands, they went to his car. David started the engine and taking a deep breath he glanced to his right at Abby.

"Ready?" he smiled.

"As I'll ever be. Let's go!"

They drove to Rosemary Point and pulled into the lot. There were no other cars this morning even though the day was sunny and warm.

"The place doesn't seem very popular today," David remarked.

"Yes, tourist season is definitely over," Abby agreed.

"It's almost noon," David said, "and there aren't any cars here. Are you sure the place open?"

"It should be," Abby replied.

"Well then, let's go," David said and started to open the door.

Abby put her hand on his arm and looked into his eyes.

"Dave, no matter what happens now, I want you to know how much I love you. If I'm wrong about this and if she's not here, then maybe I'm crazy, but we have to do this. Do you understand?"

"Sure and I know you aren't crazy. I do believe what you're saying, strangely enough. If our spirit can't help us, we'll find some way to go on. I'm with you all the way partner."

He leaned over and gave her a brief kiss. "Now," he said, "let's go spirit talking."

She smiled at him. "Okay, let's go."

They walked up the rise to the house and found the doors were locked. The house was closed.

"There's no one here," David said, "any ideas?"

"Must be some kind of screw up. Maybe today's volunteer is sick or something. We can come back later."

"Let's take a look around anyway," suggested David.

They walked down the lawn on the seaward side of the house and looked out at the ocean shinning blue and calm.

"Nothing here," Abby said.

"No, let's go around to the side of the house."

They walked, hand in hand, to the north side of the house toward the vegetable garden in the rear. They both stopped short, hearts quickening, for there was a woman in the garden weeding a row of carrots and she was dressed in period costume.

Abby spoke first, hesitant, unsure. "Grandmother?" she said not quite sure what to call the woman.

The woman stood erect and turned to face them with a smile forming on her mouth. She was of medium height, David thought as he studied her, about five five. Her eyes were royal blue and he knew it was the same woman he had seen before.

Then the woman spoke. "So, you know now, do you? You are all that I could have hoped for, you have not disappointed me."

David stood, holding Abby's hand tightly, unable to move. He shook his head in disbelief. "Are you really Abigail Steele Smith?"

She smiled again, the eyes friendly. "Yes, I know how difficult it must be for you to understand and believe, but it is true."

"How is it possible that you are here?" asked Abby in an almost reverent voice.

"This property must be protected," the woman said. "I am the only person who can do that," she sighed sadly. "I could not do it a long time ago, although I thought I had taken measures to do that."

David looked at Abby, then back at the woman. He still didn't know what to make of it. Was she real or was she some fantastic illusion or a scam?

"What happened?" asked Abby as David remained silent shaking his head trying to gauge the woman.

"Come, you two must walk with me. Much has taken place on these grounds. I think you know some of the story already, but I can tell you more as we walk. The rest you must discover for yourselves." She looked around the grounds and continued. "This land is much as it was when we bought it. It was very beautiful then and remains so now. It must be protected!"

The trio walked across the broad lawn to the flower garden with the marble benches and the woman gestured for Abby and David to sit.

"I do not know all the details because I was not here to know," the woman explained. "As I said, you must discover those. I only know that my children were robbed of their fortune."

"You mean Jacob and Content?" David asked, finally able to speak.

"Yes. You are descended from Content, are you not?"

"Yes," he said unable to take his eyes from her.

"She was very special, my Content. You know, even though I never saw her after I left her, her feelings of pain are still here and I endure them every day. She died of a broken heart you know, hurt by the injustice done to her here. You may feel them too. Oh how I wish I could have been there to comfort her!"

David looked at her. "Are you for real?"

"Yes, you may touch me if you want," she smiled and held out her hand.

David took it with both his hands and found the hand warm and firm. She seemed very much alive and he looked at the woman and smiled. "I guess you are for real."

"You are David Baker, is that not right?"

"Yes."

"Tell me about your family David, what happened to the family of my Content?"

David told her how the Baker family had moved west. He tried to do this quickly but the woman the woman asked questions at every turn, interested in all the things that had happened to his family. It was as if she was the family matriarch, catching up on years of missed information. Finally David finished.

"That is quite a story," the woman said shaking her head. "It is truly amazing what has taken place over the last two hundred years and it seems this country we helped create has indeed become something wonderful."

Then she looked at Abby and reached out to her. Abby took her hand just as David had done.

"And you are descended from my Jacob. Poor Jacob, he was very weak, but, at least, he passed on to his family what happened here. Tell me about your family. Where did they go?"

Abby related the story of her family as best she could and she included the story of David's great-great grandfather during the Civil War. This brought a look of surprise from the woman.

"My what a story! A cousin saved a cousin during that war? That is very special. I guess some things are meant to happen. Abby, you are lucky also."

Abby spoke. "I am overwhelmed by this Abigail and find this so hard to believe. Can you tell us what happened to you? All we know is you were lost at sea."

The woman blinked in the sunlight and looked away for a moment. "Yes," she said her eyes watery. "Jacob and I were lost in a great storm off of Cape Horn while we were returning from China. The voyage would have been very profitable you know, we might have made history."

"Can you tell us what happened here?" asked David.

"No, I'm sorry I can't since I was not here. I do know that that evil Jonathan Marston stole our fortune but how he did it I don't know. That is what you must find out."

"But you can help us, can't you?" asked Abby.

"I have told you what I can and that is all I can do. Because of my state, I have only been able to know what happened here. I can know nothing of what transpired elsewhere and even some things that took place here long ago I have trouble recalling."

"I understand Grandmother," Abby said, "let me ask you a question about what you did before you left for China in 1784. Is that okay?"

The woman smiled as if seeing herself in the girl with the green eyes. "I will tell you what I can."

"Grandmother, did you have new wills drawn before you went to China?"

The woman cocked her head to the side and looked sharply at Abby.

"Yes," she said, "is that important?"

"Yes," Abby replied, "when would that have been done?"

The woman thought, two hundred years was a long time to remember.

"We left in the middle of January so it must have been the first part of the month. It was the last thing I did. I did it for Jacob and my children because I did not trust Jonathan Marston. I wanted to make sure that my children were protected but somehow it did not work out as planned."

David spoke up. "When did you do the wills that the new ones replaced? I mean when were the old ones done?"

Again the woman paused, thinking.

"I believe that Jacob and I did wills sometime in 1782 before going to Europe, while I was expecting Content I think."

"You didn't do wills in the late fall of 1783?" asked Abby.

"No, I don't think so. It's so difficult to remember now, but I don't think so. We had just returned from the West Indies and were very busy getting ready for the voyage to China."

"Who did you go to to draw up the new wills?" David asked and it occurred to him just how ludicrous this was talking to what seemed to be a ghost.

"I went to a lawyer in Boston, James Read. My attorney in Portsmouth recommended him. Jacob went with me when the documents were done to sign them. We did that a week before we left."

David looked at Abby and she returned the look of surprise.

"You have just helped us more than you know," Abby said.

"I'm glad," replied the woman. "You must be having a very difficult time accepting who I am. This is so hard for me but you must understand my position. I have been here for almost one hundred ninety years since my children left. I have watched other children grown up here and then have children of their own, but I do not know what became of my family. This has been very difficult for me. You must try to understand."

Abby rose, going to her. "Could I hug you? I would like to hold you."

"Oh yes, I would like that. I have not been held by anyone in such a long time."

The two women embraced and Abby held the woman with a will, trying to give her two hundred years of love all at once. The woman responded tentatively at first, as if she could not remember how to show emotion. But within seconds, both women had tears in their eyes and all the years, no decades, of want surfacing in the woman from Rosemary Point. Abby held her close.

The woman sobbed. "I'm sorry, I did not want to do that. You have touched me deeply."

"No," Abby said quietly, "you have touched us and you have every right to have these feelings. You must have some relief from your long years of responsibility."

"Yes," added David, misty eyed himself, "you are an amazing woman. I didn't believe it possible that you could be Abigail, but I do now. We need your help so we can help you."

The woman composed herself. "Yes, we must find out what is planned for the property now."

"You warned us about the sale of the property," Abby said, "I haven't been able to find out anything that verifies the information. What else can you tell us?"

"Only what I heard. There were some men who walked the grounds one day and they spoke of dividing up the land into lots for expensive houses. One of them even talked about turning the house into a restaurant. I'm sorry, I don't know who they were but we must do something to stop them!"

David and Abby glanced at each other. "We will," David vowed.

The woman nodded, smiling. "Thank you, I know you will. Please forgive me my emotions. It has been such a long time you see."

"These men," asked Abby, "did you hear any names?"

"Why yes," recalled the woman, "I think one was called Tom and another was Dan but the name of the third one was not mentioned."

"Tom could be Thomas Sherwood?" David suggested to Abby. "It's time to check him out."

"Yes it is and I'll visit my friend Jerry Carr at the Kittery Planning Office. He may know something." She faced the woman, "don't worry, we'll help you."

"I know that," the woman replied, "you both have the spirit in you. The blood runs strong it seems and I can tell you are well suited for each other. I envy you, you know, you are very much like my Jacob and I."

The tears welled up again and David noticed that Abby's eyes were also moist.

"Can we see you again?" Abby asked.

"Oh yes, of course. I will be here to see you whenever you need me now that you know who I am."

David went to her and held her tightly in his arms. He felt her tremble in his grasp and she looked at him.

"I have not been held by a man in a long time David, I'd forgotten just how good if feels!"

David reddened but bent to kiss her on the forehead. "We'll be back. I almost hate to leave now. So much more needs to be said, so many questions to be asked."

"I will look forward to your next visit," the woman said, "this is enough for now. Just knowing I am no longer alone, and have you to help me, gives me peace of mind."

David let her go and Abby went to her to kiss her goodbye. As he watched, David thought the two women could have been sisters.

"We'll be back," Abby promised.

"And I will be here. Thank you again, both of you."

Abby and David walked toward the car. They glanced back at the woman several times, still not quite believing what had happened to them. Each time they looked the woman waved at them.

They got in the car emotionally drained and sat in silence not knowing quite what to say. The tears ran down Abby's face.

"That was something!" David said finally, "if anyone had ever told me I'd have an experience like that I'd never ever have believed them. She's one incredible woman!"

"That she is," agreed Abby, "do you believe in her now?"

"I don't know what to think," admitted David, "she certainly seems real, but is she who she says she is? Couldn't this still be some incredible fake?"

"No Dave, I don't think so. She's real Dave, anyway I'm taking her at face value. She can help us solve the mystery."

"Okay, I'll go along for now. So what do we do next?"

"I guess I'm going into town and then to the office," Abby said. "Are you going to drive home?"

"Yeah, I guess so. Maybe I'll do some checking this afternoon. One thing though, I'm glad I came, I wouldn't have missed this for anything!"

"Dave?" Abby asked.

"Yes?" he replied seeing the look on her face.

"There is one thing that bothers me and you need to know about it."

"What?"

"This fellow, Jonathan Marston, the one who apparently was responsible for taking the family fortune?"

"Yes?"

"I'm related to him Dave. That's my tie to the Sherwood family. His daughter married into the Sherwood family and I feel guilty about it. Its like I'm not worthy of the other relationships."

David took her hand. "Abby, I understand your feelings, but remember you're also descended from her," he said looking up the rise toward the house. "I'd say what we're doing more than makes up for any guilt that could possibly be left to you. The good genes far outweigh the bad ones and what happened long ago was Marston's doing, plain and simple.

Now, we've got a chance to set things straight and I think you're more than made up for anything your ancestors may have done!"

Abby took David's hand with both of hers, squeezing tightly.

"You're something, I ever tell you how much I like you?"

"I seem to recall you mentioning it," he smiled touched by her feeling.

"Come on partner, let's get a move on. We've got work to do."

She gave him a peck on the cheek and David winked at her as he started he car. Putting it into gear they drove away from what they now believed was a magical house.

*   *   *

Late in the afternoon Abigail Palmer entered the office of the Planning Board in Kittery where her friend, Jerry Carr, was the Town Planner. The secretary recognized her and she motioned Abby into Carr's office. He looked up from his work as she entered.

"Abby Palmer, how are you?"

"Good Jerry and you?"

"The same. To what do I owe the honor of this visit?"

"I need some information."

"Sure, what do you need?"

"You heard anything in the wind about Rosemary Point?"

Carr thought for a moment. "No, I haven't heard anything. Why do you ask?"

"I heard that Rosemary Point is going to be developed."

"Geez, Abby, where did you hear that?"

"From someone at the society."

"No kidding, I don't know anything about it. You know though, someone could make a ton of money off that property. But they'd have to jump through a lot of hoops to make it work. EPA, DEP, the State and the Town would all have to sign off on it. If something were happening you'd hear about it, I think."

"Yeah, you're right Jerry. I've had to jump through a lot of hoops just to do some of the deals we've done!"

"I'm surprised that Dan King or Ron Crown wouldn't know something like that. You asked them?"

"Yeah, I asked Dan, but he said he didn't know anything about it. I'm just double checking I guess, that's all."

"Sorry Abby, I don't know anything."

"Thanks anyway Jerry, I appreciate the help."

"No problem. But it's good to see you Abby."

"Thanks again," Abby said leaving.

Jerry Carr admitted to himself that the Rosemary Point story was far fetched, but someone stood to make a pile of money if it were true. He thought he would see Dan King at the Rotary luncheon on Thursday and he'd mention that Abby had been in to see him. Maybe King would tell him something.

*   *   *

David sat in Jack Pierce's office telling him about the recent events and when he finished, Pierce whistled.

"Jesus, Dave! I'm sure glad I have a normal family tree. God, I'd hate to think what the hobby would be like if everyone had your problems!"

"Thanks a lot!" David replied, "your concern is very comforting."

Pierce chuckled. "You know, I'm here to help, but you've got to admit your story is a little hard to believe. If I didn't know you so well, I'd have a tough time believing you!"

"Yeah I know, I'm still not sure I believe it."

"We should have a talk about spirits one of these days," Pierce said, "I had a Professor in the UK who was a fanatic on the subject. He was a Scotsman and he was positively convincing about the existence of ghosts. I think it was because of those old drafty castles and all those Scottish legends."

"Yeah, I'd like to talk about that," David said. "I really don't know much about the subject."

"I guess you don't have to know much but you've still got the mystery to solve," Pierce reminded him.

"Yeah I know. Jack, I need to check out this guy, Thomas Sherwood from New Rochelle. Any way you can help me?"

"Yes, I think so. I have a friend I can call. He should be able to find some things for you. Anything else?"

"What else do you suggest?"

"Well for starters, you should check to see if either of the Marston's, Jonathan or William left wills. If they did, the wills could give you some clues as to whether or not Jonathan really did take the Smith estates."

"How would that help?" David asked.

"If Jonathan's estate is significantly larger that what he inherited from his father, it would be good corroborating evidence. He may have earned a lot on his own, but it still might give you a clue."

"Okay, I'll do that tomorrow. Where do I go?"

"Come on Dave," Pierce chided him. "What have you learned?"

"Sorry, I wasn't thinking. Probate Court for Suffolk County?"

"Good guess. In this case though, start in the City Registrar's Office in City Hall in Boston. They have records going back to 1639. See if you can get a death record for both Marstons and then try the Probate Records. You may want to look for an obituary also. The public library has microfilm records of old Boston papers."

"That's a good idea," David said thinking it over. The he asked, "Jack, if the Smith wills were forgeries, any idea where the real wills might be?"

"Shit no David, I doubt if they even exist anymore. If forgeries were substituted, anyone who went to the trouble to do that would have made sure that the originals were destroyed."

"But, say they do exist. Where should I look?"

"Oh hell, I don't know," Pierce said, "I guess I'd look in the same places I told you to look for records on the Smiths. The various Marine

Museums. But Dave it really is a longshot and I wouldn't waste my time. Remember, in genealogy, if you don't have primary evidence, then the proof is the weight of the evidence. Build your case with every fact you can. That's my advice."

"Okay Jack, I hear you, but I may have a go at the museums anyway."

"Suit yourself. Anything else?"

"No, I think that's it for now. As usual, thanks for the help!"

"Gladly given. If I get a little extra time I'll try to do some legwork for you. I feel like I'm getting rusty sitting behind this desk!"

"I'd appreciate that, thanks."

David left Pierce and headed back to his office.

Jack Pierce sat for a moment deep in thought. He had a hunch that David was on to something much bigger than he knew. Jack Pierce had always thought that until you knew what you were up against it was better to be prepared to deal with an elephant rather than a mouse.

He took a worn address book from his desk and paged through it until he found the number he wanted and placed the call.

"NYPD Detectives," a voice answered.

"May I speak with Captain Nappia please?"

"Sure just a minute." The phone buzzed again.

"Captain Nappia's office. Sergeant O'Neal speaking."

"I'd like to speak with Captain Nappia please?"

"Can I say who's calling?"

"Yeah, tell the bum it's Jack Pierce."

The voice hesitated for just a second. "Just a sec."

Pierce waited about five seconds. "Jack Pierce, how the hell are you?"

"Fine Tony. Haven't been arrested yet!"

"Yeah, well, if some of those people you work with knew some of the things you've done they'd shit a brick!"

Pierce chuckled. "Tony, I need a favor."

"Anything for you my friend."

"I need to check someone out."

"You got it. Who?"

"I don't mean a once over. I want a complete package. Anything and everything you can find on this guy."

"Sure Jack, I understand."

"The guy's name is Thomas Sherwood. He lives somewhere in New Rochelle, I don't have an address and I gather he's involved in real estate somehow. He's also a partner in something called the Springbrook Partnership. That's all I know."

"That should be enough. How soon do you want this?"

"As soon as you can but no special rush."

"I'll get back to you. What's this guy done?"

"I don't know," Pierce said, "but a friend of mine is very interested in him. I appreciate the help Tony."

"Hey, what are friends for? With any luck I'll be able to tell you what color his underwear is!"

"Thanks again, Tony."

"You got it! I'll be in touch."

Pierce hung up, satisfied that he would get some answers.

CHAPTER EIGHTEEN

David was home sitting in his recliner reviewing the documents he had obtained concerning the Marstons and he knew he had made a good deal of progress.

After a long wait at the City Registrar, he found that William Marston had died in 1796 and that his son, Jonathan, had followed in 1804.

Using this information, he visited the Registrar of Probate for Suffolk County, locating wills for both William and Jonathan. The inventories for each of the estates were included and now David was rereading the documents to make sure he had the facts straight.

Jack Pierce's advice had been right on target, he thought. The inventory of William Marston's estate totaled slightly over fifteen thousand dollars, split among four children and that was a very handsome sum for those days. However, the contrast with the value of his son's estate was incredible. Just eight years later Jonathan Marston had left an estate of nearly eighty thousand dollars, a huge sum for 1804. Even allowing for a successful and profitable business career over the years, the increase in the size of the estate certainly pointed to Jonathan having acquired other assets someplace along the way. The weight of the evidence gave support to the accusation that Marston was responsible for the theft of the Smith fortune.

David sat back sipping at his beer. Tomorrow he would go to the Boston Public Library to see if he could find obituaries for either of the men. He hoped that there would be some record. It seemed important that he should tell the woman at Rosemary Point what had become of Mr. Jonathan Marston.

He thought for a moment about how events had changed the direction of his work. What had started out as simple curiosity about his ancestors had led to a two-century-old mystery with a present day secret. The woman at Rosemary Point had touched him deeply whether she was real or not and he wanted to solve the mystery for her. He went to the kitchen to fix dinner.

                    *   *   *

Abby was in her office the next morning, working intently on some project specifications when, at mid morning, the telephone rang.

"Abby Palmer," she answered.

"Abby? It's Tom Couture."

"Hi, how are you?"

"Okay. I thought I should call you. Someone just picked up the mail from the mail box."

"Oh?" her heart quickened.

"Yeah, I didn't recognize him though."

"It was a man?"

"Yeah, late forties, maybe early fifties. Thinning gray hair, medium height, kind of stocky."

"That could describe half the men in America!"

"Shit Abby, I did my best!"

"Sorry."

"It's okay. I did watch him go out to the parking lot."

"You did? Did you get the license number by any chance?"

"Sort of."

"What do you mean sort of?" She tried to control her impatience.

"Well, I was looking at the car. A green BMW, two door. He pulled out real quick, kind of like he didn't want to be seen."

"So you missed the plate number?"

"Well, no, I think I got most of it."

"What was it?" she asked hoping for the best.

"New Hampshire plate and it was a vanity plate, that's why I think I got it."

"What did it say?" Abby said waiting for Tommy to get to the point.

"BUILD." He spelled it out.

"BUILD?" she repeated.

"Yeah, BUILD. I thought it was kind of strange too. You want me to trace it for you?"

"No thanks Tommy. I can do it and thanks for the help. I owe you lunch."

"Anytime Abby. I never did ask you why you want to know who owned the box?"

"Just curiosity Tommy. Thanks again, I'll be in touch."

"Bye Abby, glad to help."

Abby put the phone back on the cradle. She could call the Department of Motor Vehicles to get the name of the owner of the car, but in this case she didn't need to. She knew who owned the green BMW. The car belonged to Dan King.

*   *   *

David arrived at the Boston Public Library and found the reference room. He inquired about the availability of old newspaper records and the librarian at the service desk reviewed what the library had to offer.

He chose two rolls of microfilm for the *Boston Gazette* for the time periods coinciding with the deaths of the two Marstons. The woman pointed David to a microfilm reader and he thanked her, going to a vacant machine.

An expert now at working with microfilm, he quickly loaded the smoke gray celluloid for the 1796 period. He paged forward to June and slowed the machine at intervals, to check his progress.

David found the issue of the paper after the date of death for William Marston. He carefully scrolled through the issue of the paper stopping occasionally to read some of the articles, fascinated with the daily events of 1796 Boston. He went through the whole issue of the paper without finding an obituary or reference to the death of William Marston.

David did notice that there were no obituaries, as he knew them. Apparently the custom of the times did not call for what David thought of as a modern obituary but he did notice several black lined rectangular ads which announced the deaths of different people. Maybe this was all he could hope to find.

Paging forward to the next issue of the *Gazette*, he began to review the pages. Six pages in, he found one of the black lined ads for William Marston. The ad contained only the barest of information that added nothing to what David was seeking. Disappointed, he made a copy of the ad anyway and rewound the roll of microfilm.

David put the roll away and reached for the other reel. He threaded the film on the reader, forwarding to the July 1804, date of death for Jonathan Marston. He examined the issue published right after the death of Marston.

Again, he paused to read the news of the day and found it very interesting. In the end though he found no ad or mention of Jonathan Marston's death.

David paged through the next issue of the *Gazette*. He carefully scanned the contents of the paper but as he went through the pages he was unable to find any reference to the death of Marston.

Frustrated, he rewound the microfilm to the issue dated on the day Jonathan Marston had died. He stopped the machine and focused on the front page, shocked and surprised by what he saw.

The headline, small by modern standards, but still stark and prominent, leaped out at him. He blinked to bring the article into perspective.

The headline read:

TWO LOCAL MERCHANTS BRUTALLY MURDERED ON THE WATERFRONT

David read on:

Two wealthy, well-respected local merchants were found murdered on the Boston waterfront today. Jonathan Marston, aged fifty-six, of Beacon Hill and his business partner, James Weaver, aged fifty, of Cambridge were discovered brutally beaten and stabbed. A night watchman, making his early morning rounds, made the grisly discovery today. The degree of violence was described as extreme by those familiar with crimes of this type. Authorities said both bodies were beaten almost beyond recognition. In addition, the victims had multiple stab wounds. The Marshall's Office speculated that both victims had been tortured before dying. One official stated that this was the most violent crime in Boston in years. As yet there are no suspects in the heinous crime.

His wife, Elizabeth, and three daughters; Tabitha, Anne and Deborah survive Mr. Marston. Mr. Weaver, an attorney in this city for nearly twenty-five years, is survived by his wife, Mary, two sons, John and Thomas, and two daughters, Samantha and Hope. Services for both victims are planned for Friday.

David let out a deep breath. "Wow!" he said out loud.

Several people working near him looked at him, wondering what was going on.

David felt a sense of elation because it looked like Marston had gotten his in the end. He couldn't wait to tell Abby and he also thought the woman at Rosemary Point would like to hear the news. He suspected there was more to the story than just the article about the crime so he made a copy of the paper and read on.

He began scrolling forward to the next several issues of the *Gazette*. Four issues later David found more information:

MAN ARRESTED IN BRUTAL DUAL SLAYING

Boston authorities have arrested a local businessman in connection with the murders of Jonathan Marston and James Weaver. Josiah Thomas, age forty-two, a silk merchant, was apprehended yesterday after evidence implicating him in the deaths of the two local merchants came to light.

Although authorities refused to talk publicly about the case, speculation suggests that Thomas was deeply in debt to both Marston and Weaver. The later two were putting pressure on Thomas to turn his business over to them. This apparently was the motive behind he brutal slayings.

The article continued on, giving more detail and David made copies of it.

He looked at his watch and saw it was almost lunchtime but he decided he didn't care, mesmerized by the story unfolding before him.

Slowly, he moved the microfilm forward, going through each succeeding issue. In a September issue he found the record of the trial of Josiah Thomas.

LOCAL MERCHANT CONVICTED OF MURDER

Josiah Thomas, of Boston, was convicted today of the murders of Jonathan Marston and James Weaver after a two day trial. Evidence presented at the trial, held in Boston Municipal Court, indicated that Thomas had borrowed three thousand dollars from Marston and Weaver. The two local merchants tried to collect on the debt by attaching Thomas' business.

Thomas, in retaliation, confronted the men in an alley near their offices on the waterfront. Thomas cornered them and attacked them

with a club. After beating them senseless, he used a knife to torture each
man before finally cutting their throats

Thomas displayed no emotion or remorse when the verdict was read.
He was given the death penalty. The sentence will be carried out at the
State Prison next month.

David was thoroughly captivated by the story and he made copies of
these pages also.

The microfilm ran out before he came to the October issues of the
Gazette. He rewound the film and returned the reels to the service desk
where he obtained the box of film containing the next issues of the paper.

Paging forward, he found the article that ended the story of revenge
on Jonathan Marston.

JOSIAH THOMAS HANGS FOR MURDERS

The convicted murderer of Jonathan Marston and James Weaver was
hanged this morning at the State Prison. The condemned man went to
the gallows quietly, accepting his fate. His final statement, issued by his
attorney, was revealing. He explained that he had to kill the evil
Marston, who in his crazed ambition to become the richest man in
Boston, had ruined many, including members of his own family.

There was more to the article, but David already had the meat of the
story. He made a copy of the material.

Rewinding the microfilm, he was surprised to see by the clock on the
wall that it was almost three and a rumbling in his stomach confirmed
the time.

He gathered up the copies he had made and stuffed them in his briefcase. He stood up and returned the microfilm to the service desk. He
felt very excited at the results of his research work and knew it had been
very rewarding day. David left the library anxious to call Abby with the
exciting new information.

*   *   *

The private telephone rang in Jack Pierce's office and he reached for the handset, answered and listened.

"Jack?" said the voice at the other end that Pierce immediately recognized.

"Yeah."

"It's Tony Nappia."

"Hey Tony, you find anything for me?"

"Shit Jack, you sure pick some beauties. This guy, Sherwood, is a real sweetheart!"

"Oh?" Pierce asked alarmed at Nappia's tone of voice.

"Yeah. He's clean Jack, but only on technicalities."

"Tell me what you got."

"You got a fax?" Nappia asked.

"Yes."

"Then I'll send all of this to you, but I'll give you the basics. Thomas Sherwood, currently of New Rochelle, New York, originally from Kittery, Maine. U.S. Army '45 to '47, mostly at Fort Dix, in New Jersey. Returned to Maine in '47 to finish school at Bates College. Graduated in '49. Left the state to go to New York and lived in Queens, working for a residential tract developer '49 to '53. Showed no particular skills or expertise as far as I can find out. Paying his dues, I think."

"What next?" Pierce asked jotting notes as Nappia talked.

"Went to work for developer Vincent Franconia '53 to '59. High rise apartments in the Bronx. Seems like he learned a thing or two and Franconia was convicted in '61 on tax evasion and extortion charges. Sherwood wasn't implicated, kept his nose clean."

"Nice company," commented Pierce.

"Yeah, but wait," said Nappia, "it gets better. '59 to '71 he was a partner in something called Springfield Associates. Owned slum properties in Brooklyn, Queens and the Bronx. Didn't pay taxes, let the buildings go to hell and finally abandoned them when they couldn't squeeze any more income out of them. Twice during this period the IRS investigated him, but did not press charges. He covered himself well."

"More?" asked Pierce.

"Oh yeah, I told you this guy's a beaut," Nappia paused and Pierce heard him turn a page in a notebook.

"1973, we got him. He threatened some tenants in a building he owned in the Bronx when they refused to pay rent. Sherwood threatened to burn them out. He was indicted and convicted, but he had a good lawyer who got him off with only a fine and a suspended sentence."

"Swell," Pierce said, "a real upright guy."

"Hey Jack, in the old days we could have wasted a guy like this and nobody would have cared!" Nappia laughed.

"Shit Tony, that was a long time ago. Don't remind me!"

"Yeah, I know. Shit, Jack, they were good times though, weren't they? he chuckled. "Okay, this guy, Sherwood gets involved next with Manhattan office space. I can't prove it, but I think he was a front for the syndicate and that lasted into '81. Then this guy branches out and starts doing deals in New England. In '82 he's involved in things in Connecticut and he's also trying to make money playing the bank takeover game, a lot of funny things going on a couple of years ago if you'll remember?"

"Yeah, I remember," Pierce said.

"Then Sherwood starts doing deals in Massachusetts, Rhode Island and New Hampshire next. As best I can figure, he made money through '87."

"What's his situation now?" Pierce asked.

"Tough to say," Tony Nappia replied. "He's got to be feeling the pressure because of the New England economic situation. I'm sure he's leveraged up the ying yang to the banks and owes them a lot of money. Probably owes a lot to the big boys too."

"Do you think he might be trying to make a final hit to bail him out?"

"Yeah that's possible. It might fit the profile. If you give me a couple of more days I'll have a financial statement on the guy."

"Yeah sure, thanks for the help Tony. I know what I'm dealing with now, you've been a big help."

"My pleasure Jack. Hey, we've got to get together soon."

"You bet, boss. I'll talk to you in the next few days, huh?"

They exchanged good-byes and Pierce hung up the phone. He would brief Dave Baker on what he had learned and he needed to make sure he gave Dave his no bullshit assessment of the man from New Rochelle. This guy was dangerous.

                          *   *   *

Abby called David first that evening and he told her about all that he had found at the library. When he finished, Abby let out an exclamation. "Wow! That's powerful stuff!"

"Yeah, I was really surprised that I found something and surprised at what I found."

"So," Abby said, "where does this leave us?"

"Well, the Marston wills certainly point to Jonathan being the person who took the Smith estate. The increase in the value of his estate does that and I don't have any doubts about that now. It had to have been Marston who took the fortune."

"Do you think he did it with a phony will?"

"Yes, I think so. I don't know what else it could have been. He could have made a lot on his own, but I don't think it could have been as much as there was in his estate."

"I agree," Abby said.

"The best part though," David said, "is that somebody did Marston in. There was some justice in the end apparently."

"We must let Abigail know," Abby said.

"Yes," David hesitated, still wondering if the woman was real. "I suppose we do. I hope that the news will give her something to ease her mind."

"Maybe it will help put her at rest," agreed Abby, "I'll try and go out to the house tomorrow."

"Let's wait until the weekend, then we can both go."

"Okay with me. Does that mean I can expect a guest for the weekend?"

"I think so," David smiled.

"I've got news too," Abby said, "I found out who picked up the mail at the Springbrook Partnership's mail box."

"Who?" asked David.

"Somehow I'm not surprised. It was Dan King."

"No shit?"

"Yes, my boss."

"I told you I didn't trust that SOB. So he's involved in this somehow?"

"I guess so, but I don't know that for sure yet. I'm going to do some snooping around."

"Okay, but, be careful, this could be dangerous."

"I'll be careful Dave, don't worry. Dave?"

"Yeah?"

"I'm curious. How was Jonathan Marston's estate divided?"

"Equally between his three daughters. Why?"

"Including Tabitha Sherwood?" Abby asked.

"Yes, she was mentioned, along with her husband, Joseph Sherwood."

"I think that became the Sherwood fortune and now it's gone. Betsey Watrous told me they lost the fortune before the Civil War in the Panic of 1857."

"Yeah, I suppose that the rest that went to the other daughters is probably gone also."

"So," Abby said, "there is no Smith fortune anymore. There's probably nothing for us to get back."

"You're right. But there is one thing left," David said.

"Rosemary Point?"

"Yes, the land must go back to the rightful owners."

"I agree. Somehow we'll do that Dave."

"We sure will," David said but wasn't sure he believed his own words. "I'll see you tomorrow night Abby."

"Okay, I can't wait."

*　　　　*　　　　*

Friday proved to be a bright and clear fall day and as David settled in at his desk sipping his morning coffee as he reviewed a new exhibit proposal. Hearing footsteps he glanced up to see Jack Pierce enter his office.

"Hi Jack."

"Morning Dave, I need to talk to you."

"Sure. What's up?" David said seeing the serious look on Jack Pierce's face.

"I've got some information on your man, Sherwood."

"Hey, that was quick!" David said as Pierce pulled up a chair.

"Helps when you know the right people. Dave I want you to be real careful with this guy. He's a bad apple and I want you to be exactly sure about what you're doing."

"Okay," David said as he saw that Pierce wasn't kidding. "What did you find out?"

Pierce went over all the information that Tony Nappia had given him. He handed David a copy of the information that had come by fax and went over each fact trying to impress on David just what he thought the man was capable of doing. When he was done David looked at Pierce with a blank look.

"He's that bad?" he asked. "He's a real threat?"

"Potentially, I think so. You've got to assume that he can go to extremes. I'm doing some more checking, but I think this guy is having financial problems so he's out looking to score big to solve his problems."

"Rosemary Point?"

"Yeah, could be," Pierce shrugged, "could be other things, but one thing I learned in the Army; expect the worst. Don't underestimate this guy!"

"I hear you. Any suggestions as to what I do now?"

"No, not at the moment. First let me see if I can find out anything more about Sherwood."

"Okay," David said then remembered. "Oh shit Jack, I almost forgot. Abby found out the name of somebody connected with the Springbrook Partnership."

"Who?" asked Pierce.

David told him of Abby's discovery.

"But you don't really know if he's a member of the partnership though?" Pierce asked.

"That's right. He could just be the guy who picks up the mail. But he has to be involved some way."

"Okay Dave, I think I'll run a check on Dan King too. What's his partner's name?"

"Ron Crown."

"I might as well check them both out, no sense leaving any stones unturned. I'll let you know if I find anything."

"Thanks Jack."

"Okay see you later," Pierce said rising from his chair.

Pierce left David's office to return to his office.

David looked after him and for the first time he felt a pang fear and he was suddenly very worried about Abby.

*   *   *

Abigail Palmer noticed it was nearly eleven as she sat at her desk jotting some notes. She had a lunch date with a friend and was looking forward to meeting her. She looked around as Dan King came out of his office and made a beeline to where she sat.

"Abby, do you have a minute?"

"Sure," she said.

"Then come into my office if you don't mind."

She followed him into his office wondering just what this was all about. He waited by the door while she entered and closed the door behind her motioning for her to sit on one of the two chairs in front of the desk. He went behind and sat in his chair.

Dan King regarded Abby closely for a moment and she returned the look warily.

"Yes?" she said, feeling uneasy at the way he was looking at her.

"Abby. I spoke to Jerry Carr at Rotary yesterday and he told me you were in his office asking questions about Rosemary Point."

"Yes, I asked him if he knew anything about the possible sale, just like I asked you," Abby said trying not to sound defensive.

"Well Abby that's not the way you came across. Jerry felt that you were spreading rumors."

"He what! He said that?" she asked incredulous at this insinuation. "Well, he didn't say that in so many words, but he implied you were trying stir up trouble. I can't have that Abby, it makes the firm look bad."

"How can you say that Dan?" Abby said wary of the implications of King's words. "I did nothing of the kind!"

"I can say it and I will Abby. I want you to stop asking questions. There's nothing happening at Rosemary Point and it's none of your business!"

"The hell it isn't!" Abby said rising to the bait. "I'm a member of the Society and besides, it's a free country! I'll do what I damn well please!"

"You're also an employee of this company," King reminded her like in a tone that suggested that she was being scolded.

"Is that a threat Dan? Because if it is, I don't like it one bit!"

"Look, Abby, I'm talking to you as a friend," King said trying to calm her as he realized he had gone too far. "I'm just asking you to back off, that's all."

"What are you worried about Dan? Why does this bother you so much?" She was determined not to let on to him that she knew he was involved with the Springbrook Partnership.

"I'm not worried about anything Abby. I'm just warning-that is I'm asking you not to take this any further."

"Warning's the word you want to use, isn't it Dan? Why are you making such a big deal out of this? You doing something you shouldn't?"

That remark hit home and King reacted angrily. "Listen you little bitch, I'm telling you that you're going to back off or you're out of here!"

Abby felt the heat of anger rise within her but she fought to keep in control. "That is a threat, isn't it Dan?" she said as calmly as she could.

King was red in the face. "Yes Abby, that is a threat and you'd better think about it too!"

Abby held her anger in check but stood her ground. "Then make good on your threat Dan, because I'm not backing off and I'm not quitting!"

"You're fired, Miss Palmer," King said flushing with anger, "now, get out! Clear your things out of your office and get out of here!"

"Yes, Mr. King, I'll go but you have not heard the last from me. You just made the worst mistake of your life bud!"

She stood eyes cold with hate and looked him straight in the eye. They stood glaring at each other for a moment and then King was forced to look away. Satisfied that she had won this last round, Abby turned, opened the door and stalked back to her office. She gathered up her belongings as the others in the office watched and wondered what had just happened.

Another project manager, Frank Davis, came over to her. "Jesus Abby, what in hell happened?"

"I just got canned Frank."

"What? You've got to be kidding!"

"No, it's true."

"What happened?"

"Call me at home Frank and I'll tell you the whole story."

"Okay," the surprised man replied.

Abby picked up her things, waved goodbye to the rest of the staff and walked deliberately to her car, settling into the front seat. Only then did the tears begin. I'll be damned if I'll let him see me cry, she thought as she turned the ignition key.

Still sitting in his office, Dan King knew that he had overreacted. He hadn't meant for things to go so far, he had only wanted to warn Abby off. Now he did not look forward to telling Tom Sherwood what had happened. He had a nagging feeling that he had screwed up and hoped he would not regret his mistake.

Chapter Nineteen

October 6, 1785 Boston, Massachusetts

Jonathan Marston knew that the *Eagle of America* was gone, lost at sea. At first it had been assumed that the ship was merely overdue. However, it was over a year since she had sailed from China and there had been no word of her from any foreign port and now it was all but certain that the ship had been lost along with her crew.

This was not quite the outcome that Marston had wanted, but it suited him well enough. His attorney, James Weaver, had filed the forged wills with the Court in Yorkshire, District of Maine and the probate process was proceeding along as expected.

Marston had solved a problem with the other attorney, John Read. Read had been reluctant to give up the original and the copies of the real Smith wills. But Marston had moved fast knowing that Read had married over his head and that his wife had no regard for money. So, in the end, Read had given in for a sum of two thousand dollars and Marston thought it was a small price to pay for the Smith assets.

He rose from his worktable and went to the window of his second floor office to inspect the busy waterfront. There was a great deal of activity on this cloudy fall morning with several ships fitting out in preparation for voyages to Europe or the Caribbean.

Looking down to the street, Marston saw James Weaver enter the first floor of the building. Marston went to the door to his office where he waited for the other man to come up the stairs.

"Good morning Jonathan," Weaver greeted him.

"Good morning James," repeated Marston, "come in."

Weaver nodded and entered Marston's office and both men sat in chairs.

"How do we stand?" asked Marston.

"Very well, I think," Weaver replied. "The wills are on the docket and I spoke to the judge three days ago during my visit to Maine. I told him we were anxious for the children's sake to have the estates probated as quickly as possible."

"And?"

"He seemed agreeable Jonathan. I think we can count on a ruling by next month."

"Excellent! And have you prepared an inventory?" asked Marston.

"Yes, it's almost done. The joint estates should come in around twenty five thousand or so."

"That much!" Marston exclaimed.

"Yes, when you add it all up. I think James Steele made a good part of it and left it to his daughter. But Abigail and Jacob were not dumb and we both know they made at least two profitable voyages to Europe."

"That's very good news," Marston said. "We can do much with assets like that!"

"Yes," Weaver smiled in agreement.

"We should start planning our next venture."

"I think that trade with China offers the best prospects," Weaver said. "I have to admit that Abigail and Jacob had the right idea about that."

"Yes," agreed Marston, "the potential for profit is good, so we shall plan a ship for the China trade."

"I'll look into it," offered Weaver, "I can talk with several shipbuilders in East Boston. I believe it should be easy to find a builder who will be anxious to work with us."

"Do that," said Marston, "it's never too early to begin to make plans."

Weaver nodded. "I must be on my way. Read has asked to see me again."

"What in blazes does he want now?" Marston asked, a look of distaste on his face.

"I don't know. I'm meeting him in my office at eleven."

"Keep me informed James, I'm afraid we may have a recurring problem with Read's conscience. Let me know what he says."

"You can be sure of it," Weaver replied and got up to leave.

As Weaver made his way down the stairs, Marston once again went to the window. A schooner was clearing the harbor and Marston watched her begin to dip and roll into the ocean swell as she left the protective shelter of the port.

Soon he would have ships flying his own flag to trade with the rest of the world and that prospect made him very happy. Jonathan had vowed to become the richest merchant in Boston and he meant to accomplish that one way or the other.

*   *   *

The next morning Jonathan Marston worked making notes for his secretary, Jonah Tyler, to turn into letters. The plans for his fleet of trading vessels were progressing rapidly and this series of letters would be the first to begin setting up a network of merchant contacts around the globe.

He paused for a moment to pick up the letter he had received that morning and reread the contents. The letter was an invitation from a friend who invited him to invest in a new textile mill to be built on the Merrimack River near New Hampshire. Marston thought that the idea had promise, seeing the manufacture of cloth and then shipping the finished product to distant ports a natural combination. He would consider the invitation very carefully.

His mind went back to the conversation he had late the previous afternoon in this office with James Weaver. Weaver's morning meeting with John Read had resulted in nothing and, try as he might, Weaver could not discover what was on Read's mind. In the end Read had demanded a meeting with Marston and Weaver had agreed to arrange this. As a result, Marston now expected John Read Esq. in half an hour.

He didn't know what to expect from the unpredictable Read. All at once he was a brilliant legal mind, specializing in estate work and at the same time, he was a henpecked greedy man, driven to try and satisfy his spoiled, aristocratic wife. Marston would hear him out and then decide what to do but he thought he already knew what would be required.

John Read arrived promptly at ten-thirty, entering the first floor, going up the stairs to Marston's office. He knocked at the open doorway and Marston motioned him to come inside.

"Hello John," Marston said and he dismissed his secretary, Jonah who scuttled out of the room. "Come and sit down," Marston motioned to the railback chair.

"Good morning Jonathan. How are you?" Read said as he sat in the chair in front of the worktable. The two men regarded each other carefully, and then Marston began.

"James Weaver tells me you have something on your mind John, what is it?"

"I have been thinking," Read said tentatively.

"Yes?"

"I hesitate to speak to you."

"Oh come out with it! What is it man? Say it!"

"I feel guilty," Read blurted out. "Jonathan, I cannot sleep!"

"Why not man?" Marston asked but he knew the answer.

"Because of what I have done! What we have done!"

"And what is it that you have done?"

"You know well enough. For God's sake Jonathan, I have stolen for you. I have stolen from a client!"

"And?" Marston said his voice edgy.

"I cannot face my family. I imagine they see the guilt on my face constantly. My God Jonathan, I cannot live this way!"

Marston eyed Read who was clearly distressed. A man in that condition could be dangerous, he thought. Yes, a distressed man could do irrational things.

"You must not feel this way," Marston soothed, "you have only helped me take better care of the Smith orphans." He tried to reason with the man.

Read glared at him not believing the lie for one moment. He was close to tears.

"Jonathan, I beg you, please restore the real wills. Have them probated. I cannot live with this!"

"Impossible," Marston replied, "they do not exist anymore. They have been destroyed."

The impact of this statement shocked Read. What? What have you done? Oh God, I cannot bear it! I cannot bear the guilt! I did not consider my actions when you proposed the idea to me. I have sold my soul to the Devil! I am guilty!"

Marston stared at Read oozing scorn and derision. "You knew damn well what you were doing John. You chose only to see the money and you were paid handsomely enough, Mister Read! You are no babe in the woods!"

The words hit Read like a splash of cold water.

"Yes by God you paid me, but with blood money! Now I have blood on my hands, just like you Jonathan!"

"I have no blood on my hands. My conscience is clear," Marston said with a calm coldness. "I'm afraid you have lost your senses Mister Read. You knew exactly what you were doing."

Read sat, breathing heavily, eyes wide. "All right, Jonathan. If I cannot have the same clear conscience, then I must have more money to rid me of the guilt! I need more money!"

Marston had expected this and in fact, he wasn't sure that Read hadn't staged this whole act to try and extort more money out of him.

"So, now it is more money?" he said, "is that all it takes to calm your guilt?"

"It will not cure the guilt, but it will make it easier to live with!"

"How much?" demanded Marston.

Read thought and this surprised Marston. He had expected Read to have a figure ready. Perhaps the guilt was real after all.

"How about five thousand?" Read suggested.

"Out of the question!" Marston spat.

"How much then?"

"Another two thousand," Marston offered.

Read thought it over. "No, five thousand," Read said.

"All right then" Marston said, "I'll raise it to three thousand."

"No," replied Read carefully, "five thousand or I go to the authorities. I'd rather go to prison with a clear conscience than live with less than five thousand."

Marston eyed him closely. So that was it and he made up his mind. "Done, Mister Read. You will get your five thousand."

The other man smiled, happy at the deal he made. "When can I get the money?" he asked eagerly.

"I don't have it here, but I'll make arrangements with James Weaver to set a meeting to get you the money."

Read got up to leave. "Thank you Jonathan, I feel better. You'll not regret this."

"I know I won't," Marston said, a false smile on his face and a cold look in his eyes.

"I will look forward to meeting James Weaver," Read said looking genuinely relieved.

"I will have him in touch with you before tonight," Marston said. "You can count on it."

"Thank you Jonathan," Read said, extending his hand.

Marston put his hand out and Read grasped it. But, as he took it, he was surprised how cold it was.

*   *   *

Marston met James Weaver for supper shortly before one o'clock at the small tavern near the end of the street. Over a glass of port Marston told Weaver of the conversation with Read that morning. A waiter came to the table and the two men ordered their mid day meal. As the waiter walked away, Weaver spoke.

"So that's what Read was after? More money?"

"Yes. Don't be surprised James, I expected it from him."

"Yes, I suppose so. I should have known that was the cause of his distress," Weaver said. "How much did you agree to give him?"

"Five thousand."

"Five thousand more to keep quiet?"

"That's right."

"I can't believe you would agree to give it to him. He'll only be back for more."

"Ah, but I did agree," Marston said with a tight malevolent smile.

"What do you want me to do?" Weaver asked.

"We make plans for you to meet with Read to pay him off. I told him he would hear from you before evening."

"All right, I'll do as you bid. When will you provide the money?'

Marston paused another smug grin forming on his face. "I won't be providing the money."

Weaver looked at him quizzically. "What do you mean Jonathan?"

"What do you think?" Marston almost laughed.

"You're not going to pay him, are you?"

"No, I think not."

"But you did promise him?"

"Yes but promises are easily broken. You know that."

"What do you want me to do?"

"Make your plans to pay him off but I'm afraid Read has become very dangerous to us. We must give him no reason to do anything irrational."

"I make plans to meet with him. Then what?" Weaver asked, already suspecting the answer.

"We kill him," Marston said easily.

"I'll make the arrangements then," Weaver smiled.

"You have someone in mind?"

"Yes. Two ex clients. They'll do it for substantially less than five thousand and also know enough to disappear."

"Good, take care of it," Marston said.

"Rest assured," Weaves said, "I will."

They both looked up as the waiter put plates of food in front of them and Marston raised his glass. "To the successful completion of another venture," he said and the two men clinked their glasses.

*   *   *

The early fall sun was just setting when John Read, Esq. left his office, closing and locking the door behind him. He walked up the street toward the corner where Weaver's note directed him to meet and he paused under the whale oil street lamp to look at his watch. He had plenty of time.

Read walked more slowly, enjoying the brisk fall night air. He was looking forward to meeting Weaver and getting the rest of the money to which he was entitled. After all, he reasoned, with what Marston stood to gain, the five thousand was more than justified. To Read the prospect of the additional money meant he could afford to buy his wife the new house that she constantly nagged him about. Yes, this was a good solution to his problems, and in the final analysis he could live with that.

Read approached a cross street and as he started to cross, he stopped short to avoid a carriage that came clattering down the street. Close behind him a swarthy stocky man also stopped to keep from bumping into Read who did not notice.

He neared a narrow alleyway in the middle of the block and a man came out of the alley to stand stood against the wall of the building on the other side. Read thought little of it, his mind focused on his meeting with Weaver.

He started to pass the man standing against the building and was suddenly aware that the man was reaching for him. Before he could run or scream out the man had him by the arm pulling him into the alley. Behind him he felt another set of hands push him and he panicked, wondering what was happening.

The two powerful men wrestled him back into the shadows, the man behind him holding him tightly and the one in front breathing heavily into his face. Read could even smell the garlic and rum on his breath. He struggled to defend himself as the man pulled a knife from his belt.

"Your money!" the man in front demanded.

"What?" Read moaned, almost begging now.

"Your money. We want your money!" the men hissed.

Read wanted to yell, to scream for help but could only pant, trying to catch his breath. He shook with fear.

"In-in my pocket," he stammered. "There isn't much."

The man in front ripped Read's coat open and roughly searched his pockets. He found the small purse and quickly opened it counting the coins with his eyes.

"Ah a tidy sum," the man said to his friend, "a nice bonus."

Behind Read, the other man grunted. "Let's get this over with!"

Read started to breathe a sigh of relief, as the man behind him eased his grip slightly.

Then suddenly, the man in front lunged, driving the blade of the knife into Read's belly. Read gasped in pain and surprise, eyes bulging with fear and terror. The pain was terrible and the man behind him viciously pulled his arms back while the other man, smiling like a demon, took his head by the forehead and pushed it back.

Read tried to cry out, but sound would not come to him. The man in front slashed out at Read's throat cutting him deeply twice and blood pumped out is spurts from a severed artery.

Read gave a low moan, his mind bordering on unconsciousness. The man behind him let him go and he slumped to the ground.

"Let's go!" the man behind said to the other.

Read heard running footsteps as the men made good their escape as he fought a losing battle for consciousness. He knew he could blame Marston for this attack and he was also sure that he was dying.

As the life bled out of him, he had the grim satisfaction of knowing that despite what Marston thought, final copies of the wills of Jacob and Abigail Smith still existed. That thought consoled him as he died.

CHAPTER TWENTY

"I'm still so angry I could just spit!" Abby said, stirring her third martini with her finger.

"I don't blame you one bit," David said, agreeing with her. "It was a shitty thing for King to do and I still don't understand what made him do it."

They were sitting on the couch in her apartment. David had arrived a little after six and he found Abby in tears. She told him what had transpired in Dan King's office that morning. David had been very surprised by King's actions and neither of them could figure out why Ron King had lost his temper so badly.

"You know," Abby lamented, "he had no reason to do that to me! No grounds! I bet I've got a good case to take to the human rights commission!"

"You probably do," David said, "but don't do anything now. Let's just wait Abby. We've got more important things to do right now like finding out what's really happening. Besides, remember the motto; don't get mad..."

"Get even!" she said with a look of satisfaction on her face as the alcohol dissipated her anger.

"You got it," David said. "We'll find a way to do just that before we're done."

"I sure hope so, it's just so damned unfair!" Abby slurred her words. "I wish I could sue the bastard!"

"Just hold on Abby, it is unfair, but think about it. King was worried enough about something to lose control and he did lose his cool. By doing that he sends a message that something really is going on."

Abby thought for a moment. "Yes, that's right. He was spooked, so we must be on the right track to worry him like that."

"I think we are," David said feeling just a bit light-headed himself.

"I'd still like to sue that bastard though! Jesus, Dave, who does he think he is?" Abby said as the anger returned.

David thought her last words over and an idea came to him. Abby watched his face, realizing that he was thinking something over.

"What are you thinking about?" she asked.

"I was thinking about the idea of a lawsuit."

"Yeah? Now you like my idea?"

"No, not an employment related suit."

"What then?"

"We turn up the heat!"

"Explain that, what do you mean?"

"Well, King is worried about something, right?"

"Yeah."

"So we give him something more to worry about."

"Oh, I think I like that idea!"

"Maybe now is the time to file suit against the Springbrook Partnership. Even if it's only a nuisance suit, it'll give them something to think about and King still doesn't know you know he's involved in the partnership?" David slurred the last few words and laughed.

"No, I was careful. I didn't say anything."

"Okay then, maybe they'll make another mistake if we put more pressure on them."

"I like that idea!" Abby said, a real smile on her face for the first time that evening. "How do we do that?"

"I want to call Jack Pierce tomorrow and talk it over with him to see what he thinks and then Monday, I'll call Jim Phillips and see what he says. Ask him how we go about filing suit."

"That sounds good. I'm going to have some time on my hands now, so I can help, can't I?" Abby giggled now, the effects of three martinis making her giddy. "Geez, martinis are good. I'm feeling better!"

David grinned at her. "I think you are feeling better."

"Yes I am, but I always feel better when you're here though."

"That's my girl," he leaned to kiss her and she tried to pull him down on top of her. David resisted.

"I want you now," she laughed, "come on!"

"No later," he said firmly.

"Okay," she pouted.

"Abby, if we're going to take this to the next level, one thing we have to do is try and find copies of the Smith wills, if they even exist. I'll start up in Maine and Jack offered to help, maybe he can go with me."

"Can I do anything?"

"Yes, it's a longshot, but you could try the Portsmouth Historical Society, maybe they have some Smith papers. Then you can try to work in some of the Boston museums. We should try everything we can think of. If there are copies, it might give a lawsuit some real meat!"

"Okay, what else?" she asked.

"We've got to visit a certain woman and give her the news about Marston."

"Oh yes! We'll go tomorrow?"

"You bet," David said.

"Now are we done planning?" asked Abby her words thicker now.

"Yes, I guess so," and he smiled at her.

"Good!" she said and threw herself at David kissing his face from top to bottom.

"Damn!" he said, "I hate a woman who can't hold her liquor!"

*   *   *

The telephone line burned between Portsmouth and New Rochelle. Dan King grimaced as the man at the other end of the line yelled at him. Thomas Sherwood was livid.

"Didn't you think about it before you did it? God, you are stupid King!"

"Yes, I thought about it. But it just happened. She pissed me off!"

King sat in his office where he had stayed late waiting for Sherwood to return the call he had reluctantly made two hours before. The private number in New Rochelle was connected to an answering machine and King had left a message then sweated out the return call, knowing how Sherwood would react.

"Do you know what you've done?" the voice hissed.

"No."

"You've tipped our hand you stupid bastard! Jesus, they had no reason to know for sure that something was going on. Now, you've given them a reason to suspect. What you did was stupid King! You must have shit for brains!"

King was silent and he heard Sherwood breathing at the other end.

"What do we do now?" King asked, reluctant to set the other man off again.

"We do damage control, and maybe we do a little intimidation, I don't know. I do know that I've got to talk with the other side now. I want to make sure that the deal is still on."

"Do you think they'd call it off?" King asked, worried again.

"I don't know. But shit, we've got too much at stake. Hell King, I've got too much at stake to let this fall through!"

"I know," King said quietly.

"Okay, first, damage control. I want you to call the Palmer woman. Apologize to her and tell her you want her back. Do whatever you have to but get her back. Tell her you lost your head and you're sorry! Crawl if you have to, but do it! Do you understand?"

"Yes, I understand. But what if she says no? Jesus, she was pretty angry."

"Then we'll have to try something else. But get her to calm down for Christ's sake!"

"Okay, I'll do it."

"You're damn right you'll do it! Call me and let me know what happens."

"All right, I'll try and call her tomorrow."

"Good, try to be convincing King and don't screw up again!"

"I won't," he started to say good-bye but the phone clicked dead.

In New Rochelle, Sherwood tried to calm his anger. He must have a clear head because this business at Rosemary Point was becoming a problem. It had seemed so very simple and he couldn't figure out how someone had found out about it in the first place.

Now these two meddlers, David Baker and Abigail Palmer were asking too many questions and it could make the buyer uneasy and panic him into backing out of the deal. And that prospect of this scared Sherwood. He was overextended with too much up in the air and the economic and real estate slump had hurt him badly. There were at least four banks threatening to give him problems, ranging from demands for more capital to outright foreclosure. He had to make the sale of the Rosemary Point property to get even and he wasn't about to let anyone or anything get in his way.

He thought carefully about what he would say when he made the next phone call. His thoughts collected, he picked up the telephone and consulting the silver address book on the desk, he dialed the number scribbled on the face page.

A voice answered on the fifth ring. "Hello?"

"It's Sherwood."

"Hello," the voice repeated.

"Can you talk?" Sherwood asked.

"Not over this phone, please. Can't tell if the line is bugged. Can't be too careful, you know."

"Then where?"

"Meet me in the lobby of the Bank of Boston Building at eleven on Monday morning."

Sherwood did not like the imposition of traveling to Boston, but he knew he had little choice in the matter.

"Okay, I'll be there."

"That's good, I'll see you then," and the line clicked dead.

Sherwood replaced the phone on the desk. How had the man sounded? He didn't think he detected anything out of the ordinary, but you could never tell. God he really needed to do this deal and he didn't even want to think about the consequences if he didn't.

*   *   *

It began to rain the next morning and Abby and David lingered over coffee in her kitchen, watching the rain pour down. She shook her head.

"Why did you let me have that second bottle of wine? My head is killing me!"

"Hey, you're over twenty-one!"

"I know, but I feel like I'm eighty-one this morning!"

She looked out the window again at the rain. "Are we still going?"

"Sure. We've got raincoats and an umbrella. Besides, it won't take too long."

"Okay, but let me take an aspirin first."

They drove to Rosemary Point, arriving at the parking lot a short time later. They walked to the house in the downpour and as they entered the house, the volunteer on duty recognized Abby. It was Norma Lord.

"Hi Abby, it's been a while. How are you?"

"Just fine Norma. You?"

"Good. Here for a look around?"

"Yes, you might say so. Norma, this is Dave Baker," she said.

"We've met before," David said.

"Sure, you're the fellow from Pilgrim Village. I remember from earlier in the summer. Did you ever join the Society?"

"Yes, I'm a member in good standing now," he smiled.

"You didn't tell me you knew Abby," Norma said.

"He didn't, then," Abby explained, "we met in July."

"Oh," replied Norma and she noticed the two of them look at each other. She smiled, so that was it.

"We'll just look around."

"Go ahead, a good day to do it I think."

Abby and David went directly to the kitchen that was empty. Abby went to the window and looked outside to the deserted garden.

"No one out there," she said.

They walked up the back stairs to the second floor where they found the woman in one of the front bedrooms, looking out the window.

"Hello," said Abby, quietly.

"Oh hello," the woman replied, not moving from the window. "I saw you come up the walk. I'm so glad to see you both."

"We're happy to be here," David returned.

"I loved days like this when I was a child," the woman mused, "I'd sit with a quilt wrapped about me to stay warm and just watch the rain. It made me happy."

"Are you happy now?" Abby asked.

"Yes, today I am, especially now that you are here," and she turned finally, a radiant smile on her face. Even in the gloomy gray light of day she seemed to be surrounded by an aura of bright beauty and tranquility.

"You look wonderful!" David exclaimed.

"Thank you," she seemed to blush.

"We need to talk with you," Abby said, "a lot has happened since we were here the last time."

Abby told the woman about what had taken place over the last few days and when she finished, she shook her head. "Oh dear, you lost your job because of me. I'm so sorry."

"It's not your fault," Abby said. "In fact getting fired helped us to confirm that something is going on here. Why else would my questions cause such a response?"

"Yes, I see. Of course you are right and that is good. But still, I am sorry for the hurt this has caused you."

"Well, we're going to find a way to solve the mystery and David also has some news!"

"What's that?" the woman asked.

"Well," David explained, "I went to find out if Jonathan Marston left a will and he did. I also found out how he died. Do you know?"

"No, how?" the woman asked anticipating his words. It seemed as if she had waited for years to hear the tale.

"He was murdered, by a someone he had cheated. He was horribly beaten and stabbed."

The woman looked at him and a smile returned to her face. "How did you find this?" she asked.

"In old newspapers at the library in Boston. It seems he was killed with his business partner, a James Weaver. It was a revenge killing."

The woman's eyes brightened. "So justice was done in the end," she said. "It is a proper ending for him. I only wish I had been the one to do it! But it is over and now only one thing remains to be done."

Abby glanced at David, then at the woman. "This place?" she said.

"Yes. I believe that will finally give me peace. I will have done what I came here to do."

"Yes," Abby said, "I feel that too. It will be an end to all of this."

"What will you do now?" asked the woman.

"We have plans," Abby replied.

"What are they?"

"We are going to file a lawsuit against the partnership that owns the property," David said, and he outlined their plans. When he finished, the woman thought for a moment.

"You say there was a covenant on the property when it was conveyed by Roger Sherwood?"

"Yes."

"He was the last Sherwoods who cared about this place," she remembered.

"He had two sons," Abby stated. "The older one died in World War II and Roger Sherwood leased the property to the Rosemary Point Society in his memory."

"There was another son too," David said, "we think that he's the one who is trying to sell the land and house now."

The woman thought again.

"I think that I remember him. The older boy was always happy and liked to play on the grounds. The younger boy was very quiet and not a happy child. I also think that Roger Sherwood's marriage was not a happy one. His family was the last to live in the house and they moved out years ago when they could no longer keep the house in repair."

"Could he have been the Tom who was here the day the men were talking about building houses on the property?" Abby asked.

"I just do not know. It was so long ago that I saw him and he was so young," the woman said.

"Well," David said, "we'll know soon enough if we can force them make another mistake!"

The woman once again regarded the couple. "May I ask you something?" she asked Abby.

"Sure."

"I see you wear no ring, yet, you two are like one. Are you planning to marry?"

Abby laughed and David smiled.

"I've been asked," Abby said, "and I've accepted, but we haven't set a date yet."

The woman continued her smiled growing wider. "Jacob Smith and I were married in this house on Christmas Day. It was the first social event held here and in spite of the war, it was a happy affair. I think it would be a good time for you to do the same."

David looked at Abby. "Why not?" he asked.

"It's fine with me," agreed Abby, "what better place?"

The woman went to them and took their right hands. She joined them together and held them with both her hands. She pressed them tightly, a sign of the love she felt for them. Her grip felt warm and strong.

"I wish you only the best in life. May you always be happy with each other. You are both very special and your lives will be blessed."

The smile formed on her face again and the aura seemed to grow even brighter.

"You will be here for the wedding, won't you?" Abby asked.

"I'm afraid I cannot promise. I'm sorry, but I just do not know."

"Why not?" David asked.

"Because it depends on how successful you are," she smiled and Abby and David could only stare, puzzled by the meaning of her words.

*   *   *

David took Abby to lunch in Portsmouth after visiting Rosemary Point and then they spent the balance of the afternoon shopping and walking through town. The returned to her apartment shortly before 4:00 and David immediately called Jack Pierce and spent fifteen minutes talking about the idea of a lawsuit. Pierce agreed that it was worth a try and told David to go ahead with it.

Now David and Abby were sitting in her living room relaxing and trying to decide what to do for dinner.

"You know, that was quite an experience today," Abby declared.

"Yes, it was. It's still hard to get used to the idea that she's not real, but she sure is quite a woman whoever she is!"

"She is persuasive," Abby agreed. "I'm happy we've set a date though, Mister Baker. At least she got us to do that."

David grinned at her. "Me too. I've been trying to coax you into doing that for a month now. You sure the date is okay with you?"

"Yes, I'm very happy and it's a wonderful thing. Besides, I'm getting a great guy, what could be bad about that?"

David smiled again and kissed her.

They broke apart and turned as the telephone rang. Abby got up from the couch, answering.

"Abby?"

"Yes?" she said recognizing the voice.

"It's Dan King."

She was surprised and glanced at David who questioned her with a silent "who is it?"

"Yes?" she said tentatively and David watched her, puzzled.

"Who is it?" he whispered again.

Abby silently mouthed the words, "Dan King".

David was surprised and watched her intently.

"Abby, I called to apologize," King explained.

She remained silent.

"Listen Abby, I'm sorry about what happened. I lost my head and I want you to come back. We need you."

"Is that so?" she said as David motioned to her.

"What's he saying?" he whispered to her.

Abby covered the mouthpiece. "He's apologizing and he wants me back," she said in a low voice.

David shook his head no and Abby nodded.

"How about it Abby?" King said, "will you come back?"

"I hear you Mister King," her voice was cold.

"Will you accept my apology? Please Abby, I want you back."

She looked at David, rolling her eyes. "Why the change of mind, Mister King?"

"I was rash Abby, God I lost my head and I'm really sorry. Don't make me beg. Please I want you to come back to work."

David moved nearer to Abby, trying to hear what King was saying. Abby again covered the mouthpiece.

"He's falling all over himself," she said covering the mouthpiece.

"Don't give in," David said quietly.

"I won't," she shook her head.

"How about it Abby, will you come back?" King pleaded.

Abby took a deep breath. "Mister King, please do not call me again. I have no desire to speak with you."

"Oh come on Abby. Please come back." King sounded desperate.

"Furthermore, Mister King, I will not accept your apology and I don't want to work for anyone like you!"

"Oh God, I apologized, Abby. Please come back!"

"Sir, I have no respect for you and I politely suggest that you go to hell!"

"Abby…" but she cut him off as she slammed down the phone.

Abby started to laugh. "That was kind of fun. I think I like being a bitch!"

"Well you convinced me," David said.

"What do you suppose brought about the change of heart?" Abby asked.

"He must have talked with someone," David replied.

"Sherwood?"

"Probably."

"But why the change?" Abby said, "why so quick?"

"He probably realized what a mistake he made and wanted to keep the damage to a minimum. I think that make's sense."

"Yeah, I guess you're right. Did I do good?" she asked.

"You did just fine Abby. That will keep them guessing and don't give in if he calls again."

"I won't," she said.

"I think we're making progress," David said. "They're nervous and I think the lawsuit may make them do something, even if we don't stand a chance."

"I hope you're right," Abby replied. "Now, where do you want to take me for dinner?"

CHAPTER TWENTY-ONE

David visited Jack Pierce early the following Monday morning and he again outlined his tentative plans for the lawsuit over the covenant.

"I've given it some thought since we talked on Saturday," Pierce said, "I think it's a good plan. In fact, it's damn good thinking. You're beginning to show some real promise Baker! I still think that looking for the Smith wills is a waste of time though, but since I am of the school of forlorn hope, I will make good on my promise of the other day and go to Maine with you."

"That's great! Thanks for the help."

"How are you going to pursue the lawsuit angle?" Pierce asked.

"Well, I'm going to talk with Jim Phillips as soon as I leave here. Since we'll have to file the suit in Maine I guess we're going to need a Maine attorney. I hope that Jim can give me some advice and the name of someone who's a member of the Maine Bar."

"That sounds good. Go with it and let me know if you need help. We can go to Maine tomorrow if you like. I'll call the Maine Maritime Museum to see if they have any material and you check with the Maine Historical Society. Maybe you can schedule a meeting with a lawyer while we're up there."

"Yeah okay, I'll try. I'll get back to you later."

"Fine," Pierce said and went back to his work as David turned to leave.

David returned to his office and called Jim Phillips. The Boston lawyer came on the line and they exchanged pleasantries.

"Remember the problem I was talking to you about three weeks ago?" David asked.

"You mean that partnership thing?" Phillips replied.

"Yeah."

"Sure I remember. Got any more information?"

"Yes, we've got a post office box number for an address."

"Shit Dave, that's not much help."

"Yeah, I know, but we also know who picks up the mail from the mail box."

"That's different," said Phillips, suddenly interested.

David told him what had happened to Abby.

"Sounds like you've made them nervous," Phillips commented.

"I think so, but now I want to turn up the heat. I want to file a suit over breaking the covenant."

"You don't have much of a case," advised Phillips, "nothing's happened yet. They haven't moved to sell the property."

"Yeah, I know, but I want to add some pressure, see what happens. We may even find out something about Springbrook. I know it's only a nuisance suit, but I want to go ahead."

Phillips thought, giving the plan a chance to sink in. "You know Dave, it might work, but you'll need an attorney from Maine."

"That's why I'm calling, I need a Maine lawyer."

"Okay, I know your man. He's a terrific litigator, went to B.C. Law School with me. His name is Edward Joseph Williams but everyone calls him Ted, just like the ballplayer. We called him the shark, like they leave him alone out of professional courtesy."

David laughed.

"He's really good," continued Phillips, "I'll call him and tell him to expect your call. One last thing. You have any idea of what you're getting into?"

"I think I have a pretty good idea," David said, sounding more confident than he felt.

"Something like this could get messy," Phillips warned. "A lot of name calling, stuff like that. You ready for that?"

"I think so," David said.

"Well okay, good luck Dave. Call me if I can help."

Phillips gave him Ted Williams' telephone number and hung up. David sat in his office, starring out the window at the Village. It was tranquil here he thought. His life was tranquil too and did he really know what he was getting into? Yes, he thought so, but in any event, he felt he had little choice. He and Abby had promised the woman they would help her and they had to see it through. The battle was beginning and he felt the call to arms. He wondered if his ancestors had the same feelings before the crucial moments in their lives.

He waited an hour before calling Williams who was busy with a client. But David spoke with his assistant and the woman recognized his name, Phillips making good on his promise to call ahead. Mr. Williams had an opening on Wednesday at ten o'clock, would that be okay? David told her it would and thanked her, hanging up.

He phoned Pierce to let him know their plans for the next two days.

*   *   *

Thomas Sherwood got off the nine o'clock New York to Boston shuttle and went into the terminal at Logan Airport. He made his way down the concourse into the main terminal building and he went out to get a cab. A taxi pulled up a moment later and Sherwood entered the car.

"Bank of Boston Building." The cabby nodded and pulled out into the airport traffic.

Boston traffic was heavy but the cab driver wheeled the cab expertly through back streets to avoid the jams on the major roads.

In the backseat Sherwood reflected on his life as he looked at his watch and saw that he had plenty of time before his meeting.

God how he hated Rosemary Point. To him it only epitomized the decline in the fortunes of the Sherwood family. He had lived in the house until he was eight but had never liked it, wishing he were some-place else. It always seemed to him that his father only had time for the old place and never for him. His father always was doing something to keep the place going and he seldom had time for his youngest son.

This made Sherwood think of his older brother, Bill. Forty-five years later it was difficult for him to remember him. Bill had loved Rosemary Point and was devastated when the depression had forced the family to move from the house. Bill had always helped his father, was always will-ing to lend a hand to repair or maintain some part of the old house and Sherwood knew that he had not felt his brother's death at all. It proba-bly should have bothered him, but it didn't. His father's actions to place the house with the Rosemary Point Society had angered him and Sherwood was frustrated by the charade of the family trying to behave like the well to do Sherwood family when most of the family fortune had been lost years before. It was this indignity that rankled him the most.

The need for money and success had made him leave Maine and go to New York after college. While he felt some satisfaction in the money he made over the years, he now feared that his whole well-planned path to success was off track. He was a victim of the economic cycle and a few mistakes.

He thought back to his last days in Maine. His father had not protested his leaving and in fact, Sherwood thought that the man was glad to see him go, his presence perhaps a reminder of the favored son who had died on Iwo Jima.

His father was an enigma and it became apparent to him early in life that his father and mother really wanted nothing to do with each other. He never could figure out why they had stayed together. Sherwood paused to think. It was his father's relationship with that other woman that really angered him. There was no attempt to hide the fact that Roger Sherwood and the Watrous woman were interested in each other. All through high school, he had to bear the brunt of schoolmate taunts about his father's open affair with the woman. In the end he had hated his father for it and now he needed to save his fragile real estate portfolio. To do that he needed to sell Rosemary Point. To Tom Sherwood, it was a just end for the property because this final family asset would rescue him from his all his problems. At the same time he would remove the hated Rosemary Point from its undeserved position of reverence.

The cab jumped over a pothole and it shook him back to the problem of the moment. He was worried about the meeting and the reaction he would get after relating what Dan King had done. While King's actions were bad enough, Sherwood didn't think it would be fatal to the deal. But he prepared himself for the inevitable tongue lashing that he knew was coming his way.

The cab arrived at the Bank of Boston Building at twenty to eleven. Sherwood got out and paid the driver. He got out and walked around the block twice to kill time before he went into the lobby of the building. He strolled to the center bank of elevators and leaned against the wall and checked his watch another time. It was five to eleven.

Tom Sherwood watched the faces of the people who went by, coming and going, to and from the elevator banks and he searched the crowd expectantly, looking for the agent for Rosemary Point's real buyer.

Ten minutes passed and the man had not arrived. Nervously, Sherwood examined his watch once more. Where was the man?

Then he was startled as a voice spoke to him from his left. "Sherwood?"

Sherwood turned quickly and recognized Nicholas Dominic. "Nick, you surprised me!"

"Tough, I had to make sure you weren't followed."

Sherwood looked around, eyes darting, worried. "And?"

"I don't think so. Let's walk."

He led Sherwood out to the street and they were soon lost in the crowd.

"What's the problem?" Dominic asked as they walked along Federal Street.

Sherwood told him what Dan King had done. "I got really pissed at him and told him he really screwed up!" he said, finishing the story.

Dominic showed no emotion. "That was stupid of him," he said slowly. "The dumb bastard has given them a reason to suspect something!"

"Yes, I gave him hell for that!" Sherwood said defensively.

"Nothing else better happen. You know Sherwood, my people won't put up with anymore screw-ups. Remember, this deal's not done yet, we can still back out."

"I know, I know. Nothing more will happen, I promise you."

"It better not. You should do something about these two snoops! Find some way to make them mind their own business. You know?"

"Yeah Nick, I'll keep an eye on them. They won't be a problem."

"Make sure you do that. You know, Sherwood, if this makes us look bad, it won't be too nice for you."

There was a threatening coldness to his voice and Sherwood felt the heat from the man's eyes.

"Heed the warning Sherwood. I think this ends our conversation."

Dominic nodded and turned, walking in the other direction.

Sherwood stopped and watched him go. Surprisingly, Dominic hadn't been that angry and this made him feel better, at least for the moment. However, he that was something to think about.

God he needed the sale to survive and once again he vowed to himself that he would not allow anything to get in his way.

*   *   *

David and Jack Pierce enjoyed the drive north into Maine the next day. It was a cool clear early fall morning and David and Pierce took Route 128 around Boston to avoid construction on the Mystic River Bridge. Once they were past the busy rush hour traffic on the heavily traveled road the drive actually became pleasant since the tourist season was over.

They entered Maine and they noticed that some of the trees were beginning to turn, even though it was only the middle of September. Pierce had called the Maine Maritime Museum the day before and determined that the facility did indeed have some papers from the post Revolutionary period that might include material on the Smiths. Doing his part, David had called the Maine Historical Society in Portland and he had talked with the executive director, who told him there might be some things of interest, although there was no detailed catalog of the material.

"What do you think?" David asked, as Pierce exited the Maine Turnpike onto I-295 that went through Portland.

"It's a longshot Dave, but it's worth trying. But shit, I'm just glad to get out of the office for a while. I don't know if we'll find anything but we'll try. Probably the most important thing we're doing is the meeting with the lawyer tomorrow."

"I'll be glad to get things moving," agreed David.

"You know this is going to cost some money?" Pierce asked.

"Yeah, I know. I've got some money saved and I'm going to get something from my mother's estate, so I don't think it's a problem."

Pierce laughed. "So it's family money helping to protect old family assets? There's a certain symmetry to that!"

"Yeah, I guess that's right, it does seem like the right thing."

Pierce was silent a moment, thinking. "I know I've told you this before, but I think you're doing the right thing and I'm with you one hundred percent."

"Thanks Jack, I can use all the help I can get," David said looking out the window at Portland as they drove by. "How much farther? I've never been to Bath before."

"Forty five minutes or so."

Pierce's estimate proved close to the truth and they pulled off of Route One by Bath Iron Works, making a right turn on Washington Street and drove south. Minutes later they drove into the parking lot of the museum. David noted that the new museum building fit in nicely with the older buildings of what had once been a shipyard.

After parking the car they entered the museum. At the front desk Pierce asked to see the executive director, a fellow by the name of Carl Thomas. He had been a student when Jack Pierce had been a professor at Yale and a few moments later a smiling young looking man dressed in chinos and a sweater came up to them.

"Jack!" the man greeted them, "God, it's good to see you!"

"Same here Carl," Pierce said to him, "say hello to Dave Baker. He's development director at the Village."

"Nice to meet you," Thomas said, then turned to Pierce. "Jack, you mentioned you were looking for information on the Smiths from Kittery. I went through our material this morning and I'm afraid there isn't much, but I've laid out what we have on one of the tables in the workroom."

"Well, we'll take a look. Which way?"

Carl Thomas gestured and led David and Pierce to the workroom.

"I'll leave you to your work," Thomas as he left. "I'll check back later."

They spent a half-hour going through the material, which proved to be mostly history material printed in the nineteenth century about the Smiths and their seafaring exploits. The only original documents were a Kittery merchant's ledger detailing shipments to Europe and a letter from Jacob Smith to a ship's chandler in Portsmouth discussing the amount of manila line necessary to replace all the *Eagle's* running rigging.

"Well?" said David, "it seems you were right. There's nothing here that will help us."

"Yeah, but you never know. We've got to try everything now, no stone unturned and all that crap."

Pierce looked at his watch. "It's nearly eleven. How about we check this place out and take Carl to lunch?"

"That's fine with me and then we'll head for Portland after lunch."

Pierce nodded in agreement and they went to find Carl Thomas.

*   *   *

The two men from Pilgrim Village went through the iron gates to the right of the Wadsworth Longfellow house on Congress Street, in Portland. The brick walk led to the library of the Maine Historical Society that was located behind the house.

They entered the building and asked to see Molly Graham, the Executive Director. The woman seated at the hallway table pointed to the stairs to the right. "Upstairs," she said.

"Thanks," David responded and he led Pierce up the stairs where another woman, sitting at a desk on the left, looked at them.

"Can I help you?" she asked.

"Yes," said David, "is Molly in?"

"She is. Is she expecting you?"

David started to speak, but he was interrupted by a tall, large boned woman about forty, who came out a door behind the seated woman.

"Dave! How are you?" she said.

David knew Molly Graham from meetings of the Organization of New England Museums. She was a knowledgeable historian, he knew and she was also a party animal who enjoyed having a good time. David remembered enjoying her company at several conferences.

"Hiya Molly," he said. "How are you?"

"Great."

"Molly, meet Jack Pierce, your counterpart at Pilgrim Village."

They shook hands. "I know you by reputation, Mr. Pierce. I've also heard you speak, you're great!"

"Ah, damned by faint praise," he said. "By the way, the name's Jack and I hope I can call you Molly?"

"Yes sure, thanks, I'd like that." She turned to David. "You said on the phone you wanted to look at our Smith material?"

"Yes."

"I'll take you down to the basement to Ellen Chase, our curator. She can help you, but I've got to warn you, we're not sure what we have. As a matter of fact, we're in the middle of a two-year project to catalog our whole collection. So I can't promise anything."

"We'll muddle through," Pierce said.

Molly Graham led them down to the basement of the building. Ellen Chase proved to be very helpful, pulling several packets of papers from steel filing cabinets and with her help, they began to go through the documents.

Among the material in the collection was a logbook belonging to James Steele that covered the Penobscot expedition. It was an interesting document, but not helpful with the immediate problem. The other material proved not to be useful either.

"Too bad," said David leaning back in his chair.

"Well, we had to try," Pierce said.

"Wait a minute!" exclaimed Ellen Chase, "there is one more thing we can try."

"What's that?" asked David.

"Our map collection. I think we have the original survey of Rosemary Point. That may not be what you're looking for, but you may find it a help."

"Sure," said Pierce, "let's have a look!"

Ellen Chase led them back up to the second floor where she searched through another steel filing cabinet.

"Here it is," she said, taking a batch of old survey maps from the drawer. She led David and Pierce to a worktable in the next room where she spread the maps out flat.

"These are the original survey maps. I think they date from 1759."

"Hey that's neat!" David exclaimed.

They examined the maps. One of the smaller detail plats was of Rosemary Point and it was titled "Land of John Rosemary".

"That's interesting!" David said, "I thought it was named after a woman."

"John Rosemary was an early settler of that area," Ellen Chase explained.

"Can we get a copy of the map?" Pierce asked.

"Sure, we can have photos made, but it'll take a week or so."

Jack Pierce looked at David nodding and David said, "Yes please do it. Do I pay you now or later?"

"Now is fine, fifteen dollars should cover it."

David took out his checkbook and wrote a check for the copy.

"Well, I guess that's it," Pierce said, finishing with the pile of maps.

"Sorry we didn't have more," Ellen Chase said. "But it's been nice to meet you Mr. Pierce. I've read your books and I like them very much. I'm glad I had the chance to meet you."

"You've been great," Pierce said.

Ellen walked them to Molly Graham's office. "Find anything?" she asked.

"Not what we were looking for, but we did find a great map that may be useful. Thanks for your help," David said.

"You're more than welcome. It's good to see you Dave."

"Same here Molly," David replied.

"And Jack, it was a pleasure meeting you," Molly said.

"Pierce smiled. "Come down and see us sometime."

"I will," Molly said and walked them to the door.

The two men left the building and walked back to their parked car. They drove over to the Holiday Inn on Spring Street and checked in.

"I'll take you on a historical tour of Portland," Pierce offered, as they went to their rooms.

"Fine with me," replied David, "but I could use a beer. You can take this history business too far, you know?"

"Yes," Pierce said, "it will be a tour limited by the time of day and it may include several stops at historic bars," he laughed.

"Ah, that's history the way I like it!" David said.

*   *   *

David and Pierce met for breakfast in the hotel restaurant the next morning and as they ate, they talked about the upcoming meeting with Ted Williams.

"Any suggestions about what to say to this guy?" asked David.

"No. Let's just give him the facts and let him tell us what to do."

"I know we don't have a good case," David lamented.

"Yeah, but there's more to this than just the lawsuit. Case or no case, we're trying to make something happen. So we tell Mr. Williams exactly what we want to do and if he won't do it, we'll find another attorney."

David nodded in agreement.

Ted Williams's law firm had offices in a bank building down the street from the Holiday Inn. The law firm was one of the biggest in Maine and David and Pierce were in the reception area at the stroke of ten. They asked the receptionist for Mr. Williams and she tapped a number on the telephone console. She spoke with someone at the other end and when she finished she looked up at them.

"Please have a seat. Mr. Williams's assistant will be out for you in a moment."

"Thanks," Pierce said.

They sat, waiting for several minutes. Then a woman dressed in a prim dark blue suit came out from a hallway.

"Mr. Baker? Mr. Pierce?" she greeted them.

"Yes," David said.

"I'm Dianne Timothy, Mr. Williams assistant. Please come with me."

She led them through another hallway down a corridor and they entered a two-office suite. She ushered them into the inner office that looked out the eighth floor over the Portland skyline.

Ted Williams was not what David Baker had expected after the build up that Jim Phillips had given him. He was short, maybe five five and he wore rumpled blue suit pants with an equally wrinkled suit jacket thrown on a chair in the corner. His tie was loose and it appeared that his hair had been styled by an eggbeater. He stood, greeting his visitors.

"Hi, I'm Ted Williams," he said, his voice heavy with a Brooklyn accent.

What had he gotten into David wondered.

They shook hands with Williams and introduced themselves. Dianne Timothy left, closing the door behind her and Williams motioned for them to sit.

"How can I help you?" he asked. "Jim Phillips mentioned a few details, but I need the whole picture." The word "picture" came out sounding "pitcher", David noted.

"Jim Phillips gave you a terrific recommendation," David said.

"Jim Phillips never did have any sense," Williams laughed, "how can I help you?"

David told Williams the story of Rosemary Point, omitting only the part about the woman at the house.

"That's quite a story!" Williams said after David finished.

"I've got some information on Thomas Sherwood," offered Pierce. He handed the attorney a copy of the written report from Tony Nappia.

Williams quickly scanned the document. "Pretty professional job," he said. "Where did you get it?"

"I know a few people," Pierce explained.

Williams looked at him a moment longer finding something in Pierce's eyes that interested him. He didn't know why, but this was a man he did not wish to confront. He shook the report.

"This is the kind of scum I like to take on. I kind of enjoy it. I must tell you though, the case is pretty thin."

"I know that," David replied, "we want to turn up the heat on these guys and see what happens."

"I understand what you want," explained Williams, "but I always believe in being up front with a client. You don't have a prayer of getting anywhere with this."

"I always thought that depended on how good a lawyer you had," said David.

Williams sized up David Baker, his estimation and respect for him growing. Both of these men had hidden strengths.

"Okay that's fair. In this case you are dealing with the best, so maybe you do have a chance. I'll see what I can do."

"How do we proceed? What happens next?" Pierce asked.

Williams tried to gauge this man and could not quite find what unsettled him. An academic by reputation, there was something more to him he could not measure.

"I'll write up the petition to the court detailing your complaint against the Springbrook Partnership. Since the case is circumstantial, I'll embellish it to make it look like we've got more than we have. Then we go to court and see what happens. To start we send a copy of the petition to the address for the partnership. You also said you know someone who's involved?" Williams asked.

"Yes," David said, "a guy named King, in Portsmouth."

"Okay then, we'll serve him in person. That might be a little more theatrical and that will help stir the pot which is what you're looking to do, right?"

"Yeah, sounds good," Pierce said.

"Who's going to serve King?" asked David.

"I'll get a process server," Williams replied.

"I know someone who would like to do it for you," David smiled.

"Who?" Williams asked.

"My friend, Abby Palmer. Dan King just fired her."

"Hey, I like your thinking, Dave! That should add to the drama also. You sure you never studied law?"

Pierce and David laughed. They decided they liked this little man from Brooklyn. Even though they had a weak case, he had inspired an optimistic confidence. If the case was thrown out they would have at least made a good try.

"Once we get the court to rule on our petition, we'll play it by ear. I think I can use this question about the Smith wills as another ploy to draw this out."

"Okay," replied David.

"I think I've got what I need," Williams said, looking at the photocopies David had given him. Then he stopped for a minute.

"There is one more thing. If there really were other Smith wills, it could be the difference between a relatively weak case and a decisively strong one. I suggest you keep looking for the elusive documents."

"Okay," agreed David.

"When will the petition be ready?" Pierce asked.

"Today's Wednesday," Williams thought for a moment, "I'll have the documents ready by Friday. We can go to court on Monday."

He looked at David. "I'll get copies to you on Friday also. Your friend can serve Mr. King on Monday too, at the same time we go to court."

"That sounds okay," David said.

"Yeah," Pierce agreed, "I'd like to be there to see it."

"The first appearance won't be anything special Jack. We only get the court to grant us the go ahead. The fireworks will come later when we have to go up against the partnership's attorney."

"Yeah, I know," Pierce said, "but, I want to see this thing get started."

"I understand. Anymore questions from you gentlemen?"

Both men shook their heads no.

"Fine," William said, "we'll file in Maine Superior Civil Court, in Biddeford. I'll be in touch to schedule the time and I will see you on Monday!"

"One last thing," David asked, "what about your fee?"

"Ah yes. Almost forgot. I'd like a one thousand-dollar retainer up front. I bill at one hundred fifty dollars an hour, but we'll see where this leads us. I have a weakness for cases that are different. That okay with you?"

"Sure, seems fair," David said, removing his checkbook from his jacket pocket. He wrote out a check for one thousand dollars and handed it to Williams.

"Thank you," the attorney said taking the check. "You know, the more I think about this, we may have a chance at that."

Jack Pierce and David shook hands with the diminutive attorney and left the office going down the hallway to the elevator bank. David pushed the down button and the elevator door opened. The two men entered and Pierce spoke first.

"Well, he certainly is something, isn't he?"

"Yes," David agreed.

"You know," Jack Pierce said, "I think you got a great recommendation. I'm going to have to remember to thank Jim Phillips for you."

"Yeah, I'll do that myself."

"Dave?" Pierce asked.

"Yeah?"

"I just want to make sure that you know what you're getting into. You know this could be like a battle and you've got to be ready for it."

"Yeah, I understand that Jack. I think I'm ready for it. If I've learned anything over the last few months it's that the Baker men and women have faced some pretty scary things over time including at least three wars. They have managed to get through things and now maybe it's my turn. I guess I owe them something."

Pierce put his hand on David's shoulder. "That, my friend, is perhaps one of the most eloquent things I have heard in a long time and you're right on target."

"Thanks, Jack. I think it's important."

The elevator reached the lobby and they walked out to the street.

"You know," said David, "it's not quite lunchtime yet, but, I think we owe ourselves a beer!"

"Yes," agreed Pierce, "after all, we are on vacation."

*   *   *

David and Jack Pierce returned to Pilgrim Village later that afternoon and went to their offices. They now planned to take time off the following week so they could attend the court hearing and, to do that, they needed to deal with the pile of work on their desks.

David sat at his desk reviewing a pile of paper and thinking of what had happened over the last past days. All at once he remembered that he had not spoken to his brother and sister since calling to tell then that he and Abby had set a wedding date. He tapped Sue's number on the telephone and she answered almost immediately.

"Sue, it's Dave."

"Hey! How are you?"

"Good. I'm sorry you missed the party at the Palmers, but I sure hope that you can make it for the wedding at Christmas."

"Yes Dave, we'll be there. God, I am so happy for you and I can't wait to meet Abby. Oh, Dave, I'm so happy for you both!"

"I think you'll like her. I hope that Jerry can come too and Beth."

"We'll all be there," Sue said. "I think you can count on it."

"That's great, and I've got more news."

"What?" Sue asked.

David brought her up to date on everything that had happened and Sue listened engrossed by what he told her.

At the other end of the second floor of the museum, Jack Pierce returned a phone call. The call went to the headquarters of the New York Police Department Detective Squad in lower Manhattan. Tony Nappia came on the line.

"Nappia speaking."

"Tony, it's Jack."

"Hiya, you been away?"

"Just for a couple of days. What's up?"

"I ran those other two guys for you and I think they're clean. They've been mixed up with your man, Sherwood, for about five years now but I don't think that any of his grease has rubbed off on them yet. They may be doing something, but it's not illegal, at least not yet."

"They've both clean then?"

"Yeah, mostly, but this guy King does have about fifteen outstanding parking tickets from Boston," Nappia laughed.

"Tony you did your usual good job. Anything else?" Pierce asked.

"No, not that I can think of. But you can tell me one thing though?"

"Sure what?"

"What's going on Jack? You need any help?"

"No, I don't think so," Pierce said, then had another thought. "Yeah maybe I do. Any way you can check and see if this guy, Sherwood has been to Boston lately?"

"Yeah, I can try."

"Okay, try it, and thanks again Tony."

"Anytime, my friend." They said good-bye and both hung up the phone.

Pierce stared out the window, thinking. He had that old feeling, the one he hadn't had in a very long time. Something was going to happen and he didn't think it would be good.

CHAPTER TWENTY-TWO

The Saturday night engagement party at the Palmer house had come as a complete surprise to David and Abby. Jan Palmer was overjoyed when Abby had told her about the plans for a Christmas wedding and she had planned the surprise party in record time.

David and Abby had arrived at the Palmer house expecting to have a quiet celebration dinner with Abby's parents. Instead, they found a house full of people, all intent on helping the couple celebrate. Abby's sister, Charity, and her husband, Scott, were there as was her brother, Tom, and his wife Martha who had driven up from New York to attend. Jack and Jennifer Pierce had come and Abby's grandmother, Susan Taylor, had brought Betsey Watrous with her. A host of other friends and relatives crowded the house and David and Abby were overwhelmed and touched by the many good wishes that were extended to them.

The fact that Abby had finally found happiness brought hugs and kisses from her older sister. "Well, Ab, you've done it! I think he's terrific!"

"Thanks Charity, I think it's been worth the wait," she said holding David's arm tightly.

"You know you've got the nicest lady in the world, Dave?"

"I do indeed," he agreed, "she's something special."

Abby's brother, Tom, came over to them. "Abby, looks like this agrees with you. It'll be a great Christmas and we'll be here with the kids. It will be fun just being together as a family again."

Abby kissed her brother. "Thanks Tom. It's so good to see you and I'm glad you came." She turned to introduce David. "Tom, this is Dave Baker. Dave, this is my brother, Tom."

Her brother looked at David and extended his hand. "Dave, I'm happy to meet you. From the looks of my little sister you do good things for her. Take care of her."

"I intend to," David replied shaking the extended hand.

Tom Palmer smiled at him. "Then welcome, welcome to the family Dave. I, for one, am glad to have you as a member."

Charity went to David and gave him a hug. "That's my welcome Dave. I'm thrilled to have another brother."

David grinned, touched by the welcome from Abby's siblings. "Thanks," he said, "it's nice to be accepted into the family. I wish my brother and sister could have come. I think you will like them."

Charity spoke. "Mom did invite them for the party, but it was just too short notice for them. I'm looking forward to meeting them in December. They'll be at the wedding?"

"I think so," David said.

"Good, then we'll meet them then."

"Come on, I'll buy you both a drink," Tom Palmer suggested.

Abby and David followed him into the kitchen where Abby's parents were holding court.

"Hi you two," her Mother gushed, "I'm just so happy for both of you!"

"Thanks for the party, Mom. This is really great!"

Bob Palmer extended his hand to David. "Congratulations Dave. I couldn't be happier for you two. In fact I'm delighted!"

"Thanks Bob, I'm kind of happy myself," David smiled.

The evening went by fast with excellent food, drink and good company combining for a great time. It was a whirlwind for Abby and David who tried to spend a moment with each guest.

As she spoke to Betsey Watrous, Abby was captivated by the sparkle in the older woman's eyes. "Abby, I'm so happy for you!" she said.

"Thank you Betsey, you look wonderful tonight. You have a look in your eye, like you're a teenager again!"

"Well it must be because of you Abby. I guess it's happiness and anticipation. Your grandmother has told me about what you and Dave are doing."

"The wedding?" Abby asked.

"No silly, the lawsuit! You're going to save Rosemary Point."

"Well, we're going to try," Abby said remembering Betsey's interest in the house.

"No, you'll do it," Betsey said, a wry smile on her face. "You'll do it for her."

"Who?" Abby asked.

"You know," Betsey smiled, "Abigail, that's who!"

Abby stared at the old woman, sensing that she knew something more than she had let on. She grinned at Betsy Watrous. "What do you mean?"

"Oh I think you know," Betsey said. "You know, no one has ever seen her, but she's there isn't she?"

Before Abby could reply and find out what Betsey knew, the older woman grabbed Abby's hand. "We'll talk later dear, you are very special, I feel it. So is your young man and I think you will be very happy together."

Abby did not know what to say and the old woman winked at her, then turned to find some food. She knew, Abby thought, but how did she know?

Later as the guests began to slowly leave Abby and David found themselves seated in the Palmer living room, talking with Jack and Jennifer Pierce.

"Well," said Jack Pierce, "are you ready for Monday?"

"Yup," David replied.

"Me too," Abby said, "I can't wait to see the look on Dan King's face when I go see him. I think I'm going to enjoy this. I only hope I do it right!"

"You'll do fine," David said and he looked at Pierce, "you staying over or going back home?"

"We're staying at the Sheraton. We're going to court on Monday with you, remember?"

"I know that. I was just curious whether you were going home or not. You two have plans for tomorrow?"

"No," said Jennifer Pierce.

"Well, yes we do," contradicted her husband, "I rather hoped that you and Abby would give us a guided tour of Rosemary Point."

Abby looked at David and they both smiled.

"I think we'd like that," she replied, speaking for them both.

"Great!" said Pierce, "pick us up that the hotel at eleven thirty tomorrow and we'll go from there."

Abby and David nodded, agreeing to the plan.

Abby looked around for Betsey Watrous but she had gone. Abby really wanted to talk to the woman and see what she knew about the mysterious woman at Rosemary Point. Had Betsey seen her too? She would have to find out.

The party finally ended after one with Abby's brother and sister the last remaining guests. Abby joined them as they talked with their parents.

"Mom," Charity said as she put her arm around Abby, "I'm really happy for my sister."

"Yes, I know. She's waited a long time, but I think it was worth it!"

Abby blushed. "Hey, quit picking on me!"

"I'm not picking on you. It's just that I think this is pretty neat," Charity protested.

Abby looked at her. "Will you be my maid of honor?"

"Sure, you know I will!" Charity said with tears in her eyes.

Tom Palmer added his thoughts. "You know, Dad, we've got to do something about these sentimental women!"

"Tom, I've put up with it for forty four years and haven't been able to change a thing. Don't expect to in the future either!"

The Palmer family laughed. It had been a great party.

*   *   *

The day was cool and crisp and it was clear that fall was coming. The late morning sun had some warmth to it but only enough to take the edge off the coolness and the foliage at Rosemary Point was alive with color, as the two couples walked the grounds. David and Abby took the Pierces to the ocean side of the property where the sea was alive this morning, shinning in the sunlight with small waves breaking on the rocks.

"It's so beautiful!" Jennifer Pierce said, clearly awed by the sight.

"Yes, it is," agreed Abby. "You know, I've been coming here for almost twenty years since I was a kid, and I never tire of this view."

They walked back to the house where David paid for the Pierces and they explored the restored residence. After finishing the tour, they went outside.

"I can see why this is such a special place," Jack Pierce said quietly.

"Yes, can you imagine living here?" Jennifer said.

"Pretty neat place, isn't it?" Abby added.

"Come on," David directed, "let's go down to the salt marsh. It's one of the few undisturbed natural waterfront areas left in the northeast."

They went down the brick path from the house to the parking lot and then followed the path leading to the boardwalk.

"We didn't see this woman you've spoken about," Pierce said.

"I know," replied Abby, "I feel she's here though. Maybe she won't show herself because you're not related to her."

"Too bad," mused Pierce, "I'd like to meet this apparition."

They walked down the boardwalk, enjoying the view.

"Truly an amazing place," Pierce declared.

"It's very special," his wife added.

They lingered in the mid day sun, savoring the experience, each of them deep in thought. Without speaking, they went back to the parking lot.

They got into David's car with David and Pierce in the front seats and Abby and Jennifer in back. As David turned the ignition key, Jack Pierce looked at his friend.

"You know," he said slowly, "a place like this is worth fighting for."

David nodded with a grin on his face. "Yes it sure is."

*   *   *

They met Ted Williams outside the Maine Superior Court, Civil Division, in Biddeford, Maine. He recognized David and Jack Pierce and greeted them. "What's this, a rooting section?"

"Yeah, something like that," David said, shaking hands with the attorney, "are we ready?"

"Should be. I had the petition delivered by courier on Friday. Here," he said as he opened his briefcase and handed a manila envelope to David, "this is the copy of the petition that needs to be delivered by hand. The other one went out by certified mail this morning."

David took the envelope and gave it to Abby.

"This your friend?" Williams asked.

"Yes, Abby, this is Ted Williams," David said and he also introduced the attorney to Jennifer Pierce.

"Okay, nice to meet you both. Shall we go inside?" the lawyer suggested.

They entered the building and Williams led them to the office of the Clerk of Court. Williams conversed with the clerk for a moment, gesturing with his hands then finally he shook the man's hand and returned to the group.

"We've got a break. Judge Andrew Carrier is going to hear the case and I know him. He's the type of judge who'll give you the benefit of the doubt so he'll give us a fair hearing. But he wants to see me in his chambers first."

"Should we stay here?" Jack Pierce asked.

"Sure, just let me get this first step out of the way. There will be plenty of things for you to see later."

"Fine, we'll wait for you to come back," David said.

Williams went down the hallway and stopped in front of a door. He knocked at the door and pausing for a second, he entered, disappearing from view.

The others returned to the front of the building and waited outside.

"What do you think?" Abby asked, fingering the envelope she held.

"I don't know what to expect," David said, "we'll see."

They waited fifteen minutes before the attorney found them. "There you are!" he said.

"What happened?" Pierce asked.

"A good beginning I think. Judge Carrier approved the petition and granted us a preliminary hearing on Friday at ten. That should be enough time for the other side to respond. Then we'll see what happens."

"Is this good?" asked David.

"Yeah sure, it's a good start I guess. We'll just have to wait and see. In the meantime, get to work. You've got to serve a man with papers! And, you've got to try and find the wills, if they exist."

"Okay," said David, "I'm glad to get things moving."

Williams saw the look of concern on his face. "Don't worry Dave. You've got the best litigator in the State of Maine on your side. We'll make out just fine, so I'll see you on Friday and it was nice to meet you ladies."

Williams left, going to his car.

"Well," said Abby, "that was interesting."

"Yeah, but kind of an anticlimax," Pierce said, "I guess I was expecting something more."

"I didn't know what to expect," said his wife.

"I am a little disappointed," David admitted, "but I'm excited that we've started the process."

The other three looked at him closely. His face was set, serious and determined. Pierce had never before seen his friend look this way. David Baker had some hidden strengths he hadn't shown and Pierce thought he would remember that.

*   *   *

David and Abby dropped the Pierces back at the Sheraton in Portsmouth and then drove directly to the offices of Crown and King where David braked the car to a stop in the parking lot.

"You sure you don't want me to go in with you?" he asked.

"No," Abby said, "we've already talked about this several times. I want to do this alone. Don't worry, I'll be okay. This is actually going to be fun."

"All right, but if you're not back in ten minutes, I'm going in."

"Just like the Marines, huh?" Abby laughed.

David smiled. "Just remember, I'm here."

"How could I forget?" Abby leaned toward him and gave him a kiss. "I'm off, wish me luck!"

She opened the car door and walked into the office. As she entered, several of her former co-workers greeted her. Abby responded to the friendly words as she walked toward Dan King's office where King's secretary, Mary Hoyt, looked up as Abby stopped in front of her desk.

"Hi Abby," she said surprised to see Abby.

"Is Mr. King in?"

"Yes?"

"I'd like to see him."

"Sure."

Mary Hoyt got up and went into King's office where she knocked on the closed door. Hearing a voice, she opened it and Abby could not hear the words spoken in King's office, but Mary Hoyt came out, followed by King.

"Abby! So good to see you. Please come into the office."

Abby nodded and followed King back through the door making sure the door stayed open. She wanted an audience.

"I hope this visit means you've reconsidered and will come back to work?" King asked hopefully.

"Well, Mr. King, it happens that's not why I'm here."

King was puzzled, he had clearly expected Abby to relent and come back to work.

"What can I do for you then?" he asked.

"Squirm," she said with a satisfied grin on her face.

"What?"

"You can squirm, Mr. King, because I have something for you." And she handed him the envelope. "Consider yourself served."

"What do you mean?" King asked, looking dumbly at the envelope.

"You're being sued, Mr. King."

"What!" he exclaimed, opening the envelope. "You can't be serious Abby, I had every right to fire you!"

"It has nothing to do with me loosing my job. That's a petition to enjoin you from selling Rosemary Point!"

King gave her a blank stare and he glanced at the document from the envelope, not really seeing the words.

"What do you mean?" he repeated weakly.

"Read the petition," Abby suggested, "you'll see."

"But I have nothing to do with Rosemary Point!" he protested.

"I know you're involved, Mr. King."

"But I'm not!"

"Oh, yes you are, Mr. King. I know you pick up the mail for the Springbrook Partnership at the Kittery Post Office."

King was shocked, the surprise and fear showing on his face. "How do you know that?"

"You'll find out in court, won't you now?"

He looked at the paper in his hand and asked her, "How long have you known?"

"As I say, Mr. King, you'll find out later. See you in court!"

She smiled and turned to walk out of the office.

"Bye, Mary, see you," she called over her shoulder at the secretary and waved to the others in the office. She opened the front door and walked to David's car, feeling like she wanted to jump up and down with joy. She sat in the front seat and leaned to David, giving him another kiss.

"Wow, I feel great!" she said, "I haven't felt this good in a long time!"

"It went well?" David asked, seeing the elation on Abby's face.

"Oh yes! Shit was he surprised!"

"Abigail's revenge?" David smiled and she nodded.

"Yeah, and does it feel good! How about some lunch Dave? I'm hungry!"

"Sure, feed the troops, you deserve it," David said and they drove off excited by anticipation of what was to come.

*   *   *

Hands shaking, Dan King went to the door to his office and closed it. How in hell did Abby Palmer know that he was involved with the Springbrook Partnership? God, he had slipped up badly and he knew Sherwood was going to be pissed.

He scanned the document the Palmer woman had given him and saw they were being sued to enjoin them from selling the property because it violated the covenant attached to the deed. Sherwood had assured him that the covenant could be broken. So what in hell did this all mean? Was there a question about the covenant now?

He knew he had to call the man from New Rochelle but didn't want to do it. Yet he knew it had to be done. So he tapped the number out on the telephone and heard it ring four times before it was answered.

"Tom?" King asked cautiously.

"Yes?"

"Dan King. We've got a problem."

"Oh shit, what now? I'm getting tired of this."

"Sorry Tom, we're being sued. I was just served with the papers."

"For Christ's sake King, what the hell is this all about?"

"We're being sued over the sale of Rosemary Point."

"Who's suing us?"

"David Baker and Abigail Palmer."

"Those two bastards again! Shit, what grounds are they suing on?"

"They cite the covenant attached to the deed to the property."

"Shit, that's breakable. God damn it King, this is nothing but a nuisance suit. It won't stand up!"

"Nevertheless Tom," King said carefully, "it's been filed and a motion for a hearing granted for this Friday."

"This Friday?"

"Yes, so we'd better be represented."

"We will be represented, I'll take care of that!" snapped Sherwood.

"Should I overnight the documents to you?"

"Yeah do that. Tell me," he hissed, "how in hell did they find you to serve the papers?"

King didn't want to answer the question. "I don't know. Somehow Abby found out that I was involved and she served me with the papers."

"You stupid shit King! You've been careless again! These two are smart and we can't underestimate them any longer!"

King was silent.

"No doubt Miss Palmer and Mister Baker are feeling very smug right now," Sherwood growled. "We're going to do something about that!"

"What do you have in mind?" King asked afraid of the answer.

"Shit, I don't know yet, but I'll think of something. You're going to have to go to court with our attorney on Friday."

"Why me?"

"Because they already know you're involved and having you there may help our case."

"But I'm only a one percent partner," King protested.

"Tough shit, you're going!"

King did not argue. The edge in the other man's voice did not encourage debate.

"Who will you use as an attorney," King asked.

"I'm going to call a fellow from Saco. His name is Harvey Veazie and I'll have him a call you so you can get your story straight. Have copies of the documents ready for him."

"Okay."

"And don't screw up again King. We've got to deal with this quickly, so it doesn't delay things."

"I understand."

"I sure as shit hope you do King." And the phone clicked dead. Dan King felt very uncomfortable at the prospect of going to court. He needed to talk with Ron Crown and knew he wouldn't be happy either.

*　　　　　*　　　　　*

Late the following morning, David was slowly working through a pile of files on his desk when the telephone rang.

"Hello?" he answered.

"David Baker please," a hoarse voice asked.

"Yes?"

"I'm calling to give you a warning."

"What?" David said instantly alert.

"A warning. I want you to stay out of trouble, so please take my advice."

"What do you mean?" David said, feeling the anger rise within him.

"You should stay away from Rosemary Point!" the voice hissed.

"What do you mean?" David responded again.

"It could be unhealthy for you."

"Is that a threat?"

"No, only a friendly warning," the voice said. "You should stay out of business that does not concern you."

"Who are you?" David demanded.

"I'm a friend and I'm concerned about you. I advise you not to press your interest in the property at Rosemary Point! You should know that you are putting Miss Palmer in danger."

"Who the hell are you?" David repeated, "what right do you have to call this way?"

"I have all the right in the world," the menacing voice almost laughed. "You should heed my words. Do not press this any further, for your own well being."

David was angry and he wanted to confront this unknown caller. "You're wasting your time, you bastard!" David yelled, slamming down the phone.

As he calmed down and thought about the call, he suspected that he had just heard from Thomas Sherwood, or someone who worked for him. That thought cheered him because it meant the plan was working.

He picked up the telephone to call Abby and warn her about the call. He tapped out the number but a busy signal came from the other end of the line. He would try calling back in a few minutes.

David looked out his window at the village and the people who were starting their visit to the pilgrim recreation and he reflected that whoever had called was worried.

Behind him the telephone rang and again he answered.

"Dave Baker."

"Dave? It's Abby." He recognized the fear.

"Abby, are you okay?"

"No, I've just had a threatening phone call!"

"Yeah, I know. I had the same call right before you."

"Who was he?" she asked, still worried.

"I don't know, but I think it may have been Sherwood."

"You really think so? God, if it was, we've struck a nerve, haven't we? We've done what we wanted to do!"

"Yeah, I think so. Are you okay?"

"Yes, just a little scared I guess," Abby said.

"I feel the same way."

"I'll be damned though if someone is going to scare me away from this!"

"I'm with you," David said, but had an empty feeling in his gut.

"You still going to Mystic?" Abby asked.

"Yeah, I'll go down on Thursday."

"Then you're up here on Friday?"

"Yes, again, and I can't wait to see who shows up in court."

"It will be interesting, but I want you to promise to be careful Dave."

"I plan on it. You be careful too, there could be some real danger behind these threats."

"I know, I'll watch out. I love you Dave," she said.

"Me too. See you Friday."

Hanging up the telephone, Abby felt a shiver of fear travel up her spine. She vowed to be very careful.

*　　　　*　　　　*

David left the Mystic Seaport Marine Museum in Connecticut late on Thursday afternoon. He wasn't disappointed because he really hadn't expected to find any useful information, much less the elusive questionable wills.

The museum staff was very helpful and even sympathetic. They had helped him search the vast archives of material that made up the museum's collection and in the end he found some information, mostly printed duplicates of what he had found elsewhere.

The drive home gave him time to think. He was anxious for the court hearing to start tomorrow but wondering how the arguments would go. He tried to think about all the things he had done over the last several months. Had he missed something? Had he overlooked a detail? He didn't think so, but he had the nagging feeling that he may have done just that.

Jack Pierce had been right. His effort to trace his family history had turned into a strange journey and he remembered the beginning of the trip back in May. Then, he had wondered where it would lead but he could have never imagined anything like what had happened.

Most people who trace their family history have to interpret it, making judgements and imagining what life was like for those who lived long ago. Now, he was defending his past from a present day danger and that was hard to put into perspective.

Whatever happened, he finally decided, he was ready for it.

*   *   *

An unexpected emergency kept Jack Pierce from attending the hearing on Friday but David and Abby were in the courtroom in Biddeford talking with Ted Williams. On the other side of the aisle sat a man in his late fifties, going through a stack of yellow legal pad notes.

"That's Harvey Veazie," Williams said, nodding to the other man.

"Who's he?" Abby asked.

"An attorney from Saco. He was a Representative to the Maine Legislature for about six terms but now he's back in practice."

"Is he good?" asked David.

"I checked up on him. He was very good and he's got a lot of political clout. I don't know how good he is now but he's representing the other side, so apparently we'll soon find out."

The bailiff spoke. "All rise! Judge Andrew Carrier presiding."

A man entered the courtroom from a side door. He was in his early fifties, salt and pepper hair, distinguished looking in is black robe.

David looked at him and thought that this was just like Perry Mason. The man sat behind the raised desk and spoke. "Clerk, please call the case."

"Baker and Palmer versus the Springbrook Partnership. Seeking a motion to enjoin the sale of property."

"Who represent s the plaintiffs?" the judge asked.

"I do your Honor," Williams said rising, "Edward Williams of Portland."

Carrier nodded once. "And for the defendants?"

The man at the other table rose. "Harvey Veazie, your Honor."

At the back of the room the door opened and Dan King entered. The few spectators in the courtroom watched him come in and take a seat near the door.

Carrier looked at his notes. "Let us proceed. Mr. Williams present your case."

Ted Williams rose and outlined the complaint as filed in the petition to the court following the line of reasoning given him by David Baker. When he finished, he thanked the court and returned to his seat.

"Mr. Veazie, how do you respond?"

The other man rose. "Your Honor. I ask that this case be dismissed for lack of evidence. In addition, the fact that no sale has taken place demonstrates that there is no cause for this suit. This is purely a nuisance suit and I ask that you dismiss it out of hand!"

"I will take that under advisement. You have a response, Mr. Williams?"

"Yes, your Honor. The plaintiffs do admit that no sale has yet taken place, but as your Honor has seen in the documents filed with the court, there is reasonable suspicion that a sale is imminent. This, in turn, would violate the covenant. We seek to prevent that from happening."

Carrier again nodded. "Mr. Veazie?"

"Again, your Honor, there is no basis for this complaint. I ask for an immediate dismissal!"

"So noted," Carrier said looking just a bit peeved at Veazie. "Mister Williams I'm inclined to agree with Mr. Veazie. Do you have anything to add?"

Williams rose once more. "Your Honor, I don't believe you can dismiss this case out of hand."

"And why not Mr. Williams?"

"Sir, you must, at least, grant a motion to allow interrogatory. So far we don't know who we are dealing with in the Springbrook Partnership. Only Mr. Veazie and," Williams pointed to King in the back of the room, "that gentleman seems to have a connection with the Rosemary Point property. We need to find out what that connection is."

"Ah, a valid point. Mr. Veazie?"

"Your Honor, we respectfully repeat that no sale has taken place. Therefore, there is no validity to the plaintiffs suit."

"You've presented that thought," Carrier said. "But do you have a response to the question raised by the plaintiffs?"

"I have no response your Honor, and I will stand by my assertion that no sale has taken place, hence there has been no violation of the covenant."

"Mr. Veazie, do you have any objection to deposition?" Carrier smiled at the man.

Veazie was taken aback. He had not anticipated this line of questioning, but he thought fast, wishing he had a better argument to this point.

Then he thought that if he accepted this request he would get to question Baker and Palmer and that seemed reasonable, even desirable.

"Ah no, your Honor. The defendants will submit to that."

"So ordered," Carrier stated and banged his gavel. "This case is continued until," he looked at his clerk.

"Thursday eleven o clock," the man answered.

"So ordered," Carrier banged the gavel again. "Next case?"

Ted Williams, Abby and David went out of the courtroom and as they left a woman approached them.

"Hi, I'm Terry Delaney from Action News in Portland," the woman explained. "I was waiting for another case to come up and heard your motion. This sounds like it could be interesting, would you consent to an interview? I'd like to know more about your suit, there might be a good story here and it may make a good human interest story."

David looked at Williams and the diminutive lawyer smiled, shaking his head yes.

"Sure," David said, "I'd be glad to talk with you."

"Then stay right here," Terry Delaney said, "my cameraman is just down the hall. I'll go get him."

She walked off and David looked at Williams.

"Did you have anything to do with her being here?" he asked as a smile formed on his face.

Williams grinned at him. "You know, Baker, you're not too dumb. I suggest that you just go with the flow. Do a good interview and it will help us."

David returned the grin. "I hear you counselor. I will try to put on a good performance."

"I'll coach him," Abby said.

Williams laughed. "I expect you could add to the performance, so Dave, let Abby do part of the interview. I think it will help."

"Okay," David agreed.

David and Abby did the interview about the lawsuit and their interest in the property at Rosemary Point. Terry Delaney took a very sympathetic slant and the story played on the six o clock and eleven o clock news in Portland. The following morning the Portland morning newspaper picked up the story and put it on the national news wire. So, the story ran in the Boston papers a day later.

Chapter Twenty-Three

Thomas Sherwood answered the ringing telephone and heard the menacing voice.

"Sherwood?"

"Yes?"

"It's Nick Dominic."

Sherwood hesitated before replying because yesterday's hearing had not gone the way he hoped.

"Yeah Nick, what can I do for you?" he said finally.

"We need to meet." No emotion in the voice.

"All right, where?" Sherwood asked.

"I want to meet you in the shuttle parking garage at Logan Airport. The lower level."

"When?"

"As soon as possible, say tomorrow at eleven?"

"Yeah, I'll be there," Sherwood said without much enthusiasm.

"Good, we don't like surprises."

"Is there a problem?" Sherwood asked.

"Have you seen the *Boston Globe*?" Dominic asked.

"No, I don't read the Boston papers."

"You should, lots of interesting things in them, you could learn a lot. I suggest you get a copy and we'll talk tomorrow."

"Shit, what happened Nick? Tell me what happened," Sherwood was worried now. What had happened?

"I said we'll talk tomorrow. Eleven o clock, shuttle parking garage, lower level, be there."

The phone clicked dead and Sherwood sat for a moment wondering what had happened to provoke the telephone call. He knew that Dominic was angry from the sound of his voice. Shit, he needed to get a copy of the Boston paper to find out.

Sherwood left his house and went to the garage to get his car. He lived alone since his wife had divorced him sixteen years before, over her suspicions of his involvement with the shady characters he knew. He didn't miss her and at the age of sixty-six, his occasional urgings for the opposite sex were satisfied by a professional. Still at times like this he wished he had someone to talk to.

As he backed the car from the garage, he reflected that the last years were totally occupied by his real estate projects. There had been little time for other things and now his financial problems threatened to destroy him. He did not like the thought of what that promised. Especially with his involvement with Dominic's friends.

He bought a copy of the *Boston Globe* at a convenience store and returning to the car, he quickly went through the paper. Near the back of the second section, he found the article.

He read the item and felt the rage building inside. The article detailed the lawsuit filed by David Baker and Abigail Palmer. The covenant on the property was mentioned prominently and he knew that was what had prompted the call from Dominic.

Sherwood tried to think this development through because it presented a real problem for him. He had not mentioned the covenant to Dominic, thinking it could be dealt with before the sale, but now he would have to do some fast talking. Still, he thought he could explain the facts without pissing Dominic off any more than he was.

He started the car and put it in gear, then headed for home. As he drove, he thought again about the article in the paper. Dominic and his people were pissed and he would have to be prepared for Dominic to do something drastic. He would drive to Logan Airport early in the morning because if he flew he would not be able to carry his pistol and that, he decided, was something he needed to have with him. He had to be prepared for the worst but one way or the other though he would deal with it.

The anger rose again and he thought of Baker and the Palmer woman. Damn it, they had gone too far and now he would have to do something to stop them. After he met Dominic, he would go to Portsmouth to see King and maybe he'd spend a few days there and find a way to solve the problem of the two meddlers. He decided he would make the trip in a rental car using one of his phony credit cards and drivers license. If an opportunity presented itself he wanted to be ready. He was going to stop the couple from doing any more damage.

He turned into his driveway and felt the anger subside as he thought of what he might do to the meddling twosome.

*   *   *

Sherwood waited against the wall on the lower level of the shuttle parking garage at Logan Airport shortly before eleven the next morning. He had driven to Boston after leaving New Rochelle at six-o clock. He looked around nervously as he waited for Dominic to show up.

Absently, he put his hand to his back to his belt, checking to see if his Colt automatic was in easy reach. Satisfied that he could grasp it with little trouble, he resumed looking for Dominic.

It was after eleven when he heard footsteps approaching and he glanced cautiously in the direction of the noise. He moved from his place against the wall and recognized Nicholas Dominic. He fought a nervous reaction to reach again behind his back and tried to smile at the man, holding out his hand. Dominic did not take it.

"My people are not happy Sherwood. You take us for fools?"

"No."

"Why is it then that we have to find out about this damned covenant from a newspaper article?"

"I was going to tell you when the time came. Besides, I thought you had done a title search and you knew," he lied.

Dominic hesitated. "We don't like surprises, Sherwood. This is a problem and I'm not sure the sale would be valid now."

"Nothing has changed," Sherwood said angrily, "The covenant does not present a problem."

"Why not?" Dominic asked.

"My attorney assures me that the covenant can easily be broken."

"How so?"

"There's a loophole," Sherwood tried to explain.

"And, what is this loophole?"

"My attorney says it will work. The partnership will cease to pay the taxes and this will cause the covenant to be null and void. The town must then accept a change of ownership."

"That sounds like a stretch to me. You sure this will work?"

"No, it's not a problem. It will work, the attorney says it won't be a problem."

Dominic looked skeptical. "I'll have my people take a look at this Sherwood. It had better check out!"

"It will," Sherwood said making his voice sound as calm as possible.

"We're still not happy with the fact that you have lied to us. You know this is the second time you've caused a problem. There won't be a third Sherwood!" Dominic's voice turned cold and cruel.

"Nothing more will happen, I promise you."

"This deal would be over already if my people didn't want this property badly," Dominic warned.

"Yes, I understand."

"Good, then take this as a warning Sherwood. Anything more happens and you will pay for it! Do you understand my meaning?"

"Yes. There will be no more problems, I promise you."

"These two in the paper, Baker and Palmer? You got plans for them? Someone should talk to them so they won't cause any more trouble."

"I'll deal with them."

"I hope so, for your own good. I'll be watching the court proceedings in Maine with interest."

"They have no case!" Sherwood blurted out. "It will be dismissed on Thursday, you can count on it!"

Dominic looked at him. "We don't count on anything, Sherwood. You would do well to do the same."

"Okay."

"We will meet again I think," Dominic said. "Soon."

Dominic smiled then turned and walked away. Sherwood let out a deep breath. He'd gotten away with it again, but he had no doubts about Dominic's intent. If there was another problem he knew he was a dead man. Yes, he had no illusions about that. He would have to do something to force Baker and Palmer to stay out of his way. He had to do that or face financial ruin.

*   *   *

Ted Williams left the Court Building in Biddeford followed closely by David and Abby. They had just finished an hour and a half of discovery testimony and Williams was not happy.

"How badly did we do?" a dejected David Baker asked.

"Not too good," replied the attorney.

"We told the truth," Abby said defensively.

"That's the problem. We don't have much of it and now Veazie knows what a slim bunch of evidence we have. It's nothing more than hearsay and we can't even produce a witness to say they heard about the sale of the property because you don't remember who it was! Veazie is going into court tomorrow and he's going to get his dismissal. There's nothing we can do!"

David and Abby exchanged glances.

"Isn't there anything we can do?" she asked.

"I don't think so. We've used up all our ammunition. Judge Carrier would have thrown this out the other day if I hadn't got lucky with the discovery ruling. Now, the only hope there is that I can get him to rule that Veazie has to disclose the names of the general partners of the Springbrook Partnership. But he'll probably throw the case out before I get a chance to do that!"

Abby and David were unhappy, the disappointment showing on their faces.

"Ted?" Abby asked, "do you have fifteen minutes to get a cup of coffee? I think it's time we told you a story."

Williams looked at her and saw the odd look on her face. What was she going to say now? "I guess so. Let's go down the street and get a cup of coffee."

Sitting in a booth in the coffee shop, the couple looked at the attorney.

"Ted," Abby began, "do you believe in spirits?"

Williams almost choked on his coffee. "What?"

"Let me tell you about something that we haven't told you yet."

She outlined the things that had happened to them, prompting them to defend Rosemary Point. She told him of the woman and about the conversation she had heard between the men who had walked the grounds. When Abby finished, Williams remained silent.

He looked up slowly. "So, that's why you can't produce a corroborating witness?"

"Yes."

"Jesus, well, I guess now I've heard everything. But, I guess I've got to believe you. You both seem like you're sane, intelligent people who believe what they've seen. Shit, now I've heard everything!" he repeated. "A ghost! Jesus Abby, what is my practice coming to?"

"Does it make any difference to the case?" Abby asked.

"No I don't think so. Jesus Abby, how in the hell am I supposed to depose a ghost! I think we're dead ducks, no pun intended."

"Isn't there anything we can do?" Abby pleaded.

Williams watched her face while he thought. Was there anything he could do? He didn't know what to make of the story the two had told him. They seemed convinced they had seen and spoken with someone. But how in hell could he believe them? He concentrated on the problem at hand.

"The only thing we can try now is raise the issue of the two wills," he said. "Ghost or no ghost, we've got to focus on the ownership of the property. That's the only thing left to try."

"Well, do the best you can," David said, "that's all we ask. No matter what Ted, you've been a big help. Thanks."

"I wish I could do more. I think your hearts are in the right place. It's just too bad we don't have any more evidence."

David shrugged, frowning. "I guess that's it then, we'll see you in court tomorrow?"

"I'll be there," Williams said.

A few minutes later Williams left the coffee shop and Abby and David sat crestfallen, saying nothing.

Finally, Abby spoke. "Don't look so sad Dave, we tried really hard."

"I know, but I feel we've let her down!"

"I feel the same way, but we have to face reality."

"You know," David said, "it's really too bad that copies of the wills don't exist. I'd still like to nail the bastards!"

"We've got one consolation thought," Abby said.

"And what's that?"

"If the place does sell, we can do this all over again." Abby laughed.

"Yeah, I guess so. That will prove we were right anyway."

Abby kissed him lightly. "Come on, cheer up. A miracle might happen!"

"Yeah," he said, "and I've got a chance to date Miss America."

"Why would you want date her when you've got me?" Abby asked.

David looked at her and saw the smile grow on her face. He grinned in return and in spite of his feelings, they both started to laugh, the dejection and frustration disappearing.

Hand in hand, with spirits renewed, they walked out of the coffee shop.

*   *   *

David and Abby drove to the court house the next morning in separate cars because David planned to go back to work after the hearing and Abby wanted to stop on her way back in Kittery to shop at the factory outlet stores.

They waited for Ted Williams to arrive and finally saw the diminutive attorney come up to them shortly before eleven.

"Good morning, you two," he said cheerfully, "no one else here today?"

"I don't know," replied David, "Jack said he would be here when I talked with him yesterday. Maybe I should call him?"

Williams looked at his watch. "Let me see where we are." He opened the courtroom door and looked inside. The case on the docket ahead of them was wrapping up.

"You've probably got about ten minutes," Williams said. "Go ahead and give him a call. There's time."

"Okay," David said and went to find a pay phone. He found one near the entry hall and made a credit card call to Jack Pierce.

Pierce answered.

"Jack, it's Dave. You're not coming up, I take it?"

"Shit no Dave, I'm sorry but I've got a financing problem on the new exhibit. I wanted to make it up, but no dice."

"You're lucky. You won't have to sit through the funeral."

"That bad huh?"

"Yeah, Ted doesn't hold out much hope."

"You tried, Dave, you really did. You've got to give yourself credit for that."

"Yeah, I know, still I feel like I failed."

"You didn't. Call me later and let me know what happens."

"I will."

David returned to the courtroom and found Abby and Williams inside, sitting at the table in front of the judge's bench. Harvey Veazie was seated at the opposite table. Dan King was there again seated near the back of the room, a smug look on his face. David looked at Williams.

"We ready?"

"Yes, just waiting on the judge."

"Listen Ted, whatever happens, I want you to know I really appreciate everything you've done for us. Thanks."

"You're welcome Dave, but we're not out of this yet!" He smiled at David and the bailiff spoke.

"All rise! Court is now in session, the honorable Andrew Carrier presiding!"

The Judge entered the room, taking his seat. "Clerk?"

"This a continuation of the hearing on Palmer and Baker versus Springbrook," the bailiff announced.

Carrier nodded. "Proceed Mr. Williams?"

"Your Honor, we completed discovery. However, Mr. Veazie did not see fit to bring forward the names of the principals in the Springbrook Partnership."

"Is that true, Mr. Veazie?"

"It is your Honor."

"You have a reason I assume."

"Your Honor, I again respectfully request that this suit be dismissed. Discovery allowed me to question the plaintiffs, and, as I think you will see in these briefs," he waved a folder, "there is little on which to base a suit. There is no corroborating evidence, so I did not respond to the question."

Carrier thought for a moment, considering the request. "Bailiff, give me the documents."

The court officer took them from the attorney and handed them to the man behind the bench. Carrier began to examine them.

The door to the courtroom opened and another uniformed court officer entered and went to the bailiff giving him a written message. The bailiff looked at it, nodded and then went to the bench where he gave it to Judge Carrier who read the note.

"Mr. Baker," Carrier said looking up toward David, "this is a phone message for you. Your office is calling about an emergency." He gave the note back to the bailiff, who gave it to David.

"Would you like a short recess, Mr. Williams?"

"If it would please the court," Ted Williams replied.

"Ten minute recess. I will review these documents in my chambers."

"All rise," the bailiff ordered and Carrier left the room.

"What is it?" Abby asked David.

He looked at the note which simply said "call the office ASAP, emergency".

"I don't know, but I'm going to find out," he said and got up going back out to the pay phone in the hall. He called his office and spoke to his secretary.

"Hi Kathy, it's Dave. You trying to get ahold of me?"

"Yes, am I glad to hear from you!"

"What's up? What's the emergency?"

"You know someone named Sherry Kaminsky?" Kathy asked.

David thought for a moment. He knew that name, but who was she? Then he remembered; the archivist at the Peabody Museum.

"Yeah sure, I know her, why?"

"She's called three times this morning Dave. She says she has to talk to you as soon as possible. It sounded real urgent!"

"She say why?" David asked.

"No, just that it was very important!"

"Okay, I'll call her. She leave a number?"

"Yes," and Kathy repeated the number to David who wrote it down on a scrap of paper he found in his pocket.

"Okay, I got it. Thanks Kathy. Anything else?"

"No that's it. I hope it's not bad news."

"Me too. I've had enough of that in the last two days!"

He returned the handset to the hook, then picked it up again and placed the call to Salem. The phone rang twice.

"Sherry Kaminsky?" the woman answered.

"Sherry, it's Dave Baker calling. What's up?"

"Hi Dave. God, I've been trying to get you all morning!"

"Sorry, I'm up in Maine. What's the problem?"

"Well, it's not a problem Dave. I read the article about you in the *Globe* on Tuesday."

"Yes?"

"Well it got me moving, made me do some checking."

"Moving on what?" David asked wishing the woman would get to the point.

"Well, I've been real busy since you were here and I felt bad that I didn't have a chance to check things out for you."

"How's that?"

"Well Dave, remember I told you we had some uncataloged material on the Smiths?"

He did remember, but he had forgotten that she had mentioned it during his visit.

"Yes, I remember."

"Well, like I said, I was busy and I never did have a chance to check it, but the article jogged my memory. I went through all our material yesterday afternoon and I've been trying to get you all morning!"

"What did you find?" David said hopefully. Could she have actually found something?

"There are some things here I think you should come look at," Sherry said.

The hairs on the back of his neck pricked up and a shiver went down his spine. "Is there anything there that looks like a will?" he asked not willing to let himself think she had found anything.

There was silence at the other end of the line

"Sherry?"

"Yes Dave, I hear you. I think there is, but I'm just not sure. Oh God, there are all kinds of things here. I really think you should get down here."

"I'm on my way," David said looking at his watch. "I'll be there in an hour or so."

He said good-bye and replaced the phone, his heart pounding. He walked back to the courtroom, hardly seeing anything around him and went to the table where Abby and Ted Williams looked at him.

"What happened?" Abby asked, "you look terrible. You're pale!"

"Are you okay?" added Williams.

David sat in a chair. "I'm going down to Salem," he said quietly, "to the Peabody Museum."

"What happened?" Abby asked again.

"I think we may have found the wills!" David whispered.

"What!" Williams exclaimed.

"I'm going down to look at the material. We're not sure but I'm going down now to take a look."

"Should I go with you?" Abby asked.

"No, you stay here. Go home and I'll call if I find anything. I don't know how long this will take but we may need you here. Besides, it will only take one of us to do this."

Abby nodded but David could see she wasn't happy about staying behind.

"If the wills are there," Williams said, "we need to think fast!"

"What about?" asked Abby.

"What this does to our case if it's true. It changes the whole focus. We need time to rethink where we're going."

"What do you suggest?" David asked.

"Call me as soon as you know anything. The office will give you my home phone or the car phone if I'm on the road. In the meantime, I'm going to try for a continuance. I just hope Judge Carrier is in a good mood!"

David kissed Abby. "See you later. I'll come back to your apartment. Wish me luck!"

"Good luck and be careful."

David left the courtroom and headed for the parking lot with his fingers crossed. Maybe he could get a date with Miss America.

*   *   *

Thomas Sherwood slammed down the telephone in the motel out-side of Portsmouth where he was registered under an assumed name. The rage surged within him because he had just spoken to Dan King, who told him that the hearing had been continued until tomorrow. Something had occurred that could affect the case, but King wasn't sure just what it was. Whatever it was, David Baker had rushed out of the courtroom and the judge had granted a twenty-four hour continuance.

Sherwood was enraged that the nuisance suit had not been dismissed out of hand. He was not going to stand by and see all his plans go down because of the two troublesome meddlers. Goddamn it, it was time he acted, time to do something. He needed to do something to send an unmistakable message that would scare off Baker and Palmer.

Quickly a plan formed in his head. It wasn't original and he wasn't sure they would fall for it, but what he had in mind would send the message he intended. He looked at his watch and saw it was nearly three-thirty. He would time it for sundown and he looked up Abigail Palmer's address and phone number in the phone book.

Sherwood picked up the Colt automatic from the dresser top and popped the clip loose. He removed the shells and then tossed them on the bed. Then he ejected the shell in the chamber and added it to the pile on the bed. He would carry the pistol with him, but didn't want to chance it discharging unless he wanted it to. He replaced the empty clip and moved the safety on.

Half an hour later Sherwood sat in the rental car and watched the front door of Abigail Palmer's apartment complex. He had a pretty good idea what she looked like and he knew from Dan King that she drove a silver Oldsmobile. He waited patiently.

The silver Olds drove into the parking lot about forty minutes later and a tallish blond haired woman got out, going into an apartment in the complex. He noted which one it was.

Sherwood waited for almost an hour as the sun sank low on the western horizon, the shadows growing longer. It was time he thought.

He picked up the cellular phone and tapped out the number he had copied earlier.

The woman answered. "Hello?"

"Miss Baker?" Sherwood said in a low voice.

"Yes?"

"My name is Johnson," he lied. "I'm a descendant of the Smith family also and I saw the article about what you are doing. I want to help and I think have some information that might help you in your lawsuit."

"What?" Abby said, "what do you know?"

"Oh, I can't talk over the phone. Could I meet you somewhere so I can give you the information?"

Abby decided she didn't like the man's voice and she didn't like what he was suggesting. "Where do you want to meet?" she asked tentatively.

He described a factory parking lot near Pease Air Force Base several miles from her apartment.

"Why can't we meet at the Fox Run Mall?" she suggested. She wanted a place where other people were present.

"I might be recognized," Sherwood said. "I have to be careful you understand. It must be the parking lot."

"What do you know?" Abby asked again.

"I'm sorry but I just can't say over the phone. I think I'm in danger but I do have some documents for you," he tried to make it sound good.

"The wills?" Abby said jumping to the suggestion.

Sherwood picked up on her interest. "Why yes, I do."

"Oh my!" Abby said, but she was still hesitant, not sure what to do. She didn't like the call or the strange request for the meeting, but on the other hand, if the man had the wills it could help them and she desperately wanted to save Rosemary Point. What would Dave do? God, she wished he were here. He hadn't even called and she wondered what he was doing. She had to make a decision, so she did.

"Okay, I'll meet you," she said. "When?"

"Twenty minutes," the voice replied.

"That's barely time to get there," she was worried again.

"Not if you leave now."

"Okay, I'm on my way. How will I recognize you?"

"I'll be waiting in a blue Caddy," he lied.

"Okay, I'll see you in twenty minutes."

As the man clicked off, she had another thought and pushed down the disconnect button on the telephone then quickly called her parents house. Her mother answered.

"Hi, it's me," Abby said.

"Abby, you sound out of breath, are you okay?"

"Yeah, listen Mom, I'm about to go meet a man who just called me who says he has the wills. I've got to go meet him," and she described where she was going.

"I don't like that," her mother said, "are you sure you want to do that? This doesn't sound right to me."

"I know Mom, it sounds like a bad TV movie, but I can't ignore anything at this point. I've got to do this. If you don't hear from me in an hour or so come looking for me. Dave should be back from Salem soon, so tell him what I'm doing, okay?"

"I'll do that, but you be careful! I still don't like this."

"I'll be careful, I promise," Abby said.

She replaced the phone and went to put on a sweater, the left the apartment. It was getting chilly she thought as she got into her car, started the engine and turned on headlights. She backed the car out of the parking space, went into drive and turned right on the street.

Behind her, the other car pulled away from the curb and followed her at a discrete distance. Abby concentrated on the road as she sped along, occasionally glancing in the rear view mirror. She did not notice the car trailing her.

Fifteen minutes later she turned left onto the service road that led to the factory parking lot and still did not notice the other car also turn behind, the headlights switching off. She drove on knowing that she had to travel about a mile before arriving at the parking lot and focused on the dirt road.

All at once she was aware of something on her left and she looked, curious to see what had caught her eye. To her surprise, she saw the shape of a car with no headlights and before she could react, the car swerved hard into her car hitting it sideways.

The cars were grinding together and she could feel the weight of the other car in the steering wheel. Abby fought for control wondering who was doing this? She was scared, felt her heart pumping fast as she tried the brakes. The other car slowed with her, pushing her off the road. She pressed the accelerator to speed up again, but the other car matched her change still pushing her toward the ditch at the side of the road.

She could think of nothing else except to try to keep the car on the road and fought the wheel, but now the other car swerved violently into her once again. She fought desperately to keep control, but knew she was losing the fight.

Her car was on the shoulder and she could see the three foot drainage ditch at the edge of the shoulder. It scared her.

Once again the other car swerved hard into her car and this time she could not control the wheel. Instinctively she hit the brakes hard, but the wheels locked and the car skidded sideways to the right, the right tires falling in the ditch. Abby could only think of what a stupid thing she had done. It was a bad TV movie.

She screamed and threw her hands to her face as the car went into the ditch. Abby was thrown toward the right door, her seatbelt restraining her and she screamed again. The car rolled on its side in the mud and gravel. It careened with metal screeching for sixty feet as the mass of metal burrowed in to the ditch. Abby could feel nothing.

The car finally stopped and nothing moved.

CHAPTER TWENTY-FOUR

January 3, 1784 Boston, Massachusetts

The *Eagle of America* sailed into Boston harbor after making a fast twelve-hour passage down from Portsmouth. On the quarterdeck Abigail Steele Smith stared at the familiar Boston shoreline deep in thought, her worries over the impending voyage now occupying most of her waking moments. She was worried about the voyage and just could not shake the sense of foreboding that disturbed her deeply.

She was concerned for her children and about what might become of them if something happened to either herself or Jacob. She planned to meet with the Boston attorney that her Kittery lawyer, Francis Lockwood, had recommended and hoped to be able to set her mind at ease with his legal help.

An hour later the *Eagle* was safely nestled against a wharf along the waterfront. Even before she was snugged up to the wharf, ship's chandlers had come aboard to begin the work of provisioning and refitting the ship. Soon laborers would start to load the cargo of mixed goods for the outward voyage.

Even though it was a warm January day, Abigail Smith wore a heavy coat over her new blue wool dress. She walked to her husband who was supervising the loading of provisions. He watched her approach.

"I'm going ashore Jacob," she announced.

"I know Abigail. Lord, you've gone over your plans with me constantly and I feel I know them as well as you," he laughed.

"You know me too well," she blushed and smiled.

"Are you sure you don't need me to go with you?" he asked.

"No, I think not. I can do this alone and you are needed here. You will need to come and sign though when the plans are completed."

He nodded. "I'll do whatever is needed."

"You usually do Jacob. It's one of the things that draws me to you."

She stood on her toes to kiss him. "I'll return later," she said.

Abigail Smith went to the gangplank, climbing the three steps of the boarding platform to reach it. It was low tide so the gangway was almost level with the wharf and she jumped down the short distance from the gangway to the cobblestones of the wharf. She walked towards the street, avoiding the muddy puddles left by the melting snow.

She walked down Commercial Street toward John Read's law office and heard church bells toll out in the distance. It was eleven-o clock. As she walked, she was amazed by the amount of traffic that moved in the busy street. She thought that the traffic had doubled, perhaps even tripled, since the end of the war. The city was becoming prosperous as the fledgling nation began to flex its economic muscles and it was exhilarating to be a part of it.

She found Read's office easily and as she entered, a tinny bell attached to the door announced her arrival. A diminutive clerk with spectacles and a long nose looked up at her.

"Mam'? Can I help you?" the man asked.

"Yes, I'd like to see Mr. Read. I wrote him for an appointment, I believe he is expecting me."

"And your name please?"

"Abigail Smith."

"Yes certainly, wait here please and I'll go tell Mr. Read."

The little man knocked at a door and then disappeared into a room to the back of the building. A moment later he returned followed by a man in his late thirties with black hair pulled back in the latest style and an aristocratic face. He was thin, which made him seem taller than he really was.

"Mrs. Smith?" he asked.

"Yes. Mr. Read?"

"It's so nice to meet you. I received your letter and the letter of introduction from Francis Lockwood. Please come into my office. Would you like some tea?"

"Yes, that would be nice," she said.

"Jeremiah, would you please get us some tea?"

"Yes Sir," the clerk said.

Read led Abigail Smith into his office and the clerk came in a moment later with a small silver tea service on a tray.

"Is there anything more you require Sir?"

Read looked at Abigail Smith, who shook her head no.

"That will be all, thank you Jeremiah."

The man gave a slight bow and left the room, closing the door behind him. Read poured tea for them.

"Sugar, milk?"

"Yes to both please," Abigail smiled.

Read added these to her cup and then handed it to her. He took his and sipped from it briefly before sitting behind his worktable.

"How can I help you?"

"I want to have new wills drawn. We are about to embark on a long voyage to China and I want to make sure that our affairs are in order and our assets protected for our children. This is a bit complicated but you came highly recommended by Mister Lockwood."

"Thank you, I believe I can help you," Read said, taking a sheet of paper from a wooden shelf. He sharpened a pen, preparing to take notes. "Tell me the details of what you would like to do."

"First, I do not trust my step-brother, Jonathan Marston. I want to keep him far away from our estate, if it were ever to come to that.

Second, I can no longer rely on my mother, I can no longer trust her either."

Read jotted notes rapidly, the pen dipping in the inkwell at intervals. "Go on," he said.

"I want our assets protected and I want to be sure they will go to our children."

"The children's names and how old are they?" Read asked.

"Our son, Jacob, is almost five and our daughter, Content, is nearly two. They are staying with our housekeeper at our home outside of Kittery."

"Minor children," Read repeated to himself, writing another note.

"I do not want my mother to act as our executor, I want that changed."

"Do you have any brothers or sisters?"

"No," she replied taking another sip of tea and Read jotted another note.

"And you don't want your step-brother to be involved?"

"Definitely not!" she was angry.

"All right Mrs. Smith, you have made your wishes very clear. Could you describe your assets for me, if you will?"

Abigail hesitated to talk of this and Read saw her pause. "I must ask so that I know how to plan for you," he explained. "It is a normal question, I assure you."

Abigail still felt on edge, but spoke slowly. "We own our ship, *The Eagle of America* and we have about four thousand invested in this voyage in cargo and other things. We own the house at Rosemary Point and two hundred twenty four acres of land there. We have other real estate in Maine, New Hampshire and near Marblehead."

"What is the value of this property?"

"I would guess about eight or ten thousand in total."

"What else is there?"

"We have gold and English notes. My husband also has land in New Hampshire in his own name."

"What is the value of these assets?"

"I would guess another ten to twelve thousand," she said.

Read looked at her. What she had just described was an incredible sum. "What would the total of your combined estates be then?" he asked with renewed interest.

Abigail Smith thought for a moment, mentally adding up each item. "I would guess about twenty five thousand or so," she said.

"That is a very large estate. You are to be congratulated for your enterprise and luck in accumulating such a sizeable fortune."

"That is why I wish to protect it!" she said sharply.

"Yes, of course," the attorney said, "anything else I should know?"

Abigail Smith considered this, her eyes searching the walls as if looking for something that was not there.

"No, not that I can think of. Do you have some suggestions to solve out problem? How can you address my wishes?"

"Well, first, I will draw new wills for both you and your husband. They will be very straightforward. In them you will leave your estate to your husband and he to you. If something happens to you both, the estate will go to your children."

"But they are so young. They cannot own property and I do not want any in the family as a guardian for them!"

"I understand that. I would propose using a testamentary trust, as part of each of your wills, to protect the estate for each of your children."

"Explain that please, Mr. Read," Abigail said trying to follow what Read was saying.

"Certainly. The assets in the estate would go into a trust, which would come into being if both you and your husband were to die. The trustee would manage the assets for the benefit of the children and the trustee would have the power to make sure the children were cared for and their needs and wants met. Do you see?"

"Yes, I think I understand. But a family member would have to be appointed trustee?"

"No, not necessarily. Anyone can act as a trustee. You could appoint me, for example, if you wanted to," Read suggested.

"But, that still means an individual would be in charge. There is no safety check? No one who would not have some interest?"

"Well I suppose you could look at it that way."

"Is there no other way to do it?" she asked not liking the options he had described.

"Well there is another possibility," Read said. "A group of local merchants are obtaining the first national bank charter for a local bank. They are planning to call the bank the Bank of Massachusetts and it is planned that the bank will have fiduciary and trust powers. You can name the bank as trustee, guardian and executor of your estates. That way there will be a group to manage the assets and that would also give you your set of checks and balances. A professional trustee would show no preferences."

The woman considered this new information carefully. "Yes," she said deliberately, "that would suit my purposes I think. None of the family would be involved in any way?"

"No, not if you used the bank. Also, because of the confidentiality of the trust, no one will be able to know what's in the trust or what the trust does. It will operate solely for the benefit of your two children and can exclude whoever else you want. Do you like that idea?"

"Yes, I want there to be no doubt that our assets are protected!"

"You can count on this Mrs. Smith. This estate plan will do all you want it to do. I think that it is a good idea to use the Bank of Massachusetts. You will be among the first to do so I would think."

"Thank you Mister Read, you have been very helpful. You may start work if you will. When can the documents be ready to sign?"

"I'll get to work on them immediately and Jeremiah can then transcribe the originals and copies. When are you planning to leave on your voyage?"

"We hope to sail before the fifteenth."

"In that case, I will have them ready a week from today. Would Eleven-o clock be agreeable with you?"

"Yes, thank you. My husband and I will be here."

"Good, and I thank you for the opportunity to serve you Mrs. Smith."

"Thank you for your kind help Mr. Read. I will see you in a week."

She turned and went out of the office, past the clerk who was busily working at his high desk. Read watched the proud woman leave, thinking that any man would be happy to have such a wife. In addition to her beauty, she was very rich, but she did not show it. Quite the opposite of his own wife he thought.

Read returned to his worktable where he picked up his pen to begin work on the Smith documents.

*   *   *

Jonathan Marston welcomed Nathan Mallin to his office, inviting him to sit and make himself comfortable. He greeted his former secretary who he had now designated as his agent and supercargo to represent him on the *Eagle's* coming voyage. It was a great opportunity for the young man.

"How are you Nathan?" he asked.

"I am well Mr. Marston, thank you."

"Are you excited about your voyage? It could prove historic you know?"

"Yes, but I am fearful Sir. I have never been to sea before."

"Ah, there is nothing to fear Nathan, the ocean will do you good and you will return a man of the world. It will help you in business when you return. You will find it opens many doors."

"I hope so Sir. I do have hopes of making something of myself."

"That you will Nathan, that you will. Are you clear about your duties Nathan, of what I require?"

"Yes Sir, I am to observe on the voyage and keep a daily journal so you may know what transpired. In addition, I am to watch over your interests to see that they are put to good use and the profit potential exploited. I am also given the authority to act on your behalf in procuring cargo upon arrival in China."

"Yes, that is very good Nathan," observed Marston.

"Thank you Sir."

"There is one more thing I want you to do."

"Yes Sir? I will try to do whatever is asked of me."

"When you arrive in Macao, you may find another American ship there."

"Oh?" Mallin was surprised.

"Yes, if the other ship arrives first and leaves before the *Eagle*, you are to do nothing."

"Yes Sir," Mallin said wondering what Marston was getting at.

"However, if the ship arrives after the *Eagle*, I want you to find some way to delay the Smiths on the return voyage."

"What do you mean?" Mallin asked.

"I want you to delay the Smiths," Marston said, "it's as simple as that. Start a slow leak or something to force them into a South American port for repairs. I want to make sure the other ship returns first."

"But, Mr. Marston, you have money invested in the *Eagle*! Why would you want the other ship to arrive here first?"

"A good question Nathan, and one that I do not have to answer, but I will. I know I can trust you," he smiled malevolently. "I am also a silent partner in the voyage of the other ship! So you see my interest?"

"But why do you do this?" the younger man asked troubled by what Marston was asking.

"It is simple Nathan. I want the other ship to have its place in history and I want to deny that place to the Smiths!"

"But isn't there danger in the plan?"

"No, I don't think so Nathan. I only want you to delay them. They, and you, will return later than expected, but without the glory. Their cargo will still fetch a handsome profit."

Marston regarded Mallin closely, an edge in his voice. "Do you understand what I am directing you to do?"

"Yes, I will carry out your wishes Mr. Marston."

"No questions?"

"No, I know your meaning," Mallin said very afraid of Marston.

"Make no mistake about it. If you do not do as I have asked, I will deal with you upon your return and you can be sure you will have no future in business!"

"You can count on me Mr. Marston."

"Good, I knew I could rely on you Nathan," Marston said rising to his feet. He went to the man and shook his hand. "Have a good voyage. Enjoy yourself."

"Yes Sir," Mallin said, also rising.

"I will see you off when you sail," Marston added.

Mallin nodded and left the room leaving Marston alone. He turned back to his window, pleased with the way his plans had fallen in place. Now, the Smiths would be denied a place in history, no matter what happened and that made him smile.

Closing the door behind him, Mallin stood, shaken by what Marston had said to him. The hate and jealously were obvious and this somehow seemed a bad omen for the upcoming voyage. He wondered if there was any way he could opt out now. But he knew he was tied to Marston now and if he ever hoped for success he had to follow through with his promise. He just hoped he could live with himself.

∗   ∗   ∗

A week after her first visit, Abigail and Jacob Smith returned to John Read's office to sign the newly drafted wills. Adam Davies, the first mate, and Caleb Brush, the second mate, accompanied them to act as witnesses.

The quartet entered the lawyer's building where John Read greeted them. Introductions were made all around and then Read led them to his office where copies of several sets of documents were on the work-table, awaiting signatures and attestations. Chairs were arranged around the room and Read invited them to sit.

"Now," he said, "the documents are ready. Mr. and Mrs. Smith, I ask that you read the documents and see that they reflect your true desires."

He handed originals to both Jacob and Abigail and they read the wills over carefully. Twenty minutes later they both had finished.

"Any questions?" Read asked.

"Yes," Jacob said, "the first part is very straight forward, but the last part of each will contains the language pertaining to the trusts. Can you explain it?"

"Certainly. There are eleven clauses in the wills concerning the trusts. These are the instructions to the trustee about how you want matters to be handled. Also, there are rules by which the trustee must abide in administering the trust. That's the gist of it, does that answer your question?"

"Yes," Jacob said, satisfied with Read's answer.

"I have one," Abigail said, "you have provided for each child to get an outright distribution of half the amount of the trusts at the age of twenty one and the balance at the age of thirty five. Is that wise? I mean what happens if the children are irresponsible?"

"A good point and we did not discuss this the other day. Perhaps we should have. The assets could remain in trust without distributing to the children. We have already given the trustee the right to distribute principal as he sees fit. If you want to make a change, I can quickly have a codicil drawn up."

Jacob Smith looked at his wife. "Well, you're the one to decide."

Abigail Smith thought for a minute. "Yes, I would like to make a change, but could we compromise? Could the children get half of the estate at age twenty five and let the rest stay in trust?"

"Certainly that can be done. Is that what you want?"

She glanced at her husband who nodded. "Yes," she said.

"Give me a few moments then. I'll write up a codicil to each will and have Jeremiah make an original and two copies. It shouldn't take too long."

The quartet waited while Read made the change and used the time to discuss the state of the vessel and the proposed time of departure. The provisioning and cargo loading were nearly completed and barring any unforeseen problems, the *Eagle* would depart in two days, sailing on the ebb, just before noon.

Read returned with the codicils that amended the wills. He fused over the documents, making notations on the wills and the copies. "All right, Mr. and Mrs. Smith we are ready. First, I want you to initial the changes I have made on the distribution clause."

Jacob and Abigail did as they were asked.

"Now, I must ask each of you a question. Mr. Davies and Mr. Brush, would you please listen to this?"

He turned to Abigail Smith.

"Ladies first," he smiled, "do you acknowledge that you sign these documents as your last will and testament of you own free will and that your actions are not influenced by others?"

"I do," Abigail said and she signed the original will, the codicil and the copies. The two ship's officers signed as witnesses.

"Now you, Mr. Smith." Read repeated the same process with Jacob Smith and when he finished, he returned to his seat.

"I think we are done," he said.

"What happens with the wills now?' Abigail Smith asked.

"Usually I give the originals to the principals and I save a copy in my vault. In your case, since you are going away, I'll hold on to the originals until I can get them to the Bank of Massachusetts when it finally opens for business. I'll keep a copy in my vault and I'll hold the third copy off premises to await your return. You can pick it up when you come back."

"Shouldn't we have a copy?" Jacob asked.

"They'll do you no good if you lose them at sea," explained Read.

"Yes, I guess so. It seems a good plan," Abigail Smith said and Jacob nodded.

"Then we are finished!" Read said and grinned.

"One last thing Mr. Read. Your bill? How much do we owe you for your services?"

"Ah yes, I am charging you twenty dollars for each will. That is my usual fee for complicated documents like these."

Abigail Smith nodded and reached for her purse. She took four ten dollar gold pieces and handed them to Read.

"I'll have a receipt drawn up and give it to you before you sail," Read said. "It will give me an excuse to see you off."

"We will look forward to seeing you," Jacob Smith said, "and thank you for your help, Mister Read, you have been very kind."

They exchanged good-byes and the mariners left the building to return to the ship. Abigail Smith admitted to herself that she felt better than she had in months.

*   *   *

The *Eagle of America* sailed just after high tide two days later. As she prepared to slip her lines and move into the channel, a small crowd of well wishers gathered to bid the ship good-bye and wish the crew good luck and godspeed.

Rebecca Marston, Abigail's Mother, was there along with her husband, William Marston. Jonathan Marston, his wife and children were there along with many merchants who had supplied cargo for the voyage. John Read Esq. also watched.

The good-byes were finally finished and the lines cast off. Slowly, the ship drifted away from the wharf and the crew set a jib and shook out the mainsail. As the ship gained steerageway, Read suddenly ran to the edge of the wharf. He looked toward Abigail and Jacob who were standing on the quarterdeck and he cupped his hands to his mouth.

"Ahoy," he yelled, "I forgot to give you your receipt!"

"Keep it!" Jacob Smith hailed in return. "We'll pick it up when we return!"

Read nodded, waving.

Abigail Smith waved back to where the others were gathered and then looked aloft as the sails began to catch the wind. When she looked back again at the wharf, she noted that Jonathan Marston had moved next to John Read and the two were talking intently.

Seeing this Abigail Steele Smith shivered in the cold winter sunlight and the sense of foreboding returned to her, more intense than ever before.

CHAPTER TWENTY-FIVE

David Baker drove north on Interstate 95, elated by what he had found because next to him on the seat were photocopies of the last will and testament of Jacob and Abigail Smith. Attached to them was a notarized statement attesting to the authenticity of the documents. Both documents were dated January 10, 1784, two months after the other wills that had been probated. It was really unbelievable and David hoped that the copies would be enough to win the lawsuit.

He knew he was late and rode the gas pedal as hard as he dared. He had arrived at the museum and immediately went to work with Sherry Kaminsky, going through the stack of files and papers that represented all the uncataloged documents. Sherry had already organized the papers that had been donated by William Read who, David guessed, was the son of John Read, the attorney who had drawn the Smith wills. This proved to be true when he found a letter with the papers saying they were "donated in the memory of my father who was brutally murdered in 1785". David wondered if this had also been Marston's work.

Sherry let him examine the documents and they appeared to be genuine. David read them quickly, raising his eyes when he came to the part that detailed the establishment of trusts with the Bank of Massachusetts, the trustee. Did that mean that the bank had actually owned the property all along he wondered?

They quickly went through the rest of the material but there didn't seem to be anything else that applied to the problem of Rosemary Point. David asked Sherry if he could get a notarized copy to take with him and she called the photographer the museum used for copying, explaining it was an emergency.

The woman arrived an hour later, delayed by a flat tire but she worked fast and David asked her to produce a copy immediately. The woman agreed after David promised a one hundred-dollar bonus if she had the copies back to him by six-o clock.

Sherry Kaminsky stayed to keep him company as they waited for the photographer to return. At David's suggestion, Sherry carefully wrapped the Smith wills in protective acid-free envelopes and put them in the fireproof vault in the museum's basement.

While they waited, David called Ted Williams and left the number at the museum where he could be reached. Next, he tried to call Jack Pierce who was busy on the Pilgrim Village grounds. Finally, he tried to call Abby but she did not answer and he assumed she was still out shopping.

Sherry Kaminsky wrote out a statement attesting to the fact that the original documents were at the Peabody Museum and that the copies were an accurate reproduction of the originals. She called her secretary in to notarize the statement.

The photographer finally returned with the still damp photocopies shortly before six. David thanked her and gave her the promised bonus. Ted Williams called back, as he was about to leave, and David told him he had found the Smith wills. He was pleased by the excitement in the other man's voice and they agreed to meet early the next day, before the hearing. The phone rang again as Jack Pierce checked in. David gave him the latest information and Pierce was clearly satisfied by developments. David tried Abby one more time but still got no answer and gave up trying.

Thanking Sherry Kaminsky, he was on the road north, shortly after six. He couldn't wait to tell Abby the good news.

As he approached the New Hampshire border he looked at his watch and saw it was nearly seven. Traffic had been heavy. But with luck, he would be in Abby's apartment in fifteen minutes. David Baker was excited and very happy indeed.

*   *   *

David turned his car into the parking place in front of Abby's apartment and thought it strange that her car was not there. Was she still shopping he wondered.

He unlocked the door to her apartment and as he entered he heard the telephone ring. He answered.

"Hello?"

"Dave!" he recognized the voice of Abby's mother and she sounded worried.

"Hello Jan," he said.

"Dave, is Abby there?" she sounded out of breath.

"No, I don't know where she is," he said, a bit uneasy.

"Oh God Dave, something's wrong! She went out to meet someone who said he had information to help you. She called me at five-thirty or so to tell me and said if she didn't call back in an hour to come for her. She hasn't called and I've been trying to call her for thirty minutes until you answered!"

"Did she say where she was going?" David asked, taking a deep breath to control the panic he felt.

Jan Palmer repeated what Abby had told her.

"Okay, I'll go after her," David said. "Could you call the cops Jan?"

"Is that necessary Dave?"

"Yeah, we'd better call them," he said, thinking of Pierce's admonition to be prepared to fight an elephant rather than a mouse. "I think we need to have them looking for her."

"Okay, I will. Please call me if you find her Dave, I'm worried sick!"

"I'll call Jan. You try to relax."

David ran back to the car the documents still in hand. He started the car and was soon following the route described by Jan Palmer. He wasn't familiar with the area and was soon lost. This delay cost him five minutes before he found his way again and he felt his anxiety grow.

Finally he turned on what he thought was the service road, driving fast as he anxiously searched the road.

Ahead he saw the reflection of flashing blue strobe lights on the trees. He began to tremble and tapped the brakes to slow the car. He drove over a slight rise in the road and his heart sank. There was a police car in the road, its door open. Next to it was a car lying on its right side in a ditch, the wheels pointing towards the road. David knew it was Abby's car.

David pulled to a stop behind the police cruiser and bolted from the car. He ran to the overturned car. There were two police officers. One was working at the driver's door while the other waited to help.

"Can I help?" David asked, afraid of what he would hear.

The officer not working at the door came over to him. "Sure, we can use some help. Who're you?"

"That's my fiancé's car," David said quietly.

"Oh shit, come on give us a hand. We just got here. My partner is trying to get the door open," he nodded toward the car door.

David hesitated. "Is she dead?" he choked on the words.

The other officer looked up at him. "No, I think she's breathing, but she's unconscious. She's still in her seatbelt and I can't get the damned door open!"

"We radioed for the rescue truck and an ambulance," the first officer added.

David heard sirens coming from down the road and a moment later a rescue truck and an ambulance skidded to a stop in front of the wrecked car. Experienced and well trained, the rescuers went right to work and quickly opened the door. One of the paramedics from the ambulance jumped up, his stomach on the rocker panel and dipped his head and torso into the car. After a few seconds he pulled himself back up.

"I think she's okay," he said. "Give me some smelling salts."

His partner searched the field kit and handed him an ampule. The paramedic on the car lowered himself back into the car and David soon heard a cough and a sneeze, then a soft whimpering. The paramedic rose again.

"Get a backboard and a neck brace, just in case," he ordered. "We'll get her out of there as soon as I get her stabilized. Looks like the seatbelt kept her out of serious trouble though!"

The paramedics, aided by the rescue team worked quickly and Abby was soon on a wheeled stretcher, her head supported by a neck brace and her back flat against a backboard. One of the paramedics gave her a quick once over as David bent to hold her hand. She squeezed it, tears in her eyes.

"Are you okay?" he asked.

"Yeah, but I've got a headache," she mumbled.

"What happened?"

Abby swallowed hard, trying to remain conscious, as one of the paramedics wrapped her in a blanket.

"Someone ran me off the road Dave!" she coughed.

Somehow this did not surprise him.

"We'll take a statement at the hospital," one of the police officers said. He touched David's arm, "why don't you follow us?"

David nodded and walked along to the ambulance holding Abby's hand. The medics expertly loaded the stretcher aboard.

"Want to ride or drive?" the same police officer asked.

"I'd better drive," David said, "what about her car?"

"A wrecker will come and take it away. Come on, we'll lead you to the hospital."

The ambulance door slammed shut and the driver spun the wheel, making a U-turn in the road and sped off.

David got into his car, the anger in him rising like hot lava because he knew who was responsible for this. Thomas Sherwood had finally responded to the pressure and had sent a message by trying to harm the person who was most dear to him.

Daivd vowed that nothing else was going to hurt Abigail Palmer, he would make sure of that.

*   *   *

Arriving at the hospital, David checked first on Abby who was being examined by the emergency room staff. It would be a while before they finished.

Next he called the Palmer house and was glad that Bob Palmer answered and not his wife. David explained what had happened and Bob Palmer thanked him, saying they would be right over.

The next call was to Ted Williams. David got him at home and the attorney was genuinely surprised when David told him what happened to Abby. He asked if she was all right. David told him he thought she was okay. They briefly discussed the newly discovered wills and Williams said he would see him in the morning.

David made a final call. This one was to Jack Pierce at home.

"Jack, it's Dave."

"You okay?" Pierce asked hearing the stress in David Baker's voice.

"No Jack, I'm not okay. Shit, someone tried to kill Abby tonight!"

"Oh no," Pierce said. "What the hell happened? Is she okay?"

"I think she's okay. Shit Jack, someone called to lure her out of the house to give her information, then tried to run her off the road. Her car rolled!"

"But she's okay?"

"Yeah, I'm at the hospital now. She's still in the emergency room but they say she's okay. Jesus Jack, I'm mad as hell and it has to be Sherwood. I want him Jack, I want the bastard!"

"Easy does it Tarzan. Time to calm down. You just stay with Abby. Where are you going to be tonight?"

"I'll probably stay at Abby's I guess. I've got to be in court tomorrow, remember?"

"Yeah. Okay, listen Dave, I'll be up first thing in the morning. I'll cancel my appointments here and I'll see you early. You just try and stay calm, stay under control. And take good care of that lady of yours!"

"Okay, Jack. I hear you."

"I'll pick you up at Abby's apartment. I think I remember the way there. Then I'll go to court with you."

David replaced the phone on the hook and went back to the waiting room where he sat staring at the wall. He felt better now that Jack Pierce was coming up in the morning.

*　　　*　　　*

Jack Pierce replaced the telephone on the cradle and looked up at the paneled wall in his den. There was a collection of photos on that wall, many of which brought back memories, some good, some bad. He thought for a moment and then rose going to the closet. From the small wooden footlocker on the floor he removed the box containing the Beretta 9mm automatic and the cleaning kit.

At his desk, he broke the pistol down, cleaning and lubricating the weapon. He reassembled the weapon and then took a box of shells from the bottom drawer of his desk, loading each of the three clips.

He jammed a clip into the pistol, checking the action. Then satisfied that all was as it should be, he wrapped the weapon in an oilskin cloth. He would let it sit overnight before placing it in his shoulder holster in the morning.

He went to the kitchen for a beer. He opened it as he walked to the living room where his wife was watching television. He told her about Abby Palmer's accident and told her that he would go help Dave Baker in the morning.

Jennifer Pierce recognized the look on her husband's face and tried to smile at him. She had not seen that determined look in years, but knew the meaning well. This was something he had to do.

She got up from the chair and went to him. She gave him a kiss and then paused to lightly touch the back of her hand to his cheek, an unspoken thought passed between them and she knew he needed to be left alone now. She nodded to him and went up the stairs to the bedroom.

Sipping the beer, Jack Pierce marshaled his thoughts, trying to think of the possible consequences his actions might bring.

                    *   *   *

David sat in the waiting room with the Palmers who had arrived a few minutes before. Jan Palmer was in tears and David tried to console her.

It was nearly 9:00 when a doctor finally came out of the emergency room and David and Bob Palmer rose as he came toward them.

"Mr. Palmer?" the doctor asked.

"Yes?" Bob Palmer replied, "how is she?"

The doctor smiled. "I'm happy to report that other than a nasty bump on the head, she seems fine. We checked her over very closely and can't find anything wrong. Just the same though, she's had quite a shock and we'll keep her over night for observation. If everything's still okay in the morning, we'll release her."

"That's good," Abby's Father said, putting his arm around his wife who joined them.

"When can we see her?" Jan Palmer asked.

"You can go in now. She's sitting up and we'll take her to a room in a moment. Follow me."

He led them into a curtained examination area where Abby was sitting on the bed, legs dangling over the side. She wore a white hospital gown. Her eyes brightened and she smiled sheepishly when she saw David and her parents enter.

"Hi," she said.

"How are you Honey?" her mother asked.

"I'll be okay. You know I've got a hard head. I've got a headache and I'm sore, but I guess I'm okay."

She looked at David who bent to kiss her.

"What happened?" he asked.

She related the story she had told to the police officers.

"So, you didn't see anything?" her Father asked.

"No. I didn't see anything until the car came up and started to push me off the road. I think he must have followed me from home, but I didn't notice him."

"You didn't see who was driving?" David questioned.

"No. It was too dark and I was too busy trying to keep the car on the road!"

"Did the police have anything to say?" her mother chimed in.

"They weren't very encouraging since I didn't see anything," Abby said shaking her head.

"We know who it was," David said, angrily, "it had to be Sherwood and he's still around here somewhere!"

Abby took his hand, trying to calm his anger and he relaxed, smiling at her. She spoke. "Did you get it? With all that's happened I still don't know?"

"Yeah, I got it," David smiled. "I got them both Abby. Jesus, it's some story!"

He told her the story of finding the wills and the Palmer's listened to the story also, surprised at the details in the wills.

"Wow!" Abby said.

"We're going to court with copies tomorrow. Ted is real excited and he says we should come out okay now."

"And I won't be there to see it!" Abby lamented.

"You just get better, so you can get out of here tomorrow," David said. "Bob, can you pick her up in the morning?"

"Hell yes, we'll be here."

David glanced back at Abby. "Jack is coming to pick me up tomorrow. He says he wants to be in on the hearing and keep me out of trouble."

"You've got to call me as soon as you know something!" she said.

"I will," David promised and they all turned as a nurse pushed a wheelchair towards them.

"Come on," the nurse ordered, "time to take you to your room."

David kissed Abby good bye and her parents followed suit.

"See you tomorrow," David said.

"I can't wait," Abby said over her shoulder as the nurse wheeled her out the door.

"That was a close thing," Bob Palmer said while they walked down the hall to the door.

"Yes," David said, "and I don't intend to let anything else happen to her."

Bob Palmer smiled. He really liked this young man and thought he would make a fine son.

*   *   *

Jack Pierce found Abby's apartment the next morning and picked David up shortly after eight. David was waiting and got into Pierce's car and slammed the door.

"How's Abby?" Pierce asked.

"She's going to be okay," David replied. Then he told Pierce what had happened after their conversation the night before.

They headed north onto the Maine Turnpike. Pierce drove, listening intently to David. When he finished, Pierce was silent for a moment, then he looked at his friend.

"Sherwood, right?" he said.

"Yeah, I think so," David replied, "who else?"

"I don't know. I suppose it could be someone who works for him maybe, but he's probably behind it."

"I want the bastard Jack! I want him to pay, God how I want to hurt him!"

"Shit Dave, you can't take the law into your own hands."

"Yeah, I know, but he tried to kill Abby. I'd like to get him by the balls and make him pay!"

"I think you're about to do that in court. Let your case do the work for you."

"Yeah, you're right, of course, but I've never experienced anything like this. I guess it's some primal protective instinct coming out. I want to pay him back for trying to hurt Abby."

"I think I know how you feel," Pierce said, "and your instincts are not uncommon."

"Well, today should be interesting anyway," David said.

"Yeah. You've done good detective work on this. You've managed to solve the mystery and done a job that any historian would be proud of."

"Coming from you, that really means something," and David smiled. Pierce returned the gesture and continued on to Biddeford.

They met Ted Williams at the coffee shop. Over steaming cups, David brought Williams up to date.

"Where are the wills?" the attorney asked.

David handed him the copies and Williams quickly scanned them, shaking his head as he read the documents.

"This is really something Dave. I'll have to write an article for the Law Journal if this turns out okay."

"You don't think it will?" Pierce asked.

Williams shook his head. "No, I'm not worried. Things should work out the way we want, but I haven't talked with Judge Carrier yet. I didn't want to give Veazie any advance warning on this."

"How are you going to handle this?" David wondered.

Williams explained his strategy and David and Pierce listened with great interest.

*   *   *

Judge Andrew Carrier took his seat and looked out at the courtroom. "Are we ready to begin?"

Both attorneys responded positively and Carrier nodded. "If you are ready to proceed, Mr. Williams? Yesterday you asked for another continuance because of new evidence. Have you been successful?"

"Yes, your Honor."

"Then go ahead and I hope this is going to be good."

"I think your Honor will find it interesting," Williams smiled and rose, glancing at the notes in front of him.

"Your Honor, the plaintiffs wish to amend their petition."

"Amend? On what grounds?" asked the Judge.

"The plaintiffs ask to enter into the record this evidence your Honor." Williams held up an envelope and Veazie was on his feet immediately.

"I object your Honor! I was not informed of this!"

"I'm sorry your Honor," Williams explained, "this has only just come to light. May I be allowed to enter this into evidence?"

"I'll allow it, but reserve the right to rule on the significance of it later. Objection is overruled. Go ahead Mr. Williams."

Ted Williams approached the bench and set the documents before the Judge.

"You Honor, these are copies of two wills. They were legally executed and witnessed on January 10, 1784, in Boston by Jacob and Abigail Smith.

"What significance is that?" protested Veazie. "What is the point of these theatrics?"

Williams continued. "Your Honor, Abigail Steele Smith was, at the time, the legal owner of the property in question in this suit. She was lost at sea a short time later along with her husband. If you will notice your Honor, in the wills she has created a testamentary trust to hold her estate and has named the Bank of Massachusetts as trustee."

"I object, your Honor! What do these theatrics have to do with this case?" Veazie exclaimed.

"Sit down, Mr. Veazie! I want to hear this!" the Judge ordered.

"Your Honor," Williams continued, "plaintiffs have good reason to believe that the other wills were substituted and probated instead of these legal and binding wills. Further, the plaintiffs amend their original motion to enjoin the Springbrook Partnership from doing anything with Rosemary Point, because they do not have legal title to the property!"

Veazie was on his feet again protesting.

"Sit down, Mr. Veazie!" Carrier said with an edge in his voice. "You will get your chance! Mr. Williams, how did these wills come into your possession at such an opportune moment? Have you been holding out on this court?" Carrier asked and a thin smile was on his face.

"Why, no, your Honor and I resent your insinuations," but Williams could not help a grin of satisfaction. "The wills were discovered at the Peabody Museum in Salem, Massachusetts, yesterday afternoon. They are in a collection of papers donated by a William Read, who was a Boston attorney. He donated them in memory of his father, John Read, who was also an attorney and drafted these wills. For some reason he apparently kept signed copies in his files. You will notice an attested and notarized statement by the Peabody Museum's archivist describing the authenticity of the documents. The originals, your Honor, are stored in the vaults of the museum and we suggest that experts will confirm to the court that the documents are real."

Carrier examined the photocopies carefully. The courtroom was silent while he did this and David looked to the back of the room where Dan King sat rigidly straight, his face deathly ashen. David smiled at him. Enjoy this, you bastard.

The Judge spoke to Veazie. "Now, Mr. Veazie, what do you have to say?"

"Your Honor, this is a grandstand play. It is preposterous and I have not seen these documents. How do we know they are real? I ask that they not be allowed into evidence!"

"I will take your objections into consideration. Mr. Williams, do you have anything else to add?"

"Two more items, your Honor. First are photocopies of the wills that were probated in Yorkshire Probate Court in 1785. They are dated November 12, 1783, two months before the wills we offer in evidence. Second, is a copy of a receipt, also obtained from the Peabody Museum, dated January 10, 1784 for legal services provided by John Read for Jacob and Abigail Smith. The plaintiffs believe that this material corroborates the authenticity of the wills offered in evidence."

The bailiff took the material from Williams and handed it to Judge Carrier. The Judge examined it closely. "We will take a fifteen minute recess. I wish to examine this in chamber."

The spectators rose as the Judge entered his chambers.

The fifteen minutes stretched to twenty-five before he returned. David, Jack Pierce and Ted Williams had spent the time talking quietly. They stood as the Judge reentered the courtroom.

Judge Andrew Carrier took his seat and placed the new evidence in front of him. He looked out at the courtroom, glancing first at Veazie, then at Williams.

"This is a very unusual case that has taken a very odd turn," he began. "I have examined these documents and reviewed several precedents."

He paused and David looked at Pierce who smiled and nodded. Carrier continued.

"In this particular case I am satisfied that the documents entered into evidence are real. The court has spoken with a Miss Kaminsky at the Peabody Museum to verify her statement and the other documents give support to this supposition. Therefore this court believes there is a real question of title to the Rosemary Point property and grants an injunction enjoining the Springbrook Partnership, or anyone else from sale of the property."

David was elated. "Yes!" he whispered. Jack took his arm, a broad grin on his face.

"Now," Carrier continued, "I have also spoken with Judge Janet Mclaine at York County Probate Court in Alfred. This court orders that this case be remanded to the Probate Court to determine the true ownership of the property in question."

He rapped his gavel. "So ruled."

Veazie was on his feet again, but most of the fight was out of him now. "Your Honor, the defense notifies the court that it will appeal this arbitrary ruling."

"That is your right Mister Veazie. So noted," Judge Carrier said, leaving his seat, going back into his chambers.

David hugged the diminutive attorney. "God damn! You did it Ted! You're terrific!"

"I'd like to take the credit Dave, but you did it. You found the wills we needed!"

"You did," agreed Pierce.

"Hey! I've got to call Abby!" David said.

The trio turned and went down the aisle toward the door. David stopped by the bench where Dan King sat, staring blankly.

David spoke his voice harsh and menacing. "How do you like that King? Go tell your friend, Sherwood. After what that bastard did to Abby, he deserves some bad news!"

The other man looked at him slowly. "What? What are you talking about?"

"Someone tried to kill Abby last night King. Someone ran her car off the road. It had to be Sherwood, or maybe it was you? Where were you last night?"

"What? I don't know anything about it! Jesus, I'd never hurt Abby," King cried out, scared.

"Then it must have been your friend King. Ask him about it!"

David felt his fists involuntarily clench and he felt like swinging at King, but Pierce grabbed hold of him and walked him out the door to the pay phone. David took a couple of deep breaths to calm down and called Abby at her parent's house to tell her of the successful conclusion. She was overjoyed at the news.

After David finished, Ted Williams made a call and that night a follow up story ran on the television news in Portland. Dutifully, the Portland morning paper and the Boston papers ran the story also.

*   *   *

At mid morning the telephone rang in Nicholas Dominic's office in South Boston.

"Hello?" he answered and then was instantly alert.

"Nick?" said the voice.

"Yes," Dominic said, recognizing the voice of one of his principals, an old friend and a man you did not mess with.

"You seen the papers?" the voice said. "Those two bastards in Maine won the lawsuit. It looks like Sherwood doesn't even own the property Nick. He's made us look like fools again and I don't like being made to look like a fool!"

"I know. The deal's off."

"Yeah, that goes without saying. The man needs an object lesson, Nick. A final lesson I think, he can't keep fucking with us this way."

"What do you want me to do?" Dominic asked.

"I think you know," the man said.

"Okay, I understand." Nick Dominic replaced the phone and tried to figure out how to do what needed to be done.

*   *   *

Thomas Sherwood sat in his home in New Rochelle where he had driven the night before in a different rental car, after abandoning the rental car he used to run the Palmer woman off the road. Since the call from Dan King the previous afternoon he had tried to figure out what to do. He was in danger and he knew he had to get out of the house. He was pretty sure he should leave the country because he had no illusions about what the people Dominic worked for were capable of doing.

The telephone startled him and he debated for a moment whether to answer it or not. He let the answering machine take the call and when the machine beeped, the voice of Nick Dominic spoke.

"Sherwood, we need to get together quickly. My people think the deal can be restructured despite what happened. We still want to go ahead with it, call me."

Impulsively, Sherwood put the phone to his ear. "Nick? It's me. I just came in," he lied, "you still want to go ahead?"

"Yes, my people want the property. They want it bad and we got a few ideas on how to do it."

"Shit, okay, I'll talk," maybe he could save himself after all, he thought.

"Meet me in the shuttle parking garage at Logan again."

"When?"

"Tonight, at seven."

"Okay, I'll be there."

After he hung up the phone, he began to think about what Dominic had said. The meeting could very well be a trap, so he would have to be careful and he needed to be prepared.

Sherwood looked at his watch. If he left in an hour, he could be in the parking garage early and that would give him time to get set, check the place out and choose his ground carefully. It would give him time to protect himself.

*   *   *

David and Abby walked up the brick pathway at Rosemary Point and David looked at Abby. She showed no signs of her experience two nights before and she smiled at him, took his hand and squeezed it.

Not finding the woman in the house, they went around to the garden in the back where they found her sitting on the back steps, her hands on her knees holding her chin, deep in thought. She was staring at the ground but she looked up, startled, as they approached.

"Oh! I did not see you. How are you?"

"We're fine," said Abby. "And we have wonderful news!"

"What is it?"

They told her everything that had taken place and when David told her about the court ruling, she jumped up to hug him.

"You have done it! You are wonderful, I knew you would help me. Oh thank you both!"

She gave Abby a hug.

"Well," David said, "we're not done yet. The probate court must rule first, but our attorney says that the property will go into the trust."

"That is good," the woman said," and you young lady, you were not hurt in your accident?"

"No, I'll be fine."

"Oh! I am so happy, so full of joy! It has been such a long time!"

"Can you rest now?" Abby asked, a concerned look on her face.

The woman thought. "Yes, it is close to being done now, but I feel there is one thing left for me to do. I just do not know what it is."

"Can we help?" David asked.

"I'm sorry, I just don't know."

They talked for a bit longer and the woman grew more excited. Finally, David and Abby reluctantly left, kissing the woman goodbye.

"You will truly be blessed for what you have done," the woman said, bidding them goodbye.

David and Abby waved to her in return, grins on their faces. They both felt a curious feeling of disappointment, it was as if something very special was ending and they did not want it to end.

*   *   *

Thomas Sherwood arrived at the shuttle parking garage at Logan Airport forty minutes early just as he had planned. He was now totally convinced that Dominic had called the meeting to kill him. He could run, but that would not allow him to accomplish what he wanted to do now. His plan was clear in his mind and to do it, he would have to kill Dominic.

He would have to let Dominic make the first move though, so he would choose his position well. He was close to the entrance he thought that Dominic would use. Sherwood made sure that he was obscured in a shadow cast by one of the overhead lights. He would have his silenced automatic in his right hand covered by his raincoat and would count on the shadows to hide this very obvious ploy.

He looked at his watch, it was seven-o clock. He expected Dominic to be late as usual, but was surprised when the man walked in a moment later looking for him. He must be anxious to get it over with, Sherwood thought and that confirmed his suspicions.

"I'm here Nick," he said trying to control his voice and his thumping heart.

The man turned, trying to find the location of the voice. "There you are," Dominic said, a nervous quiver in his voice.

"Hello Nick, what's your proposal?"

"We want to help you fight this in court. We'll give you help," he offered.

"Why?" Sherwood asked, "why go this far?"

"I told you. We want the property. Come closer Tom where I can see you better."

Dominic fingered the pistol in his coat pocket and wished Sherwood would move in the open.

"What guarantees do I have?" Sherwood asked his heart pumping even faster now.

"The usual, except because we agree to help you, the price for the property will be lower," Dominic said and knew he had made a mistake.

"How much lower?" Sherwood asked, rising anger in his voice.

"Six million," Dominic said gesturing with his hand.

"That's not enough. Eleven was the agreed price!"

"Hey, you're lucky to get six after what's happened! Come closer, we can't talk like this," Dominic said, the beginning of panic in his voice.

"I'll stay where I am," Sherwood said. "The price is eleven million!"

Dominic was getting angry, it was not going as planned. "Listen, Sherwood, you're God-damned lucky to get what we're offering. My people are not happy!"

"It's not my fault!"

"Yeah, I know that, but you know how they think. I just can't do any better now."

"Yeah, I know how they think, but as I said, eleven million."

Dominic was livid, he had screwed up letting it go on this long. He needed to end this quickly. "Sherwood, you're pushing it. You know things could get unhealthy for you!"

Outside, two shuttle buses roared by, the diesel whine piercing the air. Dominic recognized the opportunity and his hand went back to his pocket. He pulled the pistol and leveled it at Sherwood.

"Okay, Sherwood, enough is enough. Come out of there. I think it's time you and I go somewhere."

"You're going somewhere Nicholas, but not where you think!" And Sherwood pulled the trigger. The silenced automatic puffed twice.

Dominic was hit twice in the chest and he dropped his pistol, grabbing at his breast. The look of panic on his face and surprise in his eyes faded as he fell to the concrete dead.

Sherwood quickly looked around and walked cautiously to the body. He looked around again any for signs of witnesses. There were none, so he kicked the body. It did not move, Dominic was dead. Sherwood turned and walked quickly back to his car.

His blood was running hot and revenge was now foremost in his mind. He needed to settle some accounts. Mostly though, he only wanted to get even with the two people who had stolen his property from him. He had some unfinished business to attend to in Maine.

CHAPTER TWENTY-SIX

David raised his head at the sound of the ringing telephone and stumbled out of bed to answer it. He walked into the living room of Abby's apartment and picked up the handset.

"Hello?"

"Hi sleepy head," Abby said, "how are you this morning?" David looked at his watch and saw it was almost nine-o clock.

"Jesus, why are you calling now? I need to sleep."

On the couch, Jack Pierce stirred and sat up with a start.

"I'm just calling to see how you two boys are," Abby said.

The two men had stayed up very late the night before discussing what Sherwood might do next. David wasn't sure he would try anything now that they had won in court, but Pierce was convinced that he would.

"Well, it's getting late. You two should be up," Abby laughed. "Anything happen last night?"

"No," David yawned.

"Good. I told you not to worry. Jack's seen too many scary movies!" Abby said.

"No, he's right Abby. We're going to stay here for a while."

"Well, okay. You two come over for lunch though."

"Sure, we'll be there," he said and they said good-bye.

David put the phone back on the cradle and went to the kitchen to make coffee. He heard Pierce in the bathroom.

The two men had been in the apartment for two days now. Pierce had suggested that for her own protection Abby should stay somewhere else after the incident with Sherwood. Abby had reluctantly agreed and had gone to her parent's house.

Pierce came into the kitchen carrying the *Boston Globe* that had been delivered to the front door. He poured a mug of coffee and joined David at the table.

"Which section you want?" he asked.

"I'll start with sports," David replied.

"Okay. You get the feeling we're turning into the odd couple?" Pierce said only half joking.

David laughed. "No, Jack. It's just that you and I know each other too well!"

"Guess you're right. Abby's still pissed at me for making her move out?"

"Yeah. She doesn't see the danger. But I do."

"You're right. He'll be back," Jack Pierce said. "I've seen his type before and he'll be back, I know it!"

"You know, for the last couple of days it's like you've turned into Rambo. How come you think you know so much?" David asked, puzzled by the change that had come over his friend.

Pierce picked up the Metro section, folding it subway style. He looked at David. "Remember my Army time?"

"Yeah?"

"Well, I hate using this oxymoron, but I was with military intelligence. I came in contact with all kinds of scum. So trust me, he'll be back."

"Oh," said David, not knowing how impressed he should be.

Pierce read the paper, sipping at his coffee. He whistled to himself and David looked up from the sports section. "What is it?"

"Just a hunch. I need to use the phone?"

"Sure," David said as Pierce rose from the table.

Pierce went to the phone and tapped out Tony Nappia's number. The police captain was soon on the line.

"What can I do for you Jack?"

"Remember that guy, Sherwood?"

"Yeah, the guy you asked me to check on."

"I need to know if he might have had anything to do with a guy named Nicholas Dominic from Lynn, Massachusetts? Apparently he had a real estate business in Boston."

"Sure, I can do that, how soon do you need it? I've got some good friends at Boston PD."

"ASAP, Tony. I need it now, if you can do it."

"Where are you?"

Pierce gave him the number.

"Where's that?" Nappia asked.

"New Hampshire. It's a long story Tony, I'll tell you sometime."

"Okay Jack. Give me twenty minutes or so." Pierce went back to the paper.

Twenty minutes later the phone rang and Pierce went to answer it. True to his word, Tony Nappia was on the line.

"This guy Dominic got iced last night Jack. You didn't tell me about that."

"That's what the paper says Tony."

"Yeah, well, I got some funny questions from my friend in Boston. This guy Dominic was a go between for some of the boys. Fronted for them, put deals together, that sort of thing."

"Is that right?"

"Yeah, according to my friend, your Mr. Sherwood has been linked to Dominic on several occasions."

"Thanks Tony, that's what I wanted to know."

"Jack, what else do you know?"

"Nothing, just a hunch. I'll tell you later. The less you know now the better for you."

"I had to explain why I was asking Jack," Nappia continued, "my friend asked me if they should be looking for this Sherwood guy. I said yes. Did I do good?"

"You did good Tony. I'll talk to you soon. Thank you my friend!"

"You bet!"

Pierce replaced the phone and went back into the kitchen.

"He's coming," Pierce said, "he left a calling card in Boston last night. At Logan Airport. A guy named Dominic. He's dead."

David looked at Pierce, eyes wide. "How do you know?"

"I don't know for sure, but call it an educated guess. He managed to piss off the boys he was going to sell the property to because of what you and Abby did. I think they tried to get him, but he got them first. Now I think he's going to come for you."

David felt fear in the pit of his stomach. "What do we do?"

"We wait. He's got to come to us. Then we'll deal with him."

"Jesus, Jack! He's a killer!"

"Yeah, that's right," Pierce said.

"Well, shouldn't we call the police?"

"We can't yet. Nothing's happened that we can prove and they won't supply protection on a whim."

David looked at him, bothered by this turn of events.

"Don't worry Dave," Pierce said, "we'll get through this!"

Curiously, David felt a confidence and trust is his friend that he hadn't felt before.

*   *   *

Tony "Two Shoes" Zane looked at the other man who sat across from him at the McDonalds in Charlestown and wondered how he had been so unlucky to get stuck working with Willie Boy again. Tony Two Shoes was a soldier for the family from Rhode Island and often acted as a mercenary for others who needed his particular expertise. He had just received his instructions that morning.

It wasn't that Willie Boy was stupid, he thought, it was just that the kid easily lost his cool. That was the one thing that Tony did not need for this job.

Tony was smart, or at least he thought he was smart. His last name had originally been a longer one with a lot of vowels, but his father had shortened the name years before. Tony had acquired his nickname as a youngster when he had ripped off a delivery truck and in his haste had managed to get away with two right shoes. His cohorts, of course, greeted this with great derision and the nickname was forever assigned to him. He never lived this down and it still bothered him.

The job today was to clean up a mess. This mess included a dead man; Nick Dominic who had been iced at Logan Airport by a guy named Sherwood. It had happened the night before and Tony had received a call that morning giving him the job of finding Sherwood and dealing with him. Now he sat in the McDonalds with Willie Boy and they were making plans to go after Sherwood.

Tony had worked with Willie Boy before and the other man had the reputation as a loose cannon. He was apt to do anything in his zeal to do a job and this scared Tony. He worried that Willie Boy might complicate this job needlessly.

"So where do we start?" Willie Boy asked for the third time.

"Shit, I'm not sure," Tony said again, looking at the notes he had jotted down that morning. "This guy could be anywhere."

"Well, we got to start someplace."

"No shit Willie! Jesus, I know that."

Willie Boy looked away trying to hide his anger. He was tired of getting picked on by everyone. He saw himself as a fearless and hard working soldier who was not afraid to get in the trenches and get his hands dirty. Tony saw the look on Willie's face.

"Sorry. Listen, I guess our best bet is to assume that Sherwood still wants to get even with those bastards who queered his deal."

"Yeah?"

"Yeah. This Baker guy and the Palmer broad. If that's true, he should be trying to find them."

"So?"

"So we should find them too and keep an eye on them. If Sherwood finds them, then we find him."

"Okay, what about this guy and the broad?"

"What about them?"

"Do we pop them too?" Willie Boy smiled.

"That's not part of the job. We just want Sherwood."

"But if something happens and the other two get in the way?" Willie Boy said.

"Don't Willie, that's not part of the deal."

But Willie Boy just smiled and Tony Two Shoes wished again that he had someone else to help him do this job.

"Come on," he said getting up, "we got to hit the road and get up to Portsmouth."

*   *   *

Thomas Sherwood was driving north in a new rental car planning how he would take out the meddling couple who had stolen his property. He had left his car in the Logan parking lot the night before and rented the new car using his phony ID and credit cards. He had stayed in a motel off of Route One in Revere using still another alias.

He got David Baker's phone number in Duxbury from information and over the course of the evening he had tried the house a number of times getting no answer. So, he assumed that Baker was still in New Hampshire with the Palmer bitch and he was going there now with revenge on his mind.

He thought he would deal with the Palmer woman first and finish what he started three nights before. Then he would take on Baker. The thought of that made the anger and hate in him built to a crescendo. He wanted revenge because it was all he had left. If he could not have the property, then no one would.

Sherwood picked up his cellular car phone and tapped out the Palmer woman's number. It rang several times before a man answered. Hearing this he pushed the disconnect button. Someone was at her apartment.

Sherwood had anticipated the possibility that the Palmer woman would be somewhere else, hiding and the man who answered the phone was most likely Baker. If he waited long enough, Baker would lead him to her, he thought. He arrived in Portsmouth just past eleven and went directly to Palmer's apartment where he parked in the complex lot and waited.

He noticed that her car was not in the parking lot and smiled remembering the other night. He must have done a good job.

Sherwood waited only thirty minutes before two men came out of the Palmer woman's apartment. He assumed that the younger of the two was Baker, but he didn't know who the older man was. He could be a plain clothes cop, he thought, there for protection. He watched the two men get in a car and drive off. Then, after pausing for a moment, he followed at a distance.

The drive took only a few minutes and the other car pulled into a driveway beside a white frame house. The two men got out of the car and went to the front door. The door opened and he recognized the Palmer woman as she kissed the younger man. So it was Baker and he now had made them both and he knew where she was. He would come back later, after sunset and take care of her.

He put the car into gear, driving away slowly. Thomas Sherwood needed to find a place to think and make his plans.

∗   ∗   ∗

David and Jack Pierce entered the Palmer house to have lunch. Jan Palmer had set the dinning room table with cold cuts for sandwiches. As they ate, Pierce told them of the murder in Boston and the information he had, tying Thomas Sherwood to the victim.

"Of course I can't prove anything," he said, "but we've got to be careful. I'm pretty sure that Sherwood is involved."

"But, you've got Abby's apartment covered," Jan Palmer said, "surely he won't try anything?"

"Yes Jan, I think he would," Pierce said, "he's a pretty desperate man now and he doesn't care anymore. He's out for blood and I don't think he'll let anything stop him."

"He may even come here," David said looking at Abby.

"How could he know I'm here?" Abby protested.

"Simple, the phone book. He probably knows your father lives in town and he can just look up the address," Pierce explained.

"What if he does come here?" asked a very serious Bob Palmer.

"Call the police and lock the door," Pierce said. "I'm not sure there is anything else you can do."

"But we just can't call the police if he hasn't done anything," argued Abby.

"If you wait, you won't be able to call the police," Pierce said coldly.

"Why not?"

"Because you'll probably be dead!"

Abby looked at him, eyes wide, the reality of the situation finally hitting home.

*   *   *

Tony Two Shoes opened the car door and sat on the passenger side and closed the door behind him. He looked over at Willie Boy.

"Well, I got the address," he said.

"I still say we should go to the broad's apartment," Willie said.

Tony shook his head. He was losing his patience with Willie Boy. The man might be a fearless operator, but he had no imagination. They had been arguing for the past hour over where they should start. He had just finished a quick call to check on the address of Abigail Palmer's apartment and her parent's house.

"Listen, you stupid shit," he said, "we've talked about this for half the damn way up here. I told you that the broad is probably in hiding. She's not going to be at her place and the next best place is her parent's house. If Sherwood's half the dope I think he is, then he's going to go after her. So we stake out the house and wait for them to lead us to Sherwood. Or, he's going to come to us."

"Yeah, all right. But shit Tony, I think we're better off at her place."

"Just shut up and drive," Tony said.

"Okay, okay. You got the address?"

"Yeah, just drive and I'll tell you where to go," Tony Two Shoes shook his head. He really didn't like working with this guy. The faster they got this job done the better.

Willie Boy put the car in gear and they drove off. It was almost four-o clock.

*   *   *

Susan Taylor stopped to visit Abby at the Palmer house later in the afternoon. She had Betsey Watrous in tow and the three women sat in the Palmer living room, sipping tea. The bright late afternoon sunlight flooded the room yellow orange and Abby had to change seats to avoid the glare.

"Abby," Betsey Watrous said, "I want you to know what a wonderful thing you've done. All the folks at the Society owe you a debt of gratitude. I think they'll want to do something official at the next board meeting."

"Oh no," Abby said flushing, "no call to do anything special. We were just glad to do it. You know that we have an interest in this too."

The older woman eyed her oddly and smiled. "She told you to help her, didn't she?"

Abby stared at Betsey Watrous. "What do you mean?" she said slowly.

"You know what I mean," Betsey said. "I think she asked for help, didn't she? It was Abigail!"

"Oh God, how did you know Betsey?"

The older woman grinned and reached out to take Abby's arm. "I've felt her presence there many times. I always sensed I could feel it when others couldn't. You see, I think I have the gift Abby," she said. "Roger used to say that he could feel something there too, and I always wondered why she was there. I think you and Dave found the answer, but no one has ever seen her. Until now."

Abby dropped her eyes for a second and Betsey noticed the hesitation.

"But you've seen her haven't you?"

Abby nodded.

"I knew it!" Betsey was excited now. "I knew she would eventually come to someone when she needed help."

"Has Dave seen her too?" her grandmother asked.

"Yes, he actually saw her first, before I did. She chose him to help. God, it was on his first visit to the house. He thought she was an interpreter in costume."

"So she found him. She must have recognized him, sensed his heritage," Betsey said. "The combination of you two must be overwhelming to her."

"What's she like?" Susan Taylor asked.

"Grandma, she's just like us. Dave says she looks like me, but I don't know. She's very kind, deliberate I think, but she does get emotional after all these years."

"You know there's a painting of her in storage somewhere," Betsey said. "It needs work, but we really ought to put it back up at the house."

"That would be nice," Abby agreed. "I'd like to see it."

"I wonder if she's accomplished what she came to do?" Susan Taylor asked.

"She said there was something more she had to do," Abby replied.

"What was it?" Betsey Watrous asked.

"She didn't know," Abby said and wished she did know. It seemed important.

*   *   *

"Hey," Willie Boy said, "two guys leaving the house!"

Tony Two Shoes had been leaning back in the car seat, his eyes shut and now he snapped instantly awake. It was dark, the sun had set one hour before. "Yeah," he said as he watched the two men walk out to a car. "Guess one of those must be the Baker guy."

"The younger one," Willie Boy said. "Who's the other guy?"

"Shit if I know."

"What do we do?" Willie asked.

"Sit tight," Tony said. They watched as the two men got into the car and drove away.

"You don't want to follow them?" Willie Boy asked, anxious to do something. "Shit, I'm hungry Tony, I need to eat!"

"Just shut up asshole! We wait!" Tony was getting pissed at the kid.

"Aw shit Tony, nothing is happening here."

"Listen you asshole, you're getting well paid for this, so you can eat later. The broad is still here and that means that Sherwood will probably come here sooner or later."

"Yeah?" Willie challenged him.

"Yeah," Tony spat back. The other man lapsed into silence.

They waited and this time Willie started to nod off, but Tony Two Shoes watched, alert, some instinctive sense making him wary. It seemed like a long time, but it had been only about ten minutes when

Tony saw something move along the hedges that lined the street. He watched carefully for signs of movement. Had he only imagined it? Then he saw it again.

It was a man dressed in dark clothing and he moved slowly but purposefully against the shadows.

"Holy shit! Willie!" Tony said sharply and the other man was instantly awake.

"Yeah?"

"We got company."

"No shit?"

"Yeah."

"Well, let's go!" Willie said.

"Just shut up and calm down asshole. We don't know that's our man!"

"Okay, okay. What do we do?"

"We wait, now just calm down and keep cool. We'll wait and see what happens here."

"Okay, but shit Tony, we ought to do something!"

"We will Willie, we will. Let's just watch a for a second to make sure."

*   *   *

Abby helped her mother clear off the dinner table and take the supper dishes into the kitchen. David and Jack Pierce had just left the house to go back to her apartment in case Sherwood decided to show up there. Abby insisted she would be safe with everyone in the house and Jack Pierce had reluctantly agreed.

Now her father, grandmother and Betsey Watrous were in the den watching *Jeopardy* while she started the dishwater.

"I'm scared Abby," her mother said to her suddenly, looking around, "I feel like someone is watching us!"

Abby looked around the kitchen, then out the window. It was dark, but a new moon cast a pale light, leaving the suggestion of shadows. She saw nothing.

"There's no one there," she laughed nervously. "You're letting all this get to you."

"No I'm not! Damn it Abby, I've got that feeling," she said, drying her hands. "Something's going to happen, I feel it. You're not the only one with intuition, you know!"

"I know Mom, but we'll be okay," now she was trying to convince herself, she thought. "I'm safe here with you guys."

When they finished the dishes she went into the den to watch TV with the others while her mother remained in the kitchen, making a shopping list.

The doorbell rang.

Abby heard her mother go to the door and her heart pounded as she realized what was happening. She leaped from her seat, running to stop her mother before she could open the door. She made it just in time and Abby put a finger to her lips.

"Ssh! Go back to the kitchen," she whispered. Her mother looked at her, not moving, then Abby pushed her towards the room.

"Go!" she whispered urgency in here voice.

Jan Palmer went slowly back to the kitchen, where Bob Palmer and the two other women were now on their feet. Abby went to the living room window and carefully peeked around the edge, trying not to be seen.

A man in his middle sixties stood looking around nervously and he had his hand in his coat pocket.

Abby's blood ran cold, the panic rising within her because she had no illusions as to who this was. Fighting her fear, she moved quickly to the telephone and tapped out the emergency number. The phone rang.

"Portsmouth Police!"

"There's a man with a gun trying to break in!" she said gasping for breath.

"What's the address Mam'?"

Abby gave it to the woman.

"Stay calm. Find a place to lock yourself in and stay there. I'll have a car there in two minutes!"

The line clicked dead and the doorbell rang again, a voice yelling.

"Hey, anybody home?"

Abby went back to her parents and the two women.

"Come on!" she whispered, "the basement!"

They went down the stairs, feeling their way slowly in the dark and Bob Palmer locked the door behind them. As he did this the sound of two gunshots echoed from the front of the house. This was followed by the sound of splintering wood. They heard footsteps on the floor above as the intruder checked the house.

Abby wished time away. How long had it been since she phoned? A minute, thirty seconds? She didn't know and she grabbed for her father's hand, then led the group to the corner of the basement where the furnace and the oil tank were located. They huddled behind the two objects.

Abby could no longer hear footsteps and thought he must be on the second floor. Her heart pounded. He would check here next, she thought. Damn, how long had it been? She knew they didn't have long and she gripped her Father's hand again.

"I love you Dad," she whispered.

He squeezed her hand in response. "Don't worry Abby, we'll be okay." And she wanted to believe it.

They heard footsteps and creaking floorboards again on the floor above. There was a noise as the intruder tried the basement door.

Another shot rang out, the bullet ricocheting into the basement. The door flew open with a crash as the intruder kicked it in and a shaft of light illuminated the stairs.

A stair creaked and the intruder started to come down to them. God it's nearly over, Abby thought. But suddenly she felt calm and was not afraid anymore. She prepared to do whatever damage she could. She wasn't going to go quietly.

The man on the stairs stopped for a moment, as if listening for something. Then he turned going back up and three more wild shots rang out, the bullets whining through the basement.

"God damn it! You have escaped for now!" the disembodied voice screamed. "I will get revenge! I'll make you come to me! I will give you a reason you can't ignore!"

They heard rapid footsteps running and then two quick shots. Then silence.

Abby's heart pounded as she listened hard, hoping for something. Then, in the distance, the sound of a siren grew louder. So that's it, Abby thought, he had heard it first and ran.

"Is everyone okay?" she asked.

"Actually," her grandmother said, "that was quite exciting!"

The others looked at her in the dim light and as one they broke into laughter, using it as a relief from the tension of the past few minutes.

Above, they heard the sound of footsteps and they looked towards the stairs. A shadow moved across the shaft of light.

"Police officer! Is there anyone down there?" came the call.

"Yes," replied Bob Palmer, "turn on the lights!"

The lights blinked on and the harshness of the neon lighting hurt their eyes.

Abby saw a uniformed figure come carefully down the stairs. Her eyes finally adjusted to the light and she could see the man.

"You folks okay?" asked the officer.

Abby started laughing because it was the same police officer who had found her three nights before. He had a puzzled look on his face, but then he recognized her.

"Not you again?" he smiled. "If you're going to make a habit of this you ought to hire a body guard!"

*   *   *

Tony Two Shoes could not believe the shitty luck he was having on this job and was afraid it was rapidly turning into a complete fuck-up. He was back sitting in the car trying to catch his breath and make his heart stop pounding. He also wondered just were Willie Boy was.

It had all seemed too easy, he reflected. He thought they would have an easy time waxing Sherwood. They had watched while Sherwood crept up to the Palmer front door and tried to get inside. Tony and Willie saw their chance and Tony had taken the front of the house while Willie Boy had gone to cover the back door.

Tony had approached the house as Sherwood shot his way in and had stopped to make sure the noise had not attracted any unwanted attention from the neighbors. He had waited for a minute, and satisfied that nothing was amiss, he came closer to the front door. He heard shots from inside and was readying himself to go in and kill Sherwood when he heard the sound of a distant siren.

Tony Two Shoes was trying to decide which way to go when he heard three more shots inside and looked up in surprise as a man bolted from the house. It was Sherwood and he gave Tony a wild-eyed look. Tony had just a fraction of a second to react as Sherwood leveled the automatic at him and dove for the ground as two shots popped in his ears. Sherwood cursed and ran off down the street.

Tony lay on the ground for a second as the siren became louder and then he pulled himself up and ran for the relative safety of the car. He slammed the door behind him and slouched in the seat as the Portsmouth police cruiser pulled up, the blue lights flashing. He saw two cops jump out and enter the Palmer house. He cursed his damned luck. Shit, he'd almost had the bastard!

Tony turned his head as the driver's side door clicked open and Willie Boy slipped into the car breathing hard.

"Shit! What happened?" he puffed.

"Fucking cops!" Tony said. "The bastard bolted when he heard them. Almost shot me!"

"You okay?" Willie asked.

"Yeah. What the fuck happened to you?"

Willie Boy looked away. "I was climbin' a fence when I heard the shots. Fell off and then I saw the flashing lights and had to work my way back around the block!"

"Shit, anyone see you?" Tony asked, as he thought what a fuck-up Willie Boy was.

"No. We going after the bastard?"

"No. How the fuck can we? Sherwood took off and disappeared around the corner!"

"Oh," Willie said. "So what do we do?"

"Nothin' to do but wait," Tony said. "Let's see what happens now."

"Okay," Willie Boy said.

"And for Christ's sake, keep down out of sight!" Tony said, wondering what to do next.

*   *   *

The two police officers finished taking statements from Abby, her parents and the two older women. Abby thought her grandmother and Betsey were looking none the worse for wear and actually looked as if they had enjoyed the excitement. She looked at her parents talking by the badly damaged front door and saw that they looked okay too. She, however, was still shaking, the second brush with death had unnerved her.

She went to David and put her arms around him.

"Hold me please."

He held her tight and felt her tremble. "It's okay. Need to cry?"

"No, damn it, I'm not going to cry! I want that bastard's ass, that's what I want!"

Jack Pierce came out of the kitchen with one of the policemen. There were now four of them in the house because a back up unit had responded a minute behind the first to arrive. They had arrived just in the nick of time.

He and David had rushed back to the Palmer house as soon as they got a frantic call from Abby, giving only the briefest details about what had happened. Now Pierce talked with the officer for another moment, the uniformed man taking notes.

"Is that everything?" the officer asked.

"Yeah, I think that's it. Sherwood's your man," Pierce said. "I suggest you contact the Boston PD. They'll give you some help."

"Yeah, okay. We'll put out an APB on him, but who knows where the guy is. We checked the neighbors and nobody saw the guy or his car. We don't know which way he went!"

"I know."

The officer turned to the others. "You folks all sure you're okay? Anyone want to go to the hospital just in case?"

Nobody responded and the policeman spoke again. "One more time then. You all have a place to go?"

"They're coming to my place," Susan Taylor responded.

"This door needs something on it," the policeman said. "Can't leave it like this."

"We'll take care of it," David said, "there's some plywood in the garage. That should work for tonight."

"Okay," said the officer, "we'll make sure we come by and check the house during the night."

He looked around at the other officers. "We finished?" he asked.

The others nodded.

"Then, we'll go if it's okay with you folks?"

Bob Palmer came over to the officer who had been the first to arrive and he took the man's hand, shaking it.

"Thanks," he said, emotion in his voice, "you saved our lives!"

The officer blushed.

"Part of the job Sir," he said, "glad we could get here on time."

The Portsmouth Police officers left, leaving the others alone in the house.

"Anyone want a drink?" Bob Palmer asked. "I sure as hell could use one."

They all agreed that was a good idea and Bob Palmer took drink orders. While he was in the kitchen, Abby spoke. "I wonder where Sherwood went?"

"He said something when he left," her mother remembered.

"Yes," said Susan Taylor, "what was it?"

They thought as a group for a moment and finally it was Betsey Watrous who spoke, trying to remember the exact words.

"He said he'd make us come to him. He said he'd give us a reason."

"That's right," Abby agreed, "that's what he said. What does it mean?"

"I don't know," David said, "how could he make us come to him?"

They thought for a moment and it was Betsey Watrous again who broke the silence. "I know where he went," she said.

"Where?" Pierce asked.

"Where would you be certain to follow?" she asked.

"I don't know," Abby said.

"Rosemary Point," Betsey Watrous said, "he's gone to destroy the house!"

"Oh my God!" Abby exclaimed, "Abigail!"

Pierce looked at David. "Come on Dave, let's go!"

Bob Palmer came back into the living room with the drinks just in time to see the two men rush out of the house.

"Where are they going?" he asked.

"They're going to Rosemary Point," his wife replied.

"Why?"

"They think Sherwood's there," Abby said and dashed to the front door.

"Dave, be careful!" she yelled.

She watched as David and Jack Pierce squealed away from the curb in Pierce's car.

Be careful Dave, she thought, I don't want you to get hurt. Please come back to me. She watched as they drove up the street and disappeared around the corner. She did not pay any attention to the other car that followed them.

CHAPTER TWENTY-SEVEN

Jack Pierce turned into the road leading to the house at Rosemary Point. The chain that usually guarded the road after closing time was down and one of the wooden posts had been pulled out of the ground.

"He's here," Pierce said.

"Yeah it looks that way," David agreed.

"Okay Dave, here's what we do. I'm going to turn the headlights out and we'll drive in real slow. We know this guy had an automatic pistol and he may have other weapons. I want you to do everything I say Dave and if you do, you'll stay alive. Do you hear me?"

"Yes Jack," David said, respecting the authority in Pierce's voice.

"We'll go to the parking lot and block the road out with the car. Then we'll check the house and if we don't find anything we'll look around the grounds. Okay?"

"Yeah, I understand," David replied.

Pierce drove slowly down the road, the window open to the cool evening air, listening for any sound of warning. At last they came to the parking lot and Pierce pulled the car sideways in the road, shutting the motor off. He sat listening for any sound.

"There are no cars here," David said.

"Yeah, looks that way. But there are plenty of shadows to hide one in and I don't want to turn on the lights. Speaking of lights, I want you to crawl out the window after me so the courtesy lights don't go on. No sense in making an easy target."

David nodded as Pierce eased his large body out the window and crouched low on the ground. David followed him.

"What now?" he asked.

"You take the left side of the path, I'll take the right. Stay in the trees as much as you can. He must have heard us, so be careful!"

"Jack, you said he's got a gun? What do we do against that?"

"We be real careful," Pierce said and David saw a brief glint of teeth.

"That's some comfort," he said.

"Shut up and let's go."

They moved slowly up the slight rise toward the house. As they neared the top of the rise, David noticed a yellow orange flickering light from the direction of the house and he caught a whiff of smoke. Sherwood had set the house on fire! He had to put it out!

"Jack," he whispered, "the house is on fire!"

"Ssh. Just keep going!"

"But the house is on fire!"

"Shut up and let's go!"

They continued on over the rise and David could see the house where part of the front porch was burning. He had to put it out! He stood up and ran toward the house ignoring Pierce who whispered, "Stay down!"

David did not hear him, intent on extinguishing the fire. He had to save the house! He ran to the garden hose on the north side of the house and turned the tap on full. He pulled the hose and twisted the nozzle to a shower and began to spray water back and forth on the blaze. He did this for about thirty seconds and was making some progress when two shots cracked across the lawn. To his left the bullets whacked into the side of the house missing him by a close margin.

David threw himself on the ground and wildly looked around. He was lying exposed with no cover and the fire behind him made it impossible to hide. He didn't know what to do.

Another hail of bullets flew over his head, hitting the ground behind him. Holy shit! What have I gotten myself into?

＊   ＊   ＊

Tony Two Shoes and Willie Boy stumbled along the road. They had parked the car at the entrance to the road where the car they had followed had stopped and turned. The two men had no idea where they were going but Tony was sure the other two guys had gone after Sherwood.

Now Tony and Willie were cautiously moving along in the dark and Tony was excited. Beside him Willie Boy was nervous, looking around in jerks, alert to any danger. A moment later they came upon the other car parked across the road blocking it.

"So?" Willie Boy said.

"So, they're here and they don't want the other prick to get away."

"What's that smell?" Willie Boy wondered.

Tony sniffed at the air. "Something's burning," and he instinctively ducked at the sound of two gunshots.

"Shit!" Willie Boy swore. "Who's shooting?"

"Shit if I know. Let's move a little closer and see what's going on."

Carefully they crept ahead and moved up the walk toward the flickering light.

＊   ＊   ＊

David Baker looked around frantically for Pierce but he was nowhere to be seen. What should he do he thought as another bullet tore into the ground five feet in front of him. Shit, he had to move, fast!

David started to crawl on his belly towards where the path led into the trees. He moved as quickly as he could, wishing he could go back and fight the fire.

He made it to the tree line out of breath and he looked around him. In the dim moonlight he saw Pierce crouched behind a tree about twenty feet away. Pierce had a gun in his hand and he spoke without looking at him.

"You okay?"

"Yeah," David said, gasping, "what the hell is that?"

"Sssh. It's a pistol. What do you think it is?" Pierce hissed.

"What are you doing with it?"

"Quiet! I don't think he knows I'm here."

"You had a gun? Is that legal?" David asked speaking louder than he had intended.

"Shsss, I've got a permit. Jesus, Dave we're about to be killed and you're worried about breaking the fucking law!"

David took two deep breaths. "You're right. What do we do now?"

"We wait. He'll come looking for you."

"What then?"

"I shoot him!" Pierce said calmly.

"Jesus, Jack, I've never been shot at before!"

"Yeah, well, don't worry, I have, it doesn't hurt unless they hit you."

"What?"

"I'll tell you about it later," Pierce said.

"Yeah, do that. I'd like to know," David said, wondering what other secrets Jack Pierce had to tell.

The two men waited, listening. A few moments later there was a rustling sound over to the left. Someone was moving through the trees.

David watched intently and to his right, he sensed Pierce, alive, tensed and ready. He was in his element.

*　　　　*　　　　*

"Shit!" Willie Boy said as he and Tony Two Shoes went to ground at the sound of the second volley of shots. "Who the fuck is that?"

"That's got to be our man!" Tony said looking up. In the flickering light of the fire he watched as one man crawled away from the house into the trees. He thought he saw movement on the other side of the house, toward what he thought was the ocean.

"Come on!" he said to Willie Boy, "let's move off and try to circle around the house. I think our guy is on the other side."

"Okay," Willie Boy replied nervous and twitching. He pulled his own automatic from his pocket and the light briefly glinted off the metal. "Let's go get the bastard!"

"Calm down asshole!" Tony spat. "Just keep cool! Come on let's go!"

Taking the lead, Tony Two Shoes crouched and moved off to the left into the trees. He moved along slowly, followed by Willie Boy. The two men had managed to move abut fifty feet when Tony froze as behind him Willie Boy stepped on a fallen branch that cracked with a loud snap. He felt his heart begin to pound and he hoped that Sherwood had not heard them.

*   *   *

David caught a glimpse of something moving among the trees and a moment later heard a branch snap. The report of three quick shots from Pierce's pistol surprised him and made him jump. A muffled cry came from the trees, followed by a faint thud.

"Shit!" Pierce said, "I thought Sherwood was over by the house!"

"So did I," David said.

Before they could discuss this any further, a short burst of fire came from the far side of the house. David and Jack Pierce hugged the ground.

"Holy shit!" Pierce said, "there's two of them!"

"Is that possible?" David asked.

Pierce did not wait to answer, but instead he squeezed off two quick shots in the direction of the house. A scream came from the house and they heard the sound of a man running.

"Come on!" Pierce said pulling David to his feet and they ran down the rise back to the parking lot. Pierce led him to his car where they crouched, breathing hard and tried to listen. It was silent.

*　　　　　*　　　　　*

Willie Boy grimaced in pain as Tony Two Shoes cursed to himself that this could not have become more fucked up. He wasn't sure what had happened or who had shot Willie in the leg. The shots that had hit Willie had come from where he thought the two civilians were and he could not understand why unless they were armed. He hadn't thought that was likely.

"Shit," Willie Boy hissed. "This fucking hurts!"

"Yeah? Shut up!" Tony said, trying to think his way out of this mess. It was clear to him they had stumbled into something more than he had expected. He had assumed that only Sherwood had been armed, but now it looked like the civilians were also carrying.

He tried to decide what to do but then a burst of automatic fire came from the direction of the house and he saw the two men in the trees run back toward the parking lot. So, he thought, the automatic fire must have come from Sherwood and he was still by the house.

"Can you move?" he asked Willie Boy.

"Yeah, shit, I guess so."

"Okay then, get back to the car. I'm going to go and finish this. Then we're going to get the hell out of here!"

Willie Boy nodded in the dim light and he slowly started to limp back to the car. Tony took a deep breath and, pistol at the ready, he moved off toward the back of the house.

*　　　　　*　　　　　*

Satisfied that Sherwood had not followed them, Pierce went to the rear of the car and, taking the keys from his pocket, he opened the trunk a crack trying not to let light escape from the storage compartment. He reached in and pulled an object from the floor, then shut the trunk lid and returned to where David waited.

"Here," he said, handing David the object.

"What the hell is this?" David asked, taking the weapon.

"It's a shotgun. Remington eleven hundred, automatic. Five rounds in the magazine, one in the chamber. Double oh buckshot."

"Shit, Jack! What are you doing with a this?"

Pierce ignored him. "You grew up in Iowa. You know how to use one of these?"

"Yeah sure, I've been hunting."

"Good. This is an automatic, you just point it in his general direction and keep pulling the trigger when I tell you!"

"What are you going to do?"

"You stay back here by the trunk, use it for cover. I'll take the other end by the hood. Listen, Dave, Sherwood's going to try and break out of here. He's hurt and I don't think he cares about anything now! We've got to stop him right here!"

"I hear you Jack. Just tell me what to do. God, I've never done this before!"

Pierce patted him on the shoulder. "You'll do just fine, Dave! All those good genes, remember?"

David nodded and tried to smile but felt the fear in the pit of his stomach. Then they heard the sound of a car motor starting in the bushes to the right of the parking lot and Pierce went to the front of the car. As he did, a clatter of gunfire came from the sound of the motor.

A hail of bullets hit Pierce's car.

"Jesus!" David yelled, "he's got a machine gun!"

"No," said Pierce, "it's an automatic rifle. AK-47, you don't forget the sound they make. Watch out now, he's probably going to gun it and try and blow by us! When he does, open up with the shotgun. Keep him busy!"

"Okay," David said, unsure of what he would do.

He tensed behind the left rear wheel, waiting and looked toward Pierce who was concentrating on the opposite side of the parking lot. They waited.

Another shower of bullets hit the car and David ducked as low as he could hugging the ground.

"You okay?" Pierce called to him.

"Yeah, when's he coming?"

In answer to that question, headlights came on in the bushes, the motor revved and the car started towards them.

"Wait 'til I say when!" Pierce called, watching the car begin to move.

Judging the effective distance of the shotgun, Pierce waited until the car was forty yards away.

David's hands shook and he wondered when would Pierce begin. The car was coming on fast and he was worried they would be too late to stop it.

"Now!" yelled Pierce, rising from the cover of the car.

David followed suit, standing and firing in the direction of the moving car. His hands shook so badly that he was convinced he stood no chance of hitting anything.

To his left, Jack Pierce took careful aim and squeezed off three shots that went through the driver's windshield. Quickly shifting targets, he put two bullets into the left front tire.

The car came on, apparently undamaged, but then it swerved, careening back and forth. Still it was coming at them.

David continued to pull the trigger, even though he had gone through all the shells in the magazine and Pierce yelled at him.

"Move it Dave! Get out of the way!"

David came out of his trance and realized the danger. He turned and ran to the left, diving with Pierce into the bushes.

Behind them, the moving car hit the rear of Pierce's car, bouncing to the left, rolling over into a ditch where it came to a stop, the horn blaring.

Pierce got up from the ground, ejected the spent clip from his pistol and took a fresh one from his pocket, jamming it home.

David rose behind him, heart pounding and breathing in short gasps. Cautiously, they approached the overturned car and Pierce knelt to look inside. He went to the other side of the car, pistol ready. The driver of the car was half out of the window, bloody. He was unconscious. Pierce felt for a pulse. It was weak, but it was there.

"He's still alive!"

"Too bad," David said.

         *   *   *

Tony Two Shoes had carefully circled the house and now found himself on the ocean side. There was no sign of Sherwood but he saw that the fire on the porch was now fully involved and the flames were beginning to lick at the side of the house itself. He ducked to the side and moved fast across the lawn to avoid being seen in the light of the fire.

He was part way across the lawn when he heard the automatic rifle fire coming from the direction of the parking lot. He swore to himself and moved carefully in that direction. Another short burst of fire caused him to stop again and this time he heard the car rev and gravel splatter as the car's wheels dug in.

He ran down the path in time to see the car's headlights flash on and the car sped forward toward the car he had seen earlier blocking the road. He watched in awe as the car sped toward the blocked road, the driver intent on ramming his way out. It had to be Sherwood!

Tony as surprised and flinched as gunfire suddenly erupted from the road. He thought it was a shotgun and a pistol and saw that it was directed at the moving car. Well shit, he thought, the two civilians had some balls.

He saw the wild shotgun blasts hit the car and saw spider webs appear on the windshield as bullets hit the driver's side. Then the car swerved, hit the rear of the parked car and roll over. Shit, that was something!

He watched as the two civilians got up from the ground where they had thrown themselves at the last moment. He hefted his pistol and decided he needed to check out the rolled car, to make sure that Sherwood was dead.

He sauntered down the final steps to the parking lot and then ambled off toward the other two men who were examining the wrecked car.

*   *   *

Jack Pierce felt something and turned quickly to see the stranger walk slowly toward him. He hadn't seen this guy before but thought he had been in the woods earlier. The man held a pistol in his right hand and Pierce immediately leveled his own pistol at him.

"That's far enough," and the other man stopped.

"Okay."

"Who the hell are you?" Pierce asked.

David came over to stand next to him still holding the now empty shotgun.

Tony Two Shoes looked at David and the shotgun and shrugged. "You could say I'm an interested party."

David stared at the man. "Interested party? What the hell does that mean?"

Tony stared back at the younger of the two men as saw the combination of anger and excitement in his eyes. "You Baker?" he asked.

"How the hell do you know who I am?"

"I know," Tony said and looked back at Jack Pierce. "He dead?" he asked nodding at the car.

Pierce glanced briefly over his shoulder. "If he's not, he will be in a couple of minutes," Pierce lied.

Tony Two Shoes eyed Pierce closely. This man had an air about him; someone not to be messed with. "Mind if I take a look?"

"Yeah," Pierce said, "I guess I do."

Tony nodded, considering whether it was worth it to press his luck. He decided that it wasn't worth it. Sherwood was probably as good as dead and he thought he had fulfilled his contract. He started to holster his pistol and saw Pierce react to this movement by tensing on the trigger of his gun.

"Just putting it away," Tony said and saw Pierce relax.

"Probably a good idea if you were on your way," Pierce said. "My guess is there are going to be a lot of cops around here in a couple of minutes and maybe a fire truck or two. It would be a good idea if you weren't here."

Tony nodded and his eyes met Pierce's. "Yeah, you're probably right." The he looked over at David. "Nice job."

David nodded.

"I'm going to forget that you were here," Pierce said. "I've got a feeling you were only doing your job. Right?"

Tony Two Shoes smiled and nodded. "Yeah, that might be right." He smiled again and started to walk away past the wrecked car. Then he stopped and turned to look back at Jack Pierce. "You're a pro, aren't you?"

Jack Pierce nodded imperceptibly, "not anymore."

Tony grunted a short laugh and then hurried on down the road.

Jack Pierce and David watched for a second before David remembered the fire.

"Shit Jack, I got to go to the house! You okay here?"

"Sure, someone will be by soon. They've got to see the flames!"

David sprinted up the path to the house that he expected to be totally consumed by now. He didn't know what he could do, but he was going to try.

Going over the rise, he saw that the blaze was not as far along as he thought. Although the flames were licking at the house itself, the fire was still confined to the porch and he saw the reason why. A woman in a long dress was hosing down the porch with the garden hose.

He ran to her. "Here, let me finish!"

She looked at him, soot on her face and despite the grime, he thought her beautiful. David took the hose from her and began to wave it back and forth over the fire.

"Are you well?" she asked, "I heard shooting."

"I was never better Abigail! I think we've ended this business!"

David fought the fire with a will, going on the porch to get closer. He changed the nozzle setting several times to better get at the various parts of the porch. Water spilled and splashed on him, soot and ash blackening his face and clothes, he didn't care.

He fought the fire as if it were a living thing, attacking the flames, retreating and then attacking again. He fought with a will, determined to save the house. He was exhausted but ignore the fatigue and kept attacking, using the hose as a weapon. How long it took, he didn't know, but soon he realized that he had the fire under control. He continued to wet the smoldering wood and went back to the lawn in front of the house kneeling to look under the floorboards. There was no flame.

The woman came to him and David dropped the hose, taking her in his arms, hugging her. He pulled back, then kissed her.

"We did it Grandmother!" he said.

"Oh David, you saved the house! You are wonderful!"

"No," he said with tears in his eyes, "you saved it. It was because of you that Abby and I got involved. Without you the property would be gone! You have done this!"

"David, I could not have done it without you, or, your Abigail. I wish you both all the happiness in the world! You deserve it so!"

He hugged her again. "The fire is out, I think," he said.

"Yes, I think so," she agreed.

"I must go back to my friend," he said.

"I understand," she replied and they both heard the sound of sirens approaching.

"I have to go," David said again, not wanting to leave the woman.

"Yes, I know. David, I am truly proud of you, you are like a son."

"Thank you, that means a lot!" He hugged her once more and he turned to walk back down the path.

"I will be back," he promised.

Abigail waved back at the disappearing figure and she watched him go, tears welling in her eyes. They were not tears of sorrow, but tears of happiness for the joy the special couple had brought her. Her time at Rosemary Point was coming to an end. She could feel it now, her quest to right the two-century-old wrong was now complete and for the first time in over two hundred years she didn't know what to expect.

*   *   *

The ambulance carrying a badly injured Thomas Sherwood had left twenty minutes before. Sherwood had suffered two gunshot wounds, a fractured skull and a broken leg as a result of the car turning over, but the paramedics expected that he would live.

David and Jack Pierce stood in the parking lot talking with a Maine State Trooper. Two Maine State Police cruisers and a tanker truck remained in the lot, their clashing red and blue strobe lights making the scene almost surreal.

"Then what happened?" the trooper asked.

"He tried to get away by driving through us," Pierce explained.

"So you stopped him?"

"Yeah, that's right."

"So he got hurt while you were defending yourselves then?"

"Yeah, that's right," Pierce said.

"You got a carry permit for that automatic?" the cop asked Jack Pierce.

"Yeah," Pierce said and removed the permit from his wallet and handed it to the trooper.

He looked it over and returned it. "I suppose you just happened to have the shotgun with you? Lucky thing I guess."

"Yeah, wasn't it?" Pierce smiled and the trooper eyed him carefully. He was glad he did not have to face the man, because from the statement he had just taken, it was clear that what had taken place was a coldly calculated fight. The state trooper looked to his right at the two firemen who came down the path, lugging a fire hose with them. They left the hose by the truck and joined the other men.

"It's out! We'll stay for a while to make sure though," the first man said.

The other fireman looked at David. "You did a good job with just that garden hose."

The state trooper spoke, "I think I've go all I need."

"We can go then?" asked Pierce.

"Yes. I think the facts are pretty straightforward. But the DA will probably want your help in prosecuting the other guy though."

The trooper looked at Pierce's damaged car. "You two will need a ride. I'll give you a lift. Ready whenever you are."

"Could you give us a few minutes?" David asked, "I'd like to check the house."

"Sure, take your time."

David and Pierce walked up the path and David spoke. "Jack, I was terrified. That was something I'll never forget!"

"You did fine Dave and we got the bastard! He won't hurt anyone again!"

They went to the house and looked at the damaged porch.

"You did a good job putting out the fire Dave, I thought the place was ready to go up!"

"I had help."

"What?"

"She did it Jack. Abigail saved the house. She was fighting the fire with the garden hose when I came back. I only finished the job, God this whole thing is so damned confusing!"

"Well, the bottom line is that it's over with. You've solved the mystery and saved the "fortune", what's left of it anyway. You did it Dave."

"Yeah, I guess that's right."

"You remember what I told you long ago?"

"What's that?"

"You know very well now where you've been, so the rest should be easy for you and Abby. You'll know where you're going and I envy you, you're a lucky guy."

"Yeah, I guess I am. Jack?"

"Yes."

"While Sherwood was shooting at us, you said that you'd been shot at before. What did you mean by that?"

"I'll tell you Dave, but it's still kind of a secret," he laughed. "Between us, my time in the Army wasn't what you would call normal duty. I told you I was in Military Intelligence. Well, there's more to it, I worked with the CIA. I've never told anyone before, except Jennifer."

"Wow! What made you do that?"

"It was a challenge and seemed exciting, but it also gave me a chance to travel and I had a lot of free time to spend in Europe's best libraries. That's where I got to know Tony Nappia, my police buddy from New York. We ran a number of ops along the German border trying to trap agents from the other side. The early sixties were tough times in the Cold War and I did get shot at a couple of times."

"I'm glad you told me. God Jack, I'm lucky you're my friend. If you hadn't been here, I'd be dead. Thanks!"

"Hey, what are friends for?" Pierce laughed. "Come on, Dave. It's time we got you back to that lady of yours!"

He put his arm on the shoulder of the younger man. "You did good, my friend! Make no mistake about that!"

And the two friends walked back to the police cruiser.

EPILOGUE

Three weeks later, Judge Janet Mclaine looked down from her bench in York County Probate Court as Ted Williams finished speaking. David and Abby watched as Williams finished his brief summary and sat down.

"Is that all, Mr. Williams?" the Judge asked.

"Yes, your Honor."

The Judge consulted her notes and then looked around the courtroom her eyes finally stopping as she found David and Abby.

"This court is prepared to rule on this case. I'm satisfied with the authenticity of the Smith wills. I have examined the originals in Salem and the court has had experts run tests to determine age of the documents. They appear to be real. Therefore, this court sets aside the record of the previously probated wills recorded in 1785 and declares them null and void. The wills dated January 10, 1784 are now considered valid and the Bank of Boston, as successor to the Bank of Massachusetts is hereby declared trustee of the Abigail Smith and the Jacob Smith trusts. As such they will now be deemed to be the owner of Rosemary Point. Any question of title to any other assets will be determined by the Civil Court."

Judge Mclaine watched the three people sitting in front of her.

"That suit you folks?"

David and Abby smiled.

"I want you to know," the judge said, "that I've never been happier to make a ruling in my life. You two have done something very special and I want you to know that."

David and Abby nodded in response.

"Court dismissed!" Judge Mclaine said banging her gavel.

They rose and Ted Williams looked at the couple. "Well, it's over, and by God, you've done it. She's right you know, you have done something special."

"Thanks Ted, we couldn't have done it without you," David said.

Abby hugged the attorney. "Thanks," she said.

"You know," Williams mused, "I may just forget to send a bill if you do that one more time!"

Abby hugged him again.

*　　　　　*　　　　　*

Christmas Day was bright and clear and a fresh dusting of snow had fallen the night before, making the holy day picture perfect. David shaved in his room at the Portsmouth Sheraton, getting ready for the wedding ceremony that was scheduled to begin at two-o clock.

As he drew the razor over his face, he thought of all the things that had happened in the past seven months. Taken as a whole, the events fairly boggled the mind.

All the loose ends had come together though, he thought. Thomas Sherwood had been extradited from Maine to Massachusetts. He had been indicted in Maine on assault and attempted murder charges, but the Massachusetts case was viewed as more important so he would stand trial there for the murder of Nicholas Dominic after the first of the year. So far his partners in the Rosemary Point development plan had escaped prosecution but that might change as the case was investigated more extensively.

David smiled in the mirror, thinking that justice had prevailed after all. Then he heard a knock on the door and, wiping his face, he went to open it.

His brother, Jerry stood in the doorway, already dressed in his tux.

"How you doing Dave, you ready yet?"

"No, not quite Jerry. We've got plenty of time."

"I know, but I want to be sure to get you there on time. Abby would not be happy if you were late."

"I plan to be on time, thanks," David said, shutting the door, "make yourself comfortable. I'll finish dressing."

There was another knock at the door. Jerry went to open it and their sister, Sue, came in.

"Hi guys!" she was bubbling with excitement.

"What are you doing here?" asked David. "Isn't that bad luck or something?"

"No Dave, that's the bride. I'm just checking to see if you need anything."

"No, I'm fine Sue," David laughed. "Jerry can take care of me well enough."

"You know, Dave, Abby's terrific! You've lucked out in the end. I guess good things come to those who wait!"

David nodded.

"And Mom would have liked her," Jerry added.

"Yeah, I think she would have," David agreed.

"Too bad she couldn't be here to enjoy this," Sue said sadly. "But we're here and we'll be thinking of her."

"Yes," David said and saw the tears in his sister's eyes.

"You know, you've got quite a story to tell," his brother said, "given any thought to writing a book?"

"No, but that is an idea," David replied and turned at the sound of another knock at the door.

"What is this? Grand Central?" he asked.

Sue opened the door and Jack and Jennifer Pierce came into the room with broad grins on their faces. Pierce carried a brown paper bag with him.

"You ready to go?" Pierce asked.

"I will be if you all let me alone!" David said, going into the bathroom to fix his tie.

Jack Pierce pulled a bottle of champagne from the paper bag and set it on the dresser. He took out five plastic glasses and popped the bottle, pouring the wine into each glass.

David came back out of the bathroom, straightening his tie. "What's this?" he asked.

"A toast," Pierce said, handing glasses to the others.

"Me first?" Sue asked and Pierce nodded to her. "To our family. We're together and David has given us a sense of our ancestors. We're proud to be here."

Jack Pierce nodded. "Yes, that's a good thought, and I'll add more. To David and Abby and the past they discovered."

"And to the future," Sue added with a smile.

They drank the toast and David looked at them all. "Yes, to our future."

*   *   *

Abigail Palmer radiated beauty in her wedding dress and glowed with happiness. This was obvious to the crowd in the Portsmouth church as the ceremony concluded. Relatives, friends and Rosemary Point Society members were all there to help the couple celebrate their union.

As the minister finished and David kissed Abby, the sound of applause echoed in the church and the couple could not help blushing.

The newlyweds then went down the aisle to the waiting car, which took them to the house at Rosemary Point.

They went up the shoveled path, the snow glistening in the late afternoon sunlight and the sea sparkling in the distance. David noted that the porch had been rebuilt and no sign of the fire remained.

He squeezed Abby's hand and she smiled in return putting her arm around him.

"I'm so happy!" she said.

"Me too, this is perfect!"

"I wonder where she is?" Abby asked looking around.

"I don't know." They had returned to the house many times since the night of the fire but the woman had not reappeared.

They entered the house and it was almost magical. The house had been decorated for the holidays with boughs of evergreens, ribbons, flowers and ornaments, reflecting the holiday spirit.

The caterers had set up a buffet in the dinning room and a bar in the sitting room. David went to get drinks for them and returned with two glasses of champagne. He gave one to Abby and raised his glass.

"To us Mrs. Baker."

"Yes, to us Mr. Baker."

They drank, then set their glasses down and he took her in his arms, kissing her. She could only smile at him with tears of joy in her eyes.

Guests began arriving and the house was soon packed with friends.

David looked around at the crowd and saw that Abby's grandmother and Betsey Watrous were having a great time. He thought how much they had been involved in what had happened. Bob and Jan Palmer were talking with guests and grinning broadly. David thought just how close they had come to dying.

Aunt Beth had found a fast friend in Jan Palmer he noticed. Beth had been a part of the beginning of the quest so it was nice that she could be here for the end. Jack and Jennifer Pierce laughed as they talked with friends and David knew that he owed his life to his friend.

His brother, Jerry and his sister, Sue were enjoying the day. David was glad they were there to share the time with him and somehow they all seemed closer than they had ever been because of what had happened.

The adventure had ended and the journey was complete now. It had drawn him in unexpected directions and had taken his full measure. He knew that the experience had helped him understand himself better than ever and he knew he had experienced a trial by fire, like his ancestors. He was proud of his heritage.

David Baker had found his roots. They had not been far away, only hidden. Together he and Abby would somehow make a happy life, he knew it.

The reception was a wonderful time and the wedding, combined with the holiday made everyone appreciate the moment. Finally, Jack Pierce called for attention and the crowd quieted, waiting for him to speak.

"We are all here to help David and Abigail celebrate the beginning of a new life together. I don't know of a more deserving couple, so I ask you all to join me in wishing Mr. and Mrs. David Baker all the best things in life! To Abby and Dave!"

The guests responded as one. "To Abby and Dave!"

Abby smiled and kissed her husband.

On the porch the woman looked through the window, a very broad and satisfied smile on her face. Yes, she thought, those two were something special. She knew they would have a rich life together.

So she pulled her coat around her and taking one last look, she smiled again and began to walk towards the sea.

AUTHOR'S NOTE

This story is the product of my sometimes overactive imagination. The resemblance of any character to any person, living or dead, is a total coincidence.

While the book is a work of fiction, parts of it are based on historical fact. The 168th US Infantry really did exist and was a part of the Rainbow Division during WW I. The unit left a fine service record in combat. Likewise, the 74th Indiana Volunteer Regiment, the 44th Illinois Volunteer Regiment, the 1st Michigan Battery and the 15th Illinois Cavalry were real units and were part of Sherman's Army on the march to the sea.

The *Empress of China* was real and history books tell us that she was the first American ship to make the round trip to China. The trading voyages of the *Columbia* and the *Washington* also took place. While they were widely acclaimed as adventurous undertakings, they were in fact, financial failures.

Other events in the story were inspired by narratives taken from histories and journals. *Fix Bayonets*, by John W. Thomaston, Jr., Charles Scribner & Sons, 1925 provided background and gave me a sense of what it was like to assault the German trenches in World War I. *The Bark Covered House* by William Nowlin, reprinted by the Lakeside Press, 1937 suggested the Baker family adventures in Buffalo and on the steamer *Michigan* (the Nowlin's made it to Michigan). *Boston, The Place*

And The People, by M. A. DeWolfe, The MacMillan Co., 1903 and *State Of Mind-A Boston Reader*, edited by Robert N. Linscott, Farrar, Strauss and Co., 1948 were useful in imagining the City of Boston during the 1790 time period.

I also borrowed from the experiences of some of my ancestors. One of my great great grandfathers served in the 74th Indiana Volunteers. He was captured outside of Atlanta in November, 1864 while foraging. Unlike the character in the story, he did not escape and spent four months in Andersonville Prison. He survived, but the experience ruined his health. My great great great grandfather, James R. Brown, made the trip west from Delaware County, New York via the Erie Canal and Buffalo in 1835 (they also made it to Michigan). His family may have had as adventurous journey as the Baker family, I don't know.

In sum, this story is a blend of fiction and history. The fiction is the entertainment, the history the background. This story is about the United States and how it grew as the population moved west. Early on, I discovered that genealogy is really about geography. Perhaps this is what fascinates me the most.

If I have inspired anyone to be curious about their family history and heritage then I will have succeeded in meeting one of the objectives I had in writing this story. It is immensely satisfying to be able to put historical events into perspective by imagining how your own flesh and blood reacted to them.

Like Jack Pierce, I firmly believe that it helps you to know where you are going if you know where you have been.

ABOUT THE AUTHOR

James G. Brown has worked in the investment business for over thirty years. This is his first book. He is an amateur genealogist and historian and is a member of a number of hereditary, genealogy and historical societies. He has written several articles on his family. He resides in Maine.